FALLING FOR THE *Enemy*

VOLUME THREE

TARYN QUINN • ARIA WYATT
GEORGIA COFFMAN
BRIT BENSON • ELYSE KELLY

HIS FAVORITE MISTAKE

AN ENEMIES TO LOVERS ROMANCE

TARYN QUINN

ACKNOWLEDGMENTS

Sometimes we make up fictional places that end up having the same names as actual places. These are our fictional interpretations only. Please grant us leeway if our creative vision isn't true to reality.

JED

Beer. Boxing. Bed. In that order.

Idling at a light, I breathed a sigh of relief that my day was done. My dog Freddy would share the couch with me, of course, but he'd have to abstain from the beer, despite the fact that the mutt had developed a taste for it some years ago at a college frat party.

Too bad. I wasn't about to contribute to the delinquency of a geriatric dog.

A red car blitzed past me, barely waiting until the light turned green, going so fast it was clear the driver never intended to slow down. At a glance, I glimpsed dealer plates, and shit, was that a Porsche?

Up ahead it slammed on its brakes at another light, then screeched forward as soon as the light turned green.

I hit the gas, giving chase as years of training had taught me to do. A car like that in Kensington Square, operating at that rate of speed, couldn't be a good sign.

It didn't take me long to catch up with the car, in spite of how fast it was going. Coming up behind the vehicle, I switched lanes until I was right on its tail before flashing my lights several times.

Pull over, jerk.

The car slowed at the flash of my lights then sped up. Clenching my jaw, I stomped on the accelerator out of instinct.

I'd given chase a few times in my career, and the burst of adrenaline that zinged through my veins was like pure kerosene. In fact, it was one of the things I enjoyed most—

Missed most.

I wasn't a cop, not anymore. And I had no reason to be flagging down a suspicious car. This wasn't my department issued Crown Vic, and I no longer had a Detective's badge in my wallet.

I was a Dateline NBC episode waiting to happen.

Man pretends to be cop to corner innocent female victim. News at eleven.

Not that I could be certain she was female. Hell, she could've been a six-hundred pound dude in a gorilla suit for all I knew. I'd just seen someone breaking the law and reacted.

Easing off the gas, I switched lanes. I didn't back off entirely.

I'm a citizen, aren't I? I can make an arrest anyway.

Yeah, there was some rationalization. As if citizen's arrests ever held up in court. The cases that got thrown out on a technicality were a sore enough spot in the department without imagining the look on the DA's face when this file came across his desk.

I sighed, flexing my hand around the steering wheel. Pursuing this speed demon wasn't going to get me anywhere good. Even if she/he/it was still signaling in and out of lanes like a damn drag racer.

I was no longer a member of law enforcement. If I called this in, dispatch would probably blow me off. It was Friday night. They had more important things to handle than a joyrider.

The driver took a sharp right, then a sharp left, drawing us deeper into a residential area. At least the traffic was much less dense here. Fewer opportunities for the driver to do serious damage to someone else—or himself.

I continued to follow her. Arresting her wasn't an option but tailing her was. That wasn't illegal. If they didn't stop soon, I'd just call it in and be done with it.

I patted my pockets and glanced around the front seat. Where was my damn phone?

A bang up ahead made me jerk the wheel in reflex. The Porsche fishtailed in an intersection and curbed it hard enough to snap an axle. "Fucking asshole."

I finally located my phone, sending it flying to the floor in the process. "Dammit." I fumbled around the dark floorboard. I glanced up and saw a small figure jump out of the car and appear to slump over the vehicle's almost nonexistent back end.

Oh God, was she hurt?

Heart racing, I gave up on the phone and signaled toward the side street closest to the intersection before slamming on the brakes. The lack of traffic at this time of night in this neighborhood was a godsend.

Another car pulled over to help—or boost the rims off the fancy sports car. You just never knew for sure, and after the years I'd spent on the force, unfortunately, I'd lost a lot of faith in the kindness of humans.

I climbed out and stalked toward the irresponsible driver. The man from the other car swiftly got back into his vehicle and fled the scene.

Yep. So much for her good Samaritan. I might no longer be a cop, but I clearly hadn't lost my cop face.

Small favors.

As I approached, it was clear she wasn't slumped over as I'd first guessed. No, she was kicking the tire with the pointy-toed boots that ended approximately a millimeter below indecency. Her clingy dress ended just above that creamy glimpse of her thigh.

From the quick lurch of my cock, evidently some parts of me didn't give a shit if she was a little rulebreaker or not.

Worse, that was making me even harder.

"Did you boost this car?" I demanded without saying hello.

She stopped kicking long enough to give me a look of pure malevolence out of eyes that could've been blue or green. They were light in contrast to all the dark hair whipping around her shoulders like a cape. "Boost? Did we wake up in *Gone in Sixty Seconds*?"

"If we did, I want my money back, because you're sure as hell no Angelina Jolie."

So that was a bit of a half-truth. No, this woman did not look like Angelina, especially in that particular movie since Angie had been sporting blond braids. But it wasn't because this one wasn't just as beautiful. Between the wild dark hair, that curvy body wrapped in stretchy material, and the boots—Dear God, the boots—she could've given a few Hollywood starlets a run for their money.

"Yeah, well, break my heart. This car ruined my night. Popping a tire when I wasn't going more than—"

"Eighty-five?" I asked blandly, crossing my arms.

She flushed brightly enough I could her cheeks blazing in the moonlight. "Barely over eighty," she whispered, ducking her head.

Hmm. A bad girl but not comfortable with it. Bad girl in training? Or maybe bad girl on the run from something even worse?

Don't know. Don't care. Not my circus. Not my monkeys.

In spite of the hard knock of common sense in my gut, I moved closer. "Have you been drinking?"

"What? No. Not a drop."

Her vehemence seemed sincere. Or maybe I was just a sucker. "Are you hurt?"

I didn't think so, judging from the way she was still occasionally halfheartedly kicking the tire. But then she turned her face away and let out a sniffle and I couldn't help wondering what exactly was going on here.

If she'd been out for a simple Friday night joyride, it hadn't taken much to steal her joy. Then again, maybe the car really was stolen.

Fuck, I needed my phone to call this in.

"You flashed your lights at me." She lifted her chin before I could move. "You wanted me to pull over."

No, it was better altogether if I denied my intention to make her do just that. I wasn't allowed to try to corral speeders while in a civilian vehicle or otherwise.

"You're mistaken."

"No, I'm not. You slinked up behind me in traffic and screwed up my rhythm and tried to run me off the road."

"Hardly."

"Let me guess." She charged over to me. "You're one of Taylor's goons. Gotta keep the talent in line, right? So, take me back." She shifted her head and I caught the gleam of tears.

Blue. They were definitely blue.

"I don't know who Taylor is, and I'm definitely not one of his goons."

From the set of her jaw, she didn't believe me. "Don't bother lying. You've got that tough guy bodyguard look about you. Bet you even have cuffs to make it easier for you to haul me back—"

"Don't mention cuffs or you'll get what you asked for." I didn't mean to say it, didn't even realize I'd been thinking it, but man, her anger and even the slap of her hair in my face was nudging me toward a place I rarely went anymore.

I'd closed a lot of doors when I left the force. Switching careers hadn't been enough. I'd closed down some of my darker urges as well, wanting to see if time away from what had once given me pleasure would help pull off a total system reboot.

Instead, I only craved it more.

She stared at me, worrying her full lower lip between blindingly white teeth. "Are y-you a cop?"

"That's one guess," I taunted in a low voice, moving subtly closer. "The other is that I'm your worst nightmare."

I wanted to see if she shrank back, if some of the fire in her eyes banked. Words like I'd just uttered on a darkened street would make some women run.

Smart women.

But hell, I was probably already halfway to a charge of impersonating an officer, once she calmed down enough to realize that yes, I had been trying to flag her down, and no, I wasn't one of Taylor's goons. Whoever that was. And whoever *she* was that she needed to run away in such an expensive vehicle.

"Do you know who I am?" Her voice was breathless.

Oh, here we go. There was always someone who tried to posture their way out of a ticket. "No, lady, I don't have the first fucking clue who you are."

I braced for her ire. Maybe even more of her tears.

What I did *not* expect was for her to shoot me a blinding grin before she flung herself into my arms and attached her mouth to mine.

PEYTON

I WAS KISSING A STRANGER. A POSSIBLY DANGEROUS STRANGER. And oh my God, it was even better than I'd ever imagined.

I slung my arms around his neck and slipped my tongue between his lips, tasting something dark and sweet. Coffee. He tasted like a big ol' cup of java, and while I never would've guessed that flavor would set my engine purring, right now it *so* did.

He made some sort of noise in his throat, a rumble—of pleasure or warning, I wasn't sure—so I doubled down and tightened my hold on him, pressing my nipples into his big, brawny chest.

As far as adventures went, I wasn't doing so badly after one hell of a false start.

"Enough." His command sliced through me as he pushed me back, nearly sending me toppling to the pavement thanks to my insane boots. He gripped my arms to steady me and ground his teeth together loudly enough to make me shiver. "What the heck is wrong with you, lady?"

He'd called me lady twice so far. I'd only minded once.

Who was I kidding? I didn't mind anything that flew out of this sexy, hulking stranger's mouth. And oh, what a mouth it was.

Sculpted lips surrounded by a hint of stubble, white teeth, and a tongue that had given me ten seconds of glory before he shoved me back.

Next time I'd aim for twenty.

"I have a name." The haughty tone entered my voice without conscious thought. Hearing it, I cursed under my breath. I didn't want to be that girl any longer. The perfect, untouched woman everyone wanted to keep under glass because I'd made a fortune that way. I was my family's cash cow—and Bellavia Records too, for that matter—and no one wanted to jeopardize a good thing.

Except me. If I didn't jeopardize something fast, I was going to lose my mind.

The guy I'd just mouth-mauled gave me a thin smile. "Really? Me too. We're both kinda special, aren't we?" With another glance at my Porsche, he shook his head. "This needs to be reported. You had an accident. And those plates need to be run." He clamped his teeth together again audibly. "The chips will fall where they may."

"You do know who I am, don't you? That bit about not being a bodyguard was all just bullshit." I dragged out my phone from my tiny hip purse. "I'm calling a tow truck and a cab, in that order. Your threats about the police don't faze me. I'll pay the fines. You know I'm good for it."

"Wait." He gripped my wrist and I let my cell slide back in my purse. "You own that car?"

This guy must be new. If he was following me, how had he missed my trip to Walters Porsche and BMW? I'd been in there for almost an hour. And no, the car wasn't technically mine, but I'd borrowed it with an option to buy. They *expected* me to buy. I was a star after all, and stars on the verge of a downward spiral bought fancy cars and wrecked them just because they were spoiled brats.

Just like I was acting like right now.

Defeated, I sank down on the nearby curb, letting the cold from the concrete seep through my stupidly expensive dress. I was hot all over, partly from the adrenaline from the chase and partly from being kissed by a real man with a hard as hell body and no small amount of disgust in my direction.

Well-earned, because he'd pegged me accurately within a few moments. Even without knowing all the particulars, my behavior was a red flag. I might have escaped from my fortress tonight to taste freedom, but I was going to regret it all tomorrow.

I already was.

"They trusted me with the car. It wasn't its fault I curbed it and popped the tire. Hopefully, I didn't mess up the other tire too badly." Peering at the toes of my boots in the darkness, I sighed. "I'll pay whatever I owe for damages. I shouldn't have taken such a risk. It was inexcusably irresponsible."

God, it had felt so good. For those few moments, I'd felt like I was flying down the streets. I'd never driven that fast in my life. The music had been playing—not mine, never mine—and the spring night air had tossed my hair into a delightful frenzy. Nothing about me was photo shoot-ready right now. I was a mess from head to toe, and I'd never felt more alive.

Miserable at this very second, true, but alive.

"You won't hear me arguing with you." He ran his thumb along the thin chain around his neck. I'd noticed that chain and its small Saint Michael medal right away. My uncle Griff, a cop, used to wear the same medal. Supposedly, it offered protection to the wearer.

Too bad it hadn't helped Uncle Griff.

Right or wrongly, I couldn't help gravitating to this stranger because of that small sign. It seemed like a good omen. This man felt safe to me, even as he offered me an intoxicating hint of danger. Contradictory impulses aside, I couldn't deny the pull toward him.

Didn't want to.

"You could have seriously injured someone or yourself," he continued when I remained silent.

What could I say? That I'd done a full diva trip and should be embarrassed? I already knew that. Tomorrow I'd hide in bed all day and try to convince myself one more time that not making the kind of music I wanted to make was no big deal.

So what if I thought I'd die if I had to sing one more slickly produced song about falling in love for the first time? That was my job. I was no better than the thousands of people who went to work every day at jobs they hated, and most of them weren't compensated as handsomely as I was. I had absolutely no right to bitch, even in my own head.

"You're sure you didn't hurt yourself. You're okay?"

Nodding glumly, I stared at the pavement. Already the metal bars around my life were clanging shut once more.

And best of all, now I'd get to explain my reckless behavior to my parents. Which was complete bullshit. I was twenty-three. Plenty old enough to stand on my own two feet and make my own decisions.

Next time I'd start with some smart ones, just for a change of pace.

A hand appeared in my line of vision. "Get up."

As tempting as it was to say "no" and remain right where I was, I took his offered hand and rose, eyeing him warily. Just in case I'd categorized him wrong from the little bit I had to go on, I needed to lay my cards out on the table. "I'm not going to pay you off to hide this."

His rough laughter caught me off-guard. Big time. How could there be such melody in such a discordant sound? It was like sandpaper over skin, abrasive, even derogatory. Yet I shifted closer, wanting to hear it again. Desperate to see if it made his eyes flare with color and life.

I was eager for that most of all. Life. Experiences. Material to help me write the kind of edgy songs I longed for. I didn't want to be just bubblegum anymore. I wanted to grow.

And how pretentious was that? Other people were struggling just to get by, and I was worried about feeding my stupid soul.

"Honey, you couldn't afford me, I guarantee you."

I cupped my elbows and tilted my head. "Everyone has a price."

"Not me." He seemed almost smug in his assertion.

"I used to say the same thing." I gazed off into the distance, smiling wistfully at the rows of homes with the curtains pulled tight over windows backlit by the glow of lamps or TVs. We were at the edge of Kensington Square where businesses flowed into homes. A lot of windows were dark, because it was late for this neighborhood full of families.

I wouldn't know about that. I barely saw my parents except when they wanted to keep me in line, and it had been that way since I'd begun finding success with music. Not so surprisingly, *now* they were more attentive.

At least when they worried their cash cow might stop giving milk.

"What's yours?" he asked softly, surprising me into bringing my gaze back to his. He wasn't the sort of man I'd have pegged as my type. Oh, he was handsome all right, but in a brutish sort of way. His jaw was sharp under his stubble, his eyes hard and unrelenting in their perusal. And I was pretty sure I'd yet to come out on the positive side of the ledger, not that I could blame him there.

Honestly, his lack of regard toward me was rather...refreshing. He didn't act charmed or impressed or even all that aware of me as a woman. I was just a person. A bratty, petulant one at the moment, granted.

What would it take to make those unforgiving eyes warm with approval? Was it even possible?

Maybe honesty would. I could give him that, even if he turned out to be in cahoots with Taylor. What difference did it make if I told someone how I really felt? No one paid me any mind. Maybe if I told someone I could nudge the elephant off my chest so I could breathe again.

"My price was approval," I said quietly.

I hadn't changed one bit. Here I was standing on a dark street corner, trying to please some man I didn't know by telling him something real. That was my nature. People pleaser. Approval seeker.

Pop princess, go home and slip into your ivory tower. That's where you belong.

"Isn't everybody's?" His dry response teased a smile out of me. "Look, I like chatting with you and all, but we need to call this in. Even if this car is yours, you need to do an accident report. You might need to be looked at by a medical professional."

I laughed at that one. "Because I'm talking all crazy?"

"You said it, not me."

"I did." I sighed. "Yeah. We can call the cops. Might as well keep it all above board." I brightened. "Maybe this will end up in the papers?"

I probably shouldn't want that, on account of the whole diva-in-danger headline that was sure to accompany the article. Plus, it was a shitty thing to do, to borrow a car and mess it up, even in a minor, repairable way.

But maybe just maybe someone would look at me a little differently. Perhaps they'd wonder if something more lurked beneath my perfect hair and plastic smile.

Or maybe they'd just up my life insurance policy.

"You want this in the paper?" His brow furrowed. "Why?"

"Well, I'm of two minds."

He crossed his arms. "No kidding."

Swallowing hard, I strode toward the Porsche. Why was I baring myself to this stranger? Kissing him was one thing. Even going home with him—

Wait. No, I could not do that. A, he hadn't asked. B, he was showing no inclination to ask. C, if he wasn't my manager's hired muscle, he had to be in the security field. Something cop-related. He had eyes like the bodyguards I dealt with day in and day out.

Then there was the medal.

Unless he was just a dangerous man, as he'd warned. Some of

them probably had suspicious eyes and unusual jewelry too. Not that I had a lot of experience with dangerous types, but that seemed reasonable.

"Where are you going?"

"Just getting my stuff." I waved a hand over my shoulder. "Call who you need to. I'm ready to face the music." I tugged open the door of the Porsche and grabbed my guitar case out of the passenger seat.

So much for running away from my life. I couldn't even manage to do it without taking the tools of my trade. This battered case covered in a million band stamps and patches and random stickers I'd been collecting since I was a teen represented so much more than an instrument to me. It stood for the heart and soul of my music. Even if I didn't get many opportunities to play my own songs, that didn't mean I intended to give up. I'd just keep pushing.

One day I'd break through. And in the meantime, I'd collect experiences for the jar in my mind that would give me fodder to create better songs.

I couldn't create without living.

Turning back, I startled at his proximity. He moved as silently and stealthily as a cat.

"Literally," he said, staring down at the guitar case I held between us like a shield. I'd been entertaining less than innocent thoughts in his direction, but now that he was in the dominant position, looming over me, trapping me between his arms braced on the top of the car and the door, suddenly going home alone didn't seem so bad.

This was not the sort of man I was used to.

"W-what?" God, I hoped the question only sounded like a squeak in my head.

He indicated my case with the dip of his chin. His very strong, masculine chin, dark with five o'clock shadow. "You said face the music, then you whipped out a guitar."

"Oh, yeah." Blindly, I glanced down at the case and wondered how my boneless fingers didn't drop it to the ground. "I'm a singer."

"And someone gave you their Porsche." His disbelief was obvious.

"No. I kind of borrowed it. With their permission," I added hastily. "The dealership let me take it for a test drive because I told them I wanted to buy it."

"Oh, really." He set his elbow on the top of the car and leaned his cheek on his fist like he was curling up for story time. "And your say so is enough for you to just stroll out with a car like this. A car worth a hundred grand—"

I cocked a brow. "Try one twenty-five."

"Oh, so very sorry." His smirk did something not entirely unpleasant to my belly. "My original statement stands. Your word's enough to walk out—and wreck—a car like this."

"Yes." Temper licked up my spine, making my smile tight. "Have you ever heard of Peyton Pryor?"

His blank expression both annoyed and intrigued me. Either he was the finest actor I'd ever encountered or else he really didn't know my name. "No. I have not. Should I know her?"

So much for him being part of the security detail, which made him infinitely more interesting. He was an unknown quantity.

I tilted my head and softened my smile. Seduction was only part of my repertoire on stage, and only sanitized sex. I appealed to teen girls who still had posters on their walls and teen boys who had the hots for the chick next door. But I had an inner vamp somewhere down deep. The boots and the tight dress I'd bought this afternoon before my trip to the car dealership proved it.

Now I had to put that vamp to work.

Trailing a fingertip up his beefy arm, revealed by the short sleeves of his T-shirt, I gathered my courage. "Do you want to?"

JED

This night was not going the way I'd anticipated.

My beer and boxing match were fading further into the rearview mirror with every moment that passed. What I *should* do was call my buddy on the force to put this whole mess away.

I had to make sure the car was towed and returned to its rightful owner. That was my civic duty.

"Are you lucid?" I asked finally. "Did you hit your head in the crash?"

When she rolled her eyes, I tamped down on the urge to give her firm ass a not-so-gentle tap.

"No. I'm not injured. I was just suggesting that maybe we get to know each other in private." She wet her lush red lips. The brief taste I'd gotten wasn't nearly enough to satisfy my hunger in her direction. "After we contact the authorities and a tow truck, of course."

My cock veered abruptly against my zipper. Or maybe it wasn't so abrupt, since I'd been on a low simmer for the last few minutes. "Clarify get to know each other."

"That depends on you."

"No, honey, it does not."

She adjusted her hold on her guitar case, not so subtly pressing it into my chest and groin. Damn shame that my groin wasn't averse to the contact.

At least it gave me something to hide my hard-on behind.

"Hmm, not sure if I like it better when you call me lady. You could try my name though, just for kicks." She set the case on the ground between her feet and pried out her phone, holding it to her ear. "Hi, I'm Peyton Pryor and I was looking to buy a Porsche—" She stopped, her smile transforming her face.

She had such a range of them. So far I'd seen witchy smile, pissed smile and seductive smile. Now this was something else altogether. As beautiful as it was, it was utterly fake.

"Yes, that's correct. I'm afraid there was a mishap with the vehicle." She ignored my pointed stare. "Oh, no, I'm fine. Not a mark on me. The car's fine too. Well, mostly. No, really, I appreciate your concern." Her smile warmed fractionally. "Thank you, Steve. That's really sweet of you to offer to come meet me where I am. I don't want you to go to any trouble. I can just have a tow truck...oh, if you're sure it's no bother. A ride would be—"

"Unnecessary," I cut in, surprised by how much I didn't want her to disappear with this Steve guy.

Her chin lifted and she continued speaking as if I hadn't said a thing. I fisted my hands at my sides to stop myself from grabbing her phone. She wasn't mine, even for a night, and I was practicing being more easygoing.

True, my practicing hadn't yet paid off, and this one seemed to push my buttons more than most. But I was making progress.

I was also making progress on leaving police work firmly in the past, my instincts aside. Even so, I needed to deal with the police right now.

I pulled out my phone and turned away as I called my old buddy Thomas to find out the best way to handle this situation. It wasn't really one for the overtaxed 911 system, but an officer should be sent to the scene. There was a good chance they'd want to give Peyton a Breathalyzer, and of course they'd need to run her record to see if she had any outstanding warrants.

I eyed her, still chatting merrily with "Steve", while I relayed what had happened to my old pal on the force. Almost offhandedly, I mentioned the name "Peyton Pryor" and Thomas sucked in a breath.

"Not *the* Peyton Pryor," he said, his tone somehow reverent.

Husky feminine laughter made me aim a hard stare in *the* Peyton's direction. "Apparently," I muttered, hating that even her giggling was making me hard. Okay, harder, since liftoff had been achieved a while ago.

Damn her and bless her, all at once.

"So, ah, mind filling me in?" I asked in a low voice.

Peyton was too busy flipping her hair around her fingers and flirting with the dude who didn't seem to give a fig that she'd curbed his expensive car to notice how long *I* was taking on the phone.

Steve had probably been mesmerized by the boots. My gaze darted up her shapely expanse of thigh. I wasn't the only one.

"On what?" Thomas questioned, still sounding a bit dazed.

Peyton seemed to inspire that reaction in men easily. Too easily, from where I was standing.

My gaze lifted from her sexy legs to the face she'd upturned to the night. Her eyes were closed and she was still smiling as she talked, the wind playing with her long dark hair. Lifting and separating the strands before letting them fall against the bodice of her clingy sweater dress. If she were naked, her hair would coyly curve around her nipples in a naughty version of peek-a-boo.

Dammit.

Thomas started to respond but I didn't hear him, because Peyton's eyes had opened to focus on mine. From the smug little smile she wore, she knew exactly what she was doing. She was fucking teasing me, flirting with that other dude just to get my attention in spite of how inappropriate it was considering the situation. She'd just had an accident and she didn't even know my name.

I could be a serial killer. A man who collected body parts as trophies for my den. A guy who couldn't stop thinking about paddling her taut little ass.

But that hadn't stopped her from asking me home for the night. And it hadn't stopped me from being ridiculously tempted.

Thomas used the phrase "one of the biggest pop stars" and I swallowed hard, though my mouth had gone dry.

Fuck me, I was going to do this.

It had been too long, and I didn't give a shit about repercussions right now. She was a grown woman, and I was a grown man. If Steve didn't give a whit about his damaged vehicle, then neither did I.

"Get someone out here to deal with this, please. Thanks, man. Talk to you later," I said, abruptly cutting off my friend. I'd feel bad for it tomorrow, but I'd hit my limit.

Soon enough she'd understand exactly what she'd unleashed.

Pocketing my phone, I strode to her and inclined my chin. "He's coming to collect the car?"

I half-expected her to ignore me or worse, argue. Instead she gave me a shaky nod and told Steve where he could find his car. She apologized profusely, stating again that she'd pay for any damages, and then she hung up and stared at me, her pale throat working.

Not so in control now, huh, pop princess?

Silently, she waited for me to make a move.

I moved closer. Her chest lifted and fell with a quick intake of breath. At least around me, her practiced seduction faltered.

Good. I intended to see in what other ways I could knock her off her game.

"Were you serious about us getting to know each other?" I brushed against the guitar case she'd gone back to clutching like a lifeline.

She nodded.

My mouth curled. I had a feeling she wasn't quiet very often. "Cat got your tongue?"

"No." She bit the fullness of her lower lip and I nearly groaned. "I just don't want my big mouth to make you change your mind."

"Active mouths don't bother me...as long as they're used for the right things."

Her pupils widened and now that lower lip dropped as if I'd scandalized her. "You—you're not referring to— Yes, you are."

Liking her reaction entirely too much, I stepped closer and stroked my calloused thumb over her petal-soft cheek. "Look at you, dropping right into the gutter."

"I have never been in the gutter. Not one time." Her vehemence—and seeming disgust—at that fact made twin flags of color rise in her cheeks. She was so animated, every thought telegraphing across her face. It made me want to give her more experiences, just to watch her process them.

"But you want to be?" I couldn't disguise his surprise.

"Yes." No hesitation whatsoever. "I've never been anything but the good girl. I'd never even speeded before tonight." Her laughter held a note of desperation. "Hell, I hardly even get to drive myself anymore. Do you know what that's like, to lose something that's as much a part of you as your left arm?"

"Yeah." I had to clear my throat. I understood all too well.

"I used to love to drive. Now I'm herded everywhere, from appearances to interviews to shows and back to whichever hotel I'm staying in, where I hide to avoid paparazzi." As if realizing what she'd said, she glanced around and smiled faintly. "Hey, we're still alone."

"Not for long," he muttered. "So you're really a...pop star?"

I didn't really even understand what that meant. Was she like a solo Americanized version of One Direction, with the addition of breasts? I had no clue who the current pop stars were, or even what that kind of music sounded like. Probably something my niece

Jenny would listen to. She listened to bubblegum stuff that made my ears ring within a few moments of her turning it on.

She winced. "I thought you didn't know who I was."

"I didn't, but Thomas did."

At Thomas's name, her face brightened. "Tommy? I know his brother Gabe from the country club. Or at least I used to." She frowned. "A long time ago, back before everything exploded."

"Your career? Or your life?"

"Both. It seemed to happen together." Her chin trembled. "Did you call your buddies to take me in? Are you a cop?"

"Used to be," I said before my brain kicked in. I didn't want to make this personal.

What's more personal than sex? Because you know damn well you didn't want to take her home to split a beer.

Luckily, a radio car pulled up just then, lights off. The officer who stepped out, Jensen, was another old friend, and bonus, he processed the scene without becoming starstruck by *the* Peyton Prior. He didn't question her to find out if she'd been drinking, but she appeared more than coherent as she admitted matter-of-factly that yes, she'd been speeding before causing the minor accident, and yes, the car belonged to the dealership. She seemed very apologetic and Jensen made no mention of other charges, since she indicated she'd already been in contact with the dealership about making reparations.

The Pryor effect was in full force.

I was tempted to pull Jensen aside to ask if he knew who she was, but from the wink he threw her just before he got back in his cruiser, I realized I'd been outgunned again.

Everyone knew Peyton it seemed. Except me.

A fact I intended to change soon.

The equally smitten Steve arrived just as Jensen was leaving, and he didn't seem to appreciate me tugging Peyton away before he could chat her up beyond getting her insurance information and a few other particulars. Several times, she'd shot grateful looks at me that Jensen hadn't "thrown the book at her"—something she'd mentioned numerous times, as if she got a charge out of the phrase —and she didn't complain when I insisted it was time to go home.

"Your home?" she asked hopefully the moment we were out of Steve's earshot.

I glanced back. Despite the arrival of the tow truck, the other man was still staring after them unhappily, his damaged Porsche the least of his concerns. Granted, he had insurance too, and retaining someone like Peyton as a client apparently mattered more than any lost time or inconvenience.

Though I would bet a thousand bucks that Steve wasn't going easy on her in the hopes of recouping some money down the road if she purchased a vehicle.

He wanted *her*.

"Fucking boots," I muttered, unlocking my truck and pulling open the passenger door.

"What?" Baffled, she glanced up at me.

"Never mind. Get in." I took the guitar case out of her hand. Feeling her gaze on me, I opened the back door and put it gently on the seat.

Apparently satisfied that I wasn't going to rough up her prize instrument, she nodded and slipped into the passenger seat, drawing her mile-long legs up and tucking them in.

I tried not to stare. Tried not to feel the pulse of blood in my cock as I visually traced the zipper from the back of her calf to her foot.

"Problem, officer?"

Her voice was silky. Too silky for my liking, because she still thought she had the upper hand.

Time to show her otherwise.

I shut the back door. "Detective," I corrected, giving her a quick, disarming smile. It was the one I'd used dozens of times on perps to get them to let down their guard. "Ex-detective."

She caught her breath and smiled back. "As you wish."

My smile fell away. "What do you have on under that dress?"

Most other women either would've cursed at me for being so forward or they would've come back at me with a sexy response. Peyton just screwed up her mouth and appeared to think over the question. "I'm not sure, actually. I was more concerned with the wrapping than the box and this dress is new—" She broke off as I smiled, genuinely this time. "What?"

"I'm concerned enough with the box for both of us, Rule-breaker."

She flushed. "You have a filthy mouth to go with the filthy mind."

"Oh, you have no idea."

"Will I get to?"

"So eager." I touched her face again, just a quick skim of my fingers over her cheek. "I imagine in your life you've been with all kinds of men."

"I wish. Mostly self-indulgent rockstars and the occasional accountant who worked for the label."

The disparaging way she dismissed being with rockstars made me smother a grin. "How about ex-detectives? Ever been with one of those?"

Her flush deepened. "Not a one," she said softly, cupping her hand over mine against her face. "I'm hoping to change that tonight."

My heart skipped a beat. Or three. I might've been annoyed at my reaction, if not for the fact that it had been more than a year since I'd had a girlfriend...or sex.

I didn't date, ever. My interests were such that it usually didn't take me long to find out I'd be incompatible in the bedroom with someone new. Little Miss Pop Star didn't fit neatly in line with the needs I'd turned my back on, but I didn't intend to fully let them out of the box anyway.

I'd just crack the lid a little and offer her a taste.

There was another taste I wanted more than my next breath.

But I'd never take that step without making sure she was on the same page.

I glanced in the direction of the Porsche just as the tow truck hauled it down the street. Steve was already gone.

Shifting my gaze back to Peyton, I let my thumb drop to her lower lip and gave it a quick, firm stroke. She gasped as if I'd licked her nipple.

Something else I wanted to do. Fiercely.

"May I kiss you?"

I waited for her nod of acknowledgement before I pulled her around sideways on the seat. She startled, eyes going wide. They only went wider when I planted a hand on her belly and pushed her backward, looming over her until she got the message to recline on the seat. She went to her elbows, parting her legs instinctively.

Still not far enough for me.

I pushed up her dress and wrenched her thighs apart, nearly going cross-eyed at the polka dot panties that awaited me. White on black. So freaking sweet.

"You're going to kill me, baby girl."

"W-what are you—Oh God," she moaned as I bent my head to lick her through the cotton.

I couldn't stop my grin. "Call me Jed."

PEYTON

JED. WHAT A PERFECTLY WONDERFUL NAME.

I probably should've asked for his name earlier but it hadn't seemed important. What was important was this.

Just *this*.

His tongue pressed against me, dampening the fabric that didn't need much help. His rough, raspy voice was enough to start me up all on its own. Add in his penetrating stare and that smirky mouth and I was done for.

Done for on a shadowy road in small town Kensington Square. This night had certainly taken an interesting turn.

His big hands spread my thighs and I peeked over the dashboard, half expecting to see a camera crew setting up at the other end of the street. This was a quiet residential neighborhood, and I was in the front seat of a decidedly non-flashy Ford Bronco, but my jig would be up soon.

Surely someone would spot us and—

"Oh," I whispered as his teeth closed on my soft inner thigh. The flash of pain was unexpected and sent a bolt of liquid heat unfurling inside me, paving the way for his hungry licks.

Not that he'd delved beneath the material yet. Why did he need to? If he kept this up, he was going to make me soak right through it.

"Eyes on me," he commanded, and it didn't occur to me to disagree. Something about him told me he was a man not used to tolerating arguments. That irrefutable sense of authority made my riotous emotions go quiet and still, but not because he was stifling me. Quite the contrary. The way he took charge let me know I didn't have to be in control.

Right now, I could just be. He would handle everything.

Handle *me*.

"Good girl." He kissed the spot he'd just bitten, and I let my head fall back, letting the warmth of his praise and his ministrations carry me to another place. One with no worries and no responsibilities and no concerns about disappointing anyone.

I didn't care right now about record units or ticket sales or artistic integrity. There was just enjoying the insistent laps of his tongue, and the electric drag of his teeth, and the seductive slide of his fingertips on my damp inner legs. He didn't put his fingers where I needed them, just circled around and around, using his mouth to drive me insane.

He rubbed his nose against my clit while he nuzzled my swollen lower lips. I jolted at the contact, surprised at the giggle that almost escaped.

"Like that, huh?"

"It tickles."

He did it again and this time it didn't tickle at all. The pressure right where I needed it grew, becoming an ache that made me grind my hips into the seat.

I fought my impulse to pull on his hair. I didn't know how he'd react, and God, I didn't want him to stop. It had been so long, and I was so close.

"Do it," he rumbled against my drenched flesh, and I exhaled, relieved. He understood, and he didn't mind.

I sank my fingers into his dense brown hair, creating more spikes. The style was close to his scalp, but he still had enough on top to give me something to hold onto. Pulling him into me only made the slide of his tongue that more intense, and he growled as I instinctually drew my legs closer to my chest to give him more room to work.

Following my wordless lead, he flattened his mouth against my slit and did the most marvelous thing with his tongue, swirling it, alternating his outside the panties action with some playful nips and bites that didn't seem to match his personality at all. I tugged harder on his hair and he growled, causing me to cry out. My panties were going to disintegrate under all that hot, focused attention. My clit was positively throbbing, and I couldn't stop shifting restlessly against the seat.

Too much. I needed to come and he just kept going on and on, never landing long enough to allow me the release I so desperately craved.

"I bet if I slid my tongue down farther, you'd be wet back there too." His voice burned against my overstimulated flesh. "You're dripping."

I flushed, but not from embarrassment. Only excitement and anticipation fueled me now. "Don't make promises you can't keep, Detective."

Whether it was my subtle tease or the use of the term Detective that pushed him into action, I didn't know. One moment I was on my back with my toes pointing toward the roof of his truck and the next I was on my knees, ass in the air with my hands flat on the driver's seat. And my panties were gone.

I moaned as he buried his face between my legs, stabbing his tongue deep to mimic the act I longed for. He didn't stop until I was pressing my bottom against his face, helpless to stifle my cries. Just when I thought he'd finally let me climax, he slid his mouth up to the tight pucker between my cheeks and tongued me there while his fingers played a rhythm along my plump lips.

Darting in, out. Over and over.

Finally, he circled my clit with his thumb, once, twice, and I shattered, bumping my head against the steering wheel as I rode out the spasms. His fingers and tongue never stopped, taking me to the limits of my endurance and then past them.

When I'd lost the ability to even gasp, I sagged to the seat, my knees giving out. "Holy sweet mother of..."

He chuckled and scooped me up as if I was weightless, setting me back to rights on the seat. He tugged my dress down to a discreet level, then swore and pulled harder. Evidently, he wanted to cover me up, since I was pretty sure he wasn't the type to be overly concerned if I was cold.

"You asked to kiss me," I mumbled, not entirely certain I sounded lucid. My brain waves had flatlined the moment he'd kissed me down *there.*

"I did. You said yes."

I managed to lift my head far enough for our gazes to collide. I was hard-pressed to decide if I was more mesmerized by the intensity of his stare or the wetness that coated his mouth.

If I kissed him for real right now, he'd taste like *me.* Heat rushed into my face. *All* of me.

"You didn't specify where you intended to kiss me."

He chuckled again. "Nope, you assumed. And you know what they say about that."

After belting me in—since I hadn't yet recovered the ability to do it myself—and closing my door, he rounded the hood to get behind the wheel.

We drove in silence for a few moments. Then he sighed. "Do you always fidget so much?"

Guiltily, I slipped my hands beneath my legs. He hadn't bitten me in those spots, but the sting from the little love nips he'd peppered along my inner thighs traveled straight up my legs too.

I liked it. Wanted more. The flash of soreness made sure I never forgot for an instant what we'd shared—

Uh-uh. Nope. Not going there.

We hadn't shared anything, and I was *not* going to romanticize this. I didn't even know his last name or where he lived. He could be taking me to his studio apartment above a strip joint for all I knew.

Not that that would be bad. I wanted more experiences, and I'd never been to a strip joint. Though hopefully, I'd get some other experiences before that particular one. But it'd be interesting to see his response to the request in any case.

I cast a quick look at his strong profile, illuminated by the passing headlights. "If I wanted to go to a..." I fumbled around for the phrase I'd heard some of the roadies use. "...titty bar, would you come with me?"

His lips twitched. "When you break out of your shell, you go big or go home."

With a laugh, I settled back in my seat, curling my hands together in my lap. His answer soothed me immeasurably.

This was a man who would never say no to my desires, no matter how wild or outlandish. I didn't know how I knew that with such certainty, but I did.

He might laugh, he might give me that look that said he thought I was just this side of batshit, but he'd never say no.

And he'd given me an orgasm without expecting one in return.

Catching him glancing my way while he licked the inside of his lower lip, I tried not to squirm from sheer delight. *Yet.*

JED

She looked at everything. Questioned everything, even when she didn't voice those questions aloud.

I had a feeling she was probably noting things on a little checklist inside her busy brain.

Where would I rate after this night was through?

We parked in the driveway beside my house. By my best guess, the small ranch wasn't exactly the type of home she normally spent time in.

She didn't say a word as she climbed down from the vehicle. I shut the door behind her and retrieved her guitar from the back, figuring she was probably used to people holding open doors and carrying things for her. I would have anyway. My mother had taught me well.

A lady deserved to be pampered, and Peyton was definitely a lady through and through.

Following her up the solar lit flagstone walk, I grinned to myself. Lady or not, she sure could scream. I liked that about her too. She didn't have an ounce of shame in her responses. If something felt good to her, she was happy to let me know it.

It just made me more eager to make sure she was happy often.

At least for tonight.

"I like your house," she said while I searched my pockets for my keys.

"You can't even see it. It's dark out here."

"The frogs next to the walk give off some light." I heard the smile in her voice. "They're cute."

Finding the key, I shoved it in the lock and turned my face away in case she could see my flush. Somehow she'd made me blush because she liked my solar frogs. Maybe because I even *had* solar frogs. Compared to her life of limos and lounge lizards, they probably seemed hopelessly quaint.

Better hopelessly quaint than a washed-up used-to-be cop who sat around in unbuttoned jeans in front of my laptop all day, resisting the whiskey in my cabinet and the Camels I'd quit while I pounded on the keys.

I hadn't intended to choose this life, but I'd discovered along the way that it suited me. Facing myself and the character voices in my head every morning was both therapy and punishment.

Over the past two years, I'd sought both.

I pushed open the front door and flipped on the light in the foyer, stepping aside to let my guest inside. I shut the door and set down her guitar case, then I took my sweet time turning back to face her.

She must be wondering how she'd ended up in a rundown place like this with a guy like me.

A guy she'd gone home with without even asking my last name.

Unable to deny the urge, I turned back and took a long sniff of her hair. Her scent was lightly floral, as if she'd used the appropriate two spritzes of her fancy perfume before she'd gone joyriding through town.

"Do you do this often?" I growled, unable to temper my sudden possessiveness as I buried my face in the long dark waves spilling over her shoulders.

Her scent was stronger at the base of her neck and I wallowed in it, letting myself drown in the memory of her swollen clit pounding against my lips.

One thought echoed in my head.

Mine, mine, mine.

She stiffened for the first time in the last hour, but she didn't pull away. "Do what?"

"Go home with strange men. Men you don't bother asking for their names."

Her shoulders relaxed. "I know yours." She swiveled to face me. This close, her perfume clung to me like smoke. "It's Jed."

I groaned at the melodic way she said my name. It rolled off her tongue until I wanted to taste that sound just like I'd sampled the rest of her. Simply swallow it until I could carry her teasing, sexy voice with me forever.

The heavy thud of paws and click of nails on the hardwood floor heralded Freddy's arrival, if the loud bark he let out wasn't a big enough clue. A wide smile broke on her face as she turned to greet my gold and brown mutt. She dropped to her knees to circle her arms around his neck while Freddy tried to lick her into submission.

"Hey there, boy. Off the pretty girl's dress." I hooked a finger in Freddy's collar and tried to drag him back, letting out a grunt when Freddy planted his sizeable rump and refused to move.

"He's fine." Peyton laughed and continued trading kisses with my dog. She didn't balk at the way Freddy surged against her, getting his muddy paws all over her legs. Even when he pushed his wet nose in all the places he shouldn't, her grin only grew.

I rocked back on my heels and tried to ignore the tickle in my throat. Loving my boy was a serious turn-on.

"You like dogs." The understatement of the century.

"I do. I always wanted one, but with my lifestyle, it doesn't seem fair."

"Surely you have...handlers who can take care of one for you while you're away."

"I suppose." She stroked Freddy's furry cheek, some of the joy in her expression dimming. I hated that I'd done that to her, even for a moment. "It's just hard. I wouldn't want my puppy or my kid to be raised by people who wouldn't love them like I would."

"So you deny yourself entirely."

She shot me a look under her thick tangled lashes. "I'm good at that."

"That stops while you're with me." I brushed a hand over her hair and she leaned into my palm, giggling as Freddy punctuated the comment with a long lick of her hand.

She continued to stroke the dog and lean into me, seemingly content. She clearly enjoyed affectionate touches—and I was beginning to think she hadn't experienced nearly enough of them.

"On average, how much do you travel?" I asked.

Not that it mattered to me one way or the another, since this was just a one-night deal. But the idea of her never sleeping in the same bed two nights running seemed wrong. A woman like the one cavorting on the floor in front of me seemed made to own a dog with a goofy smile and a big tongue lolling out of his mouth. She should be able to run in the park and dance in the rain without having to look over her shoulder for the paparazzi.

Nor should she have to "borrow" a car to go joyriding just to evade her life.

And now I was being like Freddy, sticking my nose where I shouldn't.

She jerked a shoulder and let her forehead drop to Freddy's soft neck. "It's easier to count the days I'm home," she said quietly.

"Where is home exactly?"

"Brooklyn. I have a townhouse. But my aunt lives in Kensington Square, so I took a ride up north."

I lifted a brow. "Not a penthouse in Manhattan? You surprise me, Rulebreaker."

"When I'm on my own, I don't want to be surrounded by glitz. I want something real. I want to look out the window at the Brooklyn Bridge and watch little kids making snowmen. I don't want to be surrounded by nightclubs and famous people and faux everything." She rose and sighed as my dog laid his head against her thigh, his devotion obvious. "Can I keep him?"

If I can keep you.

I didn't know where the thought came from, and I sure as hell intended to send it right back into the ether. I wasn't a romantic—or at least I hadn't been until I'd decided to play hero and rescue a gorgeous, inexplicable brunette from her not-quite-a-wreck.

"How do you feel about joint custody?" I stepped closer and caught my fingers in her curls, pulling lightly. "He's gotten used to me."

The corner of her mouth lifted. "I can see how that could happen."

Another step forward brought my chest flush with hers, though we weren't as close as we could have been, thanks to the canine interloper between us. "He likes my bed."

"Does he now?" She licked her lips. "Again, I have to say I can see why."

"Don't say that before—" A playful tug on her hair led to it tipping precariously on her head. I blinked and reached up to slide my hand through it, absorbing her wince as I drew the mass of dark curls away to reveal a sleek fall of platinum blond.

What the hell?

I stared at the wig in my fist then looked back at her, nearly swallowing my tongue at the full effect. White-blond hair dipped over one bluer than blue eye and pale pink lips curved into a pout worthy of any pinup calendar.

Fucking A, she was glorious.

I wasn't surprised she graced teenagers' walls all over the country. What truly surprised me was that she hadn't taken over the world.

"Sorry." Her grimace intensified. "I should've told you, but I've always wanted to be a brunette."

"So commit to it. Dye your hair, don't put on this fake crap." Deliberately emphasizing the word *fake*, I tossed the hair on the table by the door.

Freddy watched the wig fly through the air and immediately rushed over to the table to seize his prize. He trotted away with it in his mouth, causing me to swear and turn to follow.

"No, let him play." Peyton laughed and grabbed my arm. "You're right. It doesn't suit me. It's also hot as hell."

"I didn't say that. Everything suits you. You make my throat hurt, just looking at you."

Her hand came up to *her* throat, and she stroked it as a wrinkle formed between her light brows. "That sounds bad."

"Try feeling it." I threaded my fingers through her fine pin-straight hair and let my gaze drift down her body. "Anything else fake that I should know about?"

Frowning, she stepped back. Maybe this was it. I'd gone too far, been a little too honest, and now she would call for a limo and sail out of my life as abruptly as she'd entered it.

Except I wouldn't be able to forget. I'd sit down at his computer and be forced to download some pop shit I normally wouldn't listen to if someone paid me, just to hear her voice in my head in reality rather than conjuring up a memory.

She reached back and unzipped her dress, letting it pool around her incredible boots. Then she flicked her fingers over the front clasp of her modest polka dot bra, causing that to fall away too.

Once she'd shed the panties I'd already savored thoroughly, she stood before me in all her blond glory, blushing in a way that told me she didn't put herself on display like this very often.

"All real from here on out," she whispered.

"That so?" I looked my fill, waiting for her to squirm and try to cover herself. But she stood tall and proud, shoulders back. My thumb circled one shell pink nipple until it beaded.

"These too?" I asked, already knowing the answer.

There was no part of her gorgeous body that hadn't been granted by nature. She had no visible piercings beyond her ears, no tattoos. Even the groomed tuft of blond curls between her legs showed that she didn't always gravitate toward artifice.

"Very real." She gave him a tremulous smile. "If I'd bought them, I'd have gone a little bigger."

"Why? You got a problem with perfection?"

Her sharp intake of breath came even before I dipped his head to take the nipple I'd stroked into my mouth. I tugged hard with my teeth, enjoying her gasp of surprise and the clutch of her fingers in my hair.

Hell, I frigging *loved* how she pulled my hair.

"You're a sweet talker. I wouldn't have guessed."

Laughter rumbled through my chest. "There's no part of me that's sweet. You'll discover that soon enough." I nipped her breast and she cried out, the sound breaking across my skin like waves at the shore.

I hadn't surfed in years, but I felt precariously balanced right now, riding a line I'd deliberately not crossed in so long.

And if I *did* cross it, I definitely shouldn't cross it with someone who smelled like some fancy Parisian perfume and had skin so pale she'd wear any mark I gave her for weeks.

That wasn't exactly a bad thing.

Her fingers clenched that much harder in my hair. "What does that mean?"

I debated painting a rosy picture for her, or better yet, sidestepping the question altogether. Then I remembered her search for reality, and what I craved was as real as it got. "Should I tell you or should I show you?"

"Show," she replied breathlessly. "Definitely show."

Shaking my head, I lifted her wrist and grazed the soft skin there with my teeth. "Are you always so lax with your safety?"

"Am I not...safe with you?"

"I won't hurt you—unless you ask me to." I let her absorb that while I studied the maze of veins under her near translucent skin.

Any makeup at all beyond mascara and lipstick would make her look garish. She had such a delicate beauty. In my grip, her arm felt fragile. But she wasn't. I could tell that just from the defiant tilt of her chin.

"But I'll push you, and I'll test you, and I won't allow you to take the easy way out."

"Okay."

Her easy acceptance baffled and aroused me. It also stirred the protective instincts I'd fought to shove down for so long. Assimilating to civilian life again had been difficult but stifling my desire to shield seemed impossible right now.

This woman made me want to stop bullets for her, even as I wanted to give her things she'd never known before. Open her eyes in a way she'd never imagined.

At least I didn't think she had. We were still strangers. Strangers who'd come together faster than the speed of doubt.

Steadily, I met her gaze. "You need a safe word."

I was risking so much by putting this on the table between us, but God, I needed to know if what I sensed between us could be true. If this path we were on was meant to go somewhere past the superficiality I'd lived with for way too long.

"What is that, exactly?"

"It's a word you'll say if what we do is too much for you. When you say it, we'll stop, no matter what point we're at." At the silent questions in her eyes, I brushed a kiss over the spot on her inner wrist I'd grazed with his teeth. "*No* always works. This is just one extra safeguard."

"I'm guessing missionary's not on the agenda tonight?"

The sparkle in her eyes made me laugh in spite of the clamp

around my chest. "It may be. There's a whole lot of things I'd love to do with you." My voice lowered. "And *to* you."

She took a shaky breath. "Music. That's my word."

"Fitting." Without saying more, I gripped her hips and spun her around to face the long table along the wall. "Hang on. We're about to go for a ride."

PEYTON

He hadn't kissed me yet. Well, on the mouth anyway.

My face flushed. I had no complaints about where he *had* kissed me, but it seemed strange that he'd started below the waist, moved on to talk of safe words, and now had me facing the wall while he caressed my naked curves.

Oh, and my wig had been absconded with by the dog. Weirdness aplenty.

"This first time will be fast," Jed said, brushing a line of kisses down my spine.

"Fast is good." I arched into the sensation, craving more.

Craving all.

His mouth incited flames to come to life beneath the surface, causing a full-body meltdown until my bones verged on melting. My knees were shaking again, and the bite of his fingers on my hips as he pressed his sizable erection against my behind did nothing to steady me.

Maybe I'd never be steady again. And wouldn't that be wonderful?

"I like fast," I added, in case he didn't grasp how much.

At some point, I should argue. Intellectually, I knew that. I just didn't want to yet.

I was responsible for so much on a daily basis that his tendency to tell me what would occur next—while always making it clear I had a choice whether or not to agree—lessened the weight that constantly hovered on my shoulders.

I never would've believed it could be freeing to be commanded, but it was when your partner somehow understood what you desired without you even having to say a word.

The sound of a zipper behind her startled me.

Oh, God. It was happening already.

My thighs were still slick from his earlier efforts, and they'd only become more so during their discussion. With one lick of my nipple, I'd been ready to go.

"You're so pink all over. Pink and wet." His fingers strummed between my legs again, and I pressed my cheek against the wall, loving this position though I'd never experienced it before.

Being able to hide my face offered me anonymity that allowed me to chase every reaction. I didn't have to hold back with him. He would catch me if I fell.

He *wanted* me to.

His finger slipped inside me and pumped deep, twisting in a way that coaxed all the simmering nerve endings back to brutal awareness. I rocked into his hand, wordlessly asking for more, and he slid in another finger, curving them and circling the spot inside that caused my knees to tremble even harder.

My thighs shook and I gasped for the air that suddenly seemed to be in short supply.

God, what was he doing to me?

He didn't continue to slide in and out. He barely even moved his fingers. But that laser-like touch right where I hadn't realized I needed it was bringing me higher than I'd ever been before.

"Jed," I moaned, digging my nails into his table. I couldn't hold on. Couldn't let go. "It's too much."

"Take more."

What choice did I have? He was still rubbing my flesh, the rough pads of his fingers insistent, and the urgency inside my core was rolling out to encompass every part of me. Every cell.

I folded over the table, caught between trying to escape his hand and to trap it inside me, rising up on my tiptoes to seek more of the impossible heat growing inside me. I couldn't bear it. My nipples dragged over the wood, and I squirmed, trying to get relief for my swollen nipples without relinquishing my hold on the table.

I needed his hands everywhere. His mouth.

His cock.

"I'm going to remove my fingers now."

I could only whimper. He'd hypnotized me with his ministrations and his voice.

God, his voice.

"As soon as I thrust inside you, you're going to come. Understand me, Peyton?"

Not Rulebreaker. Just my name, used to seduce.

I jerked my head in my best imitation of a nod, hoping it was enough. The sound of a foil packet being opened made me relax even as he drew his hand away, though the heavy wet pressure of his fingers on my hip as he positioned me reminded me without a doubt who was in charge.

Both of us.

He might make the rules, but I was the one who said if they worked. I knew he would stop if I asked.

The knowledge was improbable, considering I'd known him all of a couple of hours. That didn't mean it was wrong. I trusted my instincts.

I also trusted that the thick cock pressing against my soaked pussy was going to rock my world in ways I'd never imagined.

"Ready?" he said against my ear, his hot breath making me shiver.

I could only nod. I hadn't forgotten his command, and boy, my body was prepared to comply.

He grabbed my hips and pulled me backward, impaling me to the hilt. Somehow he dragged over that sensitive spot inside my walls just right to bring me to the edge of orgasm, though the spasms didn't fully move through me until he started to pull out, so slowly that she would've sworn his cock was finishing the work his fingers had started.

Applying pressure just *there*.

My head dropped back to his shoulder as he wrapped his arm around my midsection and hauled me upward, making me take his cock deeper even while my body clenched and released. He grunted in my ear and bent his legs, powering into me so hard that I kicked off against the table, my booted foot anchoring to the edge.

"Yes. Just like that." He closed his big hand over one of my needy breasts and my toes curled in my boots.

Quivers rolled down my legs and I couldn't find purchase. My freestanding leg wobbled, threatening to send me to the floor. Only his strong arm around my belly and the fullness of his cock driving me up again and again kept me from collapsing in a heap.

He'd fucked me boneless, and he wasn't close to through.

His teeth grazed the side of my neck and I shifted my head, offering him more. I wanted him to bite me, to give an outlet to the ache already building inside me again.

But he only teased me, licking, nuzzling. He rolled his hips with every thrust, finding new angles to blow my mind.

I should participate. I *wanted* to participate. But I also wanted to absorb. If I never got to experience this again, I needed to wring each second dry.

Besides, I didn't dare interrupt the most perfect rhythm I'd ever known. No song I'd ever composed could come close.

"That's it. Tighten up on me again." His hand found my clit and I jerked against him, driving him so deep that a cry flew from my lips. One twist of his hips and he was seated in a way that promised fulfillment lurked a stroke away.

Then his thumb skimmed my clit, almost offhandedly, and I exploded around him. Moans spilled out of my mouth as I doubled over and rode out the ecstasy that seized me.

I was barely aware of him pulling out. My body had gone into autopilot.

"Uh-uh. Not done with you yet," he said gruffly as I tried to crawl away.

I whimpered. I was too sensitive, my clit throbbing from overuse, but he didn't seem interested in granting me a reprieve.

Bless him.

He scooped me up and carried me into the next room. I opened my eyes, squinting against the lights he flipped on, then I was face-down on the couch, my ass in the air again. He slapped it and I gasped, shocked at the warmth that blossomed from the point of contact.

One more slap against the other side and I was biting the cushion beneath my cheek, wiggling my ass at him, asking for something I couldn't name and longed for with way more than my body.

"Tell me you want this." His voice sounded ragged and raw, as if his own control had thinned to a wire. I ached to trip it.

To see what happened when this man went over the edge.

"I want it." Even on my knees, I felt more powerful than I'd ever been before. I threw back my hair and shot him a look over my shoulder, making sure he understood that I was with him every step of the way. "What are you waiting for?"

He examined my position before him with a gleam in his dark green eyes that would've made me shiver if I hadn't been strung impossibly tight. Just moments after an amazing orgasm and I was already hovering on the precipice again just from the intensity in his gaze.

"Then take it." Roughly, he sank into me again, so deep that I forgot to cry out.

Forgot to breathe.

My life up to that point disappeared. I was just a body to be filled.

Just his to use. *Thoroughly.*

My cells screamed for oxygen as I bit the cushion to keep from screaming as he rammed into me again and again.

My limits disappeared. With him, I had none. I just shook for more.

"Good girl." The praise made me smile even in the midst of insanity. "So fucking good."

The pleasure mixed with a ripe pain that tore open something inside my chest. I didn't have to hold back anymore. I didn't have to lie to him. He wouldn't accept lies anyway.

There was only truth, and heat, and pleasure. And him.

Always him.

PEYTON

I woke on the same couch where I'd been banged into next Tuesday.

A fuzzy blanket covered me up to my chin, but a quick pat of my chest and hip helped me to ascertain that yes, I was indeed naked.

Normally, I would've blushed over that fact. Winding up naked on a stranger's couch after oral activities and a little spanking mid-sex wasn't exactly part of the usual setlist of my life.

Sex itself was as rare as a blue moon.

In my profession, any dalliance I had involved taking a risk. If I didn't want to end up in the gossip rags, I had to tread carefully.

Not that I had a single worry about Jed selling information about me. Every moment I spent in his company increased my sense that he was a decent guy. He obviously liked things a bit on the rougher end, which I'd enjoyed immensely.

If that was what he'd meant by pushing and testing me, I was happy to sign up for more of the same.

I hadn't been pushed or tested in so long that I'd forgotten the satisfaction afterward. That whispered "good girl" had affected me more profoundly than a thousand empty compliments.

Knowing he was sharing the pleasure with me had made me damn near euphoric. I'd given him that. My willingness to be who he needed for a night—and who I'd never dared to be before—had offered us both so much.

And now I was alone on his couch.

Sitting up, I rubbed my eyes and took in my surroundings. A small lamp shone from a table in the corner, casting the room in a soft glow. A plate and cup sat on the coffee table in front of the couch, and I grinned at the cheese and crackers and cup of tea he'd left for me.

Aww. So much for him not being sweet. Maybe he was in denial.

I reached for the cup and took a sip, unsurprised it was lukewarm. I didn't know how much time I'd been out. It could've been ten minutes or three hours. Darkness still pushed at the window behind the couch so it couldn't have been too long.

So where was my lover?

Whoa. That word didn't sit easy, probably because I hadn't had nearly enough of them. So maybe I should rectify that, huh? Now that I'd taken this step tonight, I could bang with impunity. Just say to hell with my life, throw on a wig and let fate blow me where it would.

Too bad I didn't want to be blown anywhere except in the direction of my sexy ex-cop.

Who absolutely was *not* mine. He hadn't even brought me up to his bed, for God's sake.

But he had tucked me in and left me a snack. And tea. Spiced tea, with a hint of vanilla. The kind that made me want to curl up with a novel and dream.

I took a quick glance around the room at the matching armchairs, widescreen TV, and books and newspapers stacked on every available surface. When it came to reading material, I'd have my pick here. Why didn't it surprise me that he was a reader?

My attention snagged on a cardboard box next to the couch and I leaned over the arm to poke through the contents. It was a box of books. Not different books, the same one. There had to be at least twenty-five copies.

I pried out one of them and bit my lip. *Final Justice* by Danny Markham. I'd never heard of the author, though I did enjoy the occasional suspense novel. This one had the White House on the cover and some covert spy dude hiding in the bushes.

Interesting.

So why did Jed have a box of this guy's books? Maybe he was a friend. Or maybe Jed was the author.

I frowned. Nah, that probably wasn't likely. He'd said he was an ex-Detective but he hadn't said a thing about writing.

Then again, if these were his books, he had a pseudonym for a reason. Obviously, he didn't want people to know his true identity.

Damn, I should've thought of that when I'd used Peyton as my stage name. Anything to add another layer between the real person and the public eye was a good idea. Helped save one's sanity.

"Too late now," I said under my breath, sitting back with the novel.

I flipped to the acknowledgments page, my eyes widening as I read Danny's thanks to "the boys in blue". Hmm. So maybe Jed and I weren't so far apart after all. We both dealt with the public, in very different ways.

Now to get him to admit this was really him...

Unable to stifle my curiosity, I read a few pages while nibbling on the cheese and crackers he'd left me. My growling stomach appreciated the snack, and the book fed my love of thrillers. I was on chapter three and thoroughly sucked into the female protagonist's problem of how to get into the White House to reach the endangered President before I looked up again. I set the book aside and rose, dragging the blanket with me.

If Jed wasn't coming back to me, I'd just have to find him.

I checked out the modest dining room and kitchen, smiling at the homey touches of a rooster wall clock and framed family photos. Best of all was the plaid dog bed beneath the kitchen table, full of a gold and brown sleeping pooch. And he had a tangled dark mass between his front paws that could only be my wig.

Swallowing a giggle, I padded down the hall to what must be the bedrooms as quietly as possible in my boots. I probably should just take them off, but Jed seemed to like them.

Hell, *I* liked them. They gave me a boost. Though I didn't have self-image issues most of the time, other than the relentless need to watch my weight unless I wanted to read scathing critiques in the trades, I didn't get a ton of opportunities to feel sexy. My look was more homespun than that.

These boots definitely were *not* homespun in any shape or form.

The first doorway was a small bathroom with the standard tub/shower setup and a single sink. A total bachelor's bathroom. Smiling, I moved to the next doorway and discovered what must be a guest bedroom. In the moonlight pouring through the window, I glimpsed a neatly made bed along with a nightstand and dresser. Nothing unusual there.

The final doorway led her to the jackpot. Soft, almost unintelligible music played from unseen speakers. The room was dark, and the man in bed with a laptop in his lap typed by the light from the screen. His fingers kept up an endless rhythm over the keys and I lurked in the doorway, fascinated. He'd slipped on a pair of reading glasses and his brown spiky hair looked even more so from my hands. My belly tightened and my nipples grew taut, reminding me I was still nude under my blanket.

And apparently still really horny.

"You planning on coming in or just going to stand there and watch me all night?"

His low voice startled me enough to make me waver where I

stood. He chuckled as I sucked in a breath and gripped the doorframe, evidently enjoying my surprise. "I didn't realize you knew I was here."

"Former cop," he said lightly, sparing me a brief glance that still managed to pin me in place with its intensity. "Plus hooker boots."

Biting my lip, I glanced down at them thoughtfully. "They are kind of like the ones Julia wore in *Pretty Woman*, aren't they?"

"Mmm-hmm." His noncommittal answer made me need to press for more. I already craved his praise like a junkie with a fix.

Which probably wasn't good.

"Do you like them?"

"Did I or did I not nail you in my front hall?"

"Yeah." There was no smothering my laugh as I unzipped the boots in question and wriggled out of them, abandoning them just inside the doorway. "You so did."

Giving up on any attempt at maintaining distance, I crossed the room and crawled over the distressingly neat bedding—who could be that tidy while in bed?—to curl against his side.

I wasn't surprised when he snapped his laptop closed, but I was disappointed. It would've been nice if he'd opened up to me about his true identity, especially since I already knew.

Besides, who would understand better than I would? We were both artists of a sort. Did he get to create as he saw fit or was he hamstrung by rules and standards he didn't agree with too?

But I didn't ask. I just dropped my head to his shoulder and slid my arm around his waist. "I woke up alone. I didn't like it."

"You found me well enough." He pushed his laptop aside and shifted toward me, tilting my chin upward. Even in the darkened room, I felt his probing stare. "Are you okay?"

I sighed. "You're not going to ruin some awesome sex with some *not* awesome talking about it, are you? Because really, I'm cool with putting a period on it and just not going there."

"I spanked you." His voice held a note of something dark I didn't fully understand. Nor was I sure I wanted to.

"Yeah. You did." I snuggled closer and slid my fingers into the waistband of his silky pajama bottoms. He'd skipped a shirt and I was tempted to let my hands do the walking on his ripped chest and torso. "It was fucking incredible."

"That's it? You're not unnerved?"

"Should I be?"

"No. Yes. I don't know. We don't know each other, Peyton, and I did something with you that pushed us into the realm of the familiar awfully quickly."

"What better icebreaker is there? Questions about favorite colors and meals are so tedious."

His sigh as he removed his glasses and set them on the nightstand made me grin, though I schooled my features into sober lines as he turned back to face me. "I half expected you to call a car to come get you as soon as you woke up."

A new layer of disappointment crashed into the first. I tried to suppress it. If I was going to do this—or keep doing it, since I'd already gotten that ball rolling—the key was to not get my heart involved.

Except, oops, too late. Evidently, my butt and my chest were connected. A spanking, a few words of praise and some hot lovin' later, and I thought I had a boyfriend.

Stupid, stupid, stupid.

I cleared my throat. "In case you didn't notice, I'm not in a real big hurry to get back to my life. I didn't even turn on my phone."

Forget turn on. I hadn't even looked for it yet. My purse was probably in the front hall where I'd dropped it pre-sex and I really didn't much care.

"You must have people looking for you."

"I must. Hopefully they won't be able to find me."

"So, what, you're running away?"

I snorted. "Like I could. I have a show in Edgewood next Friday night and rehearsals and meet and greets before then. Gotta give back to the fans, you know. Smaller venues are more intimate and help keep ticket prices more affordable."

"And you care about that." Doubt laced his statement.

"Of course I do. I was a fan who once went to concerts that were out of my price range too." Okay, slight exaggeration since I'd never been allowed the freedom to go to many concerts even before I was famous, but I did understand the concept.

He toyed with the ends of my hair. My real hair now since my wig had ended up as a doggie chew toy. "So this is what to you? A vacation?"

Was he trying to get a bead on how I viewed all of this? *Us*? And was that a good thing or bad?

Perhaps he'd developed feelings from our encounter and was hoping I had too. Or maybe he didn't have any and wanted to make sure I didn't either.

A pop star with as much money as the Kardashians could be trouble, and Jed probably wanted to head me off at the pass.

Sorry, sweetheart, I spank all the girls I pick up on the side of the road and bring home. You're not special.

"It's just a night I spent with a cool new guy I met," I said quietly, hoping he couldn't hear anything else in my voice. I'd spent years learning to add the appropriate inflection to the words I sang. Hopefully the reverse was true and I could keep it out when I needed to as well. "Nothing more, nothing less."

"That so?"

"That so." I snapped the waistband of his pajamas against his drum tight abs. "Unless you're getting sweet on me." Deliberately, I kept my tone light and airy. "Then we better put a stop to this, because I'm afraid that I don't have time to deal with any boyish crushes."

His growl caused a flurry of tingles to skate over my already overworked nerve endings. "I'm no fucking boy." He dragged me onto his lap and peeled away the blanket, leaning up to nibble on the eager tips of my breasts.

He didn't kiss nearly as often as he bit. I had no idea why that aroused me so.

Linking my arms around his neck, I pressed my lips to his forehead. "Tell me something I don't know."

"You're goddamn gorgeous. I've never seen an ass half as perfect as yours in thirty years."

The gruff praise against my skin made me grin. "So you were perving on bums at the preschool? Bad boy."

He growled again and moved his hand down my hip to rub the area he'd spanked before.

Even expecting the slap on my ass, it still made me jolt—and moan.

Warmth seeped through me to throb between my legs. My pussy went damp so fast that I feared I'd get his pajamas wet. I tried to press my thighs together but he just spread his legs wider, making me widen my straddling stance to accommodate him. Then he gripped my other ass cheek hard enough to bruise, his palm rubbing brisk circles for a moment before another sharp slap stung the air.

And my flesh.

"God," I whimpered, tucking my face into the crook between his neck and shoulder. "Why does that feel so incredible?"

"Because you're a kinky little thing." Wonder edged his voice, and even that was a form of praise. He seemed amazed I could be into this.

Oh, I was. So much.

"And you're a kinky big thing." I rocked against his silk-covered length, tearing a groan from his throat. "So big," I added with a purr.

"Flattery will get you nowhere but crammed full of my cock, Rulebreaker."

I nearly trembled at his dirty talk alone. Damn, this man knew how to work me over good. "Then allow me to tell you that you're not only a handsome man, but also witty and articulate—"

His laughter surprised and thrilled me almost as much as it did to find myself on my back beneath him, hips already raised.

I'd never been so primed to fuck in all my life.

Hell, I'd never even thought in those terms except when my songwriting went to a level I didn't feel comfortable expressing normally. I'd written a few songs on the naughtier end of the spectrum, ones no one would ever hear because I probably wouldn't get another chance to spread my wings.

Not after my first attempt had been such a failure.

I closed my eyes to fight back the tears. Not here, not now. *This* right here was definitely a form of growth. I'd never known anything like this night before.

And you never will again once dawn comes and your one-night-stand turns into a memory.

"Hey."

I turned up her face, hoping he'd ixnay the conversation for a kiss instead. But why would he when he hadn't kissed me yet on the mouth? Maybe that was standard one-nighter etiquette and I'd somehow skipped that chapter.

"Hey," he said again and I had no choice but to open my eyes. "Where did you go?"

For once, words weren't there. I fell back on them for so many things. To cajole, to seduce the public, to capitulate to my parents and record label. They'd never failed me before. Even when all I could do was parrot the words others had written for me, whether in speeches or in my music, I still had them, screaming away madly in my head.

Not now.

In the silence, I heard my voice come over the speakers. *My* song. One of my favorites actually, from the flop of an album that had been heavily weighted with my own material.

No more of that. Clearly you don't have your finger on the pulse.

But why was Jed listening to my pop crap?

My gaze flew to his and I clutched his shoulders at the small smile waiting for me. He obviously thought I'd be pleased to hear my own stuff while in his bed.

"Turn it off," I demanded, shoving at his immovable frame. He had the body mass of granite, especially when draped on top of me with that delicious cock pressing so intimately against me.

But I couldn't think about that, because the music was still playing, and I didn't know how to make it stop.

"Why?"

Ignoring the question, I leaned around him, trying to see in the dimness of the room. The moonlight wasn't helping much. "Dammit, where is it coming from?"

"What's wrong with it? I thought you'd be happy to hear—"

"Happy to have that intrude on us?" I knew she sounded hysterical and couldn't help it. "Tonight was about a chance to be someone else. Not to feel the same lead weights dragging me down."

He moved back, straddling my thighs in a way that still kept me firmly pinned. He crossed his arms and even without seeing it, I could just guess he'd raised an eyebrow. "Explain."

"Please," I said, more quietly now. The song was winding down, and if I kept talking I wouldn't have to hear it anywhere but in my own head. "Surely you have something else we could listen to. Or just silence."

Silence would be glorious.

His chuckle sounded anything but amused. "You think I'll ever let you be silent with me? Like hell. You're going to be panting and screaming loudly enough to drown out any music." His fingers brushed over my cheek and I shut my eyes again. "That still doesn't explain why your own music makes you so sad."

"I'm not sad. No fucking way." I let out a too loud laugh and cringed away from the sound of it. Too many sounds, and none of them were what I wanted to hear.

All I wanted was the music of Jed and I moving together like we had earlier.

He was right. I would never be silent with him. He would never allow it and thank God for that.

Before he could counter the move, I blindly reached out toward the nightstand beside the bed. I tugged on the drawer and shoved my hand inside, searching for condoms. "Protection?"

"I used one earlier."

I hadn't even noticed but I trusted him and kept digging around. What I found made me swallow a gasp.

I lifted the item and bit my lip as the moonlight glinted off metal. "So you really do have handcuffs," I managed once I'd caught my breath again.

"Former cop," he said easily, but I had a feeling he was waiting to see how I'd react.

Knowing he was watching me as I ran a fingernail along the links made my skin prickle with awareness. "So this thick padding is standard issue? I didn't realize that the police force in this jurisdiction is so concerned with comfort." I lifted my gaze to his. "Very admirable."

"Oh, sweetness, the one thing I'm not is admirable."

"Technically I was referring to the force, not you. But if that's so, even better. I think Billy Joel said it best. You know, laughing with the sinners and all that. Being good all the time kind of sucks." Catching my tongue between my teeth, I leaned up to press my breasts into his chest.

And when he lowered his head to skim his mouth over my ear, I closed the cuffs around his wrist.

He stilled. Not moving, not breathing. Then he turned his head and bit my earlobe hard enough to make me whimper. "Fast reflexes."

Uh-oh. He sounded...displeased.

Trepidation snaked through my veins and extinguished the quick glow of pride. "The crew calls me monkey," I said flippantly. "I used to climb up the lighting rigs all the time."

He cocked his head, eyes gleaming. "That so?" He tipped up my chin with his thumb. "How many positions can you get into?"

I hated that I flushed. How annoying. We'd already had sex, for God's sake. "We should figure out how many *you* can get into, since you're cuffed and at my mercy."

Even as I said it, I realized the ridiculousness of my response. He had one wrist cuffed—and it wasn't even attached to anything. He basically had the same freedom of movement as he'd had before, with the addition of an annoying piece of padded metal to slightly hamper his speed.

Jed lifted his arm and let the cuff dangle near my face. "You think so?"

That glint in his eyes was starting to freak me out. Wetness trickled down my inner thighs as I scampered backward on the bed, expecting him to lurch forward and slam into me without even giving me time to cry out. Craving that.

But he only reclined beside me, spreading out his big body over his tidy sheets. Then he reached up and snapped his cuff over the headboard.

My eyes nearly bugged out of my head. "What did you—why?"

"You wanted me at your mercy." His mouth curved. "Do your worst."

JED

Watching Peyton worry her bottom lip as she considered what she'd set in motion almost made being cuffed worth it.

Almost. Not quite.

I debated pushing down the waistband of my pajamas to give my dick room to breathe. Maybe that would spur her into action.

She'd gone stone still, her big eyes taking me in while she rubbed her palms over her hips. Clearly she hadn't expected me to adapt so readily to this change of events.

That made two of us.

"More condoms are in the back of the drawer you found these in." I jerked my chin in the direction of the nightstand. She still didn't move.

"So, ahh, what can I do to you?"

My brow lifted. "What do you have in mind, wildcat?"

A hint of a smile lifted her lush mouth before she turned to root through the nightstand. She returned with a handful of condoms and tossed them beside me before tugging my pajama bottoms down.

A moment later, they were on the floor and she was viewing me with open appreciation. She wrapped her fingers around the base of my erection, stretching them to try to get them to meet.

Between the teasing look on her face and her fluttering fingers, I should tell her right now to save her effort. At this rate, I'd keep growing until she lost her hold on me entirely.

"If I ask you to do something, you'll comply." She tilted her head. Her hand kept moving, gliding through the wetness from my seeping tip.

Wetness that only kept increasing.

"Do I need a safe word?"

I was kidding. Of course I was.

Insisting on safe words was my jurisdiction, even if I rarely allowed myself the pleasure anymore. Though after tonight, I didn't know if I'd be able to shove my needs back in the closet anytime soon.

It had been hard as hell to shut them down before Peyton. After, I felt changed in ways I wasn't sure I'd ever make it all the way back from.

And that wasn't just impossible, it was idiotic. We didn't know each other. Compatibility in the sack meant...

So fucking much.

But it wasn't just that. It was also how she smiled and laughed, along with her insatiable curiosity and urgency to live life on her own terms. Those traits not only stirred my protective instincts, they made me want to rip down the fence around my own boundaries.

I'd been locked away in a cage of my own making for so long that she represented a kind of freedom I'd never expected to get to taste again.

Peyton Pryor could easily become a dangerous addiction for me.

In every possible way.

Even her voice. I hadn't expected to like her music. I'd figured the pop princess probably couldn't sing without the help of Auto Tune or some other mechanical aid like too many of the current artists.

How wrong I was.

Maybe all her song selections weren't for me, but the voice singing those words worked for me on every level.

Sexy, husky, teasing. Coaxing me to go on the adventure of my life, if I only dared.

"Do you have one?" She cocked her head while she caressed my shaft. Her thumb circled over the tip of my erection before she darted along the underside to rub over the ridged spot that made my breath go short. "A safe word?"

"No. I'm not a switch," I bit off. From her silence, I gathered she didn't know what that was. "I'm dominant, not submissive."

She bent to lap at the liquid she'd created, making a *mmm* noise that nearly caused my eyes to roll back. "But you're cuffed right now." Lightly, she blew a stream of air over the wetness from her mouth. "At my mercy, remember?"

"Fuck." This woman. She was going to kill me, and I'd probably die happy.

With all the years I'd spent grouchy and alone, that seemed wrong.

"You said so," she said in a singsong voice that caused me to grin.

"I did. Fucking tease."

"I'm not teasing. I'm going to deliver on all promises, both direct and implied. Your safe word, Sir."

"Again," I demanded, needing to hear that word from her mouth. Needing to hear it directed at *me*.

Despite the oddness of her using it while they were discussing my need for a safe word, hearing it from her soft pink lips still satisfied something primal inside me.

"Sir?" Her voice wobbled. "Is that...is that part of this? The whole safe word deal? I've heard bits and pieces. My makeup artist is into this sort of thing, I think." She huffed out a breath. "Tell me your safe word, Sir."

I had to laugh. God, she was turning everything on its ear. Even me.

Especially me.

"Pink," I murmured, knowing she was flushing as she ducked her head. Probably between her legs too. Her liquid heat had leaked through my bottoms earlier and I could still feel how tight and wet she'd been when we'd been together the first time.

She was easily embarrassed and so seductively curious. So hot in every way.

"Speaking of pink," she released my cock to shimmy up my body, "if I were to sit on your face, what would you do?"

"Thank the God I haven't prayed to since Catholic school," I muttered, absorbing her laughter from the lie I'd told.

I'd prayed Talbot wouldn't die, and I'd been rewarded there. I'd also promised to start praying again more regularly after that, but that had turned out to be a mistruth like so many other things.

That I was okay. That walking away from the force hadn't scarred me. That I'd never faltered in choosing a new path. Thankfully that path had not only proved to be a good one, but it had also ultimately saved me.

I'd gotten lucky.

Evidently, my luck was in again tonight, because there was a warm, wet pussy inches above my mouth and all I had to do was lean up to take a long, hungry lick.

She cried out and gripped a handful of my hair, pulling the way I'd already discovered I adored. The action sent heat straight to my groin, and I could feel my cock leaking pre-cum.

Fuck, I was on the verge of coming just from eating her out, and I'd barely begun my feast.

With the cuff holding me in position more than I would've liked, I used my free hand to toy with her responsive little clit while

I licked her from top to bottom. Her excitement flowed sweetly over my tongue, so I drove deeper to scoop out more.

She rocked against me without shame, still pulling my hair while she wiggled the ass I intended to spank nice and red for this stunt.

Though in all honesty, I didn't mind that she tried to top from the bottom. Nudging her back into line would be so rewarding.

One night. This is just for one night. Don't forget that.

I pushed the annoying voice of reason out of my head and focused on my task. I licked her harder, alternating the pressure of my fingers and my tongue on her clit, offering the occasional bite to make her jolt and squeal.

She had the widest array of sounds I'd ever heard. And oh, how she panted. I might've feared she'd need oxygen soon if I wasn't in the same damn state from pressing my face into all that delicious drenched heat.

I rubbed my nose against her, drawing in a greedy breath. So good. Her smell, her taste, the uninhibited squeezes of her thighs around my head the closer she came to orgasm. Praise fell against her flesh, the kind I couldn't hold back.

She needed to know exactly how freaking sexy she was and how much I wanted her.

How I never wanted this night to end.

When the pulsing against my mouth turned into a drumbeat, I slid two fingers inside her pussy and flexed them to find the spot she'd gotten so much pleasure from earlier. Two strokes and she was coming in my mouth, her honeyed taste making me groan as I fought to swallow every drop. Even losing one would be a waste.

She sagged over me, the hand in my hair going limp. Then she lifted up and smiled down at me, her wild eyes surrounded by her angelic halo of white-blond hair. "You have a gifted tongue."

"You have a gifted pussy. I could make it come for days."

The squeeze of her thighs indicated her embarrassment—or a new rush of arousal—but she got over it quickly, offering me a soft laugh. She wiggled down my body, making sure to rub her still dripping slit over my aching cock. She laughed again at my pained grunt.

"You like torturing me, vixen?" I had so many nicknames for her already. She was like a dozen women in one, depending on which showed up to play from one moment to the next. The serious one, the petulant one, the seductive one. The one who cried so easily and laughed with even more abandon.

She'd be a wonder to watch on stage. I didn't doubt for a moment that she'd been born to own that space. That dramatic, over the top personality probably riveted crowds with the same speed that she'd riveted me.

"Maybe just a little. But don't worry. I was taught to give after I receive." Then she slipped her mouth over the straining head of my cock.

PEYTON

I HAD NEVER BEEN A HUGE FAN OF GIVING BJs.

It wasn't like I hated them or anything, and I definitely understood the "give so you can receive" theory I'd just espoused, but the guys I'd been with tended to pull on my hair—and not in a sexy way like my new lover did—while bruising my throat in the process. No finesse at all.

Jed Knight was not one of those men.

For one thing, he was partially cuffed. His free hand only stroked my hair. Never pulling. Never even tugging. Just gentle strokes that made me lean into his touches and wish he'd bump them up a notch. He'd certainly allowed me to go to town on *his* hair.

He didn't seem like he was in any hurry to rush this along though, in spite of how thick and hard he was. Pre-cum hit my tongue every time I licked him, and he seemed to lengthen with each pump of my hand. He had such control.

I wanted to decimate it.

Those limits he'd talked about testing? The time had come for me to nudge his as well.

Hollowing my cheeks, I worked my fingers over him, squeezing in rhythmic pulses. I was getting him all wet, and he wasn't the only one. It had to be obvious that I was raring to go, considering how I kept pushing my thighs together and squirming over his formerly pristine sheets. He probably could smell how much I wanted him.

I sucked him deeper, not giving myself time to flush. I hoped anyway. I was done with being embarrassed.

At least for tonight.

Bending forward, I thrust my ass in the air, circling it in time with the ripples of my throat.

God, I was actually enjoying this. Not just pretending to so it would end quicker.

He grunted and wove his fingers through my hair, leading me down closer to his groin. The combined scents of soap and a light veil of sweat made me moan and he reciprocated as the sound traveled down his cock.

Any minute now he was going to blow, and as much as I wanted to taste him, I wanted to feel him lose it inside me even more.

Reluctantly, I drew back. I continued to work his slick length with one hand—from the contorted expression he wore, he was fully enjoying the strength guitar playing had granted me—and fumbled for a condom with the other.

I ripped open the package with my teeth and stopped stroking him long enough to get it on him. It wasn't as easy as it seemed to be in the movies, but I hadn't practiced much. The few men I'd been with had always done the honors. I bit my lip as I finally got it into place, hoping I hadn't killed the mood with my slowness.

"Haven't done that much, huh?"

His low voice grazed my flesh like gravel over silk. So much for him not noticing my lack of skill in that area. I tried not to duck my head. "No."

"Hottest thing I ever saw. You pleasing me with your mouth,

then trying to make those quick fingers work even faster. Frigging perfect." His thumb smoothed over my swollen lower lip, pressing his taste deeper inside my mouth. "You're learning new things with me."

"So many." I gave up fighting my smile and crawled up his body to cup his scruffy jaw. He'd been working on five o'clock shadow all night but now it was much denser. The short hairs tingled against my palms as I lowered my head, my gaze roaming his face. I wanted to kiss him so badly. "May I?" I whispered, wanting to let him know that despite his cuffs, he still held the control.

By my choice. And his.

"May I, Sir?" I repeated when he didn't reply. With everything they'd done, something about a kiss made him hold back.

Too intimate maybe. Too...much.

He started to argue. His nostrils flared and his jaw tensed and I figured he might finally deny me.

Then he nodded, his full lips opening on an exhale. "That's cheating, you know."

Leaning closer, I smiled. I did know. I'd registered his response the first time I called him Sir, and the thickening length wedged against my belly was a strong piece of secondary evidence. "Maybe. But it's worth it if I get a kiss that tastes like both of us." I kissed the corner of his mouth. "All dirty and sweet."

"Fuck, Peyton," he groaned just before my lips slanted over his.

I tried to go slow. I didn't need much romance, but when it came to first kisses after first fucks, it seemed like maybe I should try just for the heck of it.

But the instant my tongue tentatively touched his, he sucked me inside, curling around me with a longing I wasn't strong enough to combat. One pull on my flesh and I rocked my damp slit against his belly, needing him to feel what he was doing to me. He only drew harder, his stubble branding my chin at the same time his lips, tongue, and teeth branded the rest of me.

That single kiss thrummed through me entire body, lighting me up like Christmas and the Fourth of July rolled into one. My nipples grew taut, my clit pounded. And the urge to join with him became a primitive drumbeat in my blood.

Without conscious thought, I positioned myself over him, brushing his covered length with my heat. He growled and pistoned his hips upward, driving into me so deeply that I couldn't maintain the kiss. I gasped for breath and gripped the pillow beside his head, helpless to do anything but take whatever he dished out as he grabbed my hip and thrust into me again. The cuff rattled and he swore, clearly hating his limitation.

I hated it too. I wanted him to be free to fuck me the way he craved.

Not that he seemed to be having much trouble now. Holy mother.

I wasn't going to survive this. His hips rose and fell, meeting mine relentlessly, and I couldn't even gather enough air to kiss him again. The intensity in his stare held me in thrall, and I found myself moving with him from instinct.

This was what I'd been made to do. All the other times that had seemed rushed and clumsy and not half as good as in my romance books had been the trial runs, and paltry ones at that.

This was the real deal.

"Get me wet," he whispered.

My body obliged effortlessly as he pumped in and out of me with long, slow strokes. How he could maintain such precision when I sensed every part of him was coiled to spring, I didn't know.

But I had to push him over. To know I could.

Rolling my hips, I bounced on top of him, leaning back to run my hands over my breasts. I cupped them, feeling more than a little self-conscious, but his curse swiftly killed my nerves. I twisted my nipples, pulling on them until they were tightly puckered.

All the while I continued riding him. Hard, harder. Nothing was hard enough.

When I neared the breaking point, I reached down and fingered my clit, involuntarily vising around his length deep inside me. He swore again and somehow managed to slap my ass without yanking the bedframe apart.

Talented man.

I gasped and circled my clit faster, hoping to goad him into spanking me again. I was so very close, and he felt so incredible inside me, stretching me to the edge of pain.

"Don't hold back on me." He pinched my hip and in turn I pinched my clit, needing that bite closer to where he was plowing in and out. I glanced down and bit my lip at the sight of him disappearing into my pussy before emerging soaked with my desire.

And soaked was the absolute truth.

The sounds of our bodies coming together were so sexy that I might've been able to climax from that alone.

"Next time you're going to be on your belly again. In between every thrust, I'm going to spank that tight little ass. And you're going to drench me just like you did before. Just like you're doing now." He gritted his teeth together. "Ah, just like that. Tighten up on me. Let me feel that slick little pussy fist my dick."

I couldn't speak, couldn't even open my eyes. I didn't know when I'd closed them. My fingers worked frantically in time with my hips as the pleasure inside me reached a crescendo.

I couldn't take it anymore. Teasing him had done me in too.

"Jed, I'm coming."

"Yeah, you are. Rain down on me. I want to feel every drop."

I bucked against him, dragging my nails down the tensed muscles of his abdomen as I rode out the intense spasms. I panted his name over and over, needing that link with him.

Then he was yanking out of me and slamming home one more time, tearing a cry from my throat just before he finally let go inside me. He shouted out his orgasm, the words unintelligible but one.

The most important one.

My name. Over and over.

I collapsed on top of him, so spent I couldn't even breathe.

God, this was it. I was on my way out. He'd fucked me into certain death.

Truly, I wasn't all that mad. There were worse ways to go.

"You okay?" he asked, finally pulling out of me a while later. I didn't know how long. All I knew was that we were drifting, our sweaty bodies pressed tightly together, and it was the most amazing feeling.

So much amazing tonight. I'd never be able to process it all.

I got up and disposed of the condom, since he wasn't exactly mobile yet. Then I returned to bed and sprawled on top of him again.

He made one hell of a comfy man pillow.

"Every time we do it, you ask if I'm okay." Idly, I drew patterns with my nail on his chest. I hadn't seen his back but so far, he didn't have any visible tattoos.

We were both ink-free. Pretty unusual nowadays.

"*Do it*? Have we regressed to high school?"

"That's the sandbox I live in musically, dude. Deal with it."

He chuckled, surprising me "Well, there's only been twice so far."

I tried not to let hope rear its pointy little head that he might want more. Lost cause there. He'd slipped and said *so far*, hadn't he? That had to be a good sign.

This couldn't just be one night.

We'd gone way beyond regular sex, and not just because he'd spanked me. We'd shared something so much deeper than physical intimacy, as crazy as that seemed.

And he'd let me cuff him, something I imagined he didn't allow often. Or ever.

I glanced at the metal holding him in place. I'd better unlock that soon.

Smiling, I snuggled against his damp chest. Or...not.

"I'm guessing by that Cheshire cat smile that you are. Okay, I mean." He toyed with my hair, his fingers tender against my scalp. He seemed to know intuitively when to push me for more and when to soothe.

Somehow it felt like he knew me already.

"I'm so much better than okay. I didn't know it could be like that."

"You've never orgasmed before?"

"Duh, of course I have."

He not-so-lightly patted my bottom and damn if my clit didn't sit up and take notice. "Next time you use that infernal word, at least add a *Sir* to the end of it."

Grinning, I leaned up and kissed his stubbled jaw. "Duh, Sir. Yes, I've orgasmed before. But not like that. Not even close."

"Much better."

"And that wasn't even flattery. I liked the results from that last time, by the way." I nibbled my way down his throat. "I'm hoping to —" I broke off and frowned. "Dammit, again?"

Even in the dark, I glimpsed his smile. "Turns out I'm a fan. Who'd've thunk it?"

"Yeah, right. You'd never even heard of me before tonight."

"A fan who was late to the bandwagon." Possessively, he rubbed my still smarting ass. He tended to put some power behind his slaps, and I loved it. "But I'm making up for lost time."

I couldn't argue with that.

He'd chosen yet another cut off my failed album. As if he knew. Those songs were both the brightest and most painful parts of my career. Hearing them while sprawled across his chest mitigated some of the sting, but not all of it.

Especially when I didn't know exactly why he'd put them into his musical rotation in the first place.

Soon the song ended and another song—thankfully not one of mine—begun. I couldn't wait any longer to ask.

I pulled at a loose thread on the pillowcase. One I'd probably tugged out with my nails. "Are you making fun of me by pretending to like my music?"

"No. Of course not. Why would you say that?"

I snorted. "Because it doesn't exactly seem like your thing, Mr. Gruff Dominant Ex-Cop."

And current romantic suspense author, I added mentally. Sometime soon I'd have to acknowledge I knew his secret identity, but I hoped he would voluntarily come clean before I had to.

"I'm not always gruff. Besides, you can't claim to know my *thing* already."

"Oh, you'd be surprised. I've already gotten pretty acquainted with your thing."

It was easier to act playful than to acknowledge the very real fears behind my question. I understood my music wasn't for everyone, and if he didn't go for it, that was just fine.

Half the time my music wasn't for *me* either.

No, that wasn't true. I actually enjoyed most of the material I worked with. I just wanted to do more. Stretch a little. Try different arrangements, broaden my subject matter. I didn't want to scare away all my younger more innocent fans, but they were getting older, just as I was.

Tonight had shown that to me with crystal clarity. This insulated box I'd been living in hadn't done me any favors. With all the gifts I'd been given, and opportunities I'd had a chance to enjoy, I'd lost so much else.

A chance at a normal life, with a boyfriend and a home base that actually felt like a home. I was so tired of waking up in new beds in new cities. Just once, I wanted to go to sleep with someone holding me who wanted me for who I was, not my money or fame or what I could do for them.

"Peyton."

Surprised at his somber tone, I glanced up. His gaze was trained on my face, detecting nuances. Unless I was way off, this guy had a finely honed bullshit detector.

Which meant I was in trouble, because I did the breast-stroke in poo on a daily basis.

I stifled a yawn that was half from fatigue and half a stalling tactic. "Yeah?"

His lifted brow made me reach for the title he seemed to wear so naturally. It felt like a game between them, laced with a seriousness I wasn't quite ready to accept. Getting closer, though. "Yes, Sir?"

"Good girl. Now tell me why you'd ask me if I was making fun of you by listening to music many, many other people listen to quite often. At least according to your net worth—"

My spine locked. "Why would you look up my net worth?"

"Not because I'm trying to cash in, that's for damn sure," he said in a tone that made me look away, ashamed.

I couldn't help being suspicious. Too many people wanted a piece of me. I was protected from so much of that by my body-guards and my team but I never forgot completely that I was viewed as a commodity. One with a value that rose and fell depending on factors that weren't entirely in my control.

Forget entirely. Try *mostly*.

"I'm sorry. Side effect of being—"

"You."

I nodded, sure he could read my misery. I wasn't hiding it very well. It was so hard to meet new people and trust that they cared for me, the person and not me, the performer.

Jed's lack of knowledge about me had seemed like a present. Now he was playing my songs and searching for me online and somehow that tainted what had happened between us.

And that chipped off a corner of my heart.

"I wanted to know who was in my bed." He cupped my cheek, feathering his thumb over my lower lip. Soothing me. "Not that some shiny pictures or overproduced songs or tabloid articles on how much you brought in on your last tour begin to touch who you are as a person. As a woman." His voice dipped on that word, warming it just as he warmed my skin with his hand. "I know enough about that from having you here tonight."

"From sex?"

"No. From watching the way you respond to every new thing. You have the kind of curiosity that could get you in very big trouble, Rulebreaker." He shook his head. "Going home with strange men and letting them spank you. I'm shocked."

My lips twitched but I fought the smile as I reached up to run my nail along the chain around his throat. The lack of light couldn't disguise how he braced. "This made you not a stranger to me. My uncle was a cop."

He didn't speak for a moment. "Was?"

Of course he'd get the salient point right away. That was the blessing and curse of him. "Killed in the line of duty." Somehow my voice didn't wobble. "My aunt who lives in Kensington Square lost him years ago. She never remarried. Doubt she will. But she adopted a cop." I let out a weak laugh. "Well, symbolically adopted. Jimmy has his own family but lived in the neighborhood. Now he's joining the Crescent Cove force."

"Not far from here."

"Nope, just a town over so I've heard."

Jed nodded. "I'm sorry for your loss."

"Me too. He was a good guy." I cleared my throat. "I'm glad you're not a cop anymore." I rushed ahead as he shifted, obviously preparing to speak. "I'm sorry if that makes me a heartless bitch, or stupid, or any other adjective you want to slap on there. But I'm glad you're not risking your life every day, even if I won't get to see you live them."

I hadn't meant to say the last part. Some self-preservation instinct kicking in, maybe. If I didn't act like tonight had been life-changing for me, he wouldn't be able to hurt me.

Yeah, right.

He started to say something, then he cupped my head and

pulled me down to his chest. "You're tired. You should get some rest."

Yes, my eyelids were heavy, and I'd yawned more than once. That wasn't what this was about. He didn't want to have this discussion with me. Allowing me to sleep in his bed as if I truly mattered to him was preferable to having an awkward conversation.

I understood his thought process. Couldn't stand it, but I understood it.

Arguing about our reality was a waste of time. Tomorrow, I'd go back to Brooklyn. I'd ditched my bodyguards tonight so there would be hell to pay.

My parents had probably left a dozen messages already, demanding I come visit them in Long Island. They'd talk some sense into me, or at least wear me down until I didn't have any strength left to fight.

The memory of this night would be all I'd have to remind me of the big, wide world outside my golden doors.

I let him tuck me away as so many others had before—and would do again. And I slept.

JED

I woke up to a fire in my wrist and a lead weight on my chest. Of the two, the fire bothered me the least.

A tangle of blond hair clung to my mouth. I blew it out as carefully as possible, not wanting to wake my sleeping beauty if I could help it. She didn't stir. She was snoring softly and had her fist pressed to her chin like a kid. I nearly smiled at the picture she made until reality slammed home in the form of a serious ache in my forearm.

A glance back at the bedframe made me stifle a sigh. I was still cuffed.

Add occurrences like *this* to the long list of reasons why I preferred to take the dominant role. I would never leave a submissive tied up all night in such an uncomfortable position.

Not that Peyton knew any better. This had been her maiden voyage when it came to this type of scene. Now that she'd been initiated, she could go off and find another man to—

"Like hell," I muttered, breaking the stillness.

She still didn't wake.

I looked at the alarm clock. Just past ten a.m. Sunlight streamed through the window, casting the dancing dust motes in a shimmering glow. I'd forgotten to pull the blackout curtains closed before retiring last night. With a career like mine, late nights were a necessity. I'd written into the wee hours many times when a deadline loomed too close.

"I'm glad you're not a cop anymore. I'm sorry if that makes me a heartless bitch, or stupid, or any other adjective you want to slap on there. But I'm glad you're not risking your life every day, even if I won't get to see you live them."

The last part of what she'd said had kept me up for hours. She was honest. Laid things right on the line. I had to respect her for that forthrightness, even if it made me want to punch a wall. But it wasn't as if there could be any real future for the pop princess and the cop. *Former* cop.

That was like a romance novel title gone wrong right there.

You could be her bodyguard. That would give you a reason to torture yourself with the sight of her daily. Even after she moved on to the new flavor of the moment, you could look at her and remember.

There was a maudlin idea. Besides, I'd gotten out of the security business entirely.

I liked my new career. Hell, who was I kidding? Writing had become everything to me. I needed it like I'd needed those long walks to clear my head in the days after the shooting, when the investigation had kicked into high gear.

Somewhere along the way my new career had turned into something more. A simple vocation had become a calling. Sometimes the deepest feelings were the most unexpected.

And if I kept thinking this way, I should buy a violin and set this tripe to music.

God, I needed more sleep.

To distract myself, I rubbed my fingers along her arm. At least her soft skin diverted me from mentally spouting any more half-baked poetry before I consumed a bucket of coffee.

During the night, my playlist had shut off. That was probably a blessing because Peyton certainly hadn't appreciated my musical choices. I definitely hadn't expected to enjoy any of her songs I'd downloaded on a whim while she was sleeping on the sofa. I'd expected even less that she would freak out about them.

Thinking I'd play them to make fun of her, for fuck's sake.

For a woman so confident in some ways, she had mile-wide insecurities in others.

"Artistic temperament," she'd say, flashing one of those impish grins that alternately turned my cock to stone in a second flat or made me want to laugh, *really* laugh, in a way I hadn't in too many years to count.

She was sunshine, and for so long, I'd been closed in the dark.

My alarm bleeped on. I usually went to bed after it, but that didn't mean I didn't try to keep normal hours.

As the report from the twenty-four-hour news station filled the room, I glanced at Peyton, expecting her to wake up.

She continued to doze. The girl was out.

The announcer blathered on forever about the interest rate and capital gains tax and the weather and a million other bits of useless information. I was debating nudging Peyton awake before my arm went permanently to sleep when the announcer snatched my focus.

"International pop star Peyton Pryor was in a vehicular accident last night that caused significant damage to a borrowed luxury vehicle. She was questioned and released by police. Her spokesperson assures fans that Peyton will still be attending the Pop Smash meet and greet this evening at Ridgeside Mall. The event with Ms. Pryor and Miles Barker, another pop sensation, is expected to draw thousands of fans. Extra security will be on hand at the mall this evening."

I blinked at Peyton. Happily sleeping Peyton, still snuffling through her dreams. I hated to wake her, but she had a meet and greets and fans to deal with.

Holy shit. I'd read a couple of articles last night and flipped through a couple sites online, but this was insane. Obviously, I had no grasp on her kind of fame.

Proving even more succinctly that there was no way in Hades we could have anything resembling a relationship going forward, even if I'd been prepared to take that step. Which I was not. I'd been single for a while now and that suited me as well as my new life.

Liar, liar.

Not that I was tied to a desk anymore. Writing offered me the opportunity to travel if I chose. I could pick up and meet her if—

If I lost my mind, which I clearly was on the path to doing.

We'd spent one night together. One amazing night. One night beyond compare.

I wanted to get to know her better. Definitely wanted to spend more time with her in bed. But I wasn't the kind of man to fall for someone within a matter of hours.

A couple of my buddies on the force had fallen for women just that fast—hell, Pete had met his lady at the strip club, and they were still together five years after she quit dancing—and I'd enjoyed razzing them to no end. I wasn't about to become the butt of a joke myself.

Especially when Peyton had told me flat out she wouldn't be around. That translated to she didn't *want* to be around.

No, she'd just been sowing some wild oats. If I was being honest, as much fun as Peyton was, she was entirely too wild and flighty for me. We'd had an excellent night together and that was plenty. I should be grateful I'd been there so she didn't wind up getting herself into trouble with a guy who wasn't so honorable.

You mean a guy who might spank her on the second date instead?

Shaking my head, I nudged her shoulder. She apparently had a full day ahead, and I was damn sick of my thoughts.

She didn't budge.

"Peyton." Nothing. "Hey there, Rulebreaker." Another nudge and nada. "Wake up, baby."

Like magic, her bright blue eyes opened sleepily and fastened on mine. A smile curved her mouth. "You called me baby."

Dammit, I had. Leave it to her to wake up just then. "Just a throwaway endearment."

The pleasure in her eyes dimmed, and I instantly regretted my save. "Yeah. Like sweetcheeks. Or honeybun. My mom calls my dad that when she's pissed at him, which is practically hourly." Her smile didn't mitigate how quickly she looked away.

Or the guilt that seized my gut and wouldn't let go.

"You haven't told me much about your parents," I said instead of urging her to get up and get dressed. She had a life to live, and I had stewing to do.

Something I was exceptionally good at.

"There hasn't been a lot of time."

Was that desperation in her voice or was that wishful thinking on my part? The last thing I wanted to do was read more into the situation than was there. I'd be damned if I would be her latest groupie, chasing her around for scraps. She was probably well used to that. A beautiful, single woman with so much talent—God, she must have to beat them off with sticks.

Just like I'd like to do to any man who tried to take my place in her bed.

My place. Right. As if I had one.

Delusional much, Knight?

"You need to uncuff me." My voice sounded low and rough, as if I'd gone on a bender. But nope, I'd just gone on a Peyton Pryor-induced one, worse than any alcohol.

"Oh my God. I forgot. I'm so sorry, baby."

Somehow her use of the word *baby* affected me as well. It hit me square in the chest, leaving behind a sting that didn't abate when she rose onto her knees and let the sheet I'd awkwardly pulled over her fall away like water.

That body in morning sunlight should've been a crime. Covering it in clothes would be an even bigger sin. If she was mine, I'd make sure she was naked as often as possible while we were alone. Maybe even during dinner and TV time. Just so I could watch her breasts bounce and see that adorable flush climb up her neck as she realized I was unrepentantly staring at her tits.

And all the rest of her.

"The key's in the drawer."

She nodded and scampered away to rifle through the nightstand. I watched her go, my gaze riveted on her heart-shaped ass.

Somehow I hadn't left a single mark behind. A little redness remained, but that was all.

She wouldn't even have that much of me as a reminder when she moved on to her big, busy life. Whereas I was reasonably certain that the tingle in my palm would never fully leave me again.

After she returned to my side, she made quick work of undoing the cuff. She grabbed my wrist and rubbed it briskly, regret shadowing her features. "I can't believe I didn't do this before I fell asleep. You'll never want to be submissive again."

I laughed, shaking my head. "I would never be submissive to anyone but you. It's just not my nature."

"But that tendency comes out with me?" Playfully, she nibbled the inside of my wrist. "Looks like we both broke some new ground last night."

All at once my laughter drained away. Teasing morning-after conversation was just delaying the inevitable. "Your story was on the news." I jerked a thumb toward the alarm clock, which had thankfully turned off. It was set to only play for fifteen minutes, which was usually more than enough time to rouse my lazy ass out of bed. "They mentioned the crash and the police and some meet and greet you have tonight at the mall. Your spokesperson assured everyone you would still be there."

Head down, Peyton continued to message his wrist, saying nothing.

"You planning on hiding out here forever? Because I gotta say, part of me figured you'd slither out as soon as I fell asleep."

Not cuddle in and force me to remember how it feels to snuggle with you.

"I don't slither."

"Fine, sashay," I bit off. "Whatever. You have a lot to return to, and I'm just the guy who spanked your ass and made you come hard enough to see stars."

Temper flared in her gorgeous eyes. "Boy, think a lot of yourself, don't you?"

"No, I think I'm fucking hard for you right now and you standing there naked isn't helping matters." I shot a pointed glance at my crotch and she gasped, as if just now noticing I was hard enough to drill wood. The sheet partially draped over my cock wasn't diminishing my current state either.

"So you're mad because you want to fuck me." Her voice turned throaty and if anything, I grew even harder. "Is that it?"

"I'm not mad. I'm just saying you don't need to drag this out for my sake. I'll be just fine when you move on to deal with your hordes of fans. I didn't have any illusions about last night, Peyton," I added as she lifted her head and stared me in the eye.

For a long moment, she didn't say a word. Then her lower lip trembled, something I never would've seen if I hadn't been watching her so closely. As I had been for the last twelve hours or so since she'd sped into my life.

Hell, I couldn't take my eyes *off* her. Now I knew how her groupies felt. I'd become one overnight.

"What if I did?" she whispered.

Before I could figure out if she'd really said what I *thought* she had, she picked up her abandoned boots, rushed past the nightstand then headed into the adjoining bathroom, shutting the door with a firm click.

Fabulous.

I'd stuck my foot in my mouth again. Had to be the tenth time since I'd met her. Proof positive the woman was dangerous to my mental health. She rattled me in ways I was certain I'd never been rattled before. She was a new experience unlike any other.

So much for showing her the ropes. Instead, she'd schooled *me.*

I rose, wincing more than a little at my hard-on, and pulled on a pair of clean jeans sans boxers. Some part of me still hoped she'd thaw enough for us to have a round of goodbye sex—I'd even take a spirited hate fuck at this point—and I wanted the fewest layers between us possible.

Once I stood in front of the closed bathroom door, I knocked. Loudly. "Peyton, open up."

No reply.

I knocked again. "Peyton, come on. I was just trying to make this less awkward."

A moment later, she opened the door. The hair around her face was wet, as if she'd soaped up, and she smelled of my toothpaste. All she wore were those damn boots.

My cock went from erect to stand-back-or-you-might-lose-an-eye.

Probably noticing the direction of my gaze—aka those ridiculously perky breasts capped with hard pale pink nipples—she crossed her arms over her chest. "Your plan to make this less awkward was acting like a total dick. Gotcha. Can't say I can fault your method. If you act like a big enough of a jerk, I'll forget why I ever gave a shit about more."

She reached back and grabbed something off the sink, then flung it into my hand as she pushed past me. I gripped it and tried valiantly not to watch her hips sway. Really I did. But I was so gone over her that even the tips of her blond hair skimming her shoulder blades could've prompted a wet dream. With all the rest combined?

I was toast.

"You know, I could understand your attitude about my profession if yours wasn't similar."

With her back to me, she shoved bracelets onto her wrists. I hadn't even realized she'd removed them. No, scratch that, I hadn't even noticed her wearing any. Then again, I'd been so consumed with Peyton herself that her jewelry hadn't registered.

Now her comments weren't either evidently.

"Say what?" I managed, finally discovering she'd shoved my phone into my hand. Why had she taken my phone? Probably to call her "handlers" from an unknown number.

If I ended up with a bunch of unsolicited calls, I'd be pretty—

Happy, actually, because that would be one more link to her. I was a sick bastard.

"You have a lot of nerve acting as if I'm just some kind of peddler to the masses when you do the same thing. We're both artists, just a different kind."

"Whoa, hold up. Peddler of what? I just said you have fans to meet and hordes that adore you. I saw the pictures online, Peyton. The girls crying as they waited for you to sign autographs and the men trying to get a piece of you on the red carpet. It's nothing to be ashamed of—"

"Who said I was ashamed?" Whirling to face me, she planted her hands on her spectacular hips. That she stood there so *un*self-consciously naked made me proud way down deep. She might have momentary doubts, but she fought them back.

Just like she was fighting me right now.

"In fact, *you're* the one who's ashamed, not me. At least I was honest about who I am. You, on the other hand, were not."

Did she know I'd walked away from the department after my suspension?

I'd eventually been completely cleared following the investigation into Talbot's accidental shooting, but for a while, some very uncomplimentary things had been said about me.

People still mentioned my name around New York. Maybe she'd heard of me in the security circles she ran in. God knows she dealt with plenty of bodyguards, and sec people talked.

I gripped my phone tighter. "If you wanted to know about the shooting, all you had to do was ask."

A line formed between her brows. "Shooting? What shooting?"

"What the hell are you talking about then?"

"Your books." She walked forward until she was close enough to press her hand on my chest. I'd gone stone still. "You're Danny Markham."

After suspecting she knew what had led me to walk away from the force, my career as a writer was anticlimactic. "So?"

She blinked. "So...we're more alike than different."

The bark of laughter tore out of my chest hard enough to hurt. "You have no idea who I am. I've fucked up in ways you can't imagine. I'm definitely not some lily-white pop princess. So don't tell me how alike we are, when you don't have the faintest clue who I am other than being the guy who knows how to work you just right." I couldn't help touching her cheek, unsurprised when she flinched away. I'd done that too. "That was just blind luck. Sometimes breaking the rules pays off."

Like the rule that I should've never gone near someone like her. As much as she'd seemed to enjoy what we'd done last night, I hadn't explained much to her, though she was clearly a newbie to the scene.

I'd pushed her into the deep end because I couldn't control myself.

Again.

Everything always came down to my damn control, and how little I had of it. My reckless behavior always hurt the people who mattered most. People like Talbot, and Peyton, whom I already cared about way too much.

Anything beyond concern and affection had no place in a one-night-stand, even my bastardized version of it. This was just lust, and that would fade.

I would *make* it fade.

"What rules? I'm not some neophyte. I wanted what happened

just as much as you did. Probably more because I'll never experience it again. But you...you'll just find someone else to spank."

I might've laughed at that, if the sparkle of tears on her thick lashes hadn't stopped me dead. Even my breath stalled in my chest. I refused to watch her cry. Or worse, to be the cause of a single one of those tears.

I was responsible for her, to ensure she was comfortable and happy and—

And she's not yours. Get that through your thick skull.

"Peyton," I began, gripping her arm when she shoved me away.

"You didn't break any rules I didn't dare you to. *I* asked *you* if you dared to bring me home." With one shake of her head, her tears dried. "Remember that, Jed."

She walked away from me, out the door of my bedroom and down the hall.

As tempted as I was to chase after her, to ask her to let me explain some of the muddied thoughts I'd never really voiced to another person—about the shooting and how it changed me, and my writing, and so much else—I knew that was just selfish. I was just prolonging the inevitable. It still stunned me I'd hurt her, even momentarily, but I'd already seen how responsive she was. She was genuine and emotional. *Real.*

That was why her music spoke to so many people. But it didn't begin to scratch the surface of why she spoke to *me.*

I was still standing in the same spot when the front door slammed.

PEYTON

THAT WHOLE THING ABOUT GOING HOME AGAIN BEING awesome? Complete and utter crap.

I stood outside the door to my mother's sitting room in our family home in Long Island, shredding my pale pink patent leather purse with my nails. Even knowing I was going to tell my mother to go to hell—metaphorically speaking—I'd still dressed the part of the little lady arriving for tea.

Pink purse, pink pumps, strand of pearls around my neck.

Though, wow, I'd been doing some research over the past week, and I'd learned some interesting stuff.

Pearl necklaces weren't always bought at the Tiffany counter. Who knew?

Well, evidently lots of people did. I had not. Now I was armed with knowledge of many carnal delights, and if I had her way, by God, I was going to live them out.

Maybe I'd even make up a few new sex positions, just for the hell of it. The flexibility of my thighs was the limit.

That and if I could find a willing male to help me. Not a willing male. *The* pigheaded, jackass, hot as hell man who'd saved my bacon by the side of the road then took me home to fry it up.

Or something way sexier than that.

First, I had to deal with my mother. At least I was fully fortified by a raspberry latte. I'd had to get one. It matched the whole pink theme I had going.

I knocked on the door and pushed it open once my mother instructed for me to come in. Sandra, the maid, had let me in and told me that my mother was indisposed, but that was nothing new. All that meant was that Pauline Pryor had probably been sweetening her coffee with too much Irish already, despite the fact that it was barely eleven a.m. Most likely my father was doing the same, except he'd be drinking down at the club.

"You're out and about early today, Peyton." My mother was already slurring her words. That meant this would be a conversation for the record books.

"Yes, well, I have a—"

"Show tonight. Yes, dear." She pulled at an invisible thread on her pale orange suit. She looked like a creamsicle, all cool and fresh. "Are you excited?"

This was our usual dialogue. Talking about banal, surface things was safe.

"Yes, I am." Which my mother knew. I always enjoyed performing. It was an oasis in the center of my crazy life. No matter what chased me off-stage, onstage I was happy and free. Somehow the approval of all those fans helped smooth over the rough spots inside me.

Funny how I'd discovered one man's approval mattered even more in just a few hours.

"That's good, dear. I'm pleased to hear you don't intend to go off wild-cocked again."

"Halfcocked, you mean? I didn't take off when I was due to perform. My schedule was clear." As clear as it ever was.

"Mmm-hmm," my mother replied, telling me exactly what she thought of *that*.

I forced back a sigh as my mother stared blandly out the window at the manicured grounds while she circled her silver teaspoon in her cup of "coffee". "I have something to talk to you about." I sat on the leather ottoman in front of my mother's wing-back chair. "I'm going ahead with some different material. I'm debuting two of the songs tonight. I don't want you to be surprised."

Telling her ahead of time was a courtesy. My parents wouldn't come to tonight's show. They would only grill me about it once the footage and articles surfaced.

There would be all the usual questions about why I was trying something new, and probably speculation that I was doomed to fail. After all, I'd failed on my last aborted attempt to spice it up a little.

The couple of singles off the album that had been more *me* than any other had done abysmally. As soon as I'd gone back to my usual material, my sales had rebounded.

Even increased.

Branching out was a big risk. One I had to take. I couldn't stay locked up in a cell of my own making any longer. I'd loved music once. I wanted to love it again.

Being with Jed for that one solitary night had shown me that I'd repressed so much of myself. And for what? Yes, I wanted to make other people happy, but not at my own expense. It wasn't fair to anyone.

Hopefully, my fans would understand and grow to like my new stuff too. If not, I'd still play the songs that they loved—and I would continue trying to win them over, one listener at a time.

My mother's hand rattled the cup in its saucer. "Not again, Peyton."

"Yes, again. I'm growing older and you can't expect me to still sing songs about first love until I'm middle-aged—" I broke off, realizing how ridiculous that particular argument was.

Unless I was very mistaken, I was experiencing my first love now...at twenty-three. Not at the sixteen of the girls in my songs, but still. There were plenty of parallels.

More than ever, I related to the nerves and thrills I sang about, wondering if he would call—he hadn't—or if he was thinking about me—hard to say—or if what had happened between us mattered as much to him as it had to me—doubtful.

My belly wrenched as it had every few hours over the past week. Walking away from Jed had been beyond difficult, and worse, it had felt as if I was leaving a section of my heart behind. Turning my back on happiness after finally getting my first true glimpse was nuts.

So was falling for a guy in under twelve hours. I still wasn't backing down.

If he didn't love me yet, well, he would. Hopefully. I wanted that man, and we'd had a crazy chemistry that couldn't be denied or shoved aside. As different as our lives were, we could make it work if we were willing to put in the effort.

And I was.

Tonight, after the show, I was going to put it all on the line. After that was anyone's guess, but I wasn't going to consent to being a bystander in my own life any longer. I'd been given so much, and I wanted to start giving back in ways other than holding charity benefits and donating to worthy causes.

Now I was going to try giving myself. The *real* me.

"Your fans expect a certain standard from you, Peyton." My mother didn't sound agitated, only weary. She probably knew that the easiest way to keep her daughter in line was to act as if she was just so *tedious*. "You tried some of that screaming nonsense on 'Starting Over' and what happened? You alienated the very people who've given you such a comfortable lifestyle. Would you really like it if your elderly parents had to go back to begging for scraps at our age? We've done so much for you. Made sacrifices you don't even know about."

I snorted. *Sure, like not divorcing Daddy but having an affair with your much younger tennis instructor instead? Thanks so much for keeping my happy home intact.*

"I understand that," I said evenly, "and I appreciate them. But I've sacrificed too. I lost a lot of my childhood to talent shows and trying to get that big break. Forget my teenage years. I didn't have a date until I was eighteen."

A *chaperoned* date, with three bodyguards. Because what yelled romance more than guys in dark suits with their hands on the pistols tucked in their waistbands? No wonder the guy had never contacted me again. He wasn't famous, just a regular boy, and he'd been too scared to even kiss me.

I smiled. Unlike another man I knew, who'd gone for a different kind of kiss altogether.

"So your way of making up for lost time is to wreck the career you've spent all these years building?"

My smile faded. The criticism stung. It *always* stung, because that fear of failure and letting people down had kept me rooted in place for far too long. Well, no more. I wasn't the same scared girl I'd been. One night had helped me grow up and see everything I'd been missing.

I'd dared Jed to take that next step. Now it was time to dare myself.

"I don't think I'm going to wreck my career," I said softly, stroking the cool hammered steel bracelet around my wrist until I steadied. "I think I'm going to do just fine. And if I don't, if this attempt goes up in smoke, then at least I'll be able to face myself in the mirror again. I'm tired of being a coward, Mama."

At that, my mother lifted her head. I hadn't called her that since childhood, since long before I'd started getting noticed for my singing.

"I know my success is why you love me." *If you love me.* "Risking it means I'm risking our relationship too. It's a risk I need to take, for me. For the dreams that got me here in the first place. Singing is the most important thing in my life, and I don't want to grow to hate it." I took a shuddering breath and stared hard at my new jewelry, my own unique expression of breaking free. "Or worse, to hate myself."

"You're so talented, baby."

I glanced up, shocked. "What?"

My mother smiled gently. "Your father and I don't just love you for your success. We admire you for chasing the life you wanted, no matter the cost."

"But that's just it. This isn't the life I wanted. I want to play my own music. I want..." I blew out a breath and rubbed my cheek against my shoulder, remembering how Jed's hands had felt against my skin. Every night I awakened just before dawn, straining against my nightgown, craving his touch more desperately than the water I gulped down to ease the ache in my throat. "I want so much."

"Then you need to go after it."

For a moment, I didn't move. Didn't breathe. I clutched the delicate bracelet I'd had made, wondering if it had superpowers. It had to be a special talisman, because there was no other way this conversation could be happening. "Mama?"

"You don't want to end up a bitter old woman like me, drinking coffee-flavored whiskey before lunch." With a thin smile, my mother set her saucer down on the table beside her. "I don't want that for you."

"Are you drunk?"

My mother tipped back her head and laughed, though she immediately smoothed each buttery blond strand of hair back into place.

Some things never changed. *Most* didn't. But sometimes when they did, incredible things happened.

"I'm probably more sober than ever right now, but I can't promise you I'll say the same sentiments the next time I see you. It's hard to let go of what you know. I'm comfortable where I am." Her shrewd blue eyes narrowed. "If you're not, figure out how to fix it.

And stay the course no matter who tells you to turn around. It'll make winning that much sweeter."

I nodded, swallowing hard. "When was the last time you won?"

My mother smiled. "When I had you."

I nearly asked if my mother had won simply because I was her daughter, or because I'd been so lucrative. In the end, I decided I didn't want to know. I'd already received more positive reinforcement from my mother than I'd ever expected. Why push my luck? I had plenty of other luck to push as the day wore on.

"Thank you, Mama." I rose and leaned over to kiss my mother's papery cheek. I didn't know if it was my mother's makeup or if she'd aged before my eyes, but the feel of her skin made my resolve strengthen even more.

Time spun on, whether you were ready or not. It didn't wait. Ever.

"Don't thank me." My mother squeezed my wrist, her gaze flickering to my bracelet before returning to my eyes. "Make yourself proud."

A couple minutes later, I got into my car and pulled out my phone. I'd needed that support, even if it was only temporary. Like a kid pushing off on my new training wheels, that brief hand at my back was just enough to get me going.

This would nudge me even farther.

"Hi, Taylor. I need a favor. Could you send a VIP ticket for the show tonight to a Mr. Jed Knight?" I rattled off his address. "It's important."

Indirectly, Jed had helped me stop hiding. He should be there when I took the first step to being who I truly was. I hoped I wouldn't regret inviting him.

Hoped with everything I was that he would show.

JED

My life had finally come full circle. I'd gone from being a hard-edged, take no prisoners detective to standing in the front row of a Peyton Pryor concert.

Lord help me.

The noise and crowds in this place were insane. Why hadn't I thought to bring earplugs? Maybe I should've worn a hoodie to discourage the chipper girls who surrounded me. They kept trying to talk to me as if we were old pals, brought together by our love of *the* Peyton Pryor.

Ironically enough, my feelings for the woman on the posters in the lobby of the event center crept uncomfortably close to love, as improbable as it seemed. But not because she sang "Rev Me Up", the song that the teenager beside me had declared her very favorite song ever.

I couldn't help smiling. Peyton had done damn well for herself. Perhaps one day she'd begin to appreciate her talent, rather than feel embarrassed by her success.

Like you're out so loud and proud. You couldn't even admit to her that you're a writer.

I hadn't been in denial about it exactly. It was more that so much of me was still wrapped up in being a cop. I'd thought I had let that part of my past go, but after the night I'd spent with Peyton, I'd realized swiftly that I hadn't.

Guilt was still eating me alive, still forcing me to deny my needs as a bizarre form of punishment. Being with her had shown me there was another way to live. I'd become chained by my own inhibitions—not sexual, or not entirely sexual anyway—and the time had come to unlock the damn cuffs.

A writer was who I was now.

I'd made mistakes as a cop, but I refused to let them taint the present. Peyton had reminded me of all I'd missed out on by pretending I didn't have urges beyond so-called vanilla sex. I enjoyed dominance and submission, and I had no reason to shut down that aspect of myself if I found a woman who shared my proclivities.

Strike the *if*. I was pretty sure I had found the right woman, now I just had to convince her that I was worth taking a chance on. Worthy of her.

I fingered the unused ticket in my jeans pocket. She'd sent me a VIP ticket by courier that afternoon, and I'd been both amused and irritated by the gesture. Did she think I couldn't pay my own way? I'd already bought my own damn ticket. Not front row, of course—

Because you couldn't afford it.

Whatever, I'd intended to be there anyway. Did she honestly think I would miss her show? Now that I'd heard her music, it seemed to be everywhere. When I walked into the coffee shop I liked to write at some mornings or shopped at the grocery store, she seemed to play on every speaker. Her sultry voice and her playful smile were on billboards all over the place. Those lively blue eyes would haunt me until the end of my days.

Before me, the curtain rose, and the roar turned deafening. And the eyes that haunted me were suddenly connected with mine, as if she'd sought me out the instant she stepped onstage. My heartbeat picked up pace, its beat drowning out the screams and whistles.

This past week without her had been sheer, inescapable misery. I'd tried to tell myself I was overstating things, that I couldn't feel this way after one night.

I'd been wrong. I could've felt this way about her after one hour. She'd blown into my life like a hurricane and blown out again too soon, leaving everything quiet and still. Desolate. It had felt like all the oxygen had been sucked out of my chest with the closing of my front door.

Now that she was in my sights, I could breathe again.

Onstage, she smiled and touched her wrist, a gesture I didn't understand, then offered her smile to all those that surrounded me. "Good evening, Edgewood! Are you ready to party? I said, are you ready to *party*?"

Smiling in spite of myself, I glanced down the front row of yelling, undulating girls, surprised to see two familiar faces. Jared Brooks and Preston Shaw, my old buddies from Syracuse University, along with their women, were standing at the end of the aisle, smiling wide as could be. And lo and behold, they all seemed to be enjoying the music as Peyton started to sing her latest hit, "In Your Eyes."

The words pulled at me and I had to face her again, to drink her down like a thirsty man would savor his last glass of water. She bounded across the stage, exuberance personified, her voice soaring to the rafters and beyond. Her face was radiant. This was where she was truly at home.

Hopefully, she would also find home in my bed. Under my hand, and in my arms.

By the end of the concert, the fans were on the verge of total lunacy, and Peyton was dripping with sweat and beaming. She'd changed outfits at least four times, and she'd danced and wiggled her ass until I was exhausted for her. But she showed no signs of slowing down as she announced two more songs to finish the set.

They were new ones, stuff she'd written recently, and she hoped the crowd enjoyed them.

"I have someone to thank first." She stared right at me. "Someone who helped me dare to go as far as I can with my music. And my life." Again, she touched her wrist, that mystery gesture I had a feeling I was supposed to understand but did not. "He knows who he is to me."

No, I really didn't know, not yet. But I would. Soon.

"Rulebreaker," I mouthed to her.

She nodded, grinning. She was about to break them all, and I intended to encourage her every step of the way.

From the first note, I knew these songs were different. "Caught Under Your Spell" was edgier and more intense, and Peyton played her guitar like a sexy demon throughout it. She bypassed the dancing to focus on dazzling the audience with her skills on guitar and her sexy voice, promising to lead them on a path to darker delights.

And boy, did she deliver.

The second song was just her and her guitar with only the barest of accompaniment from her backup band. Her mesmerizing vocals held everyone captive as she sung about breaking her own heart while her lonely fingerwork emphasized her pain.

Halfway through it, the girls beside him were crying and myriad cell phones had been lifted to reveal their flickering flashlight apps. I would've shook my head at the modern take on the old-fashioned lighter at a concert, if I hadn't been so enthralled by the woman sitting on a stool in the center of the stage. She was weeping softly as she sung, silent tears tracking down her cheeks.

Yet her vocals never faltered. She was simply breathtaking.

From the crowd's earsplitting applause once she'd finished, everyone in attendance knew it. She was so much more than a pop star or a flavor of the moment. She was the real deal, and I damn well intended to convince her of her talent.

I'd tell her every day if I had to, for as long as it took.

Backstage was complete chaos, but the VIP ticket she'd sent me had included a pass that got me past all the security. Not knowing exactly how these things worked, I tried to give her time to get settled. She probably needed a shower. Or maybe she had some elaborate post-show routine. I had no clue.

I stared down at his empty hands. Flowers. I needed flowers. Isn't that what people brought backstage? She deserved two bouquets of them after that performance. A *dozen* bouquets.

Glancing at my watch, I rushed down the crowded hallway, dodging bodies to get to the exit. Surely there had to be a gas station or something nearby. I didn't want to give her cheap flowers, but I also didn't want to be away from her a moment longer than necessary.

Tonight I was risking everything.

PEYTON

He wasn't coming.

I gazed at my reflection in my dressing room mirror to avoid glancing at my phone one more time. He hadn't called, and he didn't even have the excuse of not having my number because I'd saved it in his phone the morning I left. I knew the hoops people had to go through to try to reach me, and I'd wanted him to have direct access.

So much for that.

At least he'd come to the show. He'd smiled at me, and his approval had gone miles toward quelling the anxious locusts swarming madly through my belly. His quiet, steady presence had helped bolster me to get through the final two songs of my performance.

And I'd nailed them, if I did say so myself.

Even Taylor, my manager, had been abuzz after the show. The fan response was positive. Radio seemed interested. The new songs might end up on the next album.

As incredible as all of that was—beyond my wildest dreams incredible—the victory seemed hollow without Jed. He shouldn't have mattered so much to me in such a short time, but somehow he did. The backstage pass I'd given him had been a sterling sign that I wanted to talk to him.

Needed to. But he'd just walked away.

Eventually, I'd asked Taylor and the members of my band and the assorted road crew and friends who'd stopped by to leave. I hated to ruin their fun and my own. The show had taken a lot out of me, both physically and emotionally, and adding the Jed factor to the mix had drained me even further. If I made it home without crying, it would be a miracle.

Some of those tears would be happy. A lot of them, actually. Some would not.

I'd really believed he cared. Oh, I wasn't sure if he cared at the level I did. That would be asking a lot even for an optimist. I'd just hoped that he felt something beyond the usual feelings engendered from a one-night-stand. Whatever those were. I had no idea, never having had one before. All I'd had were failed short-term relationships.

Now I could add a failed one-night-stand to the list.

Somehow I managed to smile at my makeup-less reflection. Well, the sex part had been no kind of fail whatsoever. Hell to the no. That had been hallelujah chorus-worthy.

Maybe my mistake was in expecting more.

My eyes prickled, and I shut them to stave off the inevitable. Everything was going to be okay. I'd get through this, one hour at a time.

A knock on the door made me whisk my fingers over my cheeks, just in case. "Sorry, no visitors right now, please."

The only one who mattered hadn't shown.

The long pause made me wonder if they'd left. "I have a backstage pass. Surely that gives me certain rights."

His voice hit me at a visceral level, where I didn't have to think to react. Letting out a squeal, I bolted off the stool. I ran to the door and threw it open, ready to launch myself at him.

I was stopped by a forest of flowers. What the hell?

With a mouthful of petals, I drew back and tried to speak. "Jed?" I asked, peering over the profusion of red blooms. There were so many I couldn't even see him. "Thank you for the flowers. They're gorgeous."

They smelled heavenly too, but somehow his scent overrode all the rest. I swayed toward it, and him, like a bee seeking nectar.

He was *here*. Finally.

"You're more so." He stepped into the room, and it was a freaking miracle my boneless arms didn't drop the bouquet of roses altogether. He simply dominated the space. Filled it up until I backed against the door I'd just closed to try to get room to breathe.

But he didn't give me that room. Shoving the roses out of the way, he gripped my chin and lifted my face to his. "You were incredible."

Those three words were my undoing.

I barreled into his arms, trapping the roses between us as I pressed my face into his neck. The spicy scent of his soap and the ever-present aroma of coffee mashed together in my mind, smoothing away all the stress of the last week. He was here, and he was holding me, and nothing had ever been better.

Then he tipped back my chin and took my mouth, proving me a liar. *This* was as good as it got. His firm lips caressing mine, warming them before his tongue slid between them to explore. He flicked it over mine and the movement reverberated between my legs, causing my clit to pound furiously. I'd changed out of my stage costume and just wore a robe and panties, and God, I wouldn't mind making use of the couch to assuage the ache deep in my core.

The ache labeled *Jed*. He already owned that part of me just like all the rest.

But before I could guide him toward that oh so handy sofa, he shifted back and rubbed his thumb over my damp lower lip. "You always gotta look so sexy on stage?" he asked gruffly.

The light in his eyes made me grin. "Sorry. Kinda. It's my job."

He grabbed my ass and hauled me against him, kissing me one more time. Leaving me breathless when he pulled back just far enough to whisper, "And you're a damn pro."

Feeling his hardness against me, I pressed even closer, wanting it to brand her belly even through our clothes. That hot, heavy weight made me pulse and dampen, and I lifted my eyes to his, hoping he'd get the message. "If, um, it displeased you, you could always—" He was laughing before I finished the statement, and then I was laughing too.

Damn, that felt good.

"I see you haven't changed in a week."

"Oh, I have."

His eyebrow lifted. "That so?"

I pointed my thumb over my shoulder. "I couldn't have played those last couple of songs a few weeks ago. I couldn't have put myself on the line like that, knowing I might fail. That I probably would."

"You didn't fail. You were magnificent."

The pride glowing on his face and vibrating in his words caused my eyes to fill again. "I couldn't have done it without you."

"Like hell you couldn't. You've got everything you need, right here." He pushed his hand through the cluster of flowers until he finally reached my chest. He covered my rapidly beating heart with his palm, his gaze colliding with mine.

"No," I whispered, lacing my fingers with his. "Now I have everything I need."

Emotion moved over his face, and he cleared his throat. "Let's get out of here." Then he glanced around. "If you can. You probably have...stuff to do."

I had to smile. He was clearly out of his depth, but he was trying. For me. "Nope, all the stuff is done."

"Good. So, let's split."

An idea popped into my head. A *brilliant* one. If we were going to do this, I wanted to take him somewhere special to me. The first place I'd started dreaming.

"Sure." My smile grew. "I know just where we should go."

His gaze returned to mine, one corner of his mouth rising. "Does it happen to include a horizontal surface?" He glanced down at his visible erection, showcased by his snug jeans. "Pryor, we have a situation."

Laughing, I tugged on his hand. "Just let me get dressed." I winked over my shoulder. "Don't worry, I'll be sure to accommodate your request."

Under an hour later, we were staring up at the back of my childhood home in Jersey while I cursed my decision to wear low heels to the venue tonight. I knew better. My feet were always on fire after a show, but I'd been hoping to seduce Jed.

Damn vanity always screwed me over.

I gripped the trunk of the tree nearest to the house and shot him a look. His jaw was set and he kept glaring at the house—when he wasn't glaring at me. "C'mon. It's an easy climb up, I swear."

"You think climbing the tree is the part I have a problem with, Peyton?"

Uh oh. Already she'd picked up that when he used my name and not Rulebreaker or vixen or baby—I really liked that one—that he was annoyed.

My ass grew warmer. Not that his being annoyed was necessarily a bad thing.

"We won't stay long," I promised. "We aren't going inside either. Just on the roof over the back porch. See, it's flat." I couldn't keep the triumph out of my tone. "You wanted a horizontal surface, right?"

"Not on someone's roof. And I don't care if we're not going in. It's still trespassing."

"The house is for sale. No one will ever know or care." I flashed him a smile I knew my backside would pay for later. I couldn't wait. "If we get caught, I'll get us out of trouble."

"The hell you will." His hand came down on my bottom just as I boosted myself up the tree.

I laughed and just climbed higher, using the many branches for leverage. My natural athleticism came in handy, as did my muscle memory of climbing this very tree dozens of times years ago, but whoa, this was a lot harder than it had been when I was eight.

Sticking out my foot, I balanced on the edge of the roof, gathering my nerve for the final leap. I screeched a little as I jumped, but I made it without falling to my knees.

Score.

Turning back, I realized Jed was still on the ground.

"Chicken," I taunted.

"You are so getting it later."

That only made me laugh harder. "Promise?"

When he didn't respond, I fanned herself. "Whew, it's warm tonight." Actually it was quite chilly, but he would keep me warm. "Think I'll just get rid of a few layers." I tugged off my top, revealing my lacy red demi-cup bra. I sent my shirt sailing, laughing in delight as it got caught on a branch. "Damn, I'm good."

"Woman, you're on my last nerve."

"Is that the one in your cock or somewhere else?"

Growling, he ascended the tree at a speed that got me warm all on its own. He was freaking *hot.* Those muscled arms and legs made quick work of it, and he even snagged my top on the way. He planted his boot on the roof and then he was up there with me, stalking toward me with my shirt in his fist.

I nearly came on the spot.

Just before he reached me, I held up my hand. "Let me explain before you spank me into six orgasms."

His brow winged up. "Only six?"

I laughed and gave up on keeping my distance. I belonged in his arms, even when I'd pissed him off.

Much to my relief, he drew me into a tight embrace and

brushed a kiss over my forehead. "You're going to be the death of me."

"At least we'll really live first." I didn't argue when he tugged my shirt back over my head. It really was too cold to be sitting around half naked.

Dammit.

Pulling on his hand, I led him to the other end of the roof. I sat down, letting my legs dangle over the edge, waiting to speak until he sat beside me.

"This was my bedroom." I tapped the window beside us and chanced a glance inside at the darkened, empty room. Back in the old days, there had been talk in the neighborhood that my house was haunted. I'd always kind of hoped to see a ghost. "We lived here until I was ten and started getting some nibbles on the music scene. My parents said we outgrew this place, but the truth was our money had."

Not to my mind, it hadn't. I would've been happy living there throughout my childhood. My days there were the last ones it had felt like my parents and I were a real family.

Jed didn't say anything, just stroked his thumb over my knuckles. Back and forth, gently reassuring.

"I used to come out here and sing. Quietly at first, so I didn't wake up my parents or the neighbors. Eventually I'd lose myself in my music and I'd forget to be quiet. Then my dad would come outside and shush me." I smiled at the memory. "After that, I'd just make wishes on stars." I looked up and sucked in a breath at the view, as I always did. Pinprick stars studded the navy sky as if someone had tossed up a fistful of diamonds. "See how clear they are up here?"

He shifted behind me, sliding his legs along mine until they were caged in. His arms wrapped around my waist and I rested my head against his chest, more content than I'd ever been. "What did you wish for?" he asked against my temple.

"This." I gripped his strong forearm, digging in because I had to. I needed to believe he was real. "I wanted to matter to someone. I didn't really understand adult love yet, but I was already into boys." I bit my lip. "I was sorta boy crazy actually."

"No kidding."

I pushed my elbow into his gut, but he only laughed.

"I didn't actually *do* anything about it. But yeah, I was dreaming by then. I dreamed about being a famous singer too. I was already going to talent shows, and music was what I loved the most. School bored me, but music was my favorite class." I grimaced. Some of my memories weren't so sweet. "I used to sing the loudest so people would tell me I was good."

"Did they?"

"No. Most of them ignored me. Some tried to kick my ass."

"Jealous," he murmured, kissing my ear.

"No, I was a conceited little twit and they called me on it." I sighed. "In retrospect, I wish I'd held onto some of that, because I'm definitely not that confident now. I struggle constantly. Everything I do for validation threatens to destroy my confidence completely. That's melodramatic, but you understand." I twisted around to face him, unsurprised to see he'd clenched his jaw once again. "Don't you?"

"Yeah. It's different, but yeah. Anytime you put parts of yourself out there to be judged, it's hard."

"Who judged you?" I asked quietly, hoping he would tell me.

For a moment, he didn't reply. He finally began to speak in a low, emotionless voice. He told me about growing up in a family with several generations of cops and rising through the ranks in the city police department where he'd started his career. He didn't specifically tell me that he felt he'd been given promotions he didn't deserve due to his family connections but I surmised it.

"It caused some tension with me and the other guys, my partner especially. Then one day we were on an undercover mission, and we were at this tenement in the Bronx."

I fought not to shudder as he described the creepy feel of the nearly abandoned place. Dark, broken-down, decrepit. His voice dropped lower and lower as he spoke.

"There was some movement around a corner, and I reacted, thinking I'd finally spotted the perp. I was so eager to prove that I deserved my spot on the force." His Adam's apple bobbed. "I shot my partner instead. He could've died."

My first tendency was to comfort, but I sensed he didn't want that. So much of what we were together was based on instinct, on gut-level knowing, and that connection between us wouldn't fail now. "He didn't die."

"No. He spent some time in the hospital. He's okay now. Actually, he got married a few months after that." Jed smiled faintly. "Said he'd seen the light."

"Like in the tunnel or metaphorically?"

Jed laughed, shaking his head. "No clue. But they're happy together. He's got a baby on the way. Two babies. Freaking twins. Can you imagine?"

"Wow, that light must've been bright."

Jed laughed again and tightened his hold on me. It was hard to say which of us needed the connection more. "I saw the light too. A different one. I wasn't cut out to be a cop, not deep down, so I resigned."

"And started writing."

"And started writing," he agreed. "You pegged me right. I guess I just hadn't fully accepted I still wasn't a cop. I mean, I had enough to cash the checks from my publisher." He chuckled. "But beyond that? Denial fucking city."

"You're too amazing to deny it for long."

"You read something of mine?" he asked, pride filling his question.

"Uh, try two of your books already and working on the third. They're incredibly addictive. I've been sneaking in bits of them in between interviews and rehearsals." I grinned up at him. "You're awfully prolific, Mr. Not-A-Writer."

"Keeps me off the streets." He swatted my thigh. "Maybe you should try it, Rulebreaker."

"Nah, I have my own artistic outlet to pull out my hair over. You like writing?"

"I love it," he said quietly. "In a way I never loved being a cop. One more thing I felt guilty about over the years."

"So you found your way to where you needed to be." I reached up to stroke his chin, loving the way his scruff felt under my fingers. "You were—"

He caught my wrist, cutting her off. "What's this?" He stroked my bracelet. "I saw you playing with it during the show."

"Oh. Hmm. I guess we're to this part of the program already." When he only raised a brow, I plowed ahead. "I, ah, did some research on BDSM once I left you."

"Did you?"

"I did."

"And didn't run screaming," he said dryly.

"I almost ran back to you and begged you to make me scream more, but away? No." I grinned. "Anyway, I read about collars, and how they prove you're, you know, taken."

"They signify much more than that."

"Well, I didn't have you to inform me beyond the sites I found. I'm assuming you'll rectify that oversight now."

He nodded silently.

So much for no longer being a cop. The guy was downright inscrutable when he wanted to be.

"I'm not saying we're at that stage. Or even that we necessarily want to be at that stage. I don't know if you're a strict practitioner. Or if—"

"Peyton."

"The point. Right." I blew out a breath. "I heard of this up and coming designer, Presley Warren, and she does customized pieces. I asked her if she could make me a bracelet."

Turning my arm over, I showed him the clasp—two little handcuffs, locked together. The intricacy of the piece, not to mention the speed with which Presley had put it together, still awed me. I would've paid twice as much for it.

"This is your version of a collar. A pre-collar." His throat worked as he caressed the hammered steel. The simplicity and strength of the bracelet had drawn me too. It was built to last. Steel couldn't be damaged easily once it was forged.

Just like us, if the fates were kind.

"Yes. It's my way of saying I belong to you. If you want me." I tried to stop my arm from shaking, but it was impossible.

"You must realize from your research that it's the Dom who's supposed to pick out the collar for the sub. That by making this move on your own, you're stepping out of line."

"In the bad way or the good way? Because I'm never really sure."

He shook his head, smiling. "Yep, I'm a dead man."

"That was a serious question."

"And this is my serious answer. You asked me if I want you." He lifted my wrist to his mouth and kissed the bracelet's tiny clasp, his breath warm against my skin. "Baby, I can't remember ever wanting anything or anyone more."

EPILOGUE

JED

An angel was singing in my ear.

I groaned and pulled a pillow over my head to drown out the sound. Even angels were annoying at the crack of dawn after I'd been up almost all night to meet a deadline. My next book was launching in hardback, a big step up for me, and I'd been burning lots of midnight oil to get it finished. I'd also been pushing so hard to get the book done so I could join Peyton the next time she had to travel.

But now she was here, seducing me with her silky voice. Strumming the guitar, she crooned about last loves, which made me open an eye and stare at the zigzag pattern of my pillowcase. Peyton's doing.

Everything was Peyton's doing, including the fact that I'd been up so late last night. She'd just returned from a brief European tour. She was doing so well with the new songs she'd integrated into her show that she'd rushed home to head right into the studio. The plan was to get them added to her upcoming album, her dream come true. Her excitement had magnified my usual desire for her until I'd had to take her in the front hall.

Again.

Being away from her sucked. Now that she was back home for a few weeks, I planned to spoil her rotten.

Once I finished spanking her for waking me up so damn early with her sexy singing.

I rolled over and tossed aside the pillow. "You are in so much trouble—" I broke off, realizing she wasn't only singing and playing the guitar beside me in bed.

She was doing it naked, wearing only her handcuff bracelet and a smile.

"Get over here," I demanded, hooking a hand around one shapely ankle.

"Mind the guitar!" After depositing her instrument safely on the floor, she wriggled on top of me, her face lowering for her customary morning kiss.

I hadn't been much of a kisser before her, but she hadn't given me much choice except to learn to love it.

Eh, who was I kidding? I loved every chance I got to have her lips on me. Or my lips on her, wherever they might land.

"About time you wake up, old man." She poked my shoulder, giggling at the rumble in my chest. "Sleeping half the day away. We have things to do. Important things. Like—"

I flipped her over on her belly, holding her down with the press of my body into hers and my hand gently clamped on the back of her neck. "Like me paddling this sweet little ass then fucking you raw?" I grated into her ear.

Instantly, she went limp. "That's also a good plan."

I couldn't help laughing. Instead of spanking her, I eased down her body to kiss the line of her spine. She arched upward to get more of my mouth, and I dipped his hand between her legs to rub her swollen slit. "Already wet for me."

"Always," she whispered.

That was sterling truth.

As much as I wanted to continue on this path, I had something else in mind for this morning. Or afternoon. Whenever she'd so cruelly chosen to wake me up.

Moving back, I lightly tapped her perfect ass. It was still slightly flushed from the fun they'd had last night. "Stay right here."

"But—"

"Peyton."

As always, that stilled her. Her murmured, "Yes, Sir," made me smile as I rose to walk over to my dresser.

We really didn't follow most BDSM protocol, inside the bedroom or out. We'd come up with our own version of things that worked for us. Understatement. The woman left me walking around with a dopey smile half the time and a painful hard-on the rest. It had been that way for the six months we'd been together. Everything was still as chaotic and passionate between us as it had been the night we'd met, and I thanked God for it.

By far, she was the brightest part of my life.

I removed the jewelry box from the dresser and walked back to the bed. I kneeled beside her hip and opened it, then drew the intricate piece of jewelry out of its case. The handcuff charms in the center glinted in the morning sun, and my erection only thickened as I imagined her wearing her matching set.

And *only* her matching set.

"Eyes closed," I commanded, knowing she would oblige me. She always knew when to push me and when to acquiesce. Well, most of the time. Her fire was one of the things I adored most about her, and there was a long list. "Lift your head."

She did as I asked and I slipped the necklace around her neck. "Jed?" she gasped.

Her hair presented a problem. "Do something about your hair. I can't do the clasp." With a little wiggling, she managed to get it out of my way enough for me to lock it. "Sit up now, baby."

With tears in her eyes, she kneeled and turned toward me. She didn't even glance down because she understood what it signified.

Their version of a ring, though one day soon she'd have that too. "This is the best gift I've ever gotten."

"It's a gift for me too." Looking at her in my jewelry was a present I'd never hoped to wish for. I ran my fingertip over the hammered steel. "Presley changed the look this time because I wanted the handcuffs in the front. They're small, and I'm sure you can hide them under your—"

"Are you kidding? I'm showing this off everywhere." She launched herself into my arms, nearly knocking me off the bed.

Freddy whined and pawed at the door. Forget breakfast, he probably wanted to be part of the fun too. But we usually shut him out on nights we were having sex because he tended to stare.

Laughing, I brushed her hair out of her eyes. "You know what this means, don't you?"

"Yes." Her face was glowing. "It means I'm yours, forever."

"You got that right. But you already were. It also means—"

"I love you," she blurted, biting her lip once the words were out. "Whoops. I guess I should've let you finish."

"Nah, in this case, I think interruptions are perfectly acceptable." I leaned up to nibble her full lower lip. "I love you too, by the way."

"Well, duh." She grinned at my stern expression. "I mean, duh, Sir."

If you're interested in more Kensington Square goodness check out our series page!

ABOUT THE AUTHOR

USA Today bestselling author, ***Taryn Quinn,*** is the sexy and funny alter ego of bestselling authors Taryn Elliott & Cari Quinn. We've been writing together for years, but we have decided to pull the trigger on a combo name just for fun.

And so...Taryn Quinn was born!

Do you like ultra sexy small town romance full of shenanigans? Quirky office romances full of steam? Okay, look...we pretty much just love writing steamy stories. If you're all about that, we're your girls!

For more information about us...
tarynquinn.com
tq@tarynquinn.com

DEVIL IN THE DETAILS

ARIA WYATT

This is a work of fiction. Names, places, characters, and incidents are either the product of the author's imagination or are used fictitiously, and any resemblance to any actual persons, living or dead, organizations, events or locales is entirely coincidental.

ABOUT THE BOOK

She's rich. Powerful. And undeniably frigid. So why does she make me so damn hot?

Anyone who dips their toes into New York City's publishing market knows Elinora Iverson is an ice queen. The billionaire divorcee rules her empire with an iron fist. But when my best friend scores me an interview with the gorgeous mogul, she offers me a job I'm too broke to refuse—a position with Iverson Melt, her company's romance imprint.

Look, I don't know the first thing about meet cutes or falling in love. Sex? Well, that's a totally different story. One I'm more than qualified to edit, since I moonlight at The River, a water-themed kink club. My ability to bring my clients to a boil earned me a reputation as the club's gateway drug.

Enter the plot twist of a lifetime when The River hosts a masquerade party, and my new boss shows up in my private lagoon, naked and ready to submit.

Elinora doesn't know I'm the stranger behind the mask. Or that I've fantasized about her since the moment we met. The line between reality and fantasy blurs when she calls out *my* name in the darkness. And when she eventually discovers her pleasure concierge is none other than the young editor she hired, mercury *really* rises.

While I can't undo the damage her cheating ex-husband caused, I slowly thaw Elinora's frostbitten heart. It turns out she's not the ice queen she leads everyone to believe. As we melt into each other, she makes it clear she doesn't want to share me.

There's only one problem: I'm bound to another woman.

I find out the hard way that when you make a deal with the Devil herself, the Devil's in the details.

This story contains themes which may be upsetting to some readers. Please read with caution if you are sensitive to topics like divorce, mentions of the heroine's past fertility struggles and pregnancy loss, and a side character with Down Syndrome. While the following anthology piece ends with a juicy cliffhanger, the full novel (which releases on July 20, 2023, and is available for preorder) features a satisfying happily-ever-after.

ONE

Lincoln Kennedy

THE LETHAL DOSE OF CAFFEINE IS TEN THOUSAND milligrams. That means the five shots of espresso I ordered won't kill me. Will they help me stay awake? Doubtful. After last night's extracurriculars, I'd need more than a dozen to keep me going.

The strawberry blond barista hands me my jet fuel and smiles. "Do you want it dirty?"

My gaze snaps to hers. "I'm sorry, what?"

She holds up a metal carafe. "Your friend's chai. Do you want espresso in that too?"

"Oh." I shake my head to clear the imagined innuendo before I start trying to flirt like a damn fool. "Yes, please."

"Rough night?" She studies my face, her eyes lingering on the dark circles beneath mine.

I glance at her name badge. "You have no idea, Geneva."

"Well, I hope your day is an improvement." She sprinkles some cinnamon on the frothy chai before handing it over with a smile.

"Thanks. Me too," I mutter, snapping the lid onto my to-go cup.

I weave through the café to the table where my best friend awaits and place his beverage in front of him. "I still don't understand why you feel it's necessary for a pre-interview briefing."

Myles leans in. "Because I assured Elinora you were the perfect candidate for the position, and I hate looking like an idiot in front of my boss."

Settling on a stool, I swallow a few sips before answering. The high-octane refreshment is a step above river mud, but I force it down. My focus—and dwindling bank account—depends on it. I rarely order espresso, but I had a late night at the club and need all the help I can get.

"You're saying you think I'll embarrass you?"

He sighs, rubbing a pale hand over his freckled face. "I know it wouldn't be intentional, Linc."

"For the record, I plan to nail this interview and knock her socks off. You can thank me later for making you look good." I flash him a cocky smirk. "Maybe I'll nail *her* too."

While sex with my supervisor is a line I'd never cross again, it's fun to goad him because he huffs and puffs more than the big, bad wolf.

Myles snorts. "You have no idea who you're dealing with. Elinora Iverson wouldn't let you within three feet of her. Besides, Iverson Press is an industry anomaly."

"How different can it be from Cooper Press?"

The small, independent publishing house that laid me off last month is on the verge of bankruptcy. My former boss told me he was doing me a favor when he handed me my pink slip. Funny, my idea of a favor involves helping someone—not pulling the rug out from beneath them. I've been an editor for three years, and a skilled one at that, but the New York market is saturated. While I received several offers for positions on the west coast, relocation isn't an option for me.

Myles pins me with his emerald gaze. "No other woman-owned publishing house has joined the ranks of New York's Big Five this easily. Elinora is a ruthless businesswoman who will stop at nothing to reach the top. If you even *think* about nailing her, she'll trample you and feed you your balls. Then she'll eat you alive."

"You know I love surrounding myself with powerful women."

"You'll change your tune once you meet her," he mutters, sipping his drink.

"I spent a summer in Amsterdam. I think I can handle her."

"Wrong fucking country, Linc. She's from Denmark." He cocks his head to the side. "Did you research the company like I told you to?"

"A little."

"We had two editors leave this month because they couldn't handle the pressure. These are seasoned professionals with decades of experience—not somebody three years out of Emerson College. She only agreed to interview you because *I* told her you have an impeccable eye for detail, and for whatever reason, she likes me." He knots his hands in his fiery hair. "If you make me look like an asshole, she'll never promote me to the marketing executive position. This is my career on the line."

I grip his wrist. "Myles, relax. I won't let you down."

"I fucking hope not. Iverson Press is big league shit. It's nothing like what you're used to. We're talking night and day."

"Well, we both know I function better at night."

"How late did you work *last* night?" he probes, his orange brows furrowing.

I glance at my watch. "Let's see, it's eight o'clock now. I got off around five this morning, went home to shower, and here I am."

"You didn't sleep *at all*?"

I point to my cup. "Hence my vat of liquid alertness."

Myles releases a heavy sigh. "No wonder you look like shit."

"This is a new suit, asshole."

"I'm talking about the circles under your eyes. You've gotta stop this. That environment isn't healthy for you."

I love when he goes all mama hen on me. We've been friends

since kindergarten, and he knows me better than I know myself. He's right. My salacious nightlife isn't healthy, but I have no choice —my little sister's life depends on it.

Reagan was born with Down Syndrome, epilepsy, and a serious heart condition. For years I've struggled with survivor's guilt over being born healthy. Why was I given that gift when she wasn't? What made me special? Why did she deserve to endure multiple cardiac surgeries and frequent seizures, when the worst health crisis I've dealt with was a sprained wrist in ninth grade?

After our father's stroke three years ago, the family's financial situation hit rock bottom. The measly disability checks he receives from the state don't scratch the surface of Reagan's expenses. Quality assisted living requires money we don't have, so for the past two years, my second job has supplemented our income. Regardless of whether I like it, I'm stuck in this lecherous holding pattern until I've repaid my debts, or something changes with Reagan's insurance coverage, which is highly unlikely. According to my calculations, that means I'm on the hook for at least another five years. Not to mention over seventy thousand dollars. Too bad being laid off from my day job wasn't part of the equation. The surplus I'd saved is all but gone now, which is why I picked up a few extra shifts at the club. Myles knows all this, so it would be great if he'd stop riding my ass about it.

I remove my glasses and rub slow circles on my temples to combat the developing headache. While he does have a point about my lack of sleep, it's not like I can add hours to the day. "What choice do I have?"

"Have you thought about what happens if the place gets shut down and people find out you worked there? What will your parents think?"

My Irish Catholic parents would lose their shit if they had any idea about my after-dark activities. Father Ignatius DeAngelis, the principal of the Catholic school I attended through the middle of twelfth grade, would roll over in his grave and convince Jesus to hurl lightning bolts at me. Here's how I look at it: I'm already going to hell, so if I do it with good intentions, that should lessen the burn. Right?

"Who will take care of Reagan if she gets evicted from the group home for lack of payment?" I counter, raising a brow at him when he doesn't answer. Needing a distraction from the sheer panic that possibility triggers inside me, I take a long, slow sip of my espresso. "Listen, Esme doesn't cut corners. The River is a legal establishment. They won't shut us down."

Esmeralda "Madame Esme" DaVinci, the owner of the kink club where I work nights, is a keen businesswoman. Her exclusive client list features some of New York's most powerful men and women. I'm sure it works in Esme's favor that she, quite literally, has the Police Chief and District Attorney by the balls.

He lowers his voice. "Are *all* of your activities legal, Linc?"

Maybe?

I shove my glasses back onto my face. "The technicalities are above my pay grade, but Esme is fluent in loopholes and workarounds, so I'm sure we're fine." It also helps that one of her business partners is an attorney.

"This is what I mean. You're taking risks—"

"I'm an in-house escort—not a Goddamn prostitute," I whisper-shout, stiffening my spine. "And I never engage in risky behaviors."

"Fucking a stranger doesn't seem risky to you?"

"Not if I take the proper steps to mitigate said risk."

"Yeah, ok."

I jab my finger into his chest. "Look, you have your skillset, and I have mine."

"I wish you'd spend more time focusing on your editor's skillset."

"Pretty sure I got laid off, *not* fired." He opens his mouth to respond, but I cut him off. "Not to mention, Cooper Press is going under, so being out of a job was inevitable. I'm doing the best I can, bro." I lower my voice to a true whisper out of respect for the little old lady at the next table. "It's not like I sought out The River. The opportunity fell into my lap. It's not about easy pussy, it's about doing whatever's necessary to help my family. Besides, I signed a fucking contract. I'm Esme's until everything's been repaid, and I've met my time obligations. There's no way around it. You know that as well as I do. I'm a damn good editor, an excellent bartender, and an even better fuck. Until I can make it in publishing, this is my reality." Straightening, I meet his gaze. "I'll impress your boss and get you that promotion, my friend. I promise I won't let you down."

"Whatever you do, don't mention her divorce."

"Oh, for fuck's sake." I slap the edge of the table. "I may not be as brilliant as *you*, the legendary Saint Myles Callahan the second, but I'm not an idiot. Why the hell would I ask a stranger about her marital status?"

He squints. "Says the man who fucks strangers for money."

"No, I don't get paid to fuck—I get paid to *be* there. Technically, I'm on payroll as a *bartender*," I explain with air quotes. "And truth be told, the Aqua Suite bar is where I spend most of my time."

"What happens when you aren't mixing drinks?"

"Oh, you know . . . other things. According to Esme, my unofficial title is pleasure concierge, so I guess you could say it's a unique kind of mixing. But either way, I receive monetary compensation for my time. Not what I do with it."

I've never given Myles the nitty gritty details of what I do—thanks to my non-disclosure agreement—but since I listed him as my emergency contact, I've alluded to my job description. That way it won't be as much of a shock if Esme ever needs to call him. He has no clue what I deal with on a nightly basis. Over the years, I've learned it's better to keep him in the dark. We're both more comfortable this way—content to skirt around the topic like a leather-clad elephant in our friendship.

He rolls his eyes. "Whatever."

"No, it's not 'whatever.' There's a big difference."

"Your *time* entails fucking."

I shake my head. "Not always. My job is to meet the pleasure needs of our female club members, whatever they may be." His scowl tells me his misconceptions are deeply rooted, and I'm feeling chatty this morning, so I elaborate. "Yes, sometimes that involves a bit of kink."

He widens his eyes. "As in?"

"Use your imagination."

"Are you a Dom or something?"

I laugh. "Not exactly."

"So . . . you're a submissive?"

"No. Submission's not my thing." I purse my lips, trying to think of the best way to explain my River persona, since it's completely at odds with the nerdy version of me the rest of the world sees. "Let's put it this way. Esme has a team of concierges with different talents. I've been known to take control when asked. That said, there are things I will and won't do for a client, but I really can't get into specifics with you." I sip my drink and continue, "The other end of the spectrum is the lonely people who simply want someone to talk to. I've had clients where our playtime was as innocent as dinner and drinks at Oasis."

"What's Oasis?"

"The restaurant affiliated with The River."

"Oh."

"It goes beyond being a rich women's plaything." I rub my jaw, still trying to justify my employment. "Essentially, I provide *companionship* for money, with the occasional martini and cat of nine tails. The kinky fuckery is a perk, not the job itself."

Myles shakes his head. "The Devil's in the details, Lincoln."

"Good thing I'm detail oriented. Maybe I'm the breath of fresh air Iverson Press needs." Rising, I glance at my watch. "Now if you'll excuse me, I've got some Nordic ice to melt."

TWO

Elinora Iverson

I DIDN'T THINK IT WAS STILL POSSIBLE FOR MY EX-HUSBAND'S audacity to shock me, but I was wrong. Blood boiling, I clench the phone, unable to believe my ears. "Who the hell do you think you are?"

"Don't be so unreasonable."

"Unreasonable?" I screech, rocketing from my desk chair to pace the office. "I'll tell you who's unreasonable. If you think for one second my lawyers won't rip your little idea to shreds, your head is further up your ass than I remembered."

"Don't swear, Ellie," Charles chides, making my vision go red. "It's not becoming."

"Fuck you." I spit the words with enough venom to give Medusa a run for her money. Right now, I'd pay a small fortune to sprout a headful of snakes and turn that asshole to stone. It's not even ten o'clock and he's already ruined my day with his outrageous demands. The cheating bastard has the balls to ask for *more* alimony. It shouldn't surprise me though. He's always been the poster child for entitlement.

"When should I expect the deposit?"

"Go to hell." I end the call and toss the phone onto my desk, my stilettos wearing a path into the carpet. Why should I maintain his lifestyle after his third affair nearly destroyed me? Charles is still with the twenty-something supermodel he betrayed me with, and *I'm* required to shell out cash for their fancy vacations?

My eyes burn with a mix of rage and sadness. It's not fair he still has the power to hurt me, even after two years. I'm starting to wonder if I'll ever be free of him.

Rounding my desk once more, I blink back tears and sink into my chair with a defeated sigh.

When will karma get off her ass and make things right?

Freya Thorne, my fabulous assistant and one of the few people I trust, enters my office holding a clipboard. "Myles's friend is here to see you."

I blot my eyes with a tissue. "For what reason?"

"You're interviewing him, remember?"

"Shit. That was today?"

"Yes." She gives me a sheepish look. "He's been here since eight-thirty, but you were on the phone with Charles, so I didn't want to interrupt."

My lip curls at the mention of my ex's name. "If he calls again, tell him I'm out of the office."

She nods. "You ok?"

"Not really."

"Is there anything I can do?"

"Yes, actually. Can you please get me a cupcake from Compass Roasters? I need to eat my feelings." The coffee shop down the street boasts gourmet cupcakes I'd sell my soul for.

Freya grins. "Absolutely. Pick your poison."

"Surprise me."

"Will do." She points to the door. "So, do you want me to send the guy in? He's been waiting over forty-five minutes."

"He can wait for another five while I use the ladies' room." Standing, I smooth my skirt and point to Freya's clipboard. "Do you have his resume?"

"Yeah. I checked all his references for you." She cocks her head to the side. "He's only got three years of experience. You hate newbies—why would you waste your energy?"

I sigh heavily. "Because I have two positions to fill, and I trust Myles's opinion."

She snorts. "There's a shocker. You mean your golden boy's word is gospel?"

"He's not my golden boy." At her arched brow, I add, "Not that I need to justify my reasoning to you, but Myles is damn good at his job and doesn't give me any shit. If I want something done, he gets it done."

Nodding, she taps her pen on the clipboard. "Well, Clark Kent out there is getting antsy, so maybe you should get started."

"No, he can wait. Around here we operate by *my* schedule. Let him know I'll be with him shortly." I grab my cosmetic bag from my purse. I'm sure my mascara is a disaster, and I'd rather not look like a drugged-up raccoon for the rest of the day.

She holds up the resume. "Don't you want to see this?"

"I suppose I can skim it." She hands it over, and I glance at the top. "Lincoln Kennedy? What the hell kind of name is that?"

"Maybe he's American royalty." Freya pauses on her way out the door. "Oh, I should probably give you a head's up about Clark Kent."

"And that is?" I ask, perplexed by her second Superman reference in five minutes.

"He's smoking hot."

"Good for him." I couldn't care less about my interviewee's appearance. Beautiful men are trouble. I learned that the hard way. "Unless he's Henry Cavill himself, I'm not interested in smoke shows."

THREE

Lincoln

THIS IS RIDICULOUS. MY EYES HAVE BEEN BURNING A HOLE through Elinora Iverson's door for close to an hour. What sense does it make to give someone an appointment, if you plan to leave them hanging? My river mud jet fuel is long gone and I'm fading fast. I need to get this interview over with so I can go the fuck to sleep.

Finally, the door swings open, but it's her cute assistant again. Tall and curvy, with golden curls and hazel eyes, there's something familiar about her, but I can't put my finger on it.

I force a smile. "Do you think it'll be much longer?"

"Ms. Iverson will be with you shortly."

I nod and glance at my watch once more. "You said that thirty-five minutes ago."

She opens her mouth to speak, but someone else's voice comes out. "In a hurry, Mr. Kennedy?" Elinora Iverson appears at her assistant's side, and I stop breathing.

Years of Catholic school fly out the window as I stare at the porcelain goddess before me. The woman is ethereal. Resplendent. Drop dead gorgeous. It's a damn good thing I'm seated because my legs would've given out. It takes every ounce of my energy not to build her a golden pedestal and fall at her feet in worship.

Lustrous platinum blond hair cascades to the middle of her back, shimmering against the navy sheath dress showcasing her willowy frame. Silver stilettos accentuate her legs, making them appear even longer. Her only jewelry is a pair of diamond stud earrings—five times the size of my mother's engagement ring.

Courtesy of my employment at The River, I'm no stranger to provocative imagery. Whether their bodies are hugged in leather or nude, tied up or sprawled out, I've seen more beautiful women than I know what to do with. I learned to control my arousal out of necessity. Years of overstimulation dulled me to normal sexual attraction, which is likely why I don't have an actual love life. I've yet to encounter a woman who can get me out of my head enough to want something more, so I stopped trying.

Right now, staring at the ice queen that is Elinora Iverson, I'm teenage Lincoln again, sitting with my bookbag on my lap in Ms. Fisher's art class. Like the blood in my veins, every thought, rational or otherwise, follows one path. Their destination? My cock.

Elinora's ice blue gaze narrows on my face. "Hello?"

"No, I . . . uh . . . I'm good," I stutter, as my mind plays the melody for *Let it Go*.

"Then you won't mind waiting a little longer."

"Sure, that's fine," I say, even though her glacial tone makes it clear she's not asking for my permission—nor does she care that I've been waiting.

"Freya, show him to my office."

Freya. I've heard that name before, but where?

Elinora gestures to me. "Don't touch anything."

Well, fuck. There goes my plan to make a paper clip chain and put sticky notes everywhere. I open my mouth to give a sly retort but stop myself when Myles comes to mind. It doesn't matter how rude or inconsiderate I find Elinora, I refuse to jeopardize his promotion.

I follow Freya into the office, and she directs me to a chair opposite a large ebony desk. "She shouldn't be long."

"Thanks."

Our eyes meet, and hers flare in recognition. Her mouth drops open, but she quickly recovers. "Do you have questions for me?"

Realization hits me like a battering ram. Her name sounded familiar because she *is* familiar. Her sister, Anya Thorne, is a friend of mine who I met at The River. Courtesy of Anya—and whatever arrangement she has with Esme—Freya is one of the club's newer members.

Which means I'm beyond fucked.

Determined to avoid any awkwardness, or make it obvious I recognize her, I clear my throat and ask the first question that comes to mind. "Can she shoot icicles from her fingertips?"

Freya smirks. "Wait until you see what happens when she stomps her feet."

"Do I have any chance of getting this job?"

"I wouldn't count on it, but good luck." She gives me a sweet smile as she leaves.

As soon as she tells Elinora about my employment at The River, which I left off my resume for obvious reasons, my chances of being offered a position at Iverson Press will hit bottom faster than a lead sinker.

Then again, as a club member, Freya was also required to sign an NDA. I wonder if hers has the same weight as mine.

I survey the sterile room with its gray walls and sleek furniture. There aren't any pictures adorning the office—hanging, framed, or otherwise. The only décor is a massive oil painting of the Iverson coat of arms. A clock ticks away on her desk, reminding me of a silent classroom during final exams. Except this time, I didn't study.

And I'm naked.

Oh, and I have a boner.

Elinora strides in, closing the door behind her. "What brings you to Iverson Press?"

I clear my throat. "Your publishing house is among the most lucrative—"

"I'm not looking for a canned response here, Mr. Kennedy. I want to know why you left your previous place of employment."

"Cooper Press is struggling financially—"

"No kidding." She flashes a smug look and settles behind the desk. "I put them there. Anyway, you were saying?"

"I was the lowest man on the totem pole, so they laid me off."

This feels like when I told my Earth Science teacher I wasn't prepared for her midterm. How I couldn't remember the layers of the planet I'd spent my whole fucking life on. Forget the lava core—I froze after mantle.

Elinora points to my resume. "It says you've been an editor for three years. Elaborate."

"Uh . . ." The woman's a publishing mogul. Surely, she understands my job description? I shift in my seat. "I'm, uh, not sure what you mean."

She rolls her eyes. "What *kind* of editor? Line? Developmental?"

"Oh. Both, but my strength is in line editing."

"Myles praised your attention to detail." She sips her coffee. "Which genres did you work on?"

"Mainly thrillers, mysteries, and crime fiction. I recently finished a sci-fi drama, but I have little experience with sci-fi as a whole."

She gestures to my resume. "Doesn't look like you have much experience *at all*."

I stiffen my spine, pissed she's insinuating I don't know what I'm doing. "Yeah, well, that happens when someone's only been out of school three years." The snarky reply is out of my mouth before I can stop it. Fuck. Now I've really screwed myself over.

Her icy eyes narrow into slits. "I'm aware of the math, Mr.

Kennedy. But please," she flicks her hand in my direction, "go ahead and mansplain it to me. I'm sure you've got plenty of experience there."

Why did I subject myself to this level of condescension?

Reagan. She's the reason I push forward despite my wounded pride, my exhaustion, and the voice in my head screaming for me to walk out. Reagan is the reason behind everything I do, and why I can't afford to fuck up this interview.

"I apologize," I say with a heavy sigh, straightening my glasses. "But Myles gave me the impression you *wanted* to interview me."

She quirks a perfect eyebrow. "For the record, I don't do *anything* unless I want to."

"Your line of questioning seems a bit aggressive."

"If that's your idea of aggressive, you'll never make it in publishing." She taps her pen on the desk.

I can tell she's ready to dismiss me. Rich women get a certain look on their faces when they're finished with someone. I call it rueful disdain, or pity-infused annoyance. Elinora wears a mixture of both. She is moments from sending me on my merry way.

Looks like I'll be trapped in the role of pleasure concierge, kissing wealthy women's asses for the rest of my life. Living in a tiny studio apartment in New York City, while the rest of my family is upstate. Eating microwave dinners more nights than not. Missing out on conventional relationships because I'm too busy fucking the mayor's sister. Abusing my body and mind to make a better life for *my* sister. I'll do it until the day I die, but it would be nice, if just once, someone threw me a fucking bone.

Swallowing what's left of my pride, I grip the edge of her desk. "Look, I'm sorry we got off on the wrong foot. I swear I'm not an asshole."

"Could've fooled me."

"Please give me a job. I'll do whatever you want. I'll come in early, stay late. I have no problem being here on weekends." I rake a hand through my hair. "Please just give me a chance. Even if it's only a temporary position."

"While your resume is lacking, I suppose your tenacity is acceptable."

"Uh, thanks?" Hope nudges my conscience.

"It was an observation, not a compliment." Derision saturates her tone, matching her snooty face. "That said, Myles Callahan sang your praises, and his opinion is of value to me." Her frigid eyes bore into mine. "Perseverance and word of mouth don't make up for experience, but I have positions to fill. I'll give you three months to prove your worth. Against my better judgment, I'm willing to take a chance on you."

"I apprec—"

"But if you fail to meet my expectations, you're done, Mr. Kennedy."

"Thank you, Ms. Iverson. I won't disappoint you." Adjusting my glasses, I lean forward. "Please call me Lincoln."

Elinora raises an eyebrow. "Lincoln Kennedy is a bizarre name."

"My parents are history buffs with a strange sense of humor. My little sister is named Reagan."

She nods, peering down her nose at me. "You start tomorrow at nine. Freya will show you your cubicle."

"Thank you." I extend my hand to her. "I appreciate the opportunity."

"Welcome to Iverson Press." Clasping my palm with cool, delicate fingers, she thaws slightly, smiling for the first time since we met.

Its effects are devastating. My breath rushes out of me, and goosebumps bloom on my skin. Every nerve ending flares to life, sizzling my insides.

"Thank you so much."

Just when I think I'm off the glacier, she hits me over the head with a block of ice. "I think you'll be a great fit for our romance imprint, Iverson Melt."

"Romance?" I croak, blinking rapidly. "I have no experience editing romance."

"We've already established your lack of experience."

I open and close my mouth a few times. "You want me in *romance*? Sex books?"

Her icy gaze crystallizes the air in my lungs. "If you knew the first thing about publishing, you'd understand romance is a billion-dollar industry."

"I mean, I do, but—"

"Readers crave their happily ever-afters, and it's our job to give them what they want. The bottom line is sex sells."

The truth in her statement reaches a level of irony that makes me laugh aloud. Courtesy of The River, I know all about happy endings. I've done every position, acted out every kinky fantasy imaginable. From flowers and fancy dinners with aging debutants, to tying up politicians' wives, I've been there. Blindfolds, ball gags, hot wax, you name it.

While I have zero experience with the publishing end of the romance spectrum, I know sex better than anyone. You might call me a pleasure guru. Wrangler of female orgasms. Administrator of ecstasy. Superintendent of all things carnal. A bona fide *fucking* professional.

"Is something funny?"

"No, not at all." I force a straight face. "I'm just, uh, surprised you'd task me with love stories."

"If it weren't for Myles, I wouldn't task you with anything."

What's left of my ego cowers behind a rock. "You've mentioned."

She eyes me over the rim of her coffee cup before taking a slow sip. "But, like I said, I have positions that need filling. Iverson Melt is our most profitable imprint, so I can't afford any vacancies there.

We've got four manuscripts awaiting line edits and several more headed down the pike." Abandoning her mug, she stands and gestures to the door. "That's my offer, Mr. Kennedy. Take it or leave it."

Rising, I pull my shoulders back and stiffen my spine. "I'll be the best damn romance editor to ever walk through these doors."

"You've got three months to prove it." Elinora crosses her arms over her chest. "I truly hope you surprise me."

"I'll see you tomorrow, Ms. Iverson. And don't worry, I'm full of surprises."

Myles snags me on my way through the office, pulling me into a private conference room. "Well? How'd it go?"

"She spoke highly of you and offered me a position."

I leave out the part about how she stomped all over my self-esteem because I'm ashamed of how deeply her words cut me. For a moment, I could've sworn I was back in high school, reliving the torment of Sister Fitzgibbons, the cruelest nun to ever walk the Earth.

Relief floods his face. "Oh, thank fuck. I assume you're replacing Ted, our former mystery and suspense editor?"

"Nope," I say, popping the 'p' and reluctantly meeting his gaze. "I'm the new editor for Iverson Melt."

He tries to stifle his laugh, I'll give him that, but Myles's face betrays him. Whether he's angry, embarrassed, or amused, the poor guy is always red. This time's no exception. Flushing from his ears to his neck, his emerald eyes sparkle with mirth. "Wait, she seriously put *you* in romance?"

"Appears that way, doesn't it?"

"Why the hell would she do that when I told her your background was in suspense and thrillers?"

"Maybe she's setting me up to fail?"

"Iverson Melt," he murmurs, shaking his head. "That's intense. Have you ever seen any of their titles?"

"Do I look like a romance reader to you?"

"Bold of you to assume romance readers fit into a specific mold."

"That's not what I meant." Pulling off my glasses, I rub the bridge of my nose. "I don't know shit about love."

"You're right about that one." Myles chuckles. "But, you may have an advantage, given your extracurriculars. I'll forward you a few titles in each subgenre to give you an idea of what you're getting into. The most important thing you need to remember is that romance requires a happily ever after—or a 'happy for now,' where it's clear the main characters are together—in the book's conclusion. Bottom line, end of story. Don't let anyone tell you otherwise. You'll figure out the rest. Anyway, I just finished a marketing plan for the release of *Take Me,* an erotic romance that comes out in a few months. Holy fuck, I was seventeen shades of red. This shit's right up your alley."

"Just because I do it, doesn't mean I embrace my lifestyle," I mutter, wiping my lenses on my sleeve. "It's survival, Myles."

"Did she give you a probationary term?"

"Three months."

"Use your expertise wisely and I'm sure you can make your position permanent." He eyes me. "What about pay and benefits?"

"Honestly, I was so happy she offered me a job, I forgot to ask."

"The benefits package starts after someone's been employed for three months, but from what I hear, the pay's competitive."

"Either way, it gets my foot in the door. Maybe I can impress her and make a name for myself." I rub the back of my neck. "Also, you weren't kidding about the whole ice queen thing. She looks exactly like—"

"Right? The resemblance is uncanny. Last week she showed up in a baby blue pantsuit and I swear to God, I almost started singing."

"That's on brand for you." After years in our school choir, I'm shocked he doesn't break into spontaneous song more often. He certainly did back then. "So, what's Freya's story? She seems cool."

Myles nods. "Freya's her right-hand woman. She's cool as fuck, but incredibly loyal to Elinora." He lowers his voice. "I may be wrong, but I suspect something *more* is going on between them, if you know what I mean."

"Interesting. I didn't pick up on that vibe, but I'll take your word for it."

"Richard and I had dinner with them once. He also noticed their closeness."

I curl my lip at the mention of his long-time partner. I'm not a fan and never will be. Twenty years our senior, Richard Pennington acts like he's God's gift to mankind and everyone should fall at his feet—especially Myles. My best friend deserves better than some asshole Brit who thinks his shit doesn't stink. "Sorry, but I take Dick's opinion with a grain of salt."

Myles glares at me. "*Richard* is very attuned to same-sex couplings. He *is* a sex therapist, for fuck's sake."

"Methinks Dick doesn't know dick."

He snorts. "On the contrary, he *knows* dick. But I really wish you wouldn't call him that."

"I wish he'd treat you better," I counter, crossing my arms over my chest.

Myles sighs heavily. "Lincoln, please. I don't have the energy for this right now."

"It takes a lot of energy for me to watch him take you for granted, so . . ."

"Imagine the energy *I* expend worrying about some psycho kidnapping you as her sexual pet."

"I'm six foot four, two hundred and forty pounds of solid muscle. I highly doubt any woman could kidnap me without help."

"What if someone drugs you and steals your kidneys? What will you tell your parents if you wake up in a bathtub full of ice somewhere?"

"I *have* woken up in a bathtub." Smirking, I squeeze his shoulder. "I'd probably beg for one of your kidneys."

"You wouldn't have to beg, my friend." Myles shakes his head. "You know I'd give you a kidney if you needed one, but you're not getting my liver. There's far too much wine I need to experience in this lifetime."

"I certainly owe you a bottle for today. Thanks for scoring me an interview, man. I appreciate it."

He nods. "I'm glad it went well. Now, don't fuck up."

"I won't," I say, even though there's plenty of opportunity for me to fail. "Who knows? Maybe one day I'll be able to leave my extracurriculars behind."

FOUR

Elinora

Freya saunters into my office and sits on the edge of the desk, placing a massive pink cupcake in front of me. "I can't believe you gave Clark Kent a job."

While she isn't wrong with her hunky nerd description, the man I interviewed was far from Superman. His arrogance raised my hackles, and I'm still not entirely sure why I gave him a chance.

"I offered him Cindy's position for a three-month trial period."

"Wait, you seriously put him in romance?" she asks, knowing how protective I am of Iverson Melt. "I thought you told me to assign him Cindy's cubicle because Ted hasn't cleaned his out. I didn't realize you intended him as her replacement."

"Ted was caught up, so we don't have a backlog of thrillers waiting to be edited. I put Clark where I need him most."

"How long do you think he'll last?" Freya tosses her golden ringlets over her shoulder. "I give him a week before he quits."

I shrug and rearrange the papers on my desk. "He seemed pretty desperate, so maybe he'll stick it out."

She grins, her hazel eyes flashing. "At least he's nice to look at. And by that, I mean gorgeous."

"I suppose he's a bit of a visual upgrade from Cindy."

Understatement of the year.

Tall and broad, Lincoln Kennedy filled out his charcoal suit like it was hand tailored for him. His crisp navy dress shirt and silver tie made me question whether he secretly coordinated his outfit with mine. For a moment I wondered if Myles had tipped him off, but then I remembered I've been in the office since six. I doubt either of them were even awake yet.

The interview went as expected for an interviewee with little experience. My questions clearly rattled Lincoln, which was my intent, but his eye contact never faltered. That's critical for me. If someone can't look me in the eye, I know they're hiding something. Charles was a professional gaze-averter, which should've been a red flag for his infidelity. While I make my living publishing bestselling mysteries, I have no desire to live one. That holds true for every realm of my existence—from Iverson Press to my nonexistent love life.

I skimmed Lincoln's demographics while Freya showed him his cubicle. Age wise, I've got him by a decade. He's only twenty-five, yet his weary gaze held more depth than I'd expect from a man so young. Hidden behind thick black frames, inky lashes fringed a set of deep blue eyes, but it was the dark circles beneath them that struck me. Lincoln's desperation-laced tenacity reminds me of myself at his age—inexperienced and ill-equipped but driven to succeed at all costs.

Maybe he isn't perfect for the romance editor position, but something inside me insisted I give him a chance.

Besides, Freya makes a valid point. With a face carved by the gods, Lincoln is quite the physical specimen, and I could use a better view from my office. Dimples, a sculpted jaw, and a sexy chin cleft add to his Clark Kent appeal. Factor in the glossy black hair he'd swept back from his face, and I'd swear I offered the position to Henry Cavill during his tenure as Superman.

Freya rolls her eyes. "A visual upgrade? You're always so technical."

"Details and technicality make the world go around."

"I think your world needs more plot holes. Maybe a couple kinky twists. Come out with me this weekend."

"You know I don't go *out*." I unwrap my cupcake and take a bite, nearly moaning when the sweet decadence coats my tongue. "Wow. This is amazing."

"That one's called Strawberry Sex Swing. It's one of my favorites."

My insides flutter with her mention of the carnal contraption I've read about in a few of Iverson Melt's titles. While they more than intrigue me, the chances of me encountering a sex swing in the wild are slim to none. Frustrated by my nonexistent sex life, I switch topics. "Yeah, I'm not really a nightlife kind of girl. The last thing I need is to run into Charles or one of his twenty-seven mistresses."

Freya laughs. "Come to the club with me. I'll introduce you to some of my friends, and we'll get you so drunk you won't remember who you ran into, ex-husbands and mistresses notwithstanding."

"I'm too old for clubbing."

"Elinora, you're thirty-five—not dead. Throw caution to the wind and live a little. What good is building an empire if you never get to enjoy it? There's a spa we can hit up if the dancing scene's not your thing."

"A spa?" I snort. "You go from one extreme to the next. First you want to get me drunk, now we're talking pedicures?"

"Not pedicures, silly. I mean hydrotherapy and massages. If you won't let me relax you with a few drinks, maybe you'll enjoy floating in silence or allow some hot guy to rub your body."

During my marriage, I was too busy "building my empire" to relax. Our sex life suffered, and ultimately, my focus caused my husband to stray. After giving Charles the best fifteen years of my life, I'm reluctant to let another man close enough to touch me.

"No one's rubbed my body in years."

Freya leans in close. "No shit. That's why I'm suggesting it."

"Maybe I'll take you up on that. I could use a good rubdown."

FIVE

Lincoln

People need to get the fuck out of my way. Dodging a clump of tourists on the sidewalk, I hustle past Bryant Park toward Iverson Headquarters. I'm never late. Punctuality is something I value almost as much as reliability, so it would be fucking outstanding if I wasn't on the verge of being late for my first day at Iverson Press. A broken water main resulted in ungodly traffic, and I'm kicking myself for taking an Uber instead of the subway. It was so bad, I jumped out two blocks before my stop and ran the rest of the way.

I push through the front doors of the skyscraper that houses my new job and sprint over to the security desk. "Hi, I'm starting with Iverson Press today. I need elevator access please."

The guy looks over his glasses at me. "Name and photo ID?"

"I'm Lincoln Kennedy. You saw me when I interviewed yesterday, remember?"

"I remember." He points to a scanner on his desk. "But I need your ID regardless."

"Fine," I mumble, rummaging in my bag for my wallet, which is buried beneath all my shit. When I finally locate the tattered leather bundle, I withdraw it and pry my ID from its plastic sleeve. I hand it over with a forced smile. "Here you go."

He slides the card through his scanner. "Once Ms. Iverson gives us your personnel info, we can set you up in our system, so you don't have to go through this every time." He hands me back my ID and motions toward the elevators. "Eleventh floor."

"Thanks." I shove everything into my bag, and jog over there, tapping the call button. Unnerved by the additional delay, I pace the lobby while I wait. Finally, an empty car arrives, and I rush inside. Glancing at my watch, I select the eleventh floor, at the eleventh hour, and sag against a wall.

The damn thing stops on the tenth floor.

"C'mon fucker." Balling my hands into fists, I shift to the side and try to catch my breath.

Except that proves impossible when the doors slide open, and my heart stops.

Elinora stands in the doorway holding a stack of papers, the picture of sleek sophistication with her black power suit and red stilettos. Beneath her unbuttoned jacket, a blood red camisole accentuates her porcelain skin, and the lacy neckline reveals enough cleavage to make my mouth water. She'd left her hair down, the satiny strands of platinum falling past the lower curve of her breasts. I clench my jaw against the overwhelming urge to press her up against the wall and kiss her neck. My dick goes rogue again, making the situation in my dress pants tighter. I shift my messenger bag in front of me.

Stepping inside, she points to her watch and raises a brow at me. "Cutting it close, Mr. Kennedy."

Shit.

With a quick adjustment of my tie, loosening its stranglehold, I clear my throat. "I, uh, there was traffic, so I—"

"I'm not interested in your excuses." She moves to stand beside me.

"I'm sorry." I stare straight ahead, unable to meet the ice blue gaze that accompanies her frosty tone.

"When we get to our floor, I need to see you in my office."

Great, she's already firing me.

I force a swallow and pivot to face her. "Why?" Her eyes narrow, but she doesn't respond, so I backpedal. "I mean, sure. I'll be right in. Is something wrong?" Although I tower over her, I feel like I'm two feet tall, and I can't draw enough air to fill my lungs.

She cocks her head to the side. "Why would something be wrong?"

"It wouldn't. I'm just . . . uh, I was wondering," I stammer, releasing a nervous laugh.

"We never discussed your compensation yesterday," she explains, peering up at me. "I'm assuming you don't plan to work for free?"

"No, definitely not. Time is money." I cringe at my cheesy line.

"Yes, Mr. Kennedy, it is." Elinora purses her full red lips. "Which is why I expect you to be *on time*. Every day."

"I'm sorry I cut it so close. It won't happen again. When does the building open?"

"Six."

"From now on, I'll arrive by seven." My sorry ass will be here at the crack of dawn, before I even *think* about showing up late.

Her eyes widen, but she gives me a curt nod. "You need to see security for your badge before the end of business today. I'll let them know to clear you for early entrance."

We reach our floor, and I step aside so she can exit. "After you, Ms. Iverson."

"Thank you."

I follow her inside the suite like a lost puppy.

Myles waves. "Good morning."

"Good morning, Myles," she says sweetly, handing him the

stack of papers. "This is the proposal I need you to work on. Sullivan's agent wants an answer this week, but I need to know if you can market it given the controversial nature of his platform."

Myles nods. "I'll look it over as soon as I finish my meeting with the new distributor we talked about."

"Perfect." She points to her office. "Go have a seat, Mr. Kennedy. I'll be in after I grab your file from human resources."

I slump into the chair at her desk. I haven't even been employed for twenty-four hours, and I've already had two boners and roped myself into coming in early.

Freya pops her head into the office, her curls piled in a messy bun. "Hey there. You came back for more?"

I rub my jaw. "I guess I'm a glutton for a good punishment."

"Me too." She flushes. "I mean, my job isn't to punish—" Squeezing her eyes shut, she shakes her head. "Never mind. I should really be going."

I smile when she finally meets my gaze again. "I'm sure I'll see you around."

"Yeah, I float from here to there." She releases a nervous laugh. "But you already know that, apparently." Freya gives me a wave and abruptly leaves the room.

I can't figure out why she's so flustered by my knowledge of her River membership when I'm the one whose job is at stake.

After a few minutes, Elinora enters her office with a manila folder. "All right, let's get down to business." She struts to her desk and plops the file in front of me. "How much do you think you're worth?"

According to Sister Fitzgibbons, absolutely nothing.

My gaze snaps to hers, and I beat back the shitty high school memories. I open and close my mouth a few times, unable to formulate a response.

"Well?" Impatience laces her tone, but it's the look in her eyes that unnerves me. She's enjoying my discomfort.

And that doesn't sit well with me. I clench my jaw instead of answering.

"Perhaps you didn't hear me, Mr. Kennedy. I asked you how much you think you're worth."

It's a trick question. If my number is too high, she'll mock my arrogance. If I undercut myself, she wins. I'm tired of rich women winning at my expense.

Steeling myself for her rejection, I lean forward. "I made twenty-seven an hour at Cooper Press. I'd appreciate something along those lines."

"Seems vague to me." Elinora cocks her head to the side. "When you said time is money, I figured you had an exact number in mind."

"What I feel I'm worth, and what an employer is willing to pay me, seldom match up. I need this job, so the ball's in your court."

"Make no mistake, the ball is *always* in my court, Mr. Kennedy." She scans my resume once more. "I'll pay you thirty dollars an hour. *If* you make it beyond three months, there will be an associated increase, with the amount to be determined by my level of satisfaction."

"Thank you, Ms. Iverson."

"I expect my employees to *earn* what I pay them."

I straighten. "I will."

She nods, handing me a slip of paper. "Here's your email login credentials. I'll forward the manuscripts in the order I expect them done. They're all Word documents, so be sure to use change tracking so the authors know what you've edited. In addition, I'd like to view the changes for quality control purposes."

Great. Instead of letting me work, she'll be looking over my shoulder. How am I supposed to function with her breathing down my neck?

She raises a brow. "Is there a problem, Mr. Kennedy?"

"No. I'm just accustomed to my employer setting me loose on a project." Not to mention it seems pretty ridiculous the company's CEO would bother wasting her time on a mere peasant like me.

"Wipe that notion out of your head. Understand that I attach *my* name to every manuscript that makes it to publication. My standards are extremely high. I expect nothing short of excellence, and until I'm confident in your ability to perform, I'll be closely involved with your projects. Prove yourself, and I'll back off. Are we on the same page now?"

"Yes."

"Good. After you fill out all the necessary paperwork, you can jump right in."

Adjusting my glasses, I rise and sling my bag over my shoulder. "Thank you."

I head for my cubicle to discover a cup of coffee with a note from Myles.

You got this, Linc. Don't fuck up.

The Callahan brand of encouragement has always amused me. I shoot him a quick text to thank him, then fill out the required forms before diving into my work.

My first project is a steamy contemporary set in Ireland. The heroine's a sassy nurse with a guarded heart who finds herself stranded with a cocky Irish actor. I'll probably finish edits on the first few chapters today. My goal this weekend is a romance reading marathon. Maybe if I immerse myself in this world from the start, I'll have a chance at impressing Elinora.

I work straight through my breaks, which is typical for me. I'm enjoying the book more than I expected. Elinora returned from her lunch while I was reading the first sex scene. She sauntered through the suite like a fucking vixen. Powerful, confident, a force to be reckoned with.

Now I have the literary equivalent of blue balls.

Myles appears at my shoulder. "How's your first day going?"

"So far, so good." I point to my computer screen. "This one's a scorcher."

He grins. "So . . . you don't hate it?"

"Surprisingly, no. It's different from what I'm used to, but I'm adjusting."

"How's our favorite She-Devil treating you?"

I snort. "Like a toddler. I get that I'm new, but she insists on babysitting me."

"Speaking of," Myles murmurs, looking over my shoulder. "Hi, Elinora."

"Hello, Myles." She glances at me as she approaches my cubicle. "Are you making progress, Mr. Kennedy?"

"Yes, ma'am."

She cringes. "Stick with Ms. Iverson, please. Ma'am is too old a title for me."

"I'll keep that in mind. How do you want to look at my work? Chapter by chapter, or do you want the entire thing when I'm finished?"

She leans down to peer at my screen, and pieces of her hair brush my shoulder. Her perfume is a heady blend of warm vanilla and spice. I take a slow, deep breath, drawing in her scent. My cock twitches, and I force my thoughts elsewhere. If I'm not careful, I'll weave my fingers into her hair and pull her into my lap.

I've got a million reasons to resist Elinora Iverson. Not only is she rich, powerful, and gorgeous, but she's way out of my league. More importantly, she's my boss.

And the iciest ice queen who ever iced.

"You've already gotten through your edits on the first sixty pages?" she asks in surprise.

"That's a typical pace for me."

"You realize this needs to be thorough, right?"

I frown. "It's a line edit, is it not?"

"That's what I'm asking you, Mr. Kennedy." When I don't immediately answer, she purses her lips and adds, "I can't have you rushing if it means you miss out on details. If you're going to do it, do it right."

I tense. "For the record, I don't half-ass *anything*—especially not my work." Myles gives me a warning glare, but I ignore him. "I can assure you, not only is it thorough, but it's a significant improvement over what was there."

Elinora raises a brow. "No need to be defensive."

"I'm not being defensive," I snap, clenching my fists in my lap. "I'm stating a fact."

Her mouth curves into a cruel smile. "It seems like you have an issue with my authority."

"No, I have an issue with your insinuation that I'd compromise quality for speed."

Myles grips my shoulder. "Lincoln, chill."

Elinora straightens, her glacial gaze narrowing on mine. "Let me make myself perfectly clear. This is *my* company. I built this empire, therefore I can—and will—insinuate whatever the hell I want. If I'm paying you to do a job, it damn well better meet my standards. You have next to no experience. I have every right to question you *and* your process, so I'd appreciate if you'd drop your attitude. I'm the queen of this castle. If your ego can't handle my approach, I suggest you find a new kingdom."

I blink a few times before answering. "I'm sorry. I meant no disrespect."

"Could've fooled me." She turns and storms off, her stilettos clicking on the marble floor.

A slamming door rattles my skull, right before Myles smacks the back of my head. "What the fuck is wrong with you?"

"Do you want a list?"

"Are you seriously giving her shit on your first day?" He knots his fingers in his hair. "She's your *boss*, dude. Grow the fuck up."

"I'm sorry. I didn't mean to overreact, but she struck a nerve."

"Fuck your nerves. You're being an arrogant little dick. If your ego costs me my promotion, I'll kick your ass." Myles storms off in the same direction as Elinora.

"Nice one, Kennedy," I mutter under my breath. "Great first impression."

SIX

Elinora

That's it. I've finally wasted enough time to make leaving feel like the more productive option. I haven't been able to focus since my run-in with Lincoln after lunch. I release my breath in a huff, picturing the arrogance in his dark blue gaze. Who the hell does he think he is, challenging my authority on his first day? I have every right to question him—I'm the fucking boss. My top priority is to safeguard my company's reputation for quality, and his lack of experience tells me he's *unqualified* to work here.

But when he'd stared up at me as he defended himself, with his haunting eyes and perfectly sculpted face, the cocky bastard weakened my armor. I wanted to tell him to take a hike, but I couldn't bring myself to utter the words. Leave it to me to hire a man whose pride and ego rival my own. Why couldn't he be a simpering, potbellied old guy with a pockmarked face? Why does his thick, glossy hair beg my fingertips to touch it? And why do I have to see so much of my younger self in him?

I log out of my computer and stuff my phone into my purse.

After the third call from Charles, I finally took Freya's advice and put the damn thing on silent. It's funny—he calls me more now than when we were married. Not that the reason's a mystery. He wants something from me.

They all do.

Freya walks into my office, carrying her coat and purse. "Are you sure you're ok? You've been stewing all afternoon."

"Charles thinks he deserves more alimony. Maybe if the bastard worked harder, he could support himself." The words drip from my tongue like acid. I have no patience for lazy people who expect others to pick up their slack. It infuriates me when my ex thinks he's entitled to a portion of my success when he did *nothing* to get me here. I'm tired of people thinking I owe them something.

"You should block his number."

I shake my head. "He'd call the office or show up here and make a scene." I gesture to my doorway. "Did everyone else already leave for the day?" My employees have a tendency to skip out the second the clock strikes five. I get it, but it's amusing to watch them stand by the elevators like a bunch of idiot lemmings, when if they gave it a few minutes, there wouldn't be such a delay. I don't have much of a life outside of work, so I'm usually in the office until after six. My elevator ride is always smooth sailing.

Freya smirks. "No, not everyone."

I glance at my watch. "It's six thirty."

"Like your boy Myles told you, Clark Kent is extremely focused and driven," she murmurs, wagging her brows.

I curl my lip. "Clark Kent has an attitude problem."

"So, put him in his place. He'd probably like it."

"Already did," I say with a self-satisfied smile. "There's only room for one queen in this office."

"It's his first day, and you already knocked him down a few pegs?"

"He already pissed me off." I stand and slide my coat on.

"Granted, I've been on edge since Charles called, but that's neither here nor there."

Freya perks up. "Speaking of being on edge, have you given any thought to my invitation?"

"What kind of club is it again?"

"It's an elite specialty spa that provides an assortment of relaxation services for its members."

"Wait, you have to be a member to go there?"

She nods. "It's not open to the public. Lucky for you, I'm a member. You can come as my guest."

"You never mentioned being a member of some club. I thought you were kayaking?"

"Kayaking? Where'd you get that from?"

"For the past month or so, you've been talking about going to the river to float."

"The River is the name of the club, Elinora." Freya giggles. "It's, um . . . it's a water themed luxury spa with a bit of a nightclub scene. There's also an affiliated restaurant called Oasis. They serve amazing food and drinks."

"Oh. That makes way more sense," I say, shaking my head. "I knew hopping into the Hudson down here wasn't a relaxing prospect."

"Did you honestly think I drove upstate multiple times a week to paddle a kayak?"

"Yes." I laugh. "That's exactly what I imagined."

She wraps her arms around me. "Honey, you need to broaden your horizons."

"I don't have time for new horizons."

"There's *always* time to try something new. Especially if it chills you out. I'm confident The River has a cure for what ails you."

I gesture to myself. "There's no curing this."

"I wouldn't be so sure of that. Come with me tomorrow. It's new members' night, and they're having a mermaid-themed masquerade mingle."

"Seriously? Do I need to dress up as Ariel?"

She snorts. "No, not quite. Think sexy mermaids and mermen. Scantily clad hot guys with hot bodies. Besides, you'd be more like Ursula."

I give her the middle finger. "Ha. Ha. Very funny."

"Maleficent?" Freya grins. "Cruella de Vil?"

"I hate you sometimes."

She kisses my cheek. "Well, I *love* you. Which is why you're coming with me."

"Ok, fine. I'll check it out."

Freya rubs her hands together with glee. "All you need to bring is your bathing suit—I have the perfect mask for you."

"What about a towel?"

"They have towels, robes, and sandals. I'll book us for an overnight room, so we can crash after the mingle."

"You said they do massages? What types?" I rub the back of my neck.

"The spa is all-inclusive, which means you can partake in any activities you wish. As far as massages go, they offer Swedish, hot stone, deep tissue, and sensual."

I raise a brow. "Sensual?"

She nods. "They have waterfalls, hot tubs, whirlpools, a mineral pool, and much more. My personal favorites are the lazy river and private lagoons."

"What happens there?"

"You float. Water lapping at your skin, peaceful music playing—it's glorious. Sometimes, if I've had a rough week, I'll do a sensory deprivation float."

"What the hell is that?"

"There are varying degrees of flotation therapy offered, as well as elective enhancements. Picture this: silence and total darkness, you're drifting in warm water, weightless and free."

I shake my head. "I'm not loving the total darkness part."

"The float is customizable to a member's comfort level, so you can add lagoon lighting. If you don't want it silent, you can add some music or nature sounds. And if you don't enjoy being alone, you can have someone with you," Freya explains. "I'm happy to float with you for your first time."

"Yeah, let's do that. I'd feel more comfortable with you there."

"Perfect. You're gonna love it."

"Don't they worry about people drowning?" I ask, envisioning an adult water park of sorts. With a spa. And a restaurant. Oh, and a nightclub.

"Huh?"

"At the club. I mean, what if someone can't swim? Isn't it dangerous with all that water?"

"No. The salt concentration in the flotation rooms is super high, so your body is too buoyant to sink. You're encouraged to fall asleep in there. It's perfectly safe. There are lifeguards assigned to the mineral pools and lazy river as an added precaution. The owner is a stickler for safety."

"Good to know."

"Oh! I almost forgot. The River even has its own Himalayan salt cave saunas."

"This place sounds like paradise."

She grins. "You have no idea."

We make our way out of my office into the main suite, stopping near Lincoln's cubicle. He's deep in thought, immersed in the manuscript.

"Do I need to order a cot for you?" Freya chirps.

He looks up at her. "No, I'm almost done."

I point to the clock on his desk. "Quitting time was over an hour ago."

He nods. "I set a goal for myself, and I like staying on track."

"That's all well and good, but security didn't clear you for after-hours. It's time to head out."

"All right, let me log off and gather my stuff." He saves his file, emails it to himself and shuts down his computer. After shoving some items into his messenger bag, he adjusts his glasses and stands, towering over me. "I'll forward the email to you when I'm finished."

"I don't expect you to work from home." I tilt my head to meet his gaze. "Or through your lunch break."

He shrugs. "Like I said, I want to stay on track. You mentioned a backlog, so I'd like to get caught up as soon as possible."

"As long as—"

"I won't sacrifice quality, Ms. Iverson." He rakes a hand through his hair. "And I'm sorry for my behavior this afternoon."

Behind him, Freya smirks and picks at her nails.

I meet his gaze as he adjusts his glasses. "Can you understand where I'm coming from?"

"Yes."

"Good. We can start fresh tomorrow and finish our week on a positive note."

Freya shimmies her hips. "T-G-I-F."

The ghost of a smirk curves his lips. "That makes tonight Friday eve."

"I like the way you think," she says with a laugh. "Glass half full, right?"

Lincoln rubs his jaw, sighing heavily. "Hell, I'm happy to have a glass to begin with. Half empty, half full—doesn't matter to me. Even one drop is better than nothing."

His comment makes me feel like he's had to fight for his glass, his drop, his place. Like he's climbing a never-ending ladder as life removes rungs before he can grip them. His ladder sways as he clings to it, but he keeps going. The idea bothers me more than it should.

Because I've been there.

SEVEN

Lincoln

What the fuck is she staring at?

The three of us ride the elevator in silence, but I can feel Elinora's gaze on me. As much as I try to ignore it, her attention unnerves me. I stare at the lit floor numbers like they're a work of art—or a fucking lighthouse beacon—anything to keep from making eye contact. I can't look at her right now. Not her fancy suit, her red shoes, or her perfect face. None of it. She represents everything I'm not, everything I don't have. Wealth. Sophistication. Power. Today was a shitshow, and now Myles is pissed at me.

Freya breaks the silence. "Got any big plans for Friday eve?"

"Nah, just heading home." I glance at her. "You?"

"I have a yoga class tonight."

"Sounds relaxing." I don't ask Elinora what she's doing because I know she wouldn't tell me, anyway. I'm surprised she rides the elevator with peasants like me.

"Where do you live, Lincoln?" Freya asks.

"Near Madison Square Garden."

"I love seeing shows at the Garden." Freya takes another stab at small talk. "So, what do you do for fun?"

I laugh at her loaded question and the mirth in her gaze. "I'm not sure I understand."

"How do you spend your free time? Do you have any hobbies? Special talents? You know, the stuff you do when you aren't working." She elbows me. "Please tell me you have a life."

"I'm *alive.*" I meet her gaze. "But I'm always working, Freya. Even when I'm not."

Elinora peers up at me. "You like riddles, don't you?"

I shrug. "Somewhat. I'd classify them with haikus and limericks."

The She-Devil smiles, and it takes my breath away. "Do you have a favorite limerick?"

"As a matter of fact, I do."

The elevator reaches the ground floor, and the doors slide open. We step into the lobby.

"Well?" Elinora narrows her eyes on my face.

"Well, what?"

"What's your favorite limerick?"

Is she serious? I fix my glasses, even though they aren't out of place. Myles claims it's my nervous habit. I'm not currently nervous, but I'm not sure how to interpret her sudden interest. "I'll, uh, tell you some other time."

Freya nudges me and grins. "Oh, c'mon. Tell us now."

Fuck. Now I've gotta pull something from the archives. I wrack my brain for the short poems my grandmother told us as kids, but I come up empty.

Elinora shakes her head. "I'm disappointed, Mr. Kennedy. I thought you planned to wow us with your literary prowess."

Her rhyme gives me an idea. "I, um, write my own limericks."

We pass through security and make our way to the bustling sidewalk. From honking cars, to sirens, the sounds of New York

City fill my ears. I miss the quiet country evenings of my youth. It's always so fucking loud here.

Elinora stops in front of me, propping her hands on her hips. "You can't leave me hanging."

I give a halfhearted smile. "You'll have to hang until tomorrow because I'm off the clock."

"Minor details," she murmurs, her tone warming with amusement.

"The Devil's in the details, Ms. Iverson."

"Put those details to good use, Mr. Kennedy. I want a limerick on my desk tomorrow."

"Is this for extra credit, or something I missed in the company handbook?"

She actually laughs, and the sound makes my cock twitch. "Consider it as part of your orientation."

"There once was an editor named Lincoln. His boss soon got him a'thinkin.' She said give me a rhyme. Or I won't pay you a dime. The guy spewed some nonsense without blinkin.'" Both women laugh, and I'm not sure whether to be relieved or unnerved, knowing Elinora has a sliver of humanity she refused to show me earlier. I give them a dramatic bow. "Goodnight, ladies. Until the next rhyme."

"See you tomorrow, Mr. Kennedy."

Her voice skates down my spine as I make my retreat, hustling down the sidewalk to the nearest subway station.

My phone buzzes in my pocket. I peek at the screen to find my sister's name. I'm not in the mood to give her a play-by-play of my workday, but I can't bring myself to ignore the call.

"Hello?"

"Hi, Linky! How was your first day?"

I cringe at her use of my childhood nickname, but don't correct her. Reagan is the only one still allowed to use it. "It was . . . interesting. How was your art group?"

"Fun. I painted you a picture to hang in your fancy new office."

I don't have the heart to tell her it's a tiny gray cubicle. "Thanks, Reag. That was sweet of you."

"Wanna know what it is?"

I smile and step out of the way of a man dragging a rolling suitcase down the sidewalk. "Sure. Unless you want it to be a surprise."

"It's a family portrait from when we used to go fishing. But I made it so Daddy doesn't need his wheelchair."

My chest tightens, remembering how our parents took us camping in the Catskills every summer—before Reagan's epilepsy worsened. And long before our father's stroke. We'd spend hours sitting by the lake and catching fish. I always had to help her reel them in. "I can't wait to see it."

"Can you come visit this weekend?"

"I'm sorry, but I can't. I have to work all weekend, Reag."

"Oh, ok. Bartending?" There's no mistaking the disappointment in her tone.

"Yes." Guilt churns my stomach. I'm sure I'll be doing a lot more than tending bar at tomorrow night's masquerade event, but I'm not about to tell my sister. She thinks I work at an Irish pub near Times Square.

"Maybe next weekend then?"

I squeeze my eyes shut, knowing Esme owns my weekends for the foreseeable future. The best I can manage is a brief Sunday visit upstate. "We'll see. I'll ask my boss."

"How's your new boss? For your editing job, I mean."

A humorless chuckle leaves my lips. "She's a bit frosty."

EIGHT

Elinora

I LOVE MORNINGS. ENERGIZED BY COFFEE, BREAKFAST FOOD, and the untapped potential of a fresh start, I push through the revolving door to my office building. I'm not the slightest bit surprised to find a particular colleague already waiting for the elevator.

Garrett Casey owns Hudson Graphics, the design company that shares my floor, and he's responsible for the bulk of the book covers for Iverson Press. He's also the only human outside of security to ever enter the building this early. He's a brilliant artist—and businessman—with a work ethic like mine, so I have tremendous respect for him. Not to mention, the man is more gorgeous than he has a right to be. One day I'll succeed in convincing him to be a book cover model. My Iverson Melt authors would be feral if they ever caught a glimpse of him.

I wave to the security guy behind the desk and make my way over to Garrett. "Good morning."

He smiles. "Howdy. I beat you here today."

I hold up my finger in protest. "That's only because I couldn't find a spot to park."

"Valet's not your thing either?"

"No. I've found it's easier to do everything myself."

Amusement flashes in his eerie gold eyes. "Control freak."

"You know it." The elevator arrives, and we step inside. "Did you hear back from all the authors whose covers need approval?"

"All but one." He rakes a hand through his inky black hair. "I have a feeling McCarthy may be an issue for you. He's not responsive to my emails, and I have to hound him for every little thing."

"I'll reach out to his agent." I press the call button for the eleventh floor.

"Sounds good." The doors slide shut, and we fall into companionable silence for a few moments, then he pivots to face me. "Is everything all right with you?"

He's a giant like Lincoln, so I have to peer up at him. "Why do you ask?"

"Jules said she heard you crying in the restroom on Wednesday."

"Oh?"

I'd greeted his secretary when I exited my stall after a mini meltdown. Juliana is a doll, but a total busybody. I'm not surprised she reported back to him.

"She said you were in there a while, and it concerned her. And me, naturally."

"It was a rough day."

"Your ex being a dick again?"

Garrett is intuitive and easy to talk to. I've been uncharacteristically open with him over the years. It's nice to get a man's perspective sometimes.

I lean against the wall. "Yes. Very much so. He wants more alimony, and it infuriates me." I clench my jaw, refusing to acknowledge the sadness that's clung to me since Charles shattered my heart. "After everything he put me through, he's *still* trying to make my life hell."

"Want me to kick his ass?" We reach our floor, and the doors slide open. He motions for me to exit before him. "I'll add him to my list."

"As much as I'd love that, I'd hate to see you in jail for assault."

"You're assuming I'd get caught. I'll have you know I'm stealthy as fuck." He nudges me. "But in all seriousness, you know I'm here if you ever need to talk."

"I appreciate that, Garrett." We pause outside the door to my main office suite, and I release a heavy sigh. "I guess I've been a little stressed. I've let a few problematic employees go, and now we're short-staffed. I hired a new guy, but he's barely out of college."

"Lincoln's a good dude. Smart. Hardworking."

I raise my eyebrows. "You know him?"

"Yeah. I met him through my dear friend and AA sponsor, Anya. You know, Freya's sister. Anyway, I run into him all the time at Compass Roasters when I go for coffee. As I'm sure you're aware, he worked for Cooper Press."

"Yes, I know." Guilt tickles my spine. "I'm kinda putting them out of business."

Garrett flashes a wicked grin. "Because you're the Queen of Badassery."

I laugh. "Most people call me an ice queen, so I'll take that as a compliment." While I've accepted my unofficial title, it still hurts knowing people think I'm heartless. I have a heart. It's just a little frostbitten.

"It's definitely meant as a compliment." He glances at his watch. "Anywho, I've gotta run. I have a conference call that starts in a few minutes."

"This early?"

"It's a company based out of Dublin. They're five hours ahead of us." He pats my shoulder. "Happy Friday."

"You too."

He smiles and heads toward his suite, pausing to look over his shoulder after a few steps. "Give Linc a chance. He might surprise you."

"I'll try." I wave and enter Iverson headquarters.

Well, color me surprised.

It's a quarter to seven, and Lincoln is already at his desk. I didn't actually think he'd show up early to work. None of my employees—not even Freya—arrive before me. People work harder and faster when I'm around, so it impresses me that he took it upon himself to get a head start and dive in, *without* my presence. Maybe Garrett knows what he's talking about.

Lincoln glances up as I approach his cubicle. "Good morning, Ms. Iverson."

"Good morning." I tap my watch. "You're early."

"I have goals to meet today."

"Did you clock in?"

He shakes his head, his dark hair still damp from his shower. "You didn't authorize overtime, so I'll punch in at nine."

I point to the time clock across the room. "Go clock in. You're my employee—not my servant. I don't expect you to work for free. Also, you're not obligated to come in early or stay late."

"I know," he replies, rising. "But I wanted to."

God, he's tall. I'm five foot eight *with* heels and the man towers over me. He's so broad and solid. Muscular, but not bulky. He skipped the suit today, instead opting to wear a teal dress shirt and patterned tie. The greenish hue makes his irises appear a deeper blue—like a lagoon or the depths of the ocean—and I fight the urge to remove his glasses so I can lose myself in his eyes.

I shake my head to focus. "Working extra is not necessary—"

"I want to make this more than a temporary position." His gaze burns into me, laced with a desperate undercurrent that hits me in my stomach. "Understand that I'll do whatever it takes to make that happen."

Position. All it takes is that one word to leave his plush lips, and I'm out of my mind with lust, imagining all the ways our bodies could come together. His eyes . . . they warm me in places that haven't felt warmth in years. His stubbled jawline and dimples make my heart race. My mouth waters each time he moves those full, sculpted lips. His deep voice shouldn't send tingles down my spine. My breath shouldn't catch when he smiles, either. I shouldn't want him. I'm a decade older—and oh yeah—his boss.

Despite all the reasons I shouldn't be attracted to Lincoln Kennedy, we share an undeniable chemistry. It crackles in the air between us like a live wire. Its current pulses through my veins, fluttering in my chest, heating my insides. I know its voltage will destroy me, but my body aches for the shock. For the passion. I need to feel something besides emptiness. It's a position I want Lincoln to fill.

Even though I shouldn't.

"You're off to a strong start," I whisper, quickly retreating to my office. I close the door behind me and plop into my chair. Wrapping my arms around myself, I rub at the sudden chill that simultaneously feels like a hot flash.

What the hell has gotten into me?

NINE

Lincoln

I'M NOT SURE WHAT JUST HAPPENED, BUT I'D KNOW THAT flushed look anywhere. Desire. Could it really be possible *I* ruffle Elinora Iverson's feathers? Do I affect her the way she torments me?

"I'm losing it," I mutter to myself, shaking my head at my stupidity. I remove my glasses and rub my temples. Last night's lack of sleep is playing tricks on my mind.

I told Esme I'd work at The River all weekend if she let me drop my Thursday evening shift. Instead of going to bed early, like I had planned, I did some editing. By some, I mean, I stayed up until three. On the plus side, I'm nearly finished with my first pass through this manuscript. I always do at least two full passes to make sure I don't miss anything.

I've been at the office since six-thirty. After finally figuring out the ridiculously complicated espresso machine in the breakroom, I'm feeling pretty satisfied with myself. Perhaps it's the lingering effects of Elinora's breathy tone, but the confidence seeping into me reminds me of my college days, and that long lost top-of-the-world feeling I crave. *I've got this.* I know what I need to do and how to do it. Despite my concerns about the romance genre, I'm enjoying it more than I expected. I can and will make this job happen for me.

My cell buzzes with a text from Esme as I walk over to the time clock.

> Esme: Don't forget tonight's the Mermaid Masquerade. Make sure you have your sexy merman stuff.

I picture the skin-tight jammers she wants me to wear and groan. Dark teal, and patterned to look like scales, the swimwear leaves little to the imagination. I'd much rather parade around in swim trunks than have spandex plastered to my cock. Then again, it could be worse. Last year, she concocted an "Aqua Cowboy Adventure Party." My attire that evening was the Speedo equivalent of assless chaps paired with cowboy boots. I looked utterly ridiculous. Curling my lip at the memory, I quickly punch my code into the time clock before responding.

> Me: Sounds good.
>
> Esme: It's new members' night. Prepare to give them your best. The goal is to keep them coming . . .
>
> Me: You know I always do.
>
> Esme: That's why you're my favorite.
>
> Me: Correction, I'm everyone's favorite.

Sighing, I stuff my phone back into my pocket and return to my cubicle. Being the favorite is both a blessing and a curse I can't seem to escape. I doubt any of my regulars will be there. New members' night is always packed, so Gwen and Maya usually stay away.

Gwen is a widow in her late fifties, who simply enjoys my

company. We've done nothing sexual, and I consider her my friend. We have a standing dinner date on the third Thursday of each month. I'm annoyed that I missed her last night because I look forward to our talks. We discuss everything—from the environment, to politics, to our love lives. She's like the cool aunt I wish I had.

Maya, on the other hand, is a frequent fuck buddy. My friend may be my "client," but she is the one who introduced me to Esme, and most of my sexual repertoire. Maya hates chaos, so I doubt she'll show up for tonight's rendezvous, which sucks. Like my visits with Gwen, I look forward to my weekly Maya playtime—for different reasons, obviously.

Overall, I enjoy new members' night. It's an opportunity for those who are tentatively adventurous in the bedroom to test the waters. Esme always assigns me the beginners because she claims I'm The River's gateway drug—I get them hooked and keep them coming back for more. My specialty lies in pushing my clients' limits without them realizing it. Some of these women are straight vanilla when we meet. Hell, *I* was vanilla until I met Esme. Now I'm rocky road—dark, a little nutty, with some scattered soft bits.

My ability to put a woman at ease, while coaxing her beyond her comfort level, still amazes me. I don't consider myself manipulative, but my persuasion game is on point. While I may be a bumbling idiot in real life, I'm the picture of confident, smooth-talking, panty-melting swagger while at The River.

I glance up as Elinora strides into the breakroom with her coffee cup. Lucky for me, I have an unobstructed view from my cubicle. I discreetly watch her, shocked she gets her own coffee. I figured she'd have people for that. Then again, Freya isn't here yet.

Elinora is wearing a cobalt blue sheath dress. The cardigan she had on when she arrived earlier is absent, putting her lush curves on display. On her back, the zipper glints in the light like a beacon. I'd give anything to unzip that dress right now and put my hands on her porcelain skin. Bend her over my desk and grip her hips while I fuck her. Make her moan and scream my name like I'm one of the heroes in the erotic romance novels she publishes. I wonder if she actively reads my newfound genre. What positions she likes in bed. How her lips taste. If she's adventurous or docile. My cock twitches, and I shift in my chair without taking my eyes off her.

Elinora tosses her thick, white-blond hair over her shoulder and pulls the creamer out of the fridge. I want to run my fingers through those silken tresses. Tug the strands and slap her ass while she's tied up. I nearly moan at the visual as my cock stretches the material of my dress pants.

This is bad. Elinora holds my mind and body captive, which is something I haven't felt since I started at The River. I clench my jaw against the visuals dancing through my brain. I can't want her —she's my fucking boss.

"Don't even think about it." Myles's voice from right behind me jolts me back to reality.

Jumping, I nearly spill my coffee. I snatch my cup to steady it and lean forward to hide my erection. "I didn't hear you come in."

"No shit." He appears at my side. "I've been watching you for the past five minutes. You forget that I can read you like a book."

"Your point?"

"Don't. Go. There."

"Not sure what you're talking about."

He grips my shoulders. "I mean it, Linc." He lowers his voice to a whisper. "This isn't Ms. Fisher's art class. You cannot fantasize about your boss. She's forbidden fruit."

So was Ms. Fisher, the sexy teacher who unknowingly tormented me by day and gave me wet dreams on a nightly basis. Sadly, she transferred to a different school when I was a Junior.

"Is looking a crime?"

He cocks an orange brow. "I dunno. Is voyeurism what you have in mind when you say looking?"

I roll my eyes. "She's making coffee, for fuck's sake. It's not like I'm watching her shower."

"She's off-limits. Don't watch her. *At all*," he growls, in a tone that reminds me of Ignatius DeAngelis, the priest in charge of our old school.

I give him a thumbs-up. "Yes, Father Callahan. Or have you risen the ranks to Cardinal?"

Myles smirks. "Don't push your luck. I've got all kinds of priestly connections."

"I prefer nuns."

"You're going straight to hell."

"No shit. And courtesy of Dick, so are you."

"Richard is Buddhist." He scrubs a hand over his face and smirks. "And if you recall, according to Sister Fitzgibbons, I secured my place in hell when I met Henry."

Henry Winthrop was a classmate in the process of entering the priesthood. That is, until Myles "corrupted" him. Now he owns an elite gay club in Albany. He's cool as fuck, and we still keep in touch with him. Even though it's not my scene, I stop by his club to visit from time to time. Henry insists Myles did him a favor when he made him realize he was gay, but courtesy of our Catholic upbringing—and the toxic clergy at our church's helm—Myles spent years beneath a blanket of guilt. He finally got over it when Henry married Seth, the love of his life.

"You're my favorite blasphemous bastard."

"Likewise." He nods to the breakroom. "Off limits. Understand?"

"Yep," I mutter.

"What are you doing this weekend?"

"Working."

He curls his lip. "*All* weekend?"

I nod. "I missed Thursday, so I told Esme I'd be there."

"What about your Sunday date with Reagan?"

Every week I try to make the trip upstate to the group home where my sister lives outside New Paltz. I take her out for lunch and some other activity. Sometimes it's a movie or bowling, but lately, we've been going hiking. While a casual stroll around Lake Minnewaska is hardly a hike in my book, it takes a lot out of Reagan. Her heart condition makes her dizzy and out-of-breath easily, but I try to keep her active. Her fiery spirit is at war with what she's physically able to do. It kills me to see a sixteen-year-old girl trapped in her own body.

I sigh. "Don't worry, I already disappointed her." This was actually the third weekend in a row I've had to cancel.

Myles rests his hand on my shoulder. "How's she doing? I'd love to tag along on your next trip home."

I perk up. "Really? She'd be thrilled." Not to mention, it would help get me back into her good graces after our missed visits.

"Yeah, man. I haven't seen her since we went to your folks' place for Thanksgiving. I miss the little Reag-Bear."

Reagan has had a crush on Myles since she was eight. While I've made it clear he's gay, and in a relationship, my sister still insists she's going to marry him. It's sweet, really. Her face lights up whenever he's around, and he's amazing with her. I'm the family's only non-redhead, so with his red hair and freckles, he looks more like her sibling than I do. And as the youngest of four, I think Myles enjoys having someone look up to *him* for once.

I've always been grateful to my best friend for his kindness. Sadly, some other dudes we grew up with had a tendency to run their mouths. I'll never forget when I overheard Kyle Fink call my sister a retard—to her face. Reagan burst into tears, and the fucker had the audacity to laugh at her. I had the last laugh when I broke his nose and gave him a black eye. Maybe he'll think twice about being cruel to someone with disabilities.

That shit doesn't fly with me. Kindness is pretty fucking simple, and I have zero tolerance for those who behave otherwise.

"Reagan asks about you all the time." I smile and squeeze his arm. "I'll let her know you're thinking about coming to visit."

He nods. "Did you have enough for her housing this month?"

"Barely, but yeah." I clear my throat. "That's why I've been spending more time at The River."

"Let me know if you're ever in a bind. I'll gladly cover the difference."

"Thank you, man. It means a lot to me."

"I know." He grins and wags his orange brows. "That's what proper ride-or-die blasphemous bastards do for their friends."

I GLANCE AT MY WATCH. FIVE O'CLOCK MEANS QUITTING TIME. Normally, I'd stay late, but I have to be at The River by seven, which means I need to get in the right headspace for my extracurriculars.

After emailing myself the manuscript I've been working on, I stuff my phone and notes into my messenger bag. Maybe one day I'll splurge on a real briefcase. I rub the stubble on my jaw, knowing it will be a long time before that happens.

Fuck, I need to shave.

Esme demands her concierges be clean-shaven to avoid inner thigh scrapes, but that activity is on my no-fly list. Call it a hard limit if you will.

Yes, I fuck strangers. But in the unlikely event I find someone who I actually connect with, it would be nice to have something reserved for them. That's why I don't kiss anyone on the lips or give oral at work. To me, kissing is an extremely intimate act. While I have no problem using the tools at my disposal—cock included—I'm more selective with my mouth. That's not to say I *don't* use my mouth. My skills in the nipplegasm department are impressive, or so I've been told.

Speaking of nipples . . .

My mouth waters, and my cock twitches to life as Elinora floats into view. She approaches my cubicle, and since I'm still seated, her breasts are at eye level. I'd give my soul to peel off her bra with my teeth and put my tongue on her. Kiss and suck every inch of her perfect porcelain skin. Nip and nibble and mark her as *mine*.

Not that it could ever happen.

She motions to my computer. "I don't want you working from home, Mr. Kennedy. Work-life balance is important."

"Do *you* have work-life balance?" The question leaves my lips before I can stop it.

Elinora forces a laugh, her face twisting into a rueful expression. "I'm not sure I even understand the meaning of those words." She meets my gaze. "Which is why I'd like for my employees to have it."

I adjust my glasses with a smile. "Maybe you should lead by example?"

"There are a lot of things I *should* do. Sadly, I don't have the time for most of them. I'm a firm believer that balance improves productivity, even if I don't know how to apply the concept to my life."

I point to her red briefcase. "You can start by leaving work at work."

"I never bring work home. Just my laptop for safe keeping."

"Forgive me if this sounds too forward, Ms. Iverson, but you spend over sixty hours a week here. I get the feeling you make the office your home."

"You're an intuitive man." She smiles and looks me over, making my cock stiffen. "And a bit of a hypocrite."

I raise a brow. "How am I a hypocrite?"

She props her hands on her hips, and I have to clench my fists to keep from tossing her over my knee. "If I recall, you're always working—even when you're not. I believe that's a direct quote."

Shocked she'd remember anything that came out of my mouth, I blink a few times instead of answering.

Arching a perfect brow, she cocks her hip and adds, "Seeing as you're the only employee of mine still working, I'd say that qualifies as hypocrisy."

I lean forward slightly. "Maybe I enjoy working hard?"

"I appreciate hard work."

Hearing the word "hard" leave her lips makes me want to give her something hard for them. I don't think I've ever craved a woman this badly. Ever. Not even Ms. Fisher. None of my River playmates even come close to inciting this amount of lust. I can't control the way it's coursing through me, tightening my balls, and making my cock throb. I've had plenty of women, but my new boss surpasses them all.

Oh, the things I'd do to Elinora Iverson if I ever had the opportunity to be alone with her in my private lagoon at The River.

I clench my jaw and force a swallow. "Believe me, I'm no stranger to hard work. In fact, I thrive on it."

She smiles. "Yes, I've noticed this, Mr. Kennedy."

I need her to notice her way onto my cock. Preferably right now.

TEN

Elinora

Fuck. Not these guys again.

As Lincoln and I exit the building, I stiffen when I spot a trio of men congregating on the sidewalk. They've been there every day this week. I've lived in New York City for years, so I'm used to the catcalls, but something about these guys makes me uneasy.

I stare at the sign for the parking garage down the block and fish in my coat pocket for my ticket. *Shit.* I must've left it on my desk. I'm fairly certain I parked on the third level today. Spot C24. *Wait, maybe that was yesterday.* Note to self: start writing it down. I'm kicking myself for not buying a monthly permit. Or using a car service.

The attendant is in his booth, so I doubt the creeps would try anything, but still—it's days like these when I wish I wore sneakers to work.

"Where did you park?" Lincoln asks, following my gaze.

"In the garage."

His eyes narrow on the men. "I'm heading that way. I'll walk you to your car."

"Thanks," I murmur, beyond grateful I didn't have to *ask* him to escort me.

"Anytime, but you need to walk to my left." He grips my shoulders and steers me toward the inside of the sidewalk, placing his body between me and the creeps.

Tingles race down my spine. His brief touch is warm and firm, yet not overbearing. I'm suddenly at ease. Safe. Protected. Everything I never felt with Charles.

Lincoln's powerful frame towers over me as we stroll past the trio.

One man is brazen enough to let out a low whistle. "Hey, baby." Lincoln shoots him a glare, causing the dirtbag to hold his hands up in surrender. "Just whistling, bro."

Lincoln stops in front of him. "Not at her, you're not. Have some fucking class, *bro*."

Like usual, I straighten my spine and keep walking without acknowledging them. When we round the corner into the parking garage, my breath rushes out of me.

"Does that happen to you a lot?" he asks.

I nod. "I'm used to it, but that group of men is particularly aggressive with the catcalls."

Lincoln presses his lips into a grim line. "Yeah, I noticed." He points to the stairwell. "Which level?"

Gnawing my lip, I meet his gaze. "I don't remember."

Something flashes in his eyes before he runs a hand over his face. "So, you planned to wander up and down dark stairwells alone?"

"I can take care of myself, Mr. Kennedy."

"No one's questioning that." He jerks his thumb over his shoulder. "But they made *me* uneasy, so I'll be escorting you from now on."

I wave him off. "That's unnecessary."

"I'd rather not take the chance, Ms. Iverson." He pauses when we reach the landing on the second level. "Not everyone has good intentions."

"I'm aware," I murmur, suddenly wishing he had bad intentions involving me. I shake my head to clear it. "I'm pretty sure I parked on the third level. Possibly."

We reach the next landing and scan the vehicles. I spot my red Porsche and point. "That's me in the corner."

"Nice car," he says, as we approach the vehicle.

"Thanks. I hate it."

Lincoln cocks his head to the side. "Why? It's a beautiful piece of machiner—"

"My ex-husband bought it for me." I unlock it and yank open the driver's door. "After his first affair."

"As an apology?"

I shrug and toss my purse onto the seat. "Who knows? He had two more, so that negates the implied mea culpa, don't you think?"

His eyes widen. "He had *three* affairs?"

I force a smile. "Those are just the ones I know about. I filed for divorce after I caught him in our bed with his third mistress. You know, three strikes and all that." I shrug. "But he clearly didn't feel my loss since they're still an item."

"I'm sorry he did that to you." He adjusts his glasses and studies my face.

"Me too."

He touches my shoulder. "No, really. You deserve so much better."

"Thank you," I whisper.

I'm not sure what prompted me to tell Lincoln about my failed marriage or anything personal, for that matter. I don't share private information with anyone other than my mother, Freya, and Garrett. It's safer that way. People like to cozy up to the ones with money, and I learned a long time ago to stop trusting their false kindness. I won't allow myself to be duped into another financial trap. I'm tired of being used. Despite what Charles has led me to believe, I'm worth more than my bank account.

Yet here I am, still the lonely one who aches for genuine love. Disgusted by my own stupidity, I blink rapidly to dispel the moisture gathering in my eyes.

Lincoln's gaze narrows on my face. "Are you ok?"

"I'm fine." I straighten, forcing what remains of my composure. "It's just the wind."

"It's not windy today."

"I don't need a weather update, Mr. Kennedy," I snap, embarrassment clogging my throat. Charles was a professional antagonist. Last thing I need is another man contradicting everything I say and do.

He holds his hands up in surrender and takes a step backward. "Jeez. I was just making an observation. No need to bite my head off."

"Excuse me?"

"Never mind." Sighing, he rubs the back of his neck. "Forget I said that." He meets my gaze with eyes so blue, I'd swear I'm adrift in the Atlantic. "I'm sorry."

"You should be."

I can't figure out why I'm so unnerved. Better yet, why I allowed Lincoln to escort me to my car or let him stand up to those creeps for disrespecting me. I can handle myself.

I'm at a loss for why he makes my heart race and weakens my knees. How whenever I'm near him, my palms sweat, and my mouth goes dry. Then two seconds later, the cadence of his voice makes my mouth water. Most of all, I can't figure out why his apology for my ex-husband's behavior means more to me than anything Charles ever said, but I do know this: Lincoln Kennedy rattles me.

He clears his throat. "I, uh, guess I'll head out. Have a nice weekend, Ms. Iverson."

"You do the same. I'll see you Monday." I sink into the driver's seat and peer up at him. "Thank you for walking with me."

"No problem." He smiles, and my toes curl inside my stilettos. "Don't work too hard. You know, balance and all that."

"We've already established my lack of balance." Guilt nudges my conscience. "And I'm sorry for snapping at you."

"It's fine. It seems like you have a lot on your plate."

"You have no idea."

"Actually, I think I do." Something that feels like compassion colors his tone. I'm not used to anyone giving a damn about my feelings. I'm about to give my rebuttal when he rests his hand on top of my car and adds, "I've learned you can only pile your plate so high before it shatters."

Lincoln Kennedy is intelligent, driven, and intuitive. He has tenacity and wisdom beyond his years. At half Charles's age, he's the grit and integrity my ex-husband was not, all wrapped in a sexy as hell package. Equal parts nerdy and hunky, Lincoln's the picture of potent, virile male. I'd bet the future of Iverson Press that he's got stamina in bed. Heat floods my core, saturating the panties that were already damp. God knows I haven't encountered stamina—or any sex worth having—in over a decade.

With dark, glossy hair and lush lips, Lincoln is more gorgeous than any man I've seen in real life. Taller and broader too. I can't explain his effect on me, but I need to rein in my libido. Not only is he too young for me, but I've got more baggage than LaGuardia Airport.

And oh yeah, I'm his boss.

I close my car door, at a loss for what else to say. Lincoln watches me pull out of my parking spot and drive off.

One thing's for damn sure, my weekend would be a hell of a lot more enjoyable with him in my bed.

Freya reaches across our table at Oasis, the restaurant affiliated with The River, and grabs my hand. "I'm so excited you came tonight. You need this."

"Yeah, it's been years since I've had a massage."

"The River Rubdown isn't just any massage, Elle."

"A massage is a massage," I say, spearing a forkful of salad.

"Honey, this is The River. Leave your expectations—and your inhibitions—at the door."

"My inhibitions?" I cock my head to the side. "What do they have to do with anything?"

Freya giggles and wags her brows. "You'll see."

I chew on a piece of cucumber doused with green goddess dressing and eye her suspiciously.

"What the hell does that mean?"

"You'll see," she repeats, squeezing my wrist. "But I need you to promise me something."

I set down my fork. "And that is?"

"Promise you'll go with the flow. Dive in and see where the current takes you."

"I'm here, aren't I?"

She chews her lip. "Yes, but I need you to keep an open mind."

"Freya Thorne, what exactly have you gotten me into?"

She points to the far corner of the restaurant. "Look."

I turn in my seat and gasp as what appeared to be a floor-to-ceiling tank of exotic fish, suddenly slides to the right, exposing a cavernous hallway. Blue and teal lights illuminate smooth rock walls, and subversive club music with a heavy bass rhythm reaches my ears. "What's back there?"

"That, my dear, is the entrance to The River."

The music vibrates in my chest as the most beautiful woman I've ever laid eyes on steps into the restaurant. The fish wall closes behind her like a secret portal. Three massive security guards I hadn't noticed before take their places in the shadows along the room's perimeter.

"Who's that?" I ask, nodding toward the woman. "She seems important."

"Madame Esme." Freya's reverent whisper is barely audible. "She owns The River."

Madame Esme scans the room. At Freya's wave, her red lips curve into a sultry smile, and she approaches our table. Her body-hugging, teal sequined mini dress shimmers as she glides through the restaurant like a mermaid in a lagoon. Long mahogany curls, with streaks of royal blue, cascade to the middle of her back. Her olive skin is dewy, like she bathes in a fountain of eternal youth.

"Freya, baby," she croons in a lilting voice that drips of sex. "I'm so happy you made it."

"Thank you for allowing me to bring a guest, Madame."

"Anything for you, sugar." Madame Esme leans down and kisses Freya.

On the lips.

With tongue.

My jaw drops open. Freya loves men. And I mean, *loves* them. She's never given any indications she's bisexual, but here she is, passionately kissing a woman. No, make that a sexy mermaid. My nipples prick the inside of my bra, and my lower belly tightens and flutters at the sight. For a fraction of a second, I'm jealous of Freya.

Madame Esme breaks the kiss. "As sweet as always." She straightens and turns to me. "And who might this be?"

"This is my dear friend, Elinora," Freya answers, which is great because I'm still stupefied by what I just witnessed.

"Welcome, Elinora," Esme purrs, taking my hand in her silken palm.

Warmth coils inside me with her touch. *Kiss me.* The thought comes unbidden, and I shake my head to clear it.

"Hi," I murmur, my voice huskier than usual. "Thank you for letting me come." Madame Esme smiles, her honey-colored eyes glittering with amusement, and I cross my legs beneath the table when I realize what I said. "I mean—"

"Elinora, baby, you're in for a treat tonight. Freya booked you our signature service, which is a four-hour block."

"Four hours?" My longest massage was ninety minutes and that cost over two hundred bucks. I sure as hell hope Freya didn't spend her monthly bonus on *me*.

"If you desire more time, I grant extensions upon request."

"I'm sure four hours will be long enough."

"Honey, you haven't seen L yet. Trust me, no amount of time is enough." She closes her eyes for a moment, as if savoring a memory, before returning her attention to me. "Afterwards, you're free to partake in any activities you wish."

"You mean the masquerade party?" I ask.

"That's part of it. I'm referring to the other available a*men*ities, if you will." At my blank stare, she glances at Freya. "Don't tell me you didn't mention the club."

Freya flushes. "No, not exactly. I told her about the Mermaid Masquerade Mingle, and the spa stuff, but I didn't go into any details about the club amenities."

"Then tonight should be *very* interesting," Madame Esme croons, twirling a lock of my hair. The sensation sends goosebumps over my skin, and I suddenly want her to weave her fingers into my hair and drag her nails along my scalp.

"What amenities?"

Freya grips Madame Esme's other hand and points to me. "She promised to keep an open mind. Right, Elle?"

"I thought I was getting a massage?"

"Oh, don't you worry, Elinora. He'll massage you." Madame Esme runs her fingers through my hair, sending a flare of heat to my core. "The River Rubdown is a full body experience."

"Wait a minute." My gaze darts between them. "Exactly what kind of club is The River?"

ELEVEN

Elinora

I CAN'T BELIEVE FREYA BROUGHT ME TO A SEX CLUB. THEN again, knowing my friend for as long as I have, it shouldn't surprise me. We've always been opposites. She gravitates toward all things carnal, while I keep my distance. Full of warmth, passion, and adventure, she's the fire to my ice.

I want to be annoyed, disgusted even. I *should* grab my purse and run out the door. Instead, I'm intrigued. Captivated by the taboo concept and the club's beautiful proprietor. Besides, I'm tired of being the ice queen—my tundra could use some fucking flames.

Flanked by Madame Esme and Freya, I force myself to breathe as we walk arm-in-arm along the corridor. We pass a white marble arch, which opens to another, shorter hallway. Someone painted wispy clouds on the pale blue walls and curved ceiling. At the end, a massive spiral staircase seems to vanish into the heavens.

I stop short and point down the hall. "What's at the top of the stairs?"

"The members-only entrance to Vapor, our traditional spa.

When I bought this building, it was an abandoned train station. Are you familiar with Grand Central Terminal?"

"Of course."

"The setup is similar, but a little smaller. You know how when you first enter Grand Central at street level, there are upper lobbies where they frequently have exhibits and pop-up shops? I'm talking about *before* you go down the ramp to get to the main concourse with the pretty ceiling."

Envisioning the iconic station I've visited countless times since I moved to New York, I nod. "Yes."

"Well, that's where we have Oasis, our restaurant." She points to several doors further down the corridor we started out on. "Security, client dressing rooms and showers, and everyone's offices are also on the ground floor. Sadly, we don't have a fancy vaulted ceiling like Grand Central because Vapor takes up the building's entire top level. While Oasis and certain parts of Vapor are open to the public, the rest of the club is not."

"I'm assuming there are safeguards in place to ensure the general public doesn't venture into any members-only areas?"

"Absolutely. Our security team is a sophisticated network of manpower and technology. You'll see our guys patrolling all three suites—they're the ones dressed in black with our logo on their shirts. If you ever need anything, don't hesitate to approach them. No one enters this establishment without their knowledge, and we can lock this place down like Fort Knox if need be. You never have to worry about your safety here."

"Good to know."

"I'll explain the other suites in a bit when I give you the grand tour, this way I can answer any questions that may arise. But before we get started, I'll fill you in on the basics." Madame Esme punches a code into a panel on the wall, then opens the door to a women's dressing room. "Members are assigned their own unique passcodes for the boxes you'll see outside every door. Should you decide to join us, you'll be provided electronic credentials which must be kept secure." She ushers me inside with a brush of my hip, and for the life of me, I can't figure out why I want this woman's hands all over my body.

"I'm going to use the ladies' room," Freya announces, veering off to the left. "Be right back."

Madame Esme gestures to a white leather sofa. "Elinora, have a seat, baby."

I settle, the leather cooling my overheated thighs. "I'm not sure I belong at a club like this."

She slides into the empty place beside me and tilts my chin to face her. For a moment, I think she's going to kiss me. Something deep inside me hopes she does.

Cupping my face, she brushes her thumbs over my lips. "Everyone has a home at The River. It's up to you to find it."

"How do I find it?" My breathy voice makes her smile, and I press my knees together to quell the throbbing ache between my thighs.

"Use the guides. Let them be your compass."

"Guides?"

"My establishment employs men and women whose sole duties are to serve The River's patrons. I call them pleasure concierges. After I get an idea of which amenities a client is comfortable with, I assign them the concierge most equipped to meet their needs. He—or she, if that's the client's preference—serves as their personal guide. However, in your case, Freya gave me a heads-up, so I've already got somebody in mind for you."

"I've never been to a sex club," I blurt.

"This isn't *just* a sex club. It's a pleasure spa. We all have different understandings of pleasure. Some of us seek our comfort near the surface, be it companionship or affection. Maybe you simply want a man to converse with, or someone to hold your hand or rub your back. You'd be surprised by the number of clients who come here simply because they don't want to be alone all the time."

"I'll probably be one of them," I murmur, shocked by how easily the confession leaves my lips.

Madame Esme studies my face, compassion shining in her eyes. "It's easy to feel disconnected in a world ruled by technology and social media. Dating and relationships aren't what they used to be, and it takes a toll on us. Humans are pack creatures by nature. While some people prefer to lead solitary lives, they often underestimate the power of human touch. How good it feels to be held. Stroked. Kissed . . ." She stares off into the distance for a moment, the wistful look on her face making me wonder if she's describing herself. If so, we have more in common than I thought. Just as quickly, her gaze flicks back to mine, and the sultry edge returns to her voice. "If that sounds like what you're looking for, you can find it at The River. Perhaps your desires run deeper, and you want to make love. We can arrange that too. Maybe you want a thrill, to indulge in something which tantalizes and titillates your senses . . ."

"Like what?" I ask, my insides heating at the images of handcuffs and sex swings dancing in my head.

"Our concierges are skilled in a variety of activities. Many of them follow a BDSM lifestyle and are more than willing to coach interested newcomers. As long as it's one hundred percent consensual for both—or should I say *all*—parties involved, nothing is off-limits at The River. Ménage and group sex are not uncommon here, but there are designated areas for those activities."

Her statement should scare me, but it only turns me on more.

"I don't know what I like. I've never done anything like that."

"This is your safe place to test the waters, baby. Keep an open mind, and don't be afraid to express yourself. I encourage you to push beyond your comfort level, but if you have hard limits, voice them so there are no misunderstandings."

"Hard limits?" I squeak.

"Those are the acts you will not allow under any circumstances. Everyone has a threshold."

I know what hard limits are—I publish erotic romance. I've read enough of them to be familiar with the BDSM lifestyle and various kinks. I've never given any thought to my own limits because sex with Charles never pushed them. All he had in his repertoire were predictable, five-minute jackhammering sessions that did absolutely nothing for me. I got used to being the one responsible for my own orgasms, so I've never explored the concept of shared pleasure.

And I certainly never imagined stepping foot inside a sex club.

Madame Esme touches my shoulder. "I'll give you an example. While some women adore nipple clamps, I'm not a fan. A man can do anything else he wants to me, except use clamps. If there's something that's out of the question for you, let him know ahead of time."

No one's going anywhere near my back door, but how does one say that out loud? *Do I wait for him to try, and then refuse?* I grimace at the thought. "What about him?"

"I'm not sure what you're asking."

"Does the man you have in mind for me have any conditions I should be made aware of?"

She nods. "I'm sure he'll make them known, but since you're a first timer, I'll fill you in. L doesn't kiss women on the lips, nor does he perform oral sex. Those are his hard limits. They are also the only complaints I've ever received about him."

"Complaints?"

She licks her lips. "Women who have been with L *always* want more than he's willing to give. You'll understand once you see him. He's got lips to die for, so the ladies get a little frustrated when he won't kiss theirs." Her gaze drifts from my mouth to my lap, as if to illustrate her point.

My renegade brain conjures an image of her between my thighs, making me flush once more. "They seem like strange activities to have an aversion to," I murmur, forcing my attention to her eyes.

"Everybody's different, baby. I'm sure he has his reasons. Anyway, before we get started, I'll have you sign a nondisclosure agreement. It's a legal document that protects your privacy and that of the club. No one is permitted to discuss what goes on here with any nonmembers. Just like Vegas, what happens in these waters, stays at The River."

"So, no one will smear my reputation?"

Madame Esme purses her lips. "Step one. Lose your negative connotations about sex. Contrary to what you may believe, pleasure is beautiful—not dirty. If you're too worried about tarnishing your image, you won't be in the right headspace. Change your mindset. No one is here to smudge your reputation. Allow The River to flow through you, awaken and indulge the desires you might not even realize you have. All you need to do is float along and see where the current takes you. Let us polish those rough edges. Nothing shines brighter than an orgasm."

"I'm sorry." I backpedal, feeling like an ass for offending her. "It's just . . . I own a corporation, and I don't need my employees knowing about my sex life."

"Understandable, and that is the reason behind the NDA." She hands me a clipboard and pen.

"Sign your name on the line."

I scrawl my signature without reading the contract. A big no-no in business transactions. Then again, this isn't a business venture. All I can focus on is the lust coursing through my body. When the hell did I get so thirsty?

"Your first few visits are complimentary. Should you decide to join us, membership dues are paid on a quarterly basis. I can bill you, or we can arrange automatic withdrawals." She brushes the hair back from my face. "After your trial period, it's up to you whether you want to keep your concierge or test the waters yourself. Members are free to interact with whomever they choose."

"I'm nervous," I whisper.

She smiles. "That's why I'm here, baby. Any questions?"

"How do you keep the water clean?" I've always leaned toward the practical side of situations—except for my presence here tonight, obviously—and I have zero desire to contract a weird communicable disease. "I mean, it's got to be tricky for a facility of this scale."

"It is, but we make it top priority. I'm a firm believer that cleanliness is next to godliness. Rest assured we don't cut corners when it comes to public health. We follow CDC guidelines for the disinfection of our water and the establishment itself. We chemically treat and triple filter all water. The club is only open nights, so that leaves the entire day for maintenance, cleaning, repairs, what have you. A huge cleaning crew arrives every morning at eight, and they sanitize every possible surface. I'm not exaggerating when I say you could eat off the floor when they're done."

"Good to know."

Freya returns from the restroom and plops onto the couch beside me. "Are you mad at me?"

I shake my head. "Not mad. Just in shock."

"Relax." Madame Esme grips my chin. "You don't have to do anything that makes you uncomfortable." She leans in close and smiles. "We'll start you off slow, so you can dip your toes in." Tilting my chin, she brushes her lips over mine. "Then you can swim deeper." Her tongue darts out, tasting the seam of my lips, which part of their own volition. "And when you're ready, we'll take you under." She sweeps her tongue into my mouth, stroking it against mine in a sensual waltz.

I have never kissed a woman. Ever. I never had the desire to. But I'd allow this woman to do anything she wanted to me. The realization sends a flare of heat to my core. I moan into the kiss and clutch her shoulders.

"Um, this is hot as fuck," Freya murmurs from beside us. "Getting a little lonely out here, ladies."

Madame Esme breaks our kiss, leaving me breathless. "What do you say, Elinora? Are you ready to see where the current takes you?"

"Yes."

She licks her lush lips that taste of honey and chocolate-dipped strawberries. "Excellent. There are a few housekeeping points we need to go over. As I'm sure you've noticed, my establishment is water themed. Water's versatility makes it my favorite element. As vapor, water is airy like a featherlight caress. You'll find lighter activities—as in, our traditional spa amenities—in the Vapor Suite." She trails her fingertips down my throat. "On the floor below us, we have the Aqua Suite. Think of the main concourse at Grand Central, with its huge open space and train tracks branching out in every direction. Aqua's setup is very similar, except private lagoons, salt saunas, mineral pools, and a lazy river replace the platforms. Does that make sense?"

I nod. "It sounds really elaborate."

"You have no idea, baby. Water, in its fluid state, can trickle like a stream or a brook. It can flow like a winding river, or it can *rush*, surging like rapids or a waterfall. The majority of our concierges play in the Aqua Suite, which is home to our dance floor and The River's main bar. We often host special events in Aqua because it's most conducive for setting up a stage."

"What kind of events?"

"Ones like tonight's masquerade. We also hold auctions, charity benefits, and various demonstrations. Sometimes even the occasional private party."

"I can't imagine having a party at a sex club." Maybe I'll do that for my fortieth birthday in a few years. I'm sure Freya would jump all over that idea.

"Aqua is an oasis of its own. Open your mind to the possibilities." She smiles like she's keeping the world's biggest secret. "And finally, for those whose tastes run a bit kinkier, we have the Glacier."

"What's the Glacier?"

"An elite realm reserved for our most advanced players. Glacier is its own entity within The River. We will not allow you entrance at this time."

My curiosity piques like Belle in *Beauty and the Beast* when he warns her to stay out of his castle's West wing. "What happens there?"

Madame Esme shares a look with Freya, who nods and addresses me, "Things you definitely wouldn't partake in."

"Like?"

Madame Esme meets my gaze. "Glaciers are frozen rivers. Solid and unyielding. Members who follow the BDSM lifestyle are the only persons permitted in Glacier. We want it to be a safe, judgment-free space for them. Some patrons call Glacier a kink club, but I prefer pleasure lounge. Going back to our Grand Central analogy—I'm talking about the bottom floor now, where they have all the food."

"What about the lower tracks? Did this station have those?" I ask, picturing the commuter tracks at Grand Central.

"Yes. Although the setup is a bit different than how we constructed Aqua. Glacier is probably my favorite suite, mainly because I love the architecture. It's essentially an ice palace, minus the cold. So, in addition to the main lounge and several private rooms, Glacier has an underground labyrinth of chambers—we call them ice caves—with each one designed to accommodate a specific kink. There's also a much smaller bar down there."

I can't even begin to imagine the cost and complexity of The River's construction. She must have hired a team of genius architects, engineers, and contractors to make this place a reality. Not to mention the manpower required for regular deep cleaning, daily operation, *and* routine maintenance and repairs.

While I'm beyond intrigued by everything The River has to offer, I'm also a realist. "I'm a Vapor kind of girl."

She rubs circles on my knee with her thumb. "My gut says you can handle Aqua, which is why I'm sending you there."

I gnaw my lip. "I'm not sure—"

"Trust me." Madame Esme brushes her thumb over my mouth

to free my lower lip from my teeth. "Like I said, I have someone in mind for you. He's excellent with beginners."

"What if it's too much for me?"

"I'm a woman who enjoys consistency. At The River, we use a standard set of safe words across all suites."

"I thought safe words would be limited to the stuff that goes on in Glacier."

She shakes her head. "Safe words can apply to any sexual situation. When your concierge asks, 'How is the water?' you will choose one of three responses."

"How am I supposed to remember *three* safe words?"

Freya laughs. "Elle, they're self-explanatory. Now shut up and listen."

Madame Esme takes my hands in hers. "As I was saying, your concierge will check in with you periodically. If you are happy with what he's doing, your response should be 'warm.' If you like it, but want him to slow down, you will say, 'cool.' And if at any point, you want him to stop *everything*, all you need to say is 'ice.' Does that make sense?"

I nod. "Warm is like my green light, cool is yellow, and ice is red for stop."

Freya nudges her. "Since she's using a traffic light analogy, we can't leave out the strobe lighting."

Madame Esme laughs. "Good call. If you're having a *really* good time and you want your concierge to ramp up the intensity, say, 'fire.'"

"Fire and ice," I murmur, rubbing my arms to combat the sudden chill. "Hopefully I can stay at the warmer end of the spectrum."

She slides her hand up my thigh. "Don't you worry, baby. My boy L brings the heat."

TWELVE

Lincoln

I've always marveled at The River's impressive security presence, but tonight seems even more locked down than usual. Even Darius King, the club's head of security, is out patrolling the scene.

"What's good, Linc?" He claps my shoulder on his way past the Aqua Suite bar. Unlike the other security guys who roam the club dressed in all black, Esme wants Darius to blend in with the concierges like an undercover cop of sorts. Right now, wearing nothing but skin tight navy-blue jammers, and a gold mask to match the trident he carries, D is every bit the Mer king. At six foot five, the former Marine is a mountain of muscle. He's also the coolest bastard I've ever met, and one of my good friends.

"Same shit, man." I peer at my reflection in the mirrored wall and squeeze a few drops of contact solution into my eyes. I keep a bottle stashed behind the bar because thanks to long hours in front of a computer and late nights at the club, my eyes are always dry. The soothing moisture blurs my vision as I slide my silver masquerade mask back down over my face. "Still can't fucking see."

"Sounds like the sensory dep rooms are perfect for you."

I close the lid and stash the bottle in the cubby beneath the bar. "Sometimes I wonder how I don't trip over my own feet in there."

"That's why you won't catch me in one. I'm not trying to bust my ass slipping on wet marble. With my luck, I'd probably hit my head and drown." He points to the growing crowd of patrons. "Gonna be busy tonight. What's your game plan?"

"Dunno yet. Waiting for Esme to enlighten me."

"She's still upstairs prepping a member's newbie friend. My guess says you'll be over in Lagoon Seven with the newbie."

I shrug. "Works for me. You know I love broadening horizons."

He chuckles. "I caught a glimpse of her earlier, and she's smoking hot. You'd better hope I'm right because she's just your type."

"My type?"

"Blond with curves in all the right places." Darius winks and disappears through the stone archway that leads to the salt cave saunas.

I make my way behind the bar and pour myself a shot of Lagavulin, my favorite single malt whiskey. Yeah, I love blonds with curves, but lately, there's only been one on my mind.

Elinora.

I think back to the parking garage earlier, when I wanted to press her up against that little red Porsche and fuck her on the hood. How her lips quivered, and her nipples showed through the material of her dress like an invitation. I would've given my soul to hike it up around her waist and bury myself deep inside her. My cock twitches at the conjured visual. I need to chill the fuck out because these thin jammers don't stand a chance at restraining a boner.

Esme crosses the dance floor and saunters up to the bar. "I've got something special for you tonight."

"You say that before every shift."

"I really mean it this time. I just had a taste of her, and she's oh, so sweet."

"Lemme guess . . . she's a newbie?"

"She is." Esme grins and pinches my ass. "You know I reserve the tastiest treats for you, right?"

"Yeah, you take care of me." I smirk. "You know, because I'm your favorite."

She waves a finger at me. "Shh . . . don't tell anybody."

"What am I in for?" I swallow the rest of my whiskey and peer into the empty glass, annoyed with myself for finishing it so quickly. Employees are only allowed to consume one alcoholic beverage per shift, while members can have two. After the week I've had, I could use a whole bottle.

Esme straightens a stack of cocktail napkins. "I'd say she's in her mid-thirties. Drop dead gorgeous. Currently unattached, she's a recent divorcee in desperate need of a good fuck." She presses her fingertips to her red lips. "She's never been to a sex club or slept with anyone other than her ex-husband."

"Seriously? She's been with *one* dude her entire life?"

"Yep. So she claims."

"That makes my job easy."

She tilts her head to the side. "How do you figure?"

"Pretty sure I'll meet her expectations when I've only got one guy as competition."

"I wouldn't be so cocky if I were you. This woman has so much pent-up passion, she's ready to blow. I felt it when I kissed her. I'm telling you, L, she's a river herself. Except somebody put up a fucking dam and blocked her."

"How so?"

"She's gone *years* without pleasure. She's swelling to her breaking point, just waiting for someone to bust through that dam. Her desires run much deeper than she's willing to admit, so don't be fooled by her tentative façade." Esme grips my wrist. "She's *thirsty*, L, real thirsty. And she tastes like warm sugar."

"Well, you know I love sugar. And breaking barriers." I lick my lips in anticipation. "Where is she?"

"Waiting for you in Lagoon Seven." Esme smirks. "And ironically enough, she also goes by L."

I feel the wicked grin curve my lips. "We'll be like the lion and the lamb." I jab my thumb into my chest. "Hint, hint, I'm the lion."

"Yeah, something like that." She points toward the lagoons. "Now get your fine ass in there and cause a flood."

THIRTEEN

Elinora

I can't believe I'm doing this.

Iverson Melt publishes some risqué stories, so I know places like The River exist, but I never imagined I'd be sitting at the edge of a lagoon waiting for some hot stranger to fuck me. I wonder what my pleasure concierge will look like. Will he be patient with me, or will my lack of experience turn him off?

Pushing my white terry robe aside, I ease my feet into the lagoon. Beneath the robe I've got on a silver string bikini Freya talked me into wearing. The water lapping at my skin is the perfect temperature. I glance at my sparkly silver toenails and smile. I'm glad I took the time to give myself a pedicure this morning. Self-pampering is a rare luxury.

I take a deep breath and force myself to relax. Something heady, like jasmine or sandalwood greets my nostrils. The scent mingles with the hint of leather and saltwater.

Private Lagoon Number Seven has a tropical, Amazonian vibe. The space is dimly lit, save for the iridescent blue glow that emanates from the water and a strand of white lights strewn in a palm tree to my left. At the far end of the room, a tranquil waterfall cascades from the ceiling, backlit by teal-colored lights. Tall grasses like those one might see along the banks of a river, sway in the breeze coming from . . . somewhere.

A door opens behind me, and club music floods the room. My heartbeat ratchets up a few notches with the booming bass. The rhythm fades as whomever it is closes the door.

Every nerve ending flares to life, and goosebumps bloom on my skin. I shift position and adjust my royal blue mask. It obscures the top half of my face, leaving my nose and lips exposed. I draw a shaky breath and peek over my shoulder while fiddling with the end of my braid.

A figure moves through the shadows, placing something on a large, white dais. A towel or blanket, maybe. I know it's a man by the sheer size of him and the way he moves—a primal swagger that makes my inner muscles clench. My breath catches in my throat, and my hands start to tremble.

"Are you L?" I call out, my voice husky and soft.

"Are *you*?" His reply is more a vibration than anything else.

My nipples harden into peaks, and heat floods my core. My bikini bottoms don't stand a chance. "Yes."

He grunts and tosses me a bottle of water. "Drink."

"No, thank you. I'm not thirsty."

"I said, *drink*." A dark dominance laces his command, quickening my pulse.

"What if I don't want to?" I call over my shoulder.

A low chuckle rumbles from his chest as he prowls closer. "I'm the king of this castle, sugar. You'll do what I tell you, when I tell you, and not a second later."

"Is that so?" I arch my back and toss my braid behind me. "Honey, I've got a castle of my own, and I'm used to running the show, so it's gonna take a lot more than words to bend me to your will."

"Turn around," he growls. "*Now*."

Pulling my legs from the water, I pivot my body to face him and climb to my feet. I prop my hands on my hips. "You know, most people say 'please' when they want something from me."

His silhouette goes as rigid as a statue. In fact, if it weren't for his heaving shoulders, I'd think he *was* a statue. Suddenly, he backs toward the door and leaves without another word.

FOURTEEN

Lincoln

I BOLT DOWN A DARK CORRIDOR TO THE AQUA SUITE BAR, nearly knocking Esme off her stool when I finally reach her. "Name," I sputter, gripping her shoulders. "Tell me right now."

She sets down her martini. "Easy, baby. What's the matter?"

I grit my teeth. "What. Is. Her. Name?"

"Your client?"

"Who the fuck else would I be asking about?" I snap, inches from her face.

Esme raises a brow. "Watch your tone, L."

I tighten my hold on her. "Tell me."

"Elinora."

"*Fuck.* I knew it." I release her and spear my hands into my hair. "This can't be fucking happening."

"What the hell's your problem, Lincoln?"

I pace the length of the bar, muttering to myself, clenching and unclenching my fists. It's new members' night. Elinora is a newbie, likely Freya's guest. She came here to get fucked, and I'm about to get fucked out of my job.

Behind the bar, Leo, Gideon, and Rocco are hustling their asses off making drinks for the throngs of masked patrons. Maybe I can get one of the guys to swap places with me.

"I asked you a question." Esme's tone slices through the air like a whip landing on my shoulders.

I sink onto the stool beside hers. "She's my boss."

"Huh?"

"You heard me. Elinora Iverson is my boss."

"Oh my God. The publisher?"

"Yep, that'd be her." I bury my face in my hands. "You gotta get someone else. I can't fuck my boss. If she finds out it's me, I'll lose my job." My fears snowball into an avalanche that leaves Reagan without care and me as a rich women's fuck toy for the rest of eternity.

Esme snatches the schedule from behind the bar and skims her finger down the page. "The only concierge who's free right now is Z."

Zarek Petrov. As one of Glacier's resident Doms, he has a reputation for the sadomasochism end of the BDSM spectrum—not that there's anything wrong with that on principle—but Zarek is a man who doesn't play by the rules. Only experienced subs can handle what he dishes out, and even then, he's been known to take things too far. In Z's world, respecting safe words is optional. I will never understand why Esme keeps him on payroll. My blood runs cold at the thought of him with Elinora.

"Absolutely fucking not."

"Excuse me?"

I force an even tone and meet her honeyed gaze. "Anyone but Zarek." I point to my friends behind the bar. "What about them?"

"Gideon leaves in ten minutes, and Leo and Rocco are already spoken for."

"Who's bartending after them?" Most Aqua concierges work half of their shift behind the bar and spend the rest of their time in the lagoons, mineral pools, or the lazy river.

"Rhett and Silas."

"Good. Send one of them in."

She shakes her head. "They're both with clients. Besides, Elinora is here *now*. We're not about to keep her waiting, are we?"

I dodge her question with one of my own. "What about Cameron?"

"He's off tonight. There isn't anyone else, so I suggest you get your ass back in there before I call Z up to the Aqua Suite. Maybe he's not the right fit for her, but—"

"She's a newbie." I clutch the edge of the bar. "He'd be too rough for her. She can't handle his intensity."

"How do *you* know what she can handle?" Esme challenges, propping her hands on her hips. "Pretty bold of you to make those assumptions, don't you think?"

There is no way in hell I'll let that fucker near the porcelain goddess I work for. The thought of him marring her flawless skin makes my blood boil.

"You said it yourself—she's only ever been with her ex-husband. She's practically a fucking virgin." I clench my jaw. "You *know* how Z gets. Look at what happened with Maya."

Fire flashes in her gaze. "Those were entirely different circumstances."

"Right, but would you seriously set Elinora up with a Glacier Dom for her first time? That seems reckless."

"First of all, I don't appreciate you insinuating that I don't know what I'm doing." Esme grips my chin, roughly turning my head to face her. "Number two, I don't give a fuck about your opinion of Z. My focus is the bottom line. If she leaves, and we miss out on a membership opportunity, there will be hell to pay. Need I remind you of our arrangement?"

"No," I mutter, feeling sick to my stomach. "But how am I supposed to—"

"I don't care what you do, or how you do it, but you'd better make it happen. Don't forget that *I'm* your boss too. Don't you dare fuck this up." She waves a finger in my face. "I mean it, Lincoln. Be a man and give her what she needs."

FIFTEEN

Elinora

MAYBE I SHOULDN'T HAVE CHALLENGED HIM. DID MY LACK OF obedience turn him off? Toying with the end of my braid, I pace along the edge of the lagoon and try to reason through the lusty haze in my head. *Maybe I was supposed to—*

The door slides open, and I jump, nearly falling into the shimmering water. A figure enters the room and secures the door before making his way around the perimeter. His height and stature tell me he's the same man as before.

"You're back," I murmur, wrapping my arms around myself. "I thought you'd ditched me." I was moments from grabbing my shit and leaving.

"Sorry. Forgot something."

"Are we all good now?"

"Yeah." He reaches for a switch on the wall and dims the lights to near darkness. I can barely discern the outline of the lagoon. He points to the water. "Get in."

His abrupt retreat had taken some wind from my sails, so

instead of fighting him, I slide out of my robe and place it on the dais. Besides, I'm tired of being in control. This is my opportunity to relax and let somebody else call the shots. I tiptoe to the water's edge and ease in until my feet touch bottom. Water laps at my waist. It's shallower than I expected. There's a splash but I can't figure out which direction it came from.

I peer into the darkness and wait. "Esme said your name is L. What is that short for?"

"Uh . . ." He coughs. "It's . . . Elliot."

Spinning toward his voice, I blindly reach out. My fingertips brush warm flesh—a shoulder, maybe. *No, that's hair.* His chest.

"Why's it so dark in here? I can't see a damn thing."

"Just feel."

"But I want to see you," I whisper, splaying my hands against his steely pecs before sliding them lower and tracing the ridges of his abdomen. Good Lord, his body is perfection. I'd swear Aphrodite herself carved him from granite. As my fingertips explore the hidden masterpiece in front of me, I decide I don't need to see him. Feeling this man is enough for now.

His huge palms settle on top of my hands, stilling them. He brushes his thumbs over my skin. "Tell me your safe words."

"Fire, warm, cool, and ice."

"You know when to use them?"

"Yes, when you ask me how the water is," I say with a shudder.

"Correct." He lifts my knuckles to his lips and presses a kiss to each one before releasing me. "You all right?"

"Yes, I'm just a little nervous. I, uh, I've never done anything like this before."

"Relax." He clamps his hands on my hips, yanking me up against him. His erection presses into my ribcage as his hot breath tickles my ear. "Just feel, sugar. We've got all night, and I promise I won't push you too far."

"It's been years since anyone's touched me." *And I've never been up close and personal with a man this big.*

He digs his fingertips into my hips and pulls me closer. "How about we make up for lost time?"

"Yes," I whisper, clutching his shoulders.

"Keep your hands there. Don't move them, no matter what I do. Got it?"

"Yes." I can't believe how easy it is for me to obey him. I'm not a docile woman, and you'd be hard pressed to find a man who describes me as obedient. Yet here I am, following a stranger's orders like I was born to serve him. Maybe there's something in the water, but I feel like I've already been swept away by The River's current. I bite back a moan as his lips find my neck. Tasting, kissing, and sucking my skin. "Oh my God."

He grazes his teeth over my throat, and I knot my fingers in his thick, silky hair, needing him closer.

"Hands."

I jerk them back and find his shoulders once more. "Sorry."

His chuckle is little more than a rumble. "Trouble with directions?"

"I'm usually in charge."

"In here, *I'm* king. I run the show." He kisses along my jawline, sliding his grip to my waist, his thumbs rubbing circles on my hip bones. "Now, let's try again."

I can't explain it, but his dominance puts me at ease. I want his control, no, I *crave* it. I need him to bend me to his will so I can finally let go of *my* control. This faceless stranger with his hard body and soft hair, raining kisses on my skin in a dark lagoon, makes me feel . . . *safe*. Protected. Free. I can't put my finger on it, but there's something warm and familiar about him.

He reaches behind me and unties my bikini top. First the knot at the back of my neck, then the one near my shoulder blades. The halter plops into the lagoon and floats away with the rest of my inhibitions. My breath catches in my throat as he trails wet kisses across my collarbone. I clench my hands on his shoulders.

"How's the water?"

"Warm." I gasp as his mouth moves lower. His lips brush the tops of my breasts, sending a flare of heat between my legs. I clasp the back of his neck and pull his head closer.

He stills. "*Hands*, sugar."

"Shit." I slide my grip to its rightful place. "It's hard to let someone else have control."

He rolls his hips, rubbing his enormous cock against me. "Do I need to tie them behind your back?"

I can't answer him because lust obliterates my ability to speak. Does he need to tie me up? No. Do I suddenly want him to? Fuck yes.

He slides his warm palms up my torso to cup my breasts. Gasping, I press into his touch when his mouth drifts lower and brushes my nipple.

"Oh my God," I whimper, digging my nails into his shoulders.

Wet heat surrounds my nipple. He sucks it between his lips and rubs his tongue over the hardened peak. Flares of pleasure travel the length of my body, igniting me. Burning me alive. I need him to consume me, rage through me, until there's nothing left but smoke. Before I realize what I'm doing, I spear my hands into his hair once more. "*Fire.*"

He snags my waist, tossing me over his shoulder like a rag doll. "Warned you."

My blood rushes to my head as I shriek and claw at his lower back. "What are you doing?"

He makes his way through the water to the staircase at the opposite end of the lagoon. "Earned yourself some restraints."

Holy shit.

I wriggle in his hold, flailing and kicking my legs. "Put me down."

"Not a chance." He tightens his arm across my thighs and keeps walking.

"Who do you think you—" His huge palm lands on my ass cheeks with a loud crack. "Ow! Did you just *spank* me?" I sputter, shocked by how the sting sends a tidal wave of lust through my veins.

"Very observative." He squeezes my ass and snaps the waistband of my bikini bottoms.

"What, are you gonna throw me over your knee and punish me now?"

A dark chuckle leaves his chest as we approach the waterfall. "You gonna stop me?"

No. I will not stop him. I'm going to provoke him until he spanks me again. I swat him on the ass and snap *his* waistband, mirroring what he did to me.

He stops short. "This isn't a democracy, sugar. The only give and take is gonna be you," he trails his fingers up the back of my thighs, "taking what I give." He slaps my ass once more. "Got it?"

"Should I call you Sensei? Or would you prefer Captain?"

He nips my side. "How about Your Excellency?"

I snort. "In your dreams, bud."

He steps closer to the waterfall, causing me to shiver in the mist. I arch my back, contorting myself to look around him. In what little light there is, I can make out another door. *Behind* the waterfall.

"Where are we going?" I squint and crane my neck.

He presses a panel on the wall, and the door slides open. "To teach you some manners."

"Excuse me?"

He slaps my ass. "Stop talking."

We enter a silent room, leaving behind the tranquil rush of the waterfall. My hearing ratchets up a few notches in the total darkness. Our breaths and a pounding drum are the only sounds that remain. After a moment it occurs to me that the percussion is merely my heartbeat, throbbing inside my skull.

"It's too dark in here." My voice echoes around us. "Is this some sort of dungeon?"

"Shh . . . just feel," he whispers, carrying me deeper into his lair. He pauses next to what I assume is a cabinet, because I hear a drawer scrape open. He rummages inside it and retrieves something before we cross the room.

Since I can't see a fucking thing in the pitch darkness, his familiarity with the room's layout comforts me. His warmth and steady breathing put me even more at ease. None of it makes sense. I'm in a dark room with a stranger who's about to spank me, yet I feel safe.

He stops walking and sets me on my feet in front of him. The backs of my knees make contact with a piece of furniture, and its height and softness tell me it's a bed. "Give me your wrists."

I shiver when his whispered command gusts my ear, but I hold both hands out in front of me. He gently clasps my wrists, securing them with something soft. If I had to guess, I'd say it was a silk scarf. He presses me onto the bed with a nudge of my shoulders.

"Lie down and scoot back." He stretches my arms up over my head and fastens the other end of my restraints to what I assume is a bedpost. The mattress dips beside me, and fabric rustles. I gasp when he skates his palms up my torso over my breasts. Next, he removes my mask, replacing it with a blindfold.

"It's pitch black in here. Why're you blindfolding me?"

His lips find my ear. "You don't need to see. Listen, taste, and *feel.*"

"It would be nice to have a face to go with the sensations."

"I can be anyone you want me to be." His heated whisper sends a flood of desire between my thighs. "Indulge in your fantasies. Make me one of the Hemsworth brothers or Henry Cavill. Or I can be Jason Momoa, and you can call me Aquaman if you want. Trust that I'll give you what you need."

"I do trust you," I whisper, shocked by the truth in my statement.

He traces the shell of my ear with his tongue. "Tell me your safe words."

"Fire, warm, cool, and ice."

"Hard limits?"

It's a good thing he can't see me because I'd bet the heat creeping over my cheeks is in tomato territory on the redness scale. "Uh . . ."

"I need to know this." He punctuates the whispered statement with a nip of my earlobe. "Or we can't go any further."

"No nipple clamps," I say, remembering Esme's declaration from earlier. I have zero experience with the seemingly torturous devices, and I'd like to keep it that way. "And no hardcore S&M stuff."

"Not my style." He feathers his lips over my shoulders. "Anything else?"

Think, Elinora. Think.

"No butt plugs," I blurt. "Or anything there, actually."

"Got it. Now I need you to tell me how far you're willing to go tonight."

"All the way."

"Be specific. Tell me what you want."

"I . . . I want . . ." I force a swallow. While I rule the rest of my life with an iron fist and have no trouble making my demands crystal clear at the office, I've never been able to ask for what I want in the bedroom. Mainly because my needs were always shoved to the back burner. "Umm . . ."

"Do you want me to touch you?"

"Yes," I whisper.

"Say it louder."

"*Yes.*" My voice reverberates through the room.

"Good girl. That's how I want you tonight. Loud and clear. Understand?"

"Yes." I press my knees together and wait for his touch. "Are you going to make love to me?"

"I don't make love." He licks the column of my throat and brings his lips to my ear once more. "I fuck. Do you want me to fuck you, sugar?"

"Yes," I murmur, suddenly overwhelmed by the enormity of what I'm about to do.

"What was that?" He nips my earlobe.

"*Yes.*" The word leaves my lips on a moan.

"Going forward, the correct response is, 'yes, Sir.'" He palms my breasts. "Now, let's try again. Do you want me to fuck you?"

"Yes, Sir."

"Good girl." He rewards me with the brush of his thumbs over my nipples.

My back arches up off the bed, my body pressing into his touch, seeking more. "I haven't had sex in almost three years." My confession, however embarrassing, is necessary. Judging by what I felt of him in the water, he's well-endowed. If I'm not careful, I'll be begging him to skip the foreplay my body needs and fuck me this instant. "And I've only had one partner in my life."

He traces the curve of my breasts and whispers, "I won't hurt you."

I know he won't, but I need him to know how completely out-of-character this is for me. How I've spent the entirety of my life being called an ice queen. A prude. Frigid. How the man who was supposed to love me unconditionally took my loyalty for granted and betrayed me. How I've let no one close to me since.

"I'm scared."

He stills. "Of me?"

"No." My reply is unyielding, just like me—Elinora Iverson, publishing mogul. "I'm scared of how badly I need this."

Taking my statement as his call to action, he moves closer. His lips find my throat once more and claim the expanse of skin from my jawline to the tops of my breasts. His lack of stubble tells me he's clean-shaven, and I wish I could touch his face. Cup his jaw while we kiss.

He doesn't kiss, my brain reminds me. *I wonder why—*

"How's the water?" His question brings me back to the heat coursing through me.

"Fire."

He groans and grips my waistband, tugging it down. "Was hoping you'd say that."

His fingertips brush over my clit as he removes my bikini bottom. He tosses it aside and kisses my neck, flattening his palm on my lower belly. He inches his way lower and cups me before sliding a finger inside my pussy.

My hips jerk with his touch. "Oh God."

"Let me hear you, sugar." He moves in and out of me, massaging me deep inside. Awakening neglected nerve endings and stoking me hotter.

"*Fire.*"

He nips my collarbone and adds a second finger, pumping them into me. His thumb joins the party, rubbing circles on my clit. My thighs fall open and I clench around his fingers, needing more. Needing him deeper, harder, and faster. I crave a release that's so long overdue, I forget what it feels like. He kisses my neck, shoulders, and jawline. His ragged breaths gusting my skin tell me he's enjoying what he's doing to me.

"How's the water?" he grits out, his voice a deep rumble.

"Fire, Sir."

He slides a third finger inside me and increases the pressure on my clit. "Come for me, sugar."

I focus on the sensations building between my legs, loving how his thick, strong fingers fuck me, and his thumb brings me closer and closer to the edge. The room smells like leather and whiskey, and all I can hear is our ragged breathing, my moans, and the wetness coating his fingers as he moves them in and out.

I'd give my soul to taste and touch this faceless stranger. My orgasm hovers in the periphery, needing a final push before I soar. I imagine the celebrities he mentioned, but it's not enough. Their image does nothing to fan the dwindling flames.

So I focus on the one man who I shouldn't fantasize about.

Lincoln Kennedy.

Maybe I'm losing my mind, but I'd give anything to indulge in the fantasy of taking my hunky young employee to bed.

I imagine him with his tall, broad body and gorgeous face. How his deep blue eyes look at me, through me, and within me all at once. I envision myself kissing his full, inviting lips, and writhing beneath the heavy weight of his body.

The decadent visual sends me over the edge. "Oh! Yes!" My hips buck wildly as the moans rip from my throat. "Oh, God... *Lincoln.*"

SIXTEEN

Lincoln

She knows it's me.

I freeze, panic gripping my chest. Despite the darkness, the blindfold, and my attempts to deepen my voice, Elinora figured out my identity.

Which means I'm royally fucked.

"Oh my God. I—I'm so sorry. I didn't mean—" she sputters, gasping for breath. "But you—you said to fantasize about someone who—"

Wait, she was imagining me?

The guy who begged her for a job like an orphan asking for more porridge? Doesn't she notice how I trip on my words like the poster child for awkwardness whenever I'm around her? Elinora Iverson wants *me*? No, that can't be possible. I shake my head to clear it. Not only do I have my fingers inside my boss's perfect wet pussy, but now I'm losing my motherfucking mind.

She definitely said my name though.

Elinora tries again. "He's someone who—"

"Someone who?" My brain, grasping at straws, forces the words from my lips in a cautious whisper.

"You said you'd be anyone I wanted you to be."

"You want him?" I breathe, everything inside me tightening like a coiled spring.

"Yes. I—I've never done anything like this before, so I'm nervous. You told me to come for you, but I couldn't let go until my mind made you *him*. If I'm going to do this, he's who I need you to be." Her words, and the vulnerability in them, steal my breath. My sanity. What's left of my heart.

"Then he's who I'll be," I whisper, as an invisible band squeezes my chest.

Elinora wants me. She wants the real Lincoln, not the pleasure concierge who just made her come. She wants *me* to make her come. I'd give anything to reveal my identity. Pull her close and fulfill all her fantasies while making damn sure she never sought anyone else to do so.

"He's a man who—"

My lips crash down over hers, swallowing her explanation. Wedging her thighs apart, I shift to move on top of her. I cup her jaw with my free hand while the other begins its quest to wring another orgasm from her gorgeous body. Her tight, wet pussy clenches around my fingers, making me groan into the kiss.

My tongue surges into her mouth, tasting and claiming her. I can't remember the last time I kissed a woman on the lips, but it's been *years*. I never kiss my clients. Ever. It goes against all my rules. Self-preservation is critical and—while I may fuck for a living—I reserve my kiss for the rare woman I truly connect with. As pieces of my soul unravel, I realize I'd sell my soul to the fucking Devil to keep kissing *this* woman.

Elinora arches her back, thrusting her pussy onto my fingers. I love how her body responds to my touch and how she gasps and moans for me. But more than that, I love the way she said my name.

She's mine.

My cock jerks in agreement, begging to join the action, but I need to make sure she's ready. She hasn't had sex in years, and I'm a big guy. The last thing I want to do is hurt her.

I break the kiss. "Make me him again and come. *Now*."

She cries out, back arching and pussy spasming as she climaxes. "*Lincoln*."

My name leaves her lips on a moan, and I withdraw my fingers and suck them into my mouth, tasting her sweetness. A growl rumbles in my chest, and I have to force myself not to bury my face between her thighs and lick every fucking inch of her.

"I want—" she begins, gasping.

"Tell me, Elle."

"Please call me Elinora."

"I'll call you whatever you like, as long as you tell me what you want."

"I want you inside me."

I reach up and untie her wrists before snatching the condom I'd tucked in my waistband. I tear open the wrapper and place it in her hand. "Put this on me."

"Are you sure you want to do this?" she whispers.

"Huh?" Is she seriously checking for *my* consent?

"I mean, I just confessed to you that I'm imagining another man. Not to mention, I'm extremely out of practice with anything sexual. Besides, I know this is a job obligation—"

I grab her hand and press it to my cock, dragging it the entire hard length. "Does that feel like an obligation?"

She gasps. "You're huge."

I've heard it hundreds of times but hearing it from Elinora makes me want to roar. Pound my chest. Rear up like a stallion.

"Put the condom on me," I whisper, flexing my hips. "And tell me what you want Lincoln to do to you."

Her grip on my cock tightens. "Everything."

"Tell me."

"I want him to hold me, kiss me, and make love to me."

"What else?" I brush my lips over her ear.

"I want him to fuck me."

The rest of my blood rushes to my cock. "How do you want him to fuck you?" My words are more a vibration than any form of recognizable speech because I'm seconds from fucking her through the mattress. "Tell me."

"I want him to make me feel alive again." Her breath catches. "It's been so long since I've felt . . . anything."

She slides my waistband down, freeing my cock. I take over, shoving the jammers down my thighs and kicking them off. Her soft hands encircle me, and she strokes them up and down.

My eyes roll back into my head. "Condom. Now."

"Yes, Sir." As she rolls the condom on, her grip on my cock almost makes me come. "How do you want me?"

"Loud. Screaming m—" *Shit. I almost said my name.* "Screaming his name."

"I mean what position?" she clarifies.

All of them.

"On your back. Legs wide open for me. Hands on my shoulders at all times."

"What happens if I let go?"

"I'll flip you over and spank you."

Elinora's breath rushes out of her. "What if that's what I want?"

"Do you want Lincoln to spank you?"

"Yes," she whispers.

"Then that's what you'll get."

SEVENTEEN

Elinora

Need. Pure, raw need. It flows through my body, soaking deep into my soul. I've never felt desire like this, and I've certainly never felt this desirable.

"Can we try other positions?" I ask, eager to dive deeper into the feelings my stranger awakened inside me.

"We'll do every position I can bend you into." He brings his lips to my ear. "By the time tonight's over, I'll make you come on my cock so many times, you won't remember your name."

"Oh my God."

"No. Not God, sugar. There's nothing heavenly about what I'm gonna do to you." He presses my knees apart, positioning himself between them. "Hands on my shoulders."

I reach out and tug the mask covering his face. "Take the mask off."

"How do you ask?"

"Please."

"Please, what?"

"Please, Sir," I whisper. "Take it off and kiss me again." His hand brushes mine as he removes it. I stroke my fingertips along his cheeks and jaw like he's the world's most beautiful piece of Braille. "You're perfect."

He exhales roughly, pressing his cheek into my palm. I trace his features, and in this moment, it *is* Lincoln's gorgeous face. I know every curve, every angle, from his thick glossy hair to his jawline and the sexy dimple on his chin. I know his nose, his eyebrows, and those perfect pillowy lips.

"Open your legs wider for me."

My thighs fall open at his command like I was born to serve him. I'm open and vulnerable, yet somehow, I feel comfortable. Safe. *Cherished.* That's right, Elinora Iverson, a woman who trusts no man, trusts this stranger implicitly.

Like I trust Lincoln.

As the line between reality and fantasy blurs, I want the young editor even more.

Would Lincoln be domineering like my stranger, a man who's willing to bring my darkest fantasies to life? Would *he* take me over his knee and spank me? Tie me up and blindfold me, so I need to rely on touch alone? What would it feel like to be alone with Lincoln, our tongues and limbs tangling while we make love? I'll never know, but in my mind, the flipside of the nerdy, hunky gentleman I employ, is a rogue who drips of sin and sex. The thought sends a flood of arousal to my core. While I can't have Lincoln, I *can* allow my stranger to indulge me in the decadent fantasy of him.

And if that's a sin, tell the Devil to take me.

"Hands on my shoulders." His gravelly command makes my heart race.

I slide my fingers along his arms, savoring his bulging muscles. "You feel like a sexy sculpture," I murmur, finally gripping his shoulders like he commanded.

His breath rushes out of him. "And your touch feels like heaven. Now wrap your legs around me, sugar." His hand brushes my lower belly as he reaches between us and lines himself up, the broad head of his cock barely pressing inside me. "How's the water, Elinora?"

EIGHTEEN

Lincoln

It's the moment of truth. I hold my breath and await Elinora's reply. *Please don't tell me to stop. Please don't tell—*

"Warm, Sir."

Harps and trumpets be damned, her breathy whisper is more beautiful than a choir of angels, the Vatican, and the fucking Sistine Chapel.

I press forward, easing my cock inside her. As I fill her, inch by rock-hard inch, she rewards me with a throaty moan.

"The water?" I grit out through a clenched jaw.

"Still warm." She gasps and digs her nails into my shoulders.

"Don't let go of me," I command, drawing my hips back until I'm nearly free of her. I surge forward with a groan. She cries out as her tight, wet pussy takes me to the hilt. "Just like that, sugar. Take me."

"Oh, fuck." She tightens her legs around the back of my thighs. "You're so thick."

Pulling back until I'm nearly free of her body's grip, I seal my lips over hers in a slow, tender dance. While I take my time exploring Elinora's pretty little mouth, her kiss is ravenous—full of hunger and need. I rock my hips, teasing her pussy with just the head of my cock. She bucks beneath me and digs her heels into my thighs. Moaning, she knots her hands in my hair, deepening our kiss.

Esme was right—Elinora *is* a river, churning with passion, need, and emotion. Swelling past her breaking point, she flows over and through me, pulling me beneath the surface until she's all I know.

Even though my identity is still a mystery, *I'm* the man she wants and needs. And so help me God, I'm gonna bust through her dam, and make *damn* sure my plunge into her waters causes a motherfucking flood.

She cries out as I give her a powerful thrust.

"How's the water?"

She drags her nails down my back and fists my ass cheeks. "Fire."

"Hands," I remind her, rolling my hips. Instead of gripping my shoulders, she pinches my ass. Hard. I deliver a few punishing thrusts before pulling out.

"Why're you stopping?"

I pivot into a seated position and pull her across my lap instead of answering. My palm lands on her plump ass cheeks with a loud crack. A shocked cry leaves her lips, making me hope it wasn't too much, too fast. In the pitch black, I'm blind to her body's cues, so I can't use the pinking of her skin to gauge her response.

"How's the water?"

"Warm." She squirms against my legs.

Holding Elinora in place with an arm across her shoulder blades, I caress her back, hips, and thighs, my fingertips lingering on her soft bottom. God, *this ass*. I want to stroke, squeeze, and bite it. Clutch her hips while I slam into her from behind. The sultry little vixen wiggles in my lap, so I deliver another swat.

I'm sure I'll look back on this moment with the shock it

deserves, but right now, my conscience is nowhere to be found. Reason and caution surrendered to lust. I lose a little more control each minute that passes with my sexy boss naked in my lagoon. Her wanton moans spur me on, unleashing my dominant side.

I pull the elastic from the end of her braid and unravel it, running my fingers through her silken hair. Even damp, it's softer and more fragrant than I could've imagined. I gather the strands into a ponytail at the nape of her neck and gently tug her head back.

"How's the water?"

"Fire."

With one hand knotted in her hair, I slide two fingers into her pussy and stroke them in and out. I desperately want to be inside her, but she's testing the waters here, and I don't want to stop the flow.

I yank her head back and add a third finger.

She thrusts her hips to meet my strokes. "Oh, yes." I withdraw my hand, and she writhes in my lap. "Please don't stop—"

I smack her ass once more. Hard.

"*Lincoln . . .*"

My cock jerks, throbbing painfully. Hearing my name rip from her throat is the highlight of my life. Too bad I'm nothing more than a fantasy in her mind. How much further could we take this if it were real? Elinora and Lincoln, two people with a chemistry that crackles in the surrounding air. How much harder could I push her? How much louder would she scream without the smoke and mirrors?

Guilt settles in the pit of my stomach as the reality of what I'm doing comes into focus. It's bad enough my cock earns me an income—now I'm a fraud too. What kind of man knowingly deceives a woman for a fuck?

Moaning, she churns her hips in my lap. My palm collides with her ass cheeks.

"Fire."

Clenching my fingers in her hair, I deliver a few hard spanks, varying the intensity and placement. Her moans grow louder with each one until I can't fucking take it anymore. Flipping Elinora onto her back, I yank her thighs apart and settle between them, rubbing and stroking her pussy.

Her arousal coats her thighs and my fingers. I suck them into my mouth once more, growling low in my throat. "I fucking love the taste of you, Elinora."

She thrusts her hips upward. "I need you."

"I'm right here."

"Hold me and make love to me. Slowly."

My breath catches as her whispered plea cracks my heart wide open. "I've got what you need, sugar."

NINETEEN

Elinora

My ass is on fire, but that's nothing compared to the desperate ache between my thighs. The place I'd give anything to have the real Lincoln fill. My stranger grips my hips, easing his thick cock inside me, filling and stretching me to my limit. With his ragged breaths gusting my neck, he moves slowly, just like I asked. Since I can't have Lincoln, this warm, strong man is the next best thing. I wrap my arms around him and clutch his back, pulling him closer.

"How's the water?" His gritty tone rasps against my ear.

"Hot."

"Hot's not an option." He rolls his hips. "Try again."

"I want something between warm and fire."

"Tell me," he whispers, kissing my neck. "I want to hear you say it."

"I want . . ." I tighten my legs around him. "Lincoln."

His lips meet mine in a tender kiss. My tongue darts out, twining and stroking against his. He groans and picks up the pace of his thrusts, his cock rubbing places deep inside me. I'm no virgin, but I might as well be, because this feels nothing like the sex I've had in my lifetime. It's deeper. Darker. More intense than I could've imagined.

In my mind, Lincoln is the one taking me higher and higher, his thrusts growing more urgent as I near my release. He follows my body's cues, cradling me close, giving me everything I didn't know I needed. Maybe it isn't fair, wrong even, to give life to my fantasy, but in this moment, I don't give a flying fuck.

Closing my eyes, I let go of everything. All the angst, the self-damnation, the fear, and uncertainty. I need this release, this freedom to spread my wings and soar. I'm no angel, but thanks to my Lincoln fantasy, I'm flying among them.

"I'm gonna come." I gasp, clawing his back.

"Let me hear you, sugar. Scream for me."

He grinds his hips in a powerful driving rhythm and crushes his lips to mine once more. The hunger in his kiss sends me hurtling into ecstasy. He swallows my scream as the orgasm slams through me, stealing what's left of my senses. He keeps moving, pumping his hips harder and faster, all while kissing my lips with a reverence that feels like worship. No one has ever kissed me like this. Or made love to me this way. Ever.

"*Lincoln.*" As I lose myself in another climax, I know I can't live without this faceless stranger who ravages and cherishes me in pitch darkness. A man who, when I projected my deepest fantasy onto him, pulled me closer and gave me warmth instead of leaving me in the cold.

"Oh, fuck." He groans, his fingertips tightening on my hips. I feel his cock jerk and pulse before he collapses on top of me. Ragged gasps and reverent whispers of my name leave his lips as he pulls my body close. "Elinora, you're an angel."

Tears spring to my eyes at his declaration. I try to hold them back, but that dam's been broken. My physical climax heralded an emotional release so intense, I feel like I'm drowning.

TWENTY

Lincoln

If mind-fuckery was an Olympic sport, I'd hold a gold medal in every event. In every arena. Since the dawn of the games. I'm beyond fucked physically. And mentally. A sob wracks Elinora's frame, and it's clear I fucked her too.

As guilt knifes my soul, I tighten my arms around her. "Shh . . . don't cry, angel." I run my fingers through her silken hair and pull her even closer. She needs to be held, and *I* need to hold her.

How could I be so fucking stupid? I should've expected this. Sex without strings doesn't work for everyone—especially not a woman who has only ever slept with one man. I'm no better than her cheating ex-husband. I cheated her too, and that suffocating realization burns me. As her shoulders shake with her river of tears, I hope I drown in them.

"I'm sorry," I whisper.

"You did nothing wrong."

Oh, but I did. My masquerade performance hurt her. I lied to her. I've never felt dirtier than I do right now.

"Why're you crying?" I ask, even though I already know her answer.

"Because it was a lot."

"Too much?"

"No, just a lot." She burrows closer to me, pressing her damp cheeks to my chest. "I'm sorry."

"You have nothing to apologize for."

Her breath hitches. "I projected someone else onto you. It wasn't fair to you or to him."

I squeeze my eyes shut. "We can handle it."

"Yeah, but I can't." A whimper leaves her chest. More tears. Another sob.

I've seen plenty of women become emotional after sex, but never like this. As *my* eyes start to burn, I know I'm in over my head.

"Let's get you cleaned up," I whisper. "Come float in the lagoon with me."

"I don't think I can walk right now."

"I'll carry you." In my head I say a silent prayer that my legs don't give out after what was, no exaggeration, the best sex of my life. "Your job is to relax."

My orgasm was like nothing I've ever experienced. I'm supposed to give pleasure—not receive it. My time at The River isn't about me, it's about the women I serve. Over the years, I've mastered the art of climaxing without ejaculation. Now, the only client who can still force my release is my friend Maya, and *that* is solely for instructional purposes. I can't do it with anyone else. Maybe it's because my profession makes me feel dirty. My head, heart, and cock are all on different pages—of entirely different books. But with Elinora tonight, everything converged as one. I lost myself inside her. I don't think I'll ever get that part of me back, nor do I want to. Little does she know, she owns me.

"Your body felt like heaven, Elinora."

Her breath leaves her in a rush. "Heaven's no place for a woman like me."

"I hate to break this to you, but somebody'd better give you a harp, because you just brought me there, angel."

"Don't say that. I'm not an angel. Or a saint."

The self-disgust in her tone mirrors mine. She and I fit together like two halves of a puzzle. With our haphazard pieces and inability to see the picture we create, we're perfectly imperfect, and scrambled as fuck.

"Angel or demon, sinner or saint, we've all got a mix of heaven and hell in our blood."

She wipes her eyes. "Yeah, well, I'm pretty sure my blood runs hotter than most. I seem to lack that heavenly balance you speak of."

"The Devil's in the details, angel."

TWENTY-ONE

Elinora

The Devil's in the details.

I've heard that saying before. But from whom? Freya? Myles? Before I can ponder it further, my stranger scoops me off the bed and carries me across the room.

He presses something on the wall which beeps. The door to the lagoon slides open. Now it's pitch black in there too, but the rush of the waterfall gives me my bearings. He navigates around the pool to the steps and eases us beneath the water's surface, settling on an underwater ledge.

Facing him, I straddle his hips and rest my head on his shoulder. While the ache in my heart throbs deeper, the warm saltwater laps at my skin and soothes the sting between my thighs.

Neither one of us speaks. We don't have to—our bodies do the talking. Cradling me close, he clings to me, gently stroking my back. I soak up his warmth and melt into his embrace. But God, how I wish it was the real Lincoln who thawed me.

TWENTY-TWO

Lincoln

My Sunday morning coffee tastes bitter, and I can't shake the cloud of guilt that blankets me.

After spending Friday night with Elinora, my Saturday shift at The River was intolerable. How the fuck am I supposed to do my job if I can't close my eyes without thinking of her? Better yet, how can I be a pleasure concierge if my cock refuses to cooperate?

I've never had trouble getting—or keeping—an erection. Ever. Multiple rounds? Bring it. I can hold off my orgasm and suppress ejaculation. When Maya makes me come, I'm quick to recover. Not only is a refractory period unnecessary for my anatomy's repeat performance, it's all but nonexistent. My stamina and blood flow allows me to fuck all night. That's why Esme loves me so much. I'm a sex machine, and if there's one thing I've learned at The River, it's that sex sells.

Imagine my embarrassment last night when I couldn't get it up for the pretty redhead who threw herself at me.

If having my cock malfunction wasn't bad enough, a wave of nausea slammed through me, and I nearly puked on her feet. Esme sent me home after that. I called off for tonight's shift, citing nausea. While I'm not currently nauseous, the thought of being inside another woman—Maya included—makes my stomach lurch. I'd rather not humiliate myself again. I need to get my shit together before Thursday. Esme won't buy a week-long stomach bug excuse.

I swallow another gulp of bitter coffee and settle on the couch with my laptop. I've got some editing to do if I want to keep to the schedule I've set for myself. Too bad I don't have a psychological thriller to work on. Nope, I'm balls deep in an angsty erotic romance. The hero and heroine share an undeniable chemistry, but their sex scenes need some serious attention.

Is any part of my existence *not* ironic?

Like it's been doing fifty-seven times an hour since Friday, my mind drifts back to Elinora. Her warm, soft body and how tightly her pussy gripped me. The way she arched her back and thrust her hips to meet mine. How she raked her nails down my back and screamed my name when she orgasmed. Four times.

I glance at my lap as my cock stands at immediate attention, stretching the fabric of my plaid pajama pants. "Oh, so now you're not broken? Where were you last night?" It twitches at my question as if to say *I did you a favor*. "You've done me enough favors." It twitches again. "You know what? Fuck you too, bro."

My cock still works, but I'm clearly going insane. *That* concrete was mixed when I slept with my boss, poured when I lost control and allowed myself to orgasm, and it hardened to stone when I fell for her afterwards.

The way she cried in my arms and melted into me like I was her soul's only source of warmth, fucking destroyed me. How she gave me the gift of her body and fell asleep with her head on my shoulder in the lagoon, burned me alive. And when she whispered my name in her sleep as I laid her on the dais and covered her with a blanket . . . that shattered me. And freed a piece of myself I've kept locked away for years.

But I lied to her. I deceived Elinora's mind, her body, her heart, and her soul. God knows there's no freedom in deception. Then again, I am not a free man.

TWENTY-THREE

Elinora

I PEER ACROSS THE TABLE AT FREYA AND SIP MY MIMOSA instead of answering her barrage of questions. Sunday brunch is our weekly tradition—one of the few things I look forward to.

She leans in. "Well?"

"I'm thinking."

"You do too much of that." She twists a golden curl around her finger.

"I'm starting to think I don't do *enough*."

"You've done nothing but think since yesterday morning. You never came to our room at The River, didn't return my calls last night, and I'm *still* waiting for details." She reaches across the table and squeezes my hand. "Talk to me, Elle."

"It was . . ." I draw a shaky breath and blink back the moisture filling my eyes. *No more tears.* I'm done crying for something I can't have. "Intense."

"Good intense, or bad intense?"

"It was the best sex of my life."

Her hazel eyes widen. "Then what the hell's your problem?"

I want more. I imagined him as our coworker. "It was a fantasy."

Freya runs a hand over her face. "That's the friggin point."

"He was so . . . I mean, I just . . ." I squeeze my eyes shut. "I wish he was real."

"Sweetie, judging by the way you're walking, you didn't *imagine* him inside you. He *is* real." She waggles her eyebrows. "Was he super hot?"

"I don't know."

She blinks. "How can you have fantasy sex and not know if the guy's hot?"

"I couldn't see him, Freya. The room was pitch black, and he blindfolded me. He called it sensory deprivation."

"Holy fuck. I'm surprised you went for that. Did he tie you up?"

"Briefly, but then he untied me. Based on *feel* alone, his body was gorgeous, but he could've had the face of a donkey for all I knew." *Except his face felt gorgeous too.*

"How the hell did you make that work?"

"He told me he'd be anyone I wanted him to be, so I imagined him as someone else." I gulp the rest of my mimosa. "And now I'm feeling the aftershocks of it."

Her gaze narrows on my face. "Oh. My. God."

"What?"

"You envisioned Clark Kent, didn't you?"

Damn you and your intuition, Freya. As all my blood rushes to my cheeks, I curse myself for telling her I'm attracted to Lincoln.

A mile-wide grin overtakes her face. "No wonder you're all fucked up."

I roll my eyes. "You're not helping."

"What's the matter? The Lincoln fantasy lived up to your expectations?" She shimmies her hips in a seated salsa dance. "And now you want *more*?"

I hide my face. There's no sense trying to keep things from her —she'll figure it out, eventually. She always does.

Freya pulls my hands away from my face. "Just so you know, we're not leaving this table until I get every detail. And you know damn well I'll follow you home if you try to evade me."

"I hate you sometimes," I mutter with a smirk.

"It's mutual. Now start talking."

HOURS—AND FAR MORE DETAILS THAN I EXPECTED TO SHARE— later, Freya and I lounge on my couch eating ice cream. The pint of dulce de leche was doomed the second we opened my freezer.

"You know," she begins, licking some caramel off her finger. "Maybe you could go back to the club and see someone different. Esme has plenty of concierges there. She's bound to have someone who can push you further without reminding you of Lincoln."

"What do you mean?"

"I mean, test your limits, and try something new. Maybe play with someone else—with the lights on—and keep Clark out of the equation. It would be a lot harder to picture Lincoln Kennedy when you're staring into the eyes of someone like Darius."

"I don't think I could handle him." Darius is drop dead gorgeous. But he's also the tallest, most muscular man I've ever seen. "He seems intense."

"From what I've heard, he *is* intense." She grins and nudges me. "You might surprise yourself with what you can handle. It doesn't have to be Darius. I play with several guys, depending on my mood."

"Wait, several guys at the *same time*?"

She snorts. "No, I don't think I could handle group sex. Talk about sensory overload. What I mean is, I'm usually with Rocco if he's not bartending. I'm comfortable with him and we've become good friends. If he's not available, I play with Gideon, who's also a pleasure concierge. Occasionally, I'll play with another club member, instead of one of the men who works there. Like I said, it depends on my mood. Variety is the spice of life, Elle. You should explore your options. You said the spanking turned you on, right?"

I flush. "Yes."

"Well, push yourself further. Clark Kent's a gentleman, and your stranger reminded you of him. I say you skip the gentleman and take a beast for a spin."

"I dunno," I murmur, chewing my lip.

"Like I said, talk to Esme and see who's available. Maybe you'll like it, or maybe you'll hate it. Who knows? But at least this way, you'll have a *face* to work with. Maybe then you can separate your feelings better."

I take another spoonful of ice cream and ponder her suggestion.

She grins. "Or, you and Clark Kent can experiment with your sizzling chemistry." At my raised brow, she adds, "Why don't you let yourself have a fling, and work him out of your system? That's my vote, anyway."

I hold up a hand. "No. That's not an option. I'm his boss. *And* he's a decade younger than me. It would be inappropriate on so many levels. Besides, what would he possibly want with a bitter old divorcee like myself? I've got six carousels' worth of baggage." I shake my head. "Oh wait, now I remember. He'd want my money like all the other men out there. That's worth some fucking luggage, isn't it? Well, guess what? I'm done with that shit. There's no way in hell I'd open myself up to another Charles."

"I was going to say he'd want your bitter old vagina, but if you wanna make this about luggage, that's cool too." She wags her brows. "Judging by how big and strong he looks, I'm sure Clark Kent can pack a suitcase real full."

Ice cream shoots out my nose. We both cackle like idiots until tears stream down our faces.

"Where did I ever find you, Freya Thorne?"

She snorts. "Should've been a brothel, am I right?"

I elbow her. "Or a sex club."

"So . . . when are you going back for more?"

TWENTY-FOUR

Lincoln

I STARE INTO MY CUP. I'M SURE IT WASN'T INTENTIONAL ON the barista's part, but my latte's foam resembles a skull. I hope it's not an omen for today. More than a little creeped out, I snatch a wooden stirrer and swirl it around until there's no discernable design.

There. That's better.

"You afraid someone put arsenic in there or something?"

The male voice at my shoulder makes me jump and nearly drop my cup. I whirl to face my friend Garrett Casey. "Dude. Don't sneak up on people this early in the morning."

"I didn't. I said your name twice." Amusement glints in his golden eyes. "Haven't you ever heard of situational awareness?"

It's seven-thirty, and Compass Roasters is already bustling. I was so deep in my thoughts I never heard him address me.

"Yeah," I say lamely, snapping a lid onto my cup. "I guess I'm a little distracted."

"You think?" He chuckles and points to my glasses. "Keep it up, and some asshole will mug you for those. Can't do shit if you can't see, am I right?"

"Truth." I'm not exactly worried about someone jumping me for my designer frames, but clearly, Garrett thinks it could happen. I shake my head. "You really take hypervigilance to a whole new level, don't you?"

"Guilty as charged." He shrugs. "But I have my reasons."

"Why? Did someone steal something from you?"

"You have no fucking idea." A shadow darkens his expression for a fleeting moment. Just as quickly, it gives way to a smirk. "So . . . how's the new job?"

"I don't even know where to start."

He gestures to the door. "Walk with me."

When Garrett Casey tells you to do something, you do it. Unless you're an idiot. Since I have at least three functioning brain cells most days—except for when I fucked my boss on Friday—I follow him outside like the good, obedient guy I am.

I keep pace with him as we head toward our office building. "What's up?"

"She's a tough cookie, but she softens once you get to know her."

"She's . . . something."

Garrett sips his coffee. "I saw her at The River on Friday night."

I stop short and pivot to face him. "What were you doing there? Don't you have rehearsal?" He scored the lead in a Broadway production slated to open in November. How he juggles owning a business and his acting gig, I'll never know.

"Esme asked my lady to be the event photographer. She's not comfortable going there alone, so I played bodyguard."

"I didn't see you at the bar."

"Because I don't drink. It's never a good idea to put my ass on a barstool."

"Right. Sorry," I mumble, feeling like a tool for forgetting he's a recovering alcoholic.

"No worries. So, yeah, I roamed around the place, doing my typical lurk in the shadows and observe routine." He studies my face, his eerie eyes burning a hole through my skull. "Anywho, I *observed* you two going into the same private lagoon . . ."

He already knows, so it doesn't make sense to lie about what happened. Besides, I don't think it's possible for anyone to be dishonest with Garrett. His presence alone feels like truth serum.

I release a heavy sigh as we resume our walk. "Affirmative."

"I saw your masquerade getup. Did she know it was you?"

"Nope, and I'd like to keep it that way."

"How'd you manage that?" He sips his coffee, then steps out of the way of a woman pushing a stroller.

"Lagoon Seven is one of the ones we use for sensory deprivation floats."

He nods in understanding. "Did anything happen?" When I hesitate, he adds, "Not that it's any of my business, obviously, but I consider Elinora a friend." His eyes lock with mine, and the warning in them is crystal clear. "I'm very protective of the people I care about."

"Everything was consensual."

"I'm not doubting that. You're a good dude." He rubs his jaw. "I just don't want to see her get hurt again."

"I'm not trying to hurt her, Garrett."

"Are you aware of her past? I'm referring to the part about her philandering dick of an ex-husband," he clarifies as we reach our office building.

"Yeah. She mentioned his multiple affairs."

"Did she give you any other details?"

"Not really."

"Her trauma goes deeper than just being cheated on. It's not my place to elaborate, but you need to keep in mind that Elinora values honesty above all things."

"It's not like I set out to lie to her. I didn't have a choice. My situation's pretty complicated. I, uh, had to leave some details out in the name of self-preservation," I mumble, following him into the building.

We swipe our badges and cross the lobby in silence.

Garrett presses the elevator call button before turning to face me. "A lie of omission is still a lie."

GARRETT'S WORDS HAVE ECHOED IN MY MIND ALL MORNING. Even the mother of all pep talks I gave myself in the restroom earlier didn't prepare me for the cloak of uneasiness his message—and my guilt—draped over my shoulders. After Friday night, nothing could've prepared me to find Elinora in the breakroom, bent over in front of the coffee station, rummaging through boxes of tea. I still can't believe she doesn't have someone else fetch her drinks. As I stare at the luscious ass on display, the guilt dissipates, and my primal instincts roar to life.

Mine.

She's wearing a red dress and black stilettos that make my heart race. Her long platinum locks fall over her shoulders. I clench my fists at the memory of knotting my fingers in her hair while I slapped her plump, gorgeous ass.

I blink a few times and try to breathe. I can't just gawk in the doorway like a dopey Peeping Tom when I came in here to ask her a question. Funny, I can't seem to remember what that question was.

Or my own name.

I clear my throat.

Too loudly because she looks over her shoulder at me. "Good morning, Mr. Kennedy."

"Good morning."

Elinora straightens and opens a tin of teas. "How was your weekend?"

"Busy. Yours?"

Her breath catches. "Memorable."

The rest of my blood rushes to my cock. I can't breathe or think, so I point to the teabag she selected and try for small talk. "Myles likes it dirty sometimes. How about you?"

She narrows her eyes. "Excuse me?"

Fuck.

"Your chai. Espresso. Uh . . . the chai. You have a chai tea bag. It has espresso when it's dirty." I shake my head to clear it. "Myles likes chai in his espresso. I mean, espresso in his chai. Sometimes. Not always, though. Makes him jittery."

Her lips twitch with the hint of a smirk. "Did *you* have espresso this morning?"

"Yes." The barista added three shots to my latte.

"I can tell."

Not only am I stumbling over my words—far worse than usual—but she's making it known she notices my babbling idiocy. Great.

I try again. "I drink too much."

"There're services to help with that. I can get you the information if you'd like. We have alcohol treatment programs offered as part of our benefits package. I know I mentioned the three-month probation, but I'd be willing to start your coverage sooner if you need help."

"Coffee, I mean. Too much caffeine. But I like whiskey too." I rake a hand through my hair and beg my brain to function. "I only drink whiskey on weekends."

"Are you all right?" She peers up at me.

"No. I'm half left."

Elinora bursts out laughing and clutches my arm, stealing what's left of my sanity. "Thank you. I needed a laugh this morning. And to answer your question, I've never had it dirty. But who knows? I might enjoy it."

Oh, you enjoyed it, sugar. I blink a few times and open and close my mouth.

"I'm referring to a dirty chai, Mr. Kennedy."

Right. Tea. I shake my head. "You should try it sometime—it's delicious." *Like you.*

She nods. "How's the manuscript going?"

Her question jogs my memory. "That's what I was hoping to discuss when you have time."

"I have time right now," she says, squeezing some honey into her mug.

Watching her stir the honey into her chai, I nearly come when I imagine licking it off her nipples. Then she adds a splash of cream and a sprinkle of cinnamon, and I have to clench my jaw to keep from moaning. I've never had this visceral of a response to a woman. Every little thing she does, stokes the lust burning in my blood.

Elinora eyes me expectantly. "Does now work for you?"

I nod, because if I speak, I'm afraid I'll tell her how much I want her.

"Good. Come to my office."

I trail behind her and recite a few Hail Marys on our way down the hall. I haven't been to confession since I was a teen in Catholic school. Something tells me that even if I read the Bible front to back as penance—and say every prayer known to man—it won't be enough to absolve me of my sins. The more Elinora's heavenly ass sways as she walks, the less I care about redemption.

She gestures to a chair in front of her desk. "Sit."

Her authoritative tone reminds me who is in control of the monarchy right now. While I was king on Friday night, bending her to my will while I kissed, spanked, and fucked her, now we're back in her castle. Making her way to the wheeled leather throne, my sexy queen settles and sips her chai.

I ease into the seat she indicated and remove my glasses to wipe a smudge on my shirt. "I hate not being able to see," I mutter, meeting her expectant gaze.

"Did you ever try contacts?"

Shit. "No, uh, I have dry eyes."

"They make drops for that." She reaches for a pen and pad of paper. "What did you want to discuss?"

"I finished *Stranded at the Pub*, which was fabulous, but now I'm working on *Bound Hearts*. Did the previous editor do any kind of developmental edits?"

"As far as I know, yes. Why do you ask?"

"There are some issues." While I flew through the first manuscript—likely because it was set in Ireland, and I fucking love all things Irish—the second project brought my rhythm to a grinding halt. Part of me wonders if she stuck it in my lineup to test me.

"Like what?" She scrawls something on the page.

"The manuscript isn't ready for line edits."

Elinora cocks her head to the side and sets down her pen. "Oh? How come?"

"It's riddled with plot inconsistencies, unnecessary scenes, among other serious issues."

She sips her chai. "Like what?"

"Well, for starters, it feels like the book was haphazardly converted to a dual point of view. Almost like the hero's POV was thrown in there at the last minute. The heroine is outstanding. She's smart, strong, and confident. Her flaws are relatable and well-developed, and her conflict and motivations make sense. From a man's perspective, she's easy to fall for. On the other hand, I can't imagine *any* woman falling for the hero."

"I'm listening."

"He's obnoxious and far too misogynistic. The book explores BDSM, but the author clearly didn't do her research. It misconstrues the principles of dominance and submission in a way that's not only potentially offensive to the BDSM community, but it borders on dangerous. While the hero is supposed to be dominant, he lacks *any* likable qualities. He's not an alpha, he's a callous dick. His motivations aren't clear, and there's a disconnect between his actions and how they relate to the conflict. His emotional development feels flat compared to the heroine. I understand it's intended as an enemies-to-lovers romance, but aside from sex, there's no love. The happily ever after, if you can even call it that, doesn't feel earned. If the author insists on having a dual point of view narrative, the hero's perspective needs *serious* work."

She graces me with a smile. "You're brutal."

"No, I'm *honest*," I say, shaking my head. Guilt pools in my stomach as Garrett's words drift through my mind again. I clear my throat and force my brain to follow suit. "I can make the words pretty with my line edits. But in my opinion, for whatever that's worth, if you publish this developmentally flawed as is, you'd be making a colossal mistake. Forgive me for saying this but given what I know of you and your standards, I'm shocked you offered a book deal for this project."

"I didn't." Elinora squeezes her eyes shut. "I stupidly promoted your predecessor to acquiring editor last year. My gut told me she wasn't capable, but the imprint was in such outrageous demand, my romance acquisition team couldn't handle the volume of submissions. Cindy had been with me a long time, so I trusted her to make quality decisions. We've worked with that author in the past, and her platform is well established, so I allowed this deal to fly under my radar. Clearly, that was a mistake."

I nod in understanding. In my experience, many acquiring editors have the authority to make book deals, which is my absolute dream job. Maybe it's my ego, or the appeal of the inherent power in the position, but I'd love nothing more than to be a literary gatekeeper. Most publishing houses have some purchasing hierarchy in place, but Iverson Press is an independent corporation which means Elinora can run it however the fuck she wants.

I smile at the gorgeous mogul in front of me. "Well, the good news is that it's not a lost cause. With a rigorous developmental edit, I believe I can fix the issues."

She perks up. "Do you have suggestions for improvement?"

"God yes. I marked the entire thing up with comments, but I didn't want to overstep my bounds and send it back to the agent without first running it by you. I've worked with the agent before, but I haven't developed a rapport with this author, so the last thing I want to do is piss them—or you—off."

Elinora smiles. "I appreciate you coming to me first, and I'd like to read through your comments and suggestions to get a better understanding of the issues here. Depending on the amount of work involved, we may need to push out the publication date. I hate missing deadlines, but I won't allow a poorly written book to reach my readers."

"The book isn't what I'd call poorly written," I begin, feeling a twinge of compassion for the author. "Her writing style is fluid, and she has a strong voice. The story itself could work, *if* we make extensive revisions to the hero—and the sex scenes."

Elinora raises a brow. "The sex scenes?"

Hearing the words leave her lips makes my cock twitch. "Yes."

"Please elaborate."

"Well, as you'll see, my comments are specific, but like I said earlier, the author didn't research the BDSM lifestyle enough. Also, the action is very repetitive. It feels like they're having the same sex over and over again. I fought the urge to rewrite an entire scene because it was not only offensive, but boring."

"I've never heard of a sex scene referred to as boring."

"You haven't read this one yet. Honestly, if it were possible to reach through the computer and throw a thesaurus at the author, I'd do it."

She chuckles. "Is that so?"

I meet her gaze. "Put it this way, she used the term 'throbbing cock' six times in a single scene." Her face and neck flush, and I realize I should stop talking. Except my brain pushes words out of my mouth against my better judgment. "I mean, there are plenty of alternatives like pulse, twitch, or even jerk." My runaway jaw keeps accelerating, "As someone who has one, I can attest that it does *much* more than throb."

Her mouth drops open, and my verbal freight train comes to a hard stop.

Fuck.

For a moment we just stare across the desk at one another. Heat infuses her features, and it doesn't take a genius to figure out why she's squirming in her leather throne. She definitely remembers our night together. Her lips part on rapid, shaky breaths and I can see the outline of her hardened nipples through her satin dress. I'd bet her panties are damp now, saturated with the sweet arousal I'm dying to lick from her. Too bad she doesn't know it was really me who touched her. Kissed her. Spanked her. Thrust deep inside her. I shift in my seat at the memory, and it doesn't go unnoticed. Her pupils dilate, and her tongue darts out to lick her lips.

"Thank you for the visual, Mr. Kennedy."

"I didn't mean to be inapprop—"

She clears her throat. "I'll read through your comments and approach the agent accordingly, as it would be better received coming from me."

"I'll forward you the manuscript with my edits when I get back to my desk." I rake a hand through my hair. "Listen, I'm not trying to ruffle anyone's feathers, and I'm sorry if I'm overstepping my bounds. I just want to make sure we—uh—*you* publish the best possible book. I'd hate to anger the BDSM community or tarnish Iverson Melt's reputation. Especially when the issues are easily remedied. I'm happy to communicate with the author directly if she requests clarification. Also, we shouldn't need to push out the publication date, as I'm confident I can get the work done before your deadline."

"Never apologize for having my company's best interests at heart." Her gaze burns into me. "That is something I value deeply in an employee. I love the romance genre, which is why I dedicate so much of my resources to Iverson Melt. Unfortunately, my schedule doesn't allow me to give each manuscript the attention I'd like, so it's essential to maintain a quality staff. You surprise me every day, Mr. Kennedy. You've already impressed me with your tenacity, and now you're guarding the company's assets?"

"I'm just doing my job, Ms. Iverson."

"You're doing a damn good job." She rewards me with a toe-curling smile. "If your performance continues on this trajectory, you'll make that position permanent in no time."

Her praise makes me feel like I've won a gold medal. She trusts me and my editorial opinion enough to hear what I have to say, which is more than anyone's ever given me.

Sister Fitzgibbons never wanted my side of the story when Chris Boutros told her I'd vandalized the church. In actuality, I was in the wrong place at the wrong time, but she took the situation at face value. He was the one who spray-painted the chapel and carved dirty words into the pews one drunken Saturday night. But *I* was expelled for the damage he caused. I can still hear her voice after all these years. *Why should anyone listen to you? You're a disgrace. You'll never amount to anything, Kennedy.* Father DeAngelis was just as bad because he took her word as gospel. *You're an embarrassment to our parish and your family.*

I beat back the ghosts of my past and meet Elinora's gaze. "Thank you for giving me a chance."

"Thank you for covering my ass—I mean, my back."

"The pleasure's all mine, Ms. Iverson."

TWENTY-FIVE

Elinora

Lincoln's smile makes my inner muscles clench. If he had any idea I screamed *his* name while having sex with a stranger, I'd die.

I knew it would be difficult to face him after conjuring his image Friday night, but I didn't expect it to be *this* difficult. Here I'd thought indulging myself in the fantasy could work him out of my system. Nope. Now I want him even more.

He's wearing a crisp white dress shirt which conforms to the muscles of his shoulders and arms. His marine blue tie matches his eyes. *God, those eyes.* I'd give anything to stare into them while he makes love to me. I slide my hands beneath my thighs to keep from grabbing his silk tie and pulling him across my desk.

Rising, he points over his shoulder. "I'm going to head back to my cubicle now." Then, he smiles again, and I want to fall at his feet.

With his glossy black hair, oceanic eyes, and perfect teeth, my young editor is a masterpiece.

"Mm-hmm." My gaze lingers on his ass as he leaves the room, and I make a mental note to stash some spare panties in my office.

In one encounter he transformed from endearingly nervous and stumbling, to pure confidence. Intelligence and self-assuredness are huge turn-ons for me, but Lincoln discussing his work was the sexiest thing I've ever witnessed. There's no question he knows his shit. He'd already impressed me with the sample line edits he'd done. Hearing him hash out a book's developmental issues was intellectual foreplay. He claims his strength is in line editing, but I disagree. This man is the total package. Not only is he looking after my company's reputation, but he has my best interests at heart. The fact that, despite his ego and abilities, he came to me first, earns him my professional respect.

I force a few calming breaths and sip my chai. My email chimes, drawing my attention to the computer. Lincoln's name in my inbox makes my heart race.

Ms. Iverson,

Attached please find my annotated manuscript for Bound Hearts. *I've made extensive edits and suggestions for revision. If you need clarification, please let me know.*

Again, I apologize for overstepping my bounds, but there was no way I could let these developmental issues slide. Thank you for your willingness to hear me out, and I appreciate any and all feedback you have.

Best,

Lincoln

I download the attachment while the message behind his words echoes in my head. *Thank you for hearing and trusting me.* I can't imagine anyone *not* listening to this young man. I hardly trust a soul, yet I trust his assessment and I haven't even read his notations.

I open the document and smile at his first comment, which takes place midway through the third paragraph and references a block of text he'd highlighted.

I'd consider making this your book's opening line instead.

"Don't tell me I left the door unlocked again." has far more impact than, "I parked my car in the employee garage at work." Think about the questions in your readers' minds. Does Sara have a habit of not locking her door? Which door does she mean? Does she live in a dangerous neighborhood? What's making her question herself? These are the things that make your reader look for answers. Not someone parking in a garage. Public transportation notwithstanding, everyone parks. We all go to work. I want to know what's got her hackles raised about not locking the door. Hook me and pull me in. You've already got the words, just move them around. Also, the vivid description of the parking garage is excellent. I can almost hear the water dripping from the rafters and the jingling of her keys. Great job.

I'm already in love with his editing style and we're only talking about doors, keys, and parking garages. How the hell am I going to handle the throbbing cocks and sex scenes he referenced?

I've been waiting all day for this.

After stripping out of my work clothes, I adjust my reading light and slide between layers of luxe Egyptian cotton. Goosebumps bloom with the brush of the cool fabric against my bare skin.

Then again, I've had goosebumps for hours.

I spent the afternoon reading Lincoln's comments on the *Bound Hearts* manuscript. Moments from masturbating at my desk, I forced myself to close the document before the first sex scene. I rushed to the ladies' room to splash cold water on my face because I was so turned on, I could barely breathe. I'm only ninety pages in, but I know exactly how this story ends. With his ocean blue eye for detail, a permanent position at Iverson Press is in Lincoln Kennedy's future.

His edits are intricate, yet they don't interfere with the author's voice. He's equal parts blunt and thoughtful with his comments, and every developmental suggestion he's made is fabulous. Since the birth of my company, I've employed dozens of editors. None compare to this young man.

After he politely walked me to my car, and I suppressed the urge to grab his tie and yank him into my backseat, I squirmed the entire ride home. Now I'm finally in my bedroom, and I can't think of a better way to spend my Monday night than lounging naked in my bed with my laptop and a glass of wine.

I open the document and resume reading. My pulse quickens when I spot a red mark that signifies Lincoln's presence. This particular edit is a sentence rewrite where he'd changed, *"I can feel how soft her cheeks are while we frantically kiss."* to *"I cup her warm, soft cheeks and seize her lips."*

I want someone to kiss me like that. Wait, someone did. My sexy stranger at The River. My eyelids flutter closed, and I lose myself in the memory. How would it feel to kiss Lincoln? The immediate flood of heat between my thighs makes me shift, causing the sheet to brush against my clit. I gasp and tug my laptop closer, forcing my attention to his next comment.

Throughout the manuscript you've referred to Dan as an alpha. As we approach the sex scene, I'm getting some whiplash from his behavior. One moment you have him in caveman mode, and a split second later, he's aloof and disinterested. If Dan is truly an alpha, now is the time to show it. They've been dancing around the act of sex for three chapters. They're holed up in a cabin. The snow isn't letting up anytime soon. Sara's pushing him to his limits by threatening to leave and wander off in the blizzard alone. Alphas don't like their women in danger. Their instinct is to protect and claim. This isn't the occasion for tender lovemaking—it's claiming time.

You made a point of mentioning the handcuffs tucked in his police uniform. Why doesn't he use them? What better way to keep her safe than cuff her to the bed? This is Dan and Sara's first time, so it sets up the reader's expectations for the rest of the book. The way this scene's written, I had no indication Dan was a Dominant. You don't introduce BDSM stuff until the second sex scene. By the time we get there, the flogger is unexpected and not in a pleasant way. I literally scrolled back to see if I'd missed something. Nothing here even hints at the lifestyle. If Dan is truly a Dominant, that doesn't come and go. He's anxious, frustrated, and desperate to keep Sara safe. He craves her submission on every level. If you're going down the BDSM road, you need to pave the way now.

Think about what we know of Sara. She's feisty as hell but craves strength and direction. She wants Dan to assert his dominance—she's practically begging for it. Sara doesn't want to make love—she wants Dan to fuck her. She comes right out and says it. Give the woman what she needs!

There's a lot you can do to add heat here. Think of the anticipation you can infuse if he cuffs her wrists to the headboard. Maybe he spreads her legs apart before using the belt of her robe to secure them to the bedposts? The vulnerability in her forced submission would make the intimate act more intense. What if he teases her? Uses his tongue to bring her to the brink again and again until she's begging for release? Maybe he spanks her? These are just suggestions—it's totally your call, but somehow, you need to link their first time to the intensity of the future sexual encounters. Don't leave us in left field, use this scene to set the stage. This way, when the flogger and cat-of-nine-tails come knocking, we've got a door to come through.

I set my laptop aside and gulp my wine, but the flush on my skin has nothing to do with alcohol. Lincoln's words have me . . . well, hot. And wet. *Really wet*, I discover, as my fingertips glide through my arousal.

These kinds of acts are in my masked stranger's wheelhouse, not Lincoln's. Everything I know of the nerdy hunk, with his glasses and sexy dimples—and gentlemanly demeanor—is at odds with the image his written words have seared into my head. The man I'm imagining could force a woman's submission with a single word.

What if my young editor *does* have a kinky side? I moan aloud at the thought of Lincoln slapping my ass. What would it be like if *he* cuffed me to a bed, spread my legs wide, and buried his face between my thighs? What if he could make me feel the way L—Elliot—did? I picture Lincoln's face and recall my pleasure concierge's touch while rubbing slow circles on my clit. But it's not enough.

While I only just discovered this fact on Friday, I crave a man's dominance. I need him to claim me, mark me, fuck me. A flare of lust makes me snatch the vibrator from my nightstand. I seldom use it, but the wildfire surging in my blood demands a long, hard orgasm. The kind I can't achieve with my fingers alone.

Lying on my back with my eyes closed, I allow my legs to fall open and slide the toy into my pussy. While my strokes feel amazing, they aren't enough. I press the button on the end and gasp as vibrations pulse through me. I thrust it harder and faster, cranking up the intensity. It's still not enough to satisfy the empty ache that consumes me.

Desperate for my release, I roll to my stomach and pull my knees beneath me. Ass in the air, I pleasure myself with the toy the way I want Lincoln to fuck me—hard and fast—my legs spread wide while he stakes his claim. Moans and gasps spill from my lips, the cries bleeding into the mattress. My inner muscles quiver and finally send me flying. As I climax on a muffled wail, and my knees give out, I know damn well reviewing Lincoln's work will be a bedroom-only endeavor.

TWENTY-SIX

Lincoln

I PRESS MY PHONE CLOSER TO MY EAR. COMPASS ROASTERS IS packed, and I can't make out what my sister is saying over the noise. "Sorry, Reag. Can you repeat that?"

"Where are you, and why's it so loud?"

"I went out for lunch today and then made a pit stop at that coffee shop I told you about. They're super busy."

"You said your job has a fancy coffee maker though."

"We do, but sometimes it tastes better when someone else makes it." I had other reasons for stopping here, but I'm not about to share them with her.

"I don't like coffee."

I chuckle. "They have other drinks like cocoa and tea. Also, this place makes the world's best cupcakes."

"Can you bring me one on Sunday?"

I squeeze my eyes shut. "I'm sorry, Reag, but I don't think I can make the trip up this week."

"Why not?"

"I have a lot of work I need to catch up on."

"You said that last week," she whines.

"I know, and I'm sorry for disappointing you again." I run a hand over my face, adjusting the glasses that are suddenly squeezing my brain. "It's really important that I impress my new boss. She only hired me as temporary, and I want to make sure she changes her mind and keeps me."

She sniffs, and my heart cracks down the center. "Why wouldn't she want to keep you? You're the best."

Not according to Sister Fitzgibbons. Or the cop who arrested me for a crime I didn't commit. Or the school's lawyer who made my parents pay out of their assholes for damage I didn't do.

I'm about to correct her, but I don't have the heart to tell her not everyone sees me as the hero she believes I am. "Thanks, Reag. I love you."

"Love you too." She sighs. "Maybe since you can't come visit me, Mom and I can come to you? Then you can work while we're there."

"We'll see," I placate her, even though her idea is out of the question. My family has never stepped foot inside my pitifully small studio apartment, so they don't know I sleep on a lumpy twin mattress without a bedframe. They've never seen my barren cabinets or the restroom that's not much bigger than an airplane lavatory. I'd rather keep them in the dark than let them discover my "big city life" is pretty fucking pathetic. "Listen, I've gotta run. It's my turn to order. Love you."

"Love you too. Bye, Linky."

Forcing a deep breath, I knock on the door to Elinora's office.

"Come in."

I clear my throat. "Hi, Ms. Iverson. You, uh, wanted to see me after lunch?"

"Yes. Have a seat."

I nod and settle across from her. "Is everything all right?"

"Why wouldn't it be?"

I blink, unsure of how to answer. Instead, I place the chai on her desk. "This is for you."

Her eyes widen. "Oh?"

"You said you'd be open to trying it dirty, so I grabbed you. I mean, *it*. *For* you. I grabbed *it* for *you*. When I got mine." I shake my head to force the language section of my brain to cooperate. "It's a dirty chai."

Elinora's smile makes my cock twitch. "Thank you for the kind gesture, Lincoln."

"You're welcome."

Her eyelids flutter closed as she takes a long, slow sip. "Wow."

"What do you think?"

She meets my gaze. "I think I like it dirty."

"Me too," I murmur, allowing my eyes to linger on her lips as she licks foam from them. "But only when it's hot."

A flush creeps over her cheeks. "Is that so?"

"Yeah, cold espresso's not my thing."

"I also prefer it hot."

You're Goddamn right, you do. Despite how hard I try to stop them, the corners of my lips twitch into a smirk. Every time I'm alone with her, the air between us crackles. I can't tear my eyes from the heat in her gaze. *She truly wants me.* My smirk widens to a smile.

Elinora arches a brow. "Did I miss the punchline?"

"No, I'm pretty sure—"

Freya marches into the office. "Ugh. I'm sorry, Elle, but the world's biggest asshole is on the phone for you."

Elinora stiffens. "Tell him I'm in a meeting."

"Tried that. He's called six times in a row."

"What does he want?"

"He said he needs to tell you something."

"Take a message," Elinora snaps.

Freya sighs. "Tried that too. He said it's for your ears only."

Elinora squeezes her eyes shut. "Patch him through."

Freya nods and heads back to her desk.

"I'll come back later," I say, rising.

She points to the chair. "Sit. I have no intention of making this a lengthy conversation."

I settle back down like a good, obedient boy and focus on my hands. She's fucking sexy in a position of dominance. I'll submit to her here, but damn . . . I'd love to have her in my castle again.

The phone on her desk rings.

She snatches it. "What do you want, Charles? You'd better have a damn good reason for interrupting a meeting with one of my editors."

I toy with the edge of my sleeve and wonder if he's her ex-husband or someone else.

"What news?" Elinora's glacial tone makes me glance up at her. She tightens her grip on the phone. "*Excuse me?*" The words leave her lips in a pained whisper. As she listens, a single tear rolls down her cheek. Then another. "Congratulations." She hangs up the phone.

I wait in silence as more tears slide from beneath her lashes. When her shoulders shake with her attempt to breathe, I reach across the desk and touch her hand. "Are you all right, Ms. Iverson?"

With rivers running down her cheeks, eyes that look like melting ice meet mine. "I'm fine." She quickly wipes her tears away like she's pretending I don't see them.

"Is there anything I can do?"

"Can you erase time?"

"No, but if you need someone who will listen, I'm happy to lend my time."

"Do you have an extra fifteen years?" she asks, wiping her cheeks.

Ah, ex-husband it is. I glance at my watch. It's a little after two. My rescheduled dinner with Gwen is at seven. "I've got five hours until I need to be somewhere. I'm all yours until then."

"Thank you, but I'm fine. It's nothing I didn't expect. I shouldn't have allowed him to upset me and interrupt our meeting."

"Tell me." The command slips out before I can stop it. Instead of brushing me off again, her posture softens.

"My ex-husband eloped with his latest mistress." She sniffs and blots her eyes with a tissue. "She's pregnant, and he found it necessary to make that announcement to me." While the slump of her shoulders and averted gaze tell me she's embarrassed, the words spill from her lips as easily as if I demanded she tell me the weather.

"That's low," I mutter. "Did he think you'd care?"

She squeezes her eyes shut and shrugs.

"Look at me." Her gaze snaps to mine and—God help me—even though she's crying, her submission turns me on. What kind of person does that make me? *An asshole.* I shift in my seat. "Why did he call to tell you that?"

Elinora blinks back tears and sucks in a shallow breath. "He wanted to make sure I knew our fertility issues had nothing to do with his age."

"How old is he?"

"He'll be fifty in September." She wipes her face. "Anyway, our childless state was my fault. I'm the broken one—not him."

"You are *not* broken."

"Yeah, well, it solidifies the fact that my body is defective." She sighs. "I didn't mean to get upset, but that was just the gut punch I needed today."

"Nothing about you is defective. Your ex is a fucking dick."

She nods. "He's the world's biggest dick." After a moment, she smirks. "And I definitely mean *is* not has."

I chuckle at her thinly veiled insult. "Well played."

"Sadly, Lincoln, I was the one who was well played."

"It's clear he was a shitty husband, so it stands to reason he'd be an even shittier father. You're better off without him."

"I know." She sniffs and wipes her nose. "But it still really hurts."

"I'm sure it does, and I'm sorry he treated you that way. His actions reflect him. He's the defective one."

"Having a child is all I've ever wanted, but it's been the one gift consistently out of my reach. It's really hard to accept that the vision I had for my life, my future, was a fucking unattainable dream." She blots her eyes again. "And now, the person who was supposed to be my life partner is realizing that dream with someone else."

"I'm so sorry." In this moment, I'd give anything to haul her against my chest and make her pain disappear. Kick her ex-husband's ass and make him apologize for hurting her. Instead, I keep my hands to myself. It's not my place. She's my boss—not my girlfriend.

"It's fine. Thank you for listening," she whispers before clearing her throat. "Anyway, the reason I wanted to see you was to let you know I finished reading through your mark-up of *Bound Hearts*."

"That was quick."

"I'm a fast reader." She cocks her head to the side. "I thought during your interview you told me you don't have any experience editing romance?" Now that she's talking about her passion, a faint smile replaces her tears.

"I don't."

She raises a brow. "Are you sure about that?"

"One hundred percent. I'm happy to give you a list of titles I worked on at Cooper Press."

Elinora waves me off. "No, that's unnecessary. I believe you."

I straighten in my seat. "How did I do? Were you pleased with my work? Did I, uh, *it* meet your standards?"

"No."

My stomach drops, and I rub my sweaty palms on my pants. "I can take another—"

"You *exceeded* my standards and then some. I forwarded the manuscript to the agent this morning. She called me after lunch and wanted to know more about my brilliant new editor."

"Really?" I couldn't hold back my grin if I tried. "That's awesome. Thank you so much."

She smiles. "It gets better. The author wants to schedule a call with you for tomorrow."

"Was she all right with my recommendations?"

"According to her agent, she loves them but has some questions for you. What time should I tell her you're available?"

"Anytime works for me." I rake a hand through my hair. "To be honest, I thought you were about to tell me I did a shitty job."

"Far from it. You're a gifted editor, Lincoln."

My grin stretches from ear to ear. "Thank you, Ms. Iverson. You made my day."

"Thank *you* for being part of my team." She holds up her chai and gives me a warm smile. "You made my day too."

TWENTY-SEVEN

Lincoln

THE BREAKROOM IS UNUSUALLY QUIET TODAY, BUT THAT'S FINE with me. I need some silence to prepare for my call with the author of *Bound Hearts*. I'm not sure why I'm so nervous—I've worked with dozens of authors. Then again, this is my first romance author. I wonder if she knows I'm a dude. I imagine I'm among the minority there.

Brad Watson, a mystery and suspense editor who works upstairs, enters the room with a can of soda and some chips. He leans against the counter, and I quickly discover he's one of those people who crinkles the fucking bag incessantly. Annoyed that he's disturbing my solitude, I give him the side eye.

"Oh, sorry." He smears his greasy fingers on his dress pants. "How do you like it here?"

"So far so good."

"Any run ins with the matriarch?"

"Huh?"

Brad rolls his beady little eyes. "Our boss."

"What about her?" I ask, sipping my water.

"Have you had any problems with her?"

"Nope. She's cool." I cock my head to the side. "Do *you* have a problem with her?"

He sneers. "I hate that bitch."

"Sorry you feel that way." At this point I'm done with the conversation and the stupid greasy fuck. Deciding to finish my lunch at my desk, I stand.

"Back to work already?"

"Books don't edit themselves, bro."

"Which genre did she assign you?"

I stiffen my spine. "Romance."

The asshole has the balls to laugh in my face. "That shows how much she knows. Who the fuck replaces Cindy with someone like you?"

"Are you insinuating I don't know my shit?"

"Nah, man. I mean Iverson's clueless. Her ex-husband cheated on her. I'd say the Ice Queen's views on love are pretty fucked. Then the stupid bitch sticks a dude in romance?"

"First of all, Ms. Iverson's love life is none of your business. As for your opinion of me, I can assure you I'm more than qualified to edit romance." Clenching my fists, I take a step closer to him. "Call her a bitch one more time, and we're gonna have a problem."

He raises a brow. "You're *seriously* defending her?"

"Yeah, as a matter of fact, I am."

"Listen, man, I've worked here four years. All she does is bitch and nag at people until they quit. She put too much on Cindy's shoulders and now she's gone. Ted from mystery and suspense couldn't handle the pressure either."

"I work well under pressure."

Brad narrows his eyes on me. "Don't think you're immune to her wrath just because you're friends with Myles."

"Myles has nothing to do with my job performance."

"You're new. Trust me, once the honeymoon phase is over,

you'll get a taste of her shit. The first time you fuck up, she'll be on your ass. There is no satisfying her."

I satisfied her just fine. Since I can't tell him that, I snatch another bottle of water from the fridge.

The stupid fuck keeps talking, "I mean, yeah, she's hot—if frigid's your thing." He chugs his soda. "Personally, the ice queen bit doesn't do it for me. I don't care how nice her tits are, Elinora Iverson is so cold, her pussy could freeze a man's dick right off."

Before I realize what I'm doing, I grab the fucker by the throat and slam him up against the wall, pinning him in place. "Listen and listen well, because I'm only gonna say this once," I snarl, my nose inches from his. "That woman is your boss. This is her castle. If you can't handle the way she runs it, then get the fuck out." I tighten my grip and lift his body off the floor. "If I *ever* hear you disrespect her—or any other woman in this office—like that again, I'll rearrange your face. Got it?"

"Yeah," he grunts.

"I'm not fucking around. You run your mouth again, and you're gonna eat my fist. Are we clear?" When he doesn't respond, I grip his face. "I asked you a question."

"Yes."

"Yes, what?"

"Yes, we're clear."

"Good." I release him and take a step back, then fix my crooked glasses. "Now get the fuck out of here."

Brad staggers forward, gasping and wheezing. I turn and nearly collide with Elinora in the doorway. I don't know how long she was standing there, but her red face and watery eyes tell me she heard everything he said.

"Hello, Mr. Watson. I didn't realize you had such a high opinion of me."

Brad's eyes widen, and all the color drains from his face. "Ms. Iverson, I—"

"Spare me the explanation," she snaps, fire flashing in her gaze.

"Your employment with Iverson Press is terminated. Effective immediately."

"What?" Brad knots his fingers in his hair. "You can't fire me."

"It's my business, I can do whatever the hell I want. Grab your things and get out." She points to the door. "Leave in the next five minutes, or I'll have you removed from the premises."

Brad shoots me a death glare before marching from the breakroom. Once he's out of earshot, Elinora sags against the door frame.

"I'm sorry he said those things about you."

She peers up at me, her tears spilling over for the second time in as many days. "Thank you for having my back."

"Of course."

"No one has *ever* stuck up for me like that."

"Misogyny doesn't sit well with me, Ms. Iverson. Nor does blatant disrespect. Please don't cry over the bullshit he spewed. He's a dumb fuck."

A weak smile twitches her lips. "The dumbest of fucks."

I touch her shoulder. "Do you want tea or something?"

"No, thank you." She wipes her eyes. "If you want to take his job instead of the position with Iverson Melt, I'm ok with you transitioning to mystery and suspense. I know you mentioned that's your preferred genre."

"I mean, it *is*, but to be honest, I'm enjoying romance. I'd like to stay where I'm at, if that's all right?"

"Of course. Do you know any quality mystery and suspense editors who need a job?"

The only person from Cooper Press who I'd feel comfortable referring is also a romance editor. Tess McPherson is a sweet southern belle who moonlights as a Broadway actress. She'll be performing alongside Garrett in *Prodigy*, the controversial musical theater production opening in November.

"No, but I'm happy to take on a few of his manuscripts until you find someone."

TWENTY-EIGHT

Elinora

HE CAN'T BE SERIOUS.

I stare at Lincoln in disbelief. "You're volunteering to take on *more* work?"

"This," he gestures to the room behind us, "is my dream job. I may be a rarity, but I truly love what I do. Besides, if it takes some pressure off you, I'm happy to help. I can easily shoulder a few more manuscripts."

This perfect, beautiful man not only defended me, but now he's trying to make my life easier? It doesn't seem possible.

"Lincoln Kennedy, consider this my offer of permanent employment."

His eyes widen. "I thought there was a three-month probationary period?"

"This," I begin, mimicking his all-encompassing gesture from moments ago, "is my castle. I can fill it with whomever I want, in whatever time frame I choose. Your work ethic and character speak for themselves. Not to mention the superb quality of your work.

I've been doing this a long time, so I know talent when I see it. I'd be a fool not to keep you." I smile and touch his arm. "*And* you've earned yourself a raise."

Lincoln's mouth drops open. He quickly regains control and shakes his head. "While I more than appreciate your gesture, Ms. Iverson, I don't think I deserve a raise."

"Well *I* do." As his expression morphs into one of hope—and pride—I know I made the right decision. In the brief time he's worked for me, this man has lifted me up, defended, and warmed me, so the least I could do was show my appreciation. I flash him a wink. "My castle, remember?"

Lincoln's smile could melt the polar ice caps. "Thank you."

"My pleasure." I touch his arm once more. "Thank you again for sticking up for me."

"Always." His gaze burns into me, breaking what remains of my defenses.

I want to throw my arms around his neck and kiss him, but I nod instead. "Don't be late for your call."

He perks up. "Right. I'll fill you in when I'm finished."

AFTER A GOOD CRY IN MY OFFICE OVER ASSHOLE BRAD'S declaration about my frosty vagina, I head for the ladies' room to clean the mascara from beneath my eyes. I quickly reapply and fix my hair before returning to the romance suite.

Lincoln is on the phone at his desk. His call with the author of *Bound Hearts* has been going on for nearly two hours. I approach him from behind, silently admiring the confidence in his speech and posture.

He chuckles. "No, that's a common misconception about safe words."

Enticed by the opportunity to hear *his* take on the issue, I linger a few more moments.

"Safe words are an essential means of communication during sex." He sips his water, then pours a little into the plant on his desk —no doubt a gift from Myles—before picking off a dead leaf. He rolls it between his fingers as he speaks. "Not just BDSM stuff, no. They can apply to *any* sex."

Heat floods my lower belly, pooling at my core. The spare panties I tucked in my briefcase will certainly come in handy this afternoon.

"Think about it. Good sex requires open lines of communication. Most partners want the experience to be mutually pleasurable, right?" He drops the leaf into the trashcan beneath his desk. "Well, since people aren't mind readers, we need to check in periodically. With BDSM, this is especially important. When you wrote the second sex scene for Dan and Sara, you made it solely about his pleasure. Not cool. Yes, he's a Dominant, but it doesn't work like that. Not only do most Dominants want to please their subs, they get off on *giving* pleasure. It's not some 'take-what-I-give-you-and-I-don't-care-if-you-like-it' arrangement. The balance between dominance and submission is delicate and volatile. If proper techniques and good communication are lacking, the scale can quickly tip into the red zone. During the scene, Dan never once asks Sara how she's doing, which is dangerous." He gives the author an emphatic nod she can't see. "Yes, literally dangerous. Since Dan has her bound so tightly, he needs to keep her circulation in mind. An hour is not realistic because lack of blood flow can cause permanent injury. A true Dominant cares about their submissive. Their pleasure, safety, *and* emotional wellbeing. While some techniques may be heavier handed than others . . . pun intended." He laughs again, and the deep rumble tickles my spine. "Yeah, I know. I couldn't help myself. Anyway, regarding the pain side of pleasure, a Dominant's goal is not to harm the other person. Physically *or* emotionally."

As I listen to Lincoln's conversation, an awareness bubbles in my veins. He's got firsthand experience with the concepts of dominance and submission. Images of him pinning Brad to the wall flash through my mind. The authoritative tone he used yesterday, when he forced me to confess the reason behind my tears. The way my body and mind submit to him without question.

Lincoln is a Dominant.

The thought zings through my brain—which is currently hard-wired to my pussy—and my body's reaction is instantaneous. I'm a mess of tingles as every nerve ending between my legs flares to life.

He and Elliot are not that different after all.

Lincoln runs a hand through his hair, and I clench my fists to keep my fingers from following suit. "Exactly. That's where the safe words come in. Some people only have one. In that case, when a submissive says the agreed upon word, all activity must cease. Other techniques involve the use of multiple words, usually in a scale."

My nipples harden at his confident tone, and I ghost closer.

"Picture a stop light. That's a pretty universal example because even children know that green means go, yellow means slow down, and red means stop. In fact, plenty of couples use those exact words. If that's not Sara's style, maybe she and Dan can agree to words that suit them better." He sips his water and twists into a stretch.

I cover my mouth to stifle a moan at witnessing the bunch and flex of his shoulders. Even hidden beneath a dress shirt, his body is a thing of beauty.

"Ok, here's an example using temperature. Let's say a couple is having sex. For the purposes of keeping it relevant to your book, we'll make it a heterosexual couple with the male partner in a position of dominance. Instead of green, maybe they use warm. Yellow can be cool, and she can say 'ice' when she wants him to freeze or stop. Does that make sense? And if things are going *really* well, and she wants him to crank up the intensity . . ." He takes another sip of water.

My inner muscles clench in anticipation of his next words. The auditory foreplay is nearly as arousing as reading his comments in the manuscript. "If Sara wants *more,* she'll say, 'Fire.'"

Oh my God, he's been to The River.

"Not only does Dan need to pay attention to visual cues, but he can't just wait for Sara to blurt out a safe word. The lines of communication must be open. By that, I mean, he needs to check in with her."

Like Elliot did with me.

He nods. "Exactly. Or he can say something like, 'How's the water?'"

My heart skids to a stop. Those exact words, uttered in that same low tone, have haunted me all week. Unable to breathe, I slowly back away and slip into my office.

I sag against the closed door and force my brain to function.

It's him. It has to be—it's *his* fucking voice. Lincoln and Elliot are the same person. That's why Elliot blindfolded me and kept his voice at a whisper. That's why he encouraged me to say Lincoln's name. Why I felt so comfortable with him. Why his face felt familiar to my touch.

"I fucked my employee." I wheeze, clutching my chest before sinking into my desk chair and rubbing my temples.

No. It can't be possible. There has to be an explanation. *Think, Elinora. Think.*

Maybe they're brothers—or cousins. Yeah, that's it. Family. This is a crazy coincidence. My decade younger employee didn't *actually* spank and fuck me last weekend—it was only a fantasy. Since I so desperately wanted it to be Lincoln in that lagoon, I'm hung up on the reverie. My mind is still blurring the boundaries of reality.

I chug some water and try to stop my runaway fantasy train in its tracks, but my brain won't be derailed.

What if it's really him?

Desperate for answers, I lurch to my feet and head for Lincoln's cubicle but stop short when I find Myles dangling an open bag of

Skittles in front of his face. Lincoln must have just finished his call during my mini freakout.

"What's this?" Myles demands, propping his other hand on a hip.

"Uh, Skittles . . ."

"I *know* it's Skittles. I'm talking about what's *in* the bag."

"My answer's still Skittles." Lincoln grins. "You're only just discovering them? I put the bag there this morning."

"I've been at a meeting." Myles drops the candy onto Lincoln's desk. "I don't want your leftovers."

"My leftovers?"

"Lincoln Elliot Kennedy, if you think I don't know you ate everything but the green ones, you forget that I'm on to your games."

It's him.

The air inside my lungs crystallizes, and I stagger backward, unable to rip my gaze from the pair of men.

Lincoln pats Myles on the shoulder. "Get your facts right—I saved you the yellows too."

Myles flicks the side of Lincoln's cheek. "Minor details, Linc."

"It's like I always say . . ." Stretching his arms over his head, Lincoln leans back in his seat and grins. "The Devil's in the details."

The End

Continue Lincoln and Elinora's story in DEVIL IN THE DETAILS, which releases on July 20, 2023, and is available for preorder.

ABOUT THE AUTHOR

Aria Wyatt is a pharmacist mom who spends the inhumane predawn hours with a cup of coffee and her laptop, gleefully indulging in her passion for romance. Her novels range in heat from steamy to scorching, and she doesn't shy away from writing flawed characters with real life issues.

She resides with her husband and two children in New York's picturesque Hudson Valley, near the Catskills and iconic Woodstock. The avid reader balances marriage, motherhood, her pharmacist career, and her romance author dream. When not writing, she dabbles in photography, using the natural beauty of the region to her advantage. She's a self-proclaimed cat lady who cannot live without coffee, chocolate, music, and books.

Read More from Aria Wyatt

www.ariawyatt.com

ABOUT THE AUTHORS

CAN'T HAPPEN AGAIN

GEORGIA COFFMAN

ABOUT THE BOOK

Working with the enemy is one thing. Secretly sleeping with him is an entirely different predicament.

Theo is the Devil in a Greek god's body.
I was fooled by his charm once. Then I found out what a pig he truly is, and I want nothing to do with him.
Unfortunately, we have to work together, and due to the nature of our job, it's nearly impossible to maintain boundaries.
As romance book cover models, our goal is to depict fantasy, not reality, but it's not long before the lines are blurred. Every time we get in front of the camera, strange things happen. Some might call it chemistry. Some might call the butterflies in my stomach attraction.
But I call it a curse—a very tall, dark, and handsome curse.
The thing is, I'm only human. I have thoughts, feelings, and worst of all—needs. And Theo is all too good at fulfilling the latter.
When he shows me a new side to him, I can't resist the man I vowed to despise.
Before I know it, I'm falling for the enemy.

ONE

RAEGAN

I STEP INTO THE WELL-LIT STUDIO, CAREFUL TO PEEL AWAY A strand of hair from my lips without smearing the obscene amount of lip gloss coating them. Even though I told my roommate, Dakota, not to use so much, she insisted it would show up better in the images this way.

And I trusted her judgment, as I have for years.

Plus, she has several sample tubes of the stuff since she started selling it as a side gig. In order to survive in New York City and afford to have fun too, it's all about the side gigs, and even those have branches dipping into other financial avenues.

Another NYC life hack I've learned since I made the switch from Long Island is that it's great to have connections. It's why I'm doing the photoshoot today.

The photographer is my friend Stormie, who took Dakota and me under her wing in college. Since she's the only one of us three who grew up in the city, we hitched our wagon to her confidence, and we haven't looked back.

Today, I'm here for an exclusive book cover image photoshoot, which I haven't done many of in the past, but the few I've posed for have been exciting. It's good money too, although the waiting and uncertainty can be excruciating. Depending on the contract, I might not get paid until the images are sold.

But if I could establish a stream of income with these cover shoots to add to what I make with wedding photography and the occasional contract for freelance work, I can tuck enough away in savings and hopefully live without the constant constraint of money woes.

That would be a huge relief.

A buzz vibrates against my shoulder, and I slide to the side to check my phone, still unseen as Stormie and her assistant rearrange the lights on the other side of the room.

Dakota: I know how much you love to lick your lips, so I stuck a tube of lip gloss in your backpack. You can pay me back later. ;)

I find the pink tube and turn it in my fingers. The silver Annalisa Hughes logo covers most of it, glistening under the lights overhead. If I weren't already aware of how extra the Hollywood starlet could be, given the boisterous content on her socials, I'd be surprised by the gaudy branding. But this is in line with the large neon-framed sunglasses the actress loves and the brightly colored patterns she wears.

Dakota thinks it's great, but it's more her style. *Over-the-top* is her own brand too.

In any case, I'm glad she's focusing on more productive things than seeing how long she can stay in pajamas and eat only toast out of grief.

It's her breakup MO. Every time a guy she believes to be *the one* ends things, she sinks into a pit of despair faster than it takes a slice of bread to pop out of the toaster. The latest "soul mate" of hers sounded like a real dick, though, so it's probably for the best that he ghosted her. I mean, the asshole abandoned her when she sprained her ankle during their date, and he never even called to check on her.

But after nearly a month, my hopelessly romantic roommate is finally coming around and seeing the light.

"Raegan!" Stormie calls out, drawing my attention to where she stands next to a tall, dark, and extremely handsome man.

Handsome isn't enough to describe him, actually. I'd say the more appropriate word is *yummy*, which I mainly reserve for delicious actors like Ian Brock and tasty dishes like cheesy lasagna.

The guy in front of me runs his thick fingers through his dark brown hair, barely flattening the wild strands into submission.

The muscles in his quads wink and wave at me as he loosens each leg to the side, his attention never straying from whatever Stormie whispers to him.

His shirt is unbuttoned at the top, giving us all a peek of his velvety tan chest. Did someone have the honor of lathering lotion on it?

And if so, where do I sign up for that job?

If the guy wasn't already posing for the covers of romance books, I'd say he missed out on the perfect opportunity. Whatever divine being led him on this path knew what they were doing.

When he locks his eyes on mine, my mouth dries as if he heard me thinking all this out loud.

"Raegan!" Stormie calls again and waves me over. "Come meet your leading man for the day."

My feet move to close the distance between us, my body hovering outside itself as I enter the ridiculously hot model's atmosphere.

He's even sexier up close.

"This is Theo," Stormie says beside me, but it sounds like she's speaking to me through water.

Instinctively, I reach out to shake his hand. Could I be any lamer? This isn't a freaking business meeting.

"Theo, this is my good friend, Raegan," she finishes, as he meets me halfway for our painfully formal handshake.

As it turns out, I *could* be lamer.

Because I'm still holding my phone in the hand I reach out... and I drop it on his foot.

"Oh!" I cover my mouth and snap out of my dazed trance. "I'm so sorry. Are you okay?"

He flicks his wrist toward me in a reassuring gesture. "I'm fine. Only got my toe. Your phone, on the other hand..." Kneeling in front of me, he scoops up the device and checks it over as he stands upright again. "It's fine too, actually."

"Not surprised. It's as hard as my head," I joke—and immediately regret it.

Theo's full lips twitch in the corners, and next to me, Stormie's eyes bulge.

On an exhale, I say, "My mother claims I was a hardheaded kid. Never mind. It's nice to meet you, Theo." I force a smile and refuse to meet Stormie's inquisitive gaze.

I've never been so damn flustered because of a guy. What is wrong with me?

"Go easy on her today," she tells Theo as she takes a step back.

Did she just wink? What the hell does any of that mean?

The last time I posed with a male model was for a custom shoot for a quirky rom-com, and there was barely any touching. I've seen my friend's work for other, much hotter covers, though.

Is that what *this* is?

When I agreed to do this, she didn't give me many details, other than I'd be done in time to make my Orangetheory class later. I'm going for a ten-day streak.

"I'll be gentle," Theo says, his voice light and playful, but there's a gruff hint that tugs at my heart like puppet strings.

"Get acquainted and comfortable while I finish up," Stormie instructs. "Then, we make magic."

She leaves us with a pair of jazz hands, her eyes sparkling

under a line of thick bangs. She's the only woman I know who can pull those off. Dakota tried soon after Stormie cut hers, but it was "such a miserable fail," as she lamented. I had to stay home with my roommate for three days straight because she apparently couldn't leave the house looking "like a twelve-year-old girl from the sixties." I wouldn't have humored her, but she's done a lot for me over the years.

She makes me soup when I'm sick, does my makeup for these shoots, and never complains when I want to binge *Bridgerton* over and over again. Beyond that, she also indulges my interest in making crystals at home. We don't have any pets, but who needs the fur and slobber when we can have shiny crystals? They're fun and easy to make, and they're the perfect, inexpensive décor.

"How many shoots have you done like this?" Theo asks and steps toward me, closing the triangle we'd formed when Stormie was here.

I clear my throat, desperately hoping I give a simple answer without choking. "About three or so. I'd like to do more. It's fun, and even though I'm also a photographer on the side, I enjoy being in front of the camera too."

"Is that how you know Stormie—because you're both photographers?"

"Yes," I confirm. "We took a lot of the same courses in college. How do you know her?"

"She and a friend chased me down outside my gym. Said if I could work the camera like I do the dumbbells, we're both in luck." He chuckles. The sound is easy and a bit raspy, like he just woke up. If that's not sexy enough, the way his smile brightens his otherwise dark eyes makes something flip in my stomach.

Are those butterflies?

"Sounds like Stormie."

"I've only done three others too, but Stormie claims I'm a natural. I don't think I agree," he says, teetering on his heels.

I smile over his confession. It seems genuine, and he scratches his head while he glances around. Is he nervous? I find it hard to believe that he could have any shy or sheepish bone in his body, but clearly, there's more to him than meets the eye.

"I bet you're better than you think," I say unevenly and hoist the strap of my backpack higher on my shoulder, my body going slack as I attempt to do what Stormie said and get comfortable.

Harder said than done when I'm standing next to someone like Theo. He might be the hottest man I've ever talked to.

"Let me take that for you." Theo gestures a large hand toward my bag. "My mom would smack the back of my head if she knew I hadn't already offered."

"Oh." My cheeks heat as I release the bag of clothes and beauty products. "Manners. That's refreshing. The last guy I met elbowed me out of the way for the last scone at a coffee shop."

"I'd say I'm surprised, but since I grew up in the city, I've seen it all."

"You're from New York?"

"Born and raised. All four of my siblings and I were." He slings the strap of my backpack over his shoulder, and the sight is rather adorable. Theo is pretty large to be so lean, and he makes my purple and turquoise backpack appear smaller than a clutch.

I'm so distracted by the charming juxtaposition that I almost don't register what he just told me. "There are five of you?" I gape.

"Big Greek family—what can I say?" He chuckles again.

Of course he has Greek in him.

Is it possible that he's *too* good-looking and interesting?

"I was friends with a girl in college who was Greek," I say, recalling Anna, who lived in the dorm room next to mine and Dakota's. I could never pronounce her last name. In my defense, it had twenty letters in it, and when she'd say it, they sounded like they were mostly consonants. Trying to repeat it was like trying to teach my mouth and tongue the acrobatic moves of Cirque du Soleil. "She always used to complain about the way people pronounced the letters of sororities and fraternities."

He nods like this isn't the first time he's hearing this. He clearly understands Anna's dismay on a deeper level than I ever did.

"You two would probably have a lot to talk about."

He flicks his searing gaze up to meet mine, then leans in, his tone flirtatious when he quips, "I'd like to talk to *you*. Drinks later?"

My stomach does that weird fluttery thing again. "Sure," I say quickly.

Orangetheory can wait. Who cares about a ten-day streak when a date with a Greek god hangs in the balance?

Stormie announces they're ready and calls us over, where we begin with shots back-to-back. Theo's body is as hard as I imagined as he presses his backside against mine, the ridges of his muscles rubbing against me each time either of us moves.

There's friction.

Electricity.

And fuck, does he smell good.

When we face each other, and he touches my bare arm, heat radiates throughout the rest of my body.

When was the last time I've been so pathetically enamored by a man? Ever?

It's too good to be true. It has to be.

As we smile and grow more comfortable with each pose, my mind races with potential bombshells he could drop while we're having drinks later.

He's a drug dealer.

Head of the Greek mafia.

Soaks his hairy feet in milk.

What if it's all of the above, and he's a shady drug dealer in the Greek mafia who has disgusting feet?

"Try pressing your foreheads together," Stormie instructs, and it's followed by a quick succession of snaps of the shutter on her camera.

We do as she says, and I close my eyes.

Theo's minty breath is simultaneously hot and cool against my mouth, and his manly scent envelops me as Stormie's camera goes wild.

Whether he's hiding gross habits or not, he's hot and charming.

When he cups his hand around my cheek, I lean into his inviting palm, peering into the depths of his eyes. There's something comforting about him underneath his chiseled exterior that makes me feel like I've known him for longer than a few minutes.

It's why I have the craziest idea of kissing him.

I *could* kiss him.

Somewhere in the back of my mind, I even rationalize that this is a controlled setting, and it would be perfectly acceptable to kiss this leading man for the sake of romance books everywhere.

"Ah!" someone shrieks from the side.

I jerk in place and nearly trip over Theo's foot. We were standing so close, and I was totally entranced.

My fuzzy mind takes a moment to register a spill.

"I'm so sorry!" Stormie's assistant apologizes profusely, as if she dropped a cup of coffee onto the equipment, but it just got on the wall and floor. It's nothing a few paper towels can't handle.

No harm done, but the disappointment flooding my stomach over an interrupted near-kiss disagrees.

"Seriously, it's fine," Stormie reassures her and adds a smile. "The coffee smell is actually pretty welcomed. It's much better than the faint smell of meth. Know what I mean?"

She addresses me with the last question, and I freeze. Do I know? I didn't notice anything other than Theo's intoxicating cologne.

The spicy bergamot scent is too strong this close. I don't even smell the coffee from here.

"I should really revisit the idea of getting my own, more permanent studio," Stormie mutters, and it seems like it's more for her own benefit.

As the assistant races across the room, a roll of paper towels flying behind her like a cape, we continue on as if I wasn't practically begging to make out with this stranger.

I don't even know the guy's last name. How is it possible to be so wrapped up in him? Then again, how could I not be? Physically, Theo is absolute perfection, and I'd be insane *not* to want to kiss him.

There's also the fact that I haven't been out on a real date since my disastrous attempt at New Year's Eve, and that was over three months ago. I was horny as hell before I ever dropped my phone onto Theo's foot.

We take a few individual shots each, then change into different outfits before coming back together for couple's shots.

With miraculous self-control and strength, I manage to survive the rest of the session without throwing myself at Theo. But by the time my friend snaps the last shot, I'm flushed and practically breathless, which I hope isn't obvious in the images. As one of my oldest friends, Stormie would've told me had I appeared too blotchy and sweaty, right?

It's too late to fix it now.

We're done on schedule, as Stormie promised me, and I'm eager to have Theo to myself.

While Stormie and her assistant—the clumsy girl still offers apologies for the coffee splatter—tear down the backdrops and other equipment, Theo sidles next to me, his twinkling eyes hopeful. "Still on for drinks?"

The only thing that could stop me from showing up to this date would be a 9.5 earthquake, but I don't say as much out loud.

"Sure," I say as breezily as possible. It's extra difficult to do so since I feel the exact opposite of breezy. "Let me just check if Stormie needs help."

"Of course." He scratches the back of his head, and his previously flirty grin slips into a sheepish one. "I should've thought of that."

Adorable.

I skip toward the genius behind the camera and grab her by the shoulders. "What can we do to help you?"

My mischievous friend talks out of one side of her mouth. Thankfully, her voice is low enough for only me to hear. "What would help me is you getting out of here and into that hunk of a man's pants."

I mock gasp. "If that's what you really want..."

"Babe, go. Get out of here." She reaches around and swats my ass, but before we part ways, she adds, "And tell Dakota to call me. I haven't seen or talked to her in over a month. I want to hear about the new guy she's seeing."

"Actually, they broke up a few weeks ago. As it turns out, he was a real jerk." I frown.

"Ouch." She glances over my shoulder, and her smile reappears. "Hopefully you and Theo have a much better outcome."

I shimmy in place, the butterflies in my stomach very similar to the ones I had with my very first crush. I was thirteen, and the boy next door made me all kinds of giddy.

But Theo is no boy. He's all man, and the excitement coursing through me is R-rated.

Stormie blows me an air kiss and pleads, "Call me tomorrow with all the deets."

I hold up my crossed fingers and suppress the zealous bounce in my step as I reach Theo, who's already slung my backpack over his shoulder again.

Is he always this much of a gentleman? Or is he... an animal in the bedroom?

As we make our way downstairs and onto the sidewalk outside, I ache to find out for myself.

But first—drinks.

Yes. Drinks. Hanging out together will tell me all I need to know, re: grotesque habits.

We keep a respectful distance during our short walk to the bar of his choosing, and when we stop in front of a little place wedged between an Italian restaurant and a bodega, I applaud his taste.

This bar looks fun and laidback, with its colorful décor and cozy booths. It's also well -lit, and the lively music drifting through the speakers is loud enough to enjoy without hindering conversation.

As we settle into a booth and I listen to him order, I don't detect any hint of an accent, although he did say he was born and raised here. Are his parents from Greece? Has he visited before?

Would he whisper sweet nothings in Greek if we were to end up in bed tonight?

Oh, God.

The thought alone sends shivers down my spine.

"Nice choice," Theo says, playfully drumming his fingers on the table as the server sets the house version of a hurricane in front of me. It's dressed in all the things—cherries floating in the orange liquid, a lime hugging the rim, and an orange slice clinging to the straw like a koala bear does a tree.

It's the perfect beach drink, and the best way to celebrate the warmer spring weather we've been graced with.

I take a sip and hum. "It *is* a nice choice. I don't usually keep any kind of juice in our refrigerator since my roommate hates most kinds, so I have to indulge when she's not around."

"Who hates all juices?" He hikes a brow toward his hairline and stops swirling the whiskey in his glass.

"Someone who believes fruits should be eaten, not drunk."

"Sounds like something my dad would say." He chuckles into his drink before taking a sip. "He's the kind of person who always needs to make a point or give a lesson. Years ago, I brought a, um... never mind."

"What?" I press. "This is the land of no judgment. Go forth, and be open."

A soft laugh escapes, but it's a nervous sound, like he regrets bringing it up. "I was just going to say that I introduced him to a, um, friend once. She was a psychology major, and my dad lectured her. He tried to convince her that the human brain isn't to be studied or understood—far too dangerous."

"He's not wrong," I tease.

"Yes, well, she didn't appreciate it."

"Was this friend... a special someone you may have dated?"

He squirms, shifting in his seat and disturbing the leather material. "Not really. We went out a couple times, but ultimately, let's just say, we had different expectations."

What does he mean by that? I search his expression but come up empty.

"Not sexually," he blurts. "I mean, the expectations weren't anything sexual."

"Much better," I say with a grin.

"I'm sorry. I don't know why I brought this up. It's far too early in the evening to discuss that kind of stuff." He clears his throat and smooths his shirt down.

He wants this to go well. It's obvious, and my heart rate spikes to an obnoxiously dizzying rhythm.

I'm far more comfortable now after a few hours of having his arms wrapped around me for Stormie's camera, so I reach across the table and grab his hand to reassure him he didn't do or say anything to turn me off. In fact, it makes me like him even more.

"What kind of stuff should we talk about, then? I can share things about my past dates, if that would make you feel better."

This earns me a genuine laugh, which fills the booth with vibrant energy once again. "Anything about your hobbies or your childhood will suffice."

"If you want to get right down to the nitty-gritty," I joke, and he turns his palm over to play with my fingers.

Our skin is hot.

And it's hard to focus on things like moving to Long Island as a junior in high school and growing up in Rhode Island before that.

To me, it sounds mundane, but it all seems to fascinate him. He's never been there. He's never even left the state.

"We have a lot of family in Greece," he says. "My parents have visited them a few times over the years. My sisters have gone too, but my brother and I always had other obligations with school sports or work."

"Do you speak the language?"

"No." A shadow darkens his features as he slumps against the back of the booth. "My big sister and brother do, but the rest of us never learned. My youngest sister, Kia, tried to pick up the language during her visit to Greece, and while a few words stuck, she just never got the hang of it."

As the music plays and other patrons come and go, Theo shares what it was like to grow up with so many siblings. It's very different from my own upbringing, as I'm the only child. I relied on neighborhood kids for company, whereas Theo grew up sharing a room with his brother, so he didn't need to go far for a friend.

According to him, he just needed to cross the Spider-Man rug separating their beds.

As I got older, I made friends, especially in college. Stormie and Dakota became my family. They're the reasons I've stayed in the city and haven't moved back to Long Island, or some other place that's more affordable and requires less use of the subway. Although it's practical, the subway gives me the creeps worse than any haunted house or horror movie.

In any case, Stormie and Dakota are more like my sisters, and I can't imagine living far away from them.

Besides, I'm living the dream. I feel like I'm a character in *Sex and the City* with all the excitement around me. There's never a dull moment, and I have to admit, no matter the challenges, it's too fun to give up.

I'm surprised when I reach the bottom of my drink. I've been so lost in conversation with Theo that I don't realize there's no more alcohol until I attempt a sip and get a gurgling sound in response.

"I'm empty too." He holds his glass up as if I need proof. "Want another, or should we..."

He leaves the suggestive question hanging in the air as he pins me under a scorching gaze, and I'm glad his train of thought is on the same path as mine.

"We should." I slide the empty glass toward the middle of the table and gather my backpack and phone as he settles the bill.

Outside, we climb into a taxi and give the driver two different addresses.

"Shit. Sorry. We didn't—" he starts at the same time as I say, "My roommate will be gone for a couple hours."

Am I being too bold? Probably. But his coy and pleased grin indicates he doesn't mind it one bit. As he entwines his fingers with mine in the middle of the back seat, my heart races with anticipation. When was the last time a date went so well for me? Two dates from over a year ago come to mind, but neither compares with tonight.

The familiar buildings and shops blur as we pull up to the one I've called home for the last three years.

"Wait here." Theo finishes paying and exits the cab, rounds the back of it, and opens my door.

"I don't think anyone's ever opened a door for me." I beam as I rise to my full height.

My chest skims his as he closes the door, and again, his smell wraps me in an intense embrace.

We remain standing close as the taxi rides off, the rolling tires along the asphalt a distant memory as blood roars in my ears.

Is he going to kiss me now?

"I'm going to go out on a limb and say you've dated a lot of jerks," he whispers.

"Hmm?" My eyelids flutter.

Jerks? Who? What?

There's no room for jerks here. Not when I'm with Theo, who might be the best first date I've ever been on.

"Never mind." He cups my cheek in one large and confident palm, much like he did during the photoshoot, but instead of an interruption by a treacherous coffee spill, this time leads to a toe-curling kiss.

He presses his lips to mine, and my body melts against his, my arms limp at my sides. Theo steps closer, shielding my body from the evening chill, and he falls more deeply into this kiss in the process.

His lips leave zero room to breathe, and I'm happily suffocating.

Instantly, I'm glad we didn't share this intimate moment during the photoshoot. It's not one for witnesses.

It's hot and heady and so very promising as to what lies ahead for us.

If our kiss is this powerful, I fear I won't survive sleeping with him, but I'm more than thrilled to test that theory.

Giggling to our side interrupts us and pulls us apart. My eyes open in slow motion, taking three times as long to pry my lids wide as it does when I wake up in the morning, which is usually a difficult task.

When I do open them, I find Dakota, but she's not looking back at me.

Instead, her smile morphs into something much less playful. She's glaring murderously at Theo.

Clearing my throat, I manage, "What are you doing here? I thought you had to work late."

"What is *he* doing here?" she shoots back at me, then directs her next question to him. "Is this some kind of sick joke?"

"No... I... What's going on?" Theo's confused gaze bounces between Dakota and me, and I wish I had answers.

I have no clue what's going on, or why my friend is staring at him like she's trying to light him on fire.

"This is my roommate, Theo," Dakota clips, folding her arms over her chest. "If that's even your real name."

"Of course it's my real name." He scoffs and puts more distance between the two of us.

Dakota turns her wide-eyed stare on me. "This is the asshole who abandoned me when I sprained my ankle."

Fuck.

"Hang on. That's not what happened," Theo cuts in.

Fuck, fuck, fuck.

"We went out after Stormie and I met him at the gym. He's the one I've been talking about for weeks." Her voice rises, filling the quiet evening with alarm.

I hold my hands up, my head spinning. "Let's take a breath," I whisper. It's more to myself, although we could all use one.

They still try to talk over each other, but I don't register any of it. It might as well be sounds of the city, aka background noise I usually sleep through at night.

Stormie didn't say anything to me about Dakota going out with Theo. Does she even know they did? If she hasn't talked to Dakota in a month, I'm betting she has no idea.

Why didn't Dakota say anything about Theo? I search the recesses of my brain for any moment where she might've mentioned his name, but I come up empty. She never even told me she went out with a freaking Greek guy. She tells me every time she unexpectedly finds money in her pockets, so how could she have kept a Greek man to herself?

I have a lot of questions, thoughts, and concerns, but only one thing matters right this second.

It's over between Theo and me.

I can't date the guy Dakota's been moping over for weeks. Even if she hadn't cared about the breakup at all, I wouldn't be able to date him knowing the dickish things he did to her.

He'd do them to me too.

And just like that, my whirlwind romance has turned into a not-so-happily ever after.

TWO

THEO

"How are you all so hungry today?" My dad leans back in his chair and fishes remnants of lunch out of his teeth with a toothpick. Rubbing his swollen stomach, he adds, "I'm still full from Easter last weekend."

A nearly empty plate of boiled horta rests in front of him. I've always hated the smell of them. The lemon juice does nothing to cover the musty odor, but my dad eats them up like candy. Says it's the perfect light and healthy meal to keep people strong. He does always complain that they're not like the kind they'd eat in his village years ago, but he does that with everything.

At Easter dinner, he went on and on with our extended family about how different it is to roast the lamb in the kitchen of the family restaurant instead of a pit they dug in the ground for a rotisserie-style barbecue.

He finishes his light but brutal lunch—the word for his meal in Greek is literally *weeds*—while the rest of us scoop up the last of our pastitio onto forks and homemade bread. It's all the work of my mother's loving hands.

She hasn't sat down once to eat her own food. Instead, she's run around the table with my oldest sister, Catherine, on her heels. Both have been making sure we all have plenty to drink and that the customers are also taken care of. The restaurant is still open, but the back corner is always reserved for us every Wednesday, Sunday, and any holiday, birthday, or name day.

My parents may not have taught me or my youngest sisters, Kia and Angie, the language, but most of the Greek customs and traditions are ingrained in us all. In fact, I was in first grade by the time I realized Americans don't celebrate name days, which we do to honor the saints we're named after.

"I think it's time for my nap." My dad heaves himself out of the chair with more difficulty than usual. "My back is killing me."

Catherine rushes to his aid and grips his upper arm with two hands to help him up, but he shoos her away.

"I'm not a vegetable yet," he grumbles.

"You've been complaining about your back for days. It's either that, your arm, clogged ear, or restless leg." She exhales, clearly exasperated. The dark circles under her eyes could be from her toddler keeping her on her toes at home, or from our father listing each ache and pain in his body.

I'd bet it's mostly the latter.

"I'm old. This is what happens when you're old."

"You're sixty, not a hundred," she shoots back. "Did you go to the doctor I recommended? You need a physical."

"What I need is a nap."

Niko and I share a knowing look over our squeaky-clean plates. Dad hates doctors, and if Catherine keeps on, he's going to lecture us all on taking care of ourselves with one nap a day and a glass of red wine, along with boiled horta. He'll also argue for the use of olive oil over butter.

According to the stubborn man, there's no better medicine than those four things.

Niko leans halfway over the table to say directly to me, "Put that on the list of things we need to cover on our podcast—an endless list of ailments."

"Most of which are figments of his imagination," I add and snap my fingers in agreement. Then I pull out my phone, click on the Notes app, and type two words when my father cuts in.

"Are you writing about me again? What is it this time?" he clips.

Kia grips my shoulder and peers over it at my screen, the rest of the idea typed out. After a beat, she giggles and settles back into her seat.

"This is the great respect I get," my father laments. He points to the mural on the opposite wall near the front door, which is a tribute to the village he's from.

The church at the top of the mountain overlooks the rolling hills of olive trees and a few scattered houses. It's the only reason I know what his place of birth and upbringing looks like since I've never been there myself, and he doesn't have many pictures. The two he's shown me of him as a kid with his parents are both black and white, and the backgrounds aren't distinct. Those photographs could've been taken anywhere.

Since he's pointing to the mural now, it can only mean one thing—a self-righteous rant is coming on.

Here we go.

"I came to this country forty years ago with only a bag of two shirts and a pair of pants to my name before I met your mother. When I was a child the same age as Catherine's daughter, I wore underwear my mother sewed together herself using dishcloths. You all grew up wanting for nothing because of the sacrifices I made, and what do I get in return? Skits and jokes at my expense on your little podcast." He wiggles his fingers condescendingly at us.

"The podcast is nearing five thousand subscribers with three times as many downloads," I argue. "It's not little, nor is it about laughing at you, Dad. It's about life in New York as a Greek family, and we—"

"Don't even get me started on you." He flicks his wrists and dismisses me.

Typical.

He turns, and I believe I'm safe from his rampage. I guarantee he didn't get enough sleep last night, and he's definitely still hungry. No bowl of weeds could satisfy anyone's hunger, especially not his. The man put away half a lamb himself last weekend—and he still went back for a big plate of dessert. Claimed he couldn't resist his sister's baklava or my mother's galaktoboureko.

And it's true. The two women make the best desserts I've ever tried.

But I'm surprised he didn't make himself sick.

"You and your hobbies." My father spins back around. I guess I'm not safe from his fussy wrath, after all. "When are you going to come work here full-time? Your mother and I want to retire before we're unable to walk, you know."

"Dad, the podcast and modeling are my livelihood now. They might've been hobbies at first, but modeling is a real career. So is the podcast, which we've generated enough interest in that we have two sponsors lined up to give us their money as soon as we hit five thousand subscribers."

Niko flashes his hopeful gaze up to meet mine, but he remains silent. He knows the drill as well as I do, given the number of times we've been through this, or something similar, with our father.

I'm not even sure why I'm arguing with him now. It won't change his mind, nor will it earn me the prideful clap I secretly hope for.

As a teenager, this same lecture from our father made me feel guilty and hollow, not that I could do much at the time. When I was old enough, I'd help around the restaurant, but even that didn't stop him from pushing me to do and be more.

At twenty-eight, I've now heard the speech over a thousand times. The guilt is much fainter at this point.

Contrary to what he might believe, I do respect the man—we all do. It's why it stings so much when he can't return the sentiment, especially since I figured he'd understand the desire to pave the way for myself and my future.

He worked tirelessly to do the same many years ago. My father didn't even know English when he arrived in this country, but over the years, he's mastered it and much more. He helped his first cousin with construction jobs around the city, and in turn, Uncle Niko—there are so many of the same names around here—helped my father open this restaurant and forge his own path in the US.

Uncle Niko also introduced him to my mother way back when. She was in the same boat as him as a Greek new to this city, so they hit it off right away.

"Modeling." My dad scoffs. Of course that's the only thing he heard.

I open and close my mouth, my nerves tightening in every corner of my body as thoughts of my last shoot course through me. It was the one with Raegan.

I'd had her in my arms for an entire afternoon. The scent of her sweet and floral perfume invaded my senses, and I swear I can still smell it.

But it doesn't matter. None of it should. I haven't heard from her in three damn weeks.

My dad throws his hands up. "You take pictures and call yourself a successful entrepreneur. Why can't you be more like Niko? He's going to take over this restaurant soon, but he can't do it alone. Or your sister, Catherine? She's married with a beautiful daughter, and she still has time to come here to help us out. She can't do everything, either, though." He claps Niko's shoulder. "If I could just find you a nice Greek girl to marry." His voice trails off as he loses himself in the dream he's had for the last six years—since Niko turned thirty.

My dad is hitting all the hot topics at once. This is one cranky man today, and we're all paying the price. Well, everyone except the women. My sisters could lie on the couch all day, and he'd applaud them. He's always had a soft spot for those three, as do Niko and I, but our father has always taken his affections for them to the next level.

Once, I overheard him telling our mother that Niko and I would always take care of our sisters, no matter what, so it relieved him of some of the pressure to be hard on them.

The excess pressure of which he's put on Niko and me, instead.

"Vasili, quit pestering your sons and go upstairs for a nap," my mother—ever the family referee—intervenes. "I'll wake you up before the dinner rush. *Άντε*."

She pats him on the shoulder before he takes slow strides toward the side door, through which are the stairs to their apartment above the restaurant. It's not where they currently live full-time, but it's an easy reprieve from the hustle and bustle of the restaurant when they need it.

Niko convinced them to rent it last year when it became available, and I agreed it was a good idea.

Another point in Niko's favor.

In fact, our podcast and remaining wifeless are the only two things about my big brother that our father wishes would be different. On the other hand, my dad wants to change everything about me.

The target of my ambition.

My lack of interest in the restaurant.

My clothes. Last week, he actually told me my black T-shirt was too dark.

No matter what jabs he makes, though, his patience holds more bandwidth with me than it does for Niko—it's all I have going for me in order to avoid being squashed by my father's thumb.

His expectations to carry on the family name with a *nice Greek girl* are much higher for Niko, as the oldest son, than they are for me.

Years ago, my dad rooted for us all to settle down with Greek spouses, but that came to a screeching halt when Catherine met Todd and wanted to marry him. He wasn't stoked over the idea, but he eventually caved. She got off easy, but I doubt he'd show Niko the same courtesy—or mercy—unfortunately.

But that's a problem for another day, as my brother hasn't dated in years, Greek women or other.

Once the door chimes with my father's exit, my mother kisses the top of my head as if I were still five and tsks. "Don't pay your father any mind. As long as you're happy and healthy, that's all we truly care about."

"Thanks, Ma," I offer, grateful for her sympathetic and nurturing spirit. She's the sweet honey to Dad's sharp stinger, that's for sure.

Catherine stacks the dirty plates in front of us, and over her shoulder, she says to our mom, "I'm going to need to leave in a half hour to pick up Lydia from Thea Dimitra's, okay?"

Ma claps her hands. "Please bring the little angel by before you go home, will you? I haven't seen her all day."

"I won't have time. Todd's brother and his wife want us to come over." Catherine rushes the dishes to the back while my mother grumbles over the in-laws hogging her only grandchild. "I can hear you mumbling all the way from the kitchen, Ma," Catherine chides as she returns to continue tidying up.

I help her by taking the empty salad bowl and the plate of half-eaten Feta cheese to the back. When I return, the two women are arguing over who spends more time with Lydia.

"I'm just saying, I wanted to take her birthday shopping last weekend, but Todd's family got priority." My mom shrugs as she scans the few patrons currently in the restaurant—always one eye on the family and the other on its legacy.

"That's because you constantly spoil her rotten like every day is her birthday," Catherine shoots back.

As soon as she disappears again to check out a customer at the register, my mom winks at me. "That's why I'm Lydia's favorite grandma," she teases before she grabs the last thing on the table—what's left of the pastitio—and disappears into the kitchen.

I shake my head. She actually argues over who gets to love my little niece the most.

"We should go if we want to brainstorm our next episode before the dinner rush," Niko says, nodding toward the door as Angie and Kia burst into a fit of giggles over something on their phones.

I push my chair back and stand, my stomach full and satisfied from a home-cooked meal. "Let's do it."

My mother scurries back over with two to-go boxes and other items I can't see through the bags. "Here. Take some food with you for later. I put oranges and apples in here too. You need to eat more fruit."

We accept the bags and give her one-armed hugs before we say goodbye to our sisters. Catherine gives us a quick wave from behind the register, and we escape just in time before our sister and mother get into it over our aunt Dimitra babysitting all morning. The game of jealousy is all in good fun, but I can't imagine Catherine enjoys it. Of course, she and Todd love the free and convenient babysitters, but she's confessed on a few occasions that it's exhausting to ensure everyone gets to see their daughter.

"I can't wait until she starts school, and we have a rock-solid excuse to set up boundaries with everyone," she'd said then.

And I don't blame her.

I also don't blame everyone for wanting their time with Lydia. The three-year-old is adorable, with chunky legs and wild, curly hair. My parents particularly eat up her lispy attempts at pronouncing Greek words.

At the apartment Niko and I share, I settle into the corner of our living room where our equipment is set up, and I take a moment to bask in the peace and quiet. Family meals are great, and I love seeing my sisters all in one place, but the dizzying chatter and multiple conversations happening at once are surefire ways to give me a headache.

My temples throb with remnants of Catherine scolding Angie for not helping her and Ma, the buzz of the other patrons carrying on between themselves, and my father talking business with Niko.

He plops down next to me, and I pull up the notes I've made over the last week. My brother does the same, but before we compare, I set my phone down and ask, "What the hell was up with Dad today?"

Niko barely spares me a glance. "He's wound up because the health inspector popped in last week and gave him hell over the Easter lamb in the cooler."

"Shit."

"Eugene went easy on us, but I'm afraid that was our only get-out-of-jail-free card." He frowns.

"You won't need any more," I offer encouragingly.

"I wouldn't if I had my way," he grumbles, and I detect a bitter edge to his tone.

"What do you mean?"

He checks the time on his phone and sighs. "We should get moving. I have to be back at the restaurant in a couple hours."

I open my mouth to insist he talk to me, but he moves on to the notes on his phone. I don't make a habit of pressing my brother on things he doesn't want to share, anyway. He's reserved, and I respect it, even though my curiosity is champing at the bit.

"We definitely need to do a follow-up to our last segment on Greek Easter. We got a lot of comments on the red egg tradition."

"For sure. We can talk about Angie being a sore loser—middle-child problems."

Niko laughs. "Relatable for any culture—perfect. I'm writing that down."

I scroll on my laptop to the comments under our video on *YouTube*. "Oh, and we had a few people asking what we do with the eggs that break."

"Our father and his cousins eat them until they get sick," he answers.

"Or, they eat them until they get dangerously close to sprouting feathers themselves," I say, adjusting the line for us to use.

"That's why you're the funny one of the family."

"The only thing I've got going for me." I roll my eyes, annoyed that my father is in my head once again.

He never fails to make me question my life choices, but I always end up recalling my mother's words.

As long as you're healthy and happy...

And I am.

I have my family. My jobs, however unconventional they might be. And I'm single, which means more free time to focus on the former two points.

"Dad will feel far better after his nap. Stop by the restaurant tonight, and you'll see."

"What I'll see is him pretending everything's fine and ignoring how rude he was," I toss back.

"He's earned the right to be... outspoken."

"Nice way of putting it." I sway in my chair, keeping my gaze trained on the computer.

In my periphery, Niko scratches his dark hair. It's similar to mine, but he keeps his much shorter than I do. He also keeps his jaw shaved and clean, but I tend to leave mine scruffy unless I have a photoshoot coming up that requires a different look.

Stormie and a couple of the other photographers I've worked with like my chaotic appearance, though. According to them, chaos sells.

Thinking of Stormie instantly reminds me of Raegan again.

She and I laughed a lot during our date. I wanted to hear more of that sound—and I definitely wanted to taste her again—but I haven't heard from her in weeks.

After we realized I'd gone out with her roommate, I sent her two texts, both of which went unanswered. And it's annoyed the shit out of me, not that I'd admit it to anyone. I haven't even said as much to Niko. Although he rarely shares what's going on in that thick head of his, I tell him mostly everything. I just can't stand to say aloud how much it bothers me that a woman I hardly know has completely ghosted me.

More than that, I'm insulted that she believes I abandoned her roommate during a crisis, which is not what happened.

Raegan didn't give me a chance to explain, but that's her own problem. I just wish I could stop thinking about it—and her.

I've thought about her every day since our date, even though I know I shouldn't. Will that ever fucking go away?

Over the next hour, Niko and I finish up planning our next episode and jot down the rest of our notes, creating a loose script to keep us on track. He's about to get ready to return to work when my laptop pings with a notification.

I don't normally jump at a new email, but the sender and subject catch my eye.

Stormie wants to do a custom shoot for a contemporary romance author. My eyes bug out of my head when I read the name.

Pia Matthews.

I don't read romance, or much of any genre at all, and even I know the name. She's Elijah Hastings's new wife. The lead singer of Faint of Heart is on the cover of one of her books, and it's plastered all over TikTok, Instagram, and the rest of the internet.

And she wants *me* on her next cover.

"Holy shit," I repeatedly mutter under my breath as I reread the top of Stormie's email, making sure I understand this correctly.

"What's going on?" Niko slides his rolling chair toward me and tilts the computer screen enough to read the email. "Who's Raegan Peters?"

The shock of what this could mean for me instantly evaporates. "Why do you ask?"

He points a finger to the end of the email—the part I hadn't yet reached because I was stuck on Pia Matthews. "Says here you'll be doing this shoot with her."

His tone is calm and collected, but I feel the exact opposite.

Another shoot with Raegan? For the love of—

"Whoa. She's hot." Niko scrolls on the laptop, completely taking over my space.

"Give me that." I snatch the computer back and nudge him aside.

When I glance at what he's pulled up, I groan. It's Raegan's social media. Her face stares back at me from thirty different pictures.

Some with her hair flowing down both shoulders, loose over her breasts, and some with her hair pulled up.

A few show her in athleticwear, while in others, she wears sleek dresses and holds a fun drink in her hand like the one she ordered during our night out.

Smiling. Laughing. Beaming. Pursing her full lips—it's all on her Instagram profile.

I hate that Niko's right. Raegan is gorgeous, and seeing her again, even just online, has my blood pumping.

She'd invited me into her apartment the night of our date. I knew good and well where it would lead, and my pants had never been tighter.

I was so sure there would be a second date before we'd ever reached her apartment—that's how fucking crazy I was. Because it turned out too good to be true, just as this email is.

"I can't do it," I tell Niko and shut the laptop closed.

"Why?"

Sighing, I push away from the desk and stand to pace in front of my wise older brother. Maybe he can shed light on this and talk some damn sense into me. I know I need a kick in the pants, and he's definitely the one to give it.

The ass might even be happy to do so.

I scratch the back of my head. "Working with Pia would put my name on the fucking map. She's Elijah Hastings's new wife."

"Oh?" Niko leans back in his chair, folding his arms over his lean chest. We're both fans of the band, so I don't need to explain the exact caliber of how awesome it would be to do this cover.

"I have no doubt my schedule would fill up like *that*." I snap my fingers, spin, and pace along the same line I've been treading.

"Then what's the problem?" he asks, completely oblivious to the worst part of this.

"Raegan is the problem."

"So, you *do* know her."

"We worked together a few weeks ago, and..."

He lurches forward on the desk, clearly more interested in this than getting back to the restaurant on time.

"We got drinks after the shoot, and I haven't heard from her since then. Not since Raegan realized I went out with her roommate a couple of times, but she and I didn't even sleep together. We went out for drinks, and that's it. It was completely casual."

"And Raegan is all about some chick code that says she can't date you because of the roommate?" he ventures a guess, and he's not far off.

I stop pacing and face him. "Not only that, but the roommate told her I was a dick. I think that's the real reason she's avoiding me."

"She didn't give you a chance to argue your side of things," Niko says, catching on to the shitty ending of this little tale. He knows me well, and he just hit the nail on the damn head.

"I don't even care," I blurt. "If Raegan wants to believe her sad little roommate, then that's her choice and her problem. Not mine."

"Then why are you letting her keep you from doing the shoot?"

I stare at him for several seconds, then snap my fingers again. "I'm not. I'm fucking going, and she can deal with it. Because again, what Raegan Peters does or doesn't do is *not* my problem. I'll show her how much I really don't fucking care."

"It doesn't sound like *she* cares, little bro."

"She will."

"Do you want her to?"

"No." I scoff. "Drama is for the birds."

"What does that even mean?" He sways in his chair, and the smug expression he wears pisses me off.

My blood boils as I backpedal for an explanation to my suddenly tongue-twisted narrative. "Isn't that some shit Dad and Ma say? Some Greek allegory I'm supposed to find useful?"

"There's the one about the goat and a stick. One about sitting on your eggs like a chicken too."

"You can't make this shit up," I mutter.

"Someone did. These sayings originated somewhere," he rationalizes, but I'm clearly beyond all logic.

"Well, I'm *originating* this one—drama is for the birds. Write it down."

"For the podcast, or as a general life hack?"

I grind my teeth and bite out, "And you always say *I'm* the funny one."

"Look at that—I have jokes too," he muses with the sarcasm of an annoying parrot.

The ass.

Before I embarrass myself further, I clamp my big mouth shut and practically leap back into my chair to type out a reply to Stormie, my fingers shaking as I agree to the dates and terms of the custom shoot.

Next month, I'll be posing for a cover that has the potential to change my life, and I'm not going to let one woman derail me.

Even if that woman crawled deep under my skin after a single date.

THREE

RAEGAN

"I WISH I DIDN'T NEED THIS JOB SO BADLY," I SAY TO KYLE, who's stretched across my bed and scrolling through his phone. I stuff a blouse and jeans into my tote, along with an extra jumpsuit and a few accessories.

I never know what I'm going to need for a photoshoot. For this, Stormie asked me to wear something sleek and trendy, as if I were attending a gala with Manhattan's elite.

So, I raided the side of my closet that houses the dresses and jumpsuits I wear when photographing weddings around the city. I hope a couple of these will do.

I've been strapped for cash the last few weeks since Dakota lost her main job at a small art gallery, and thus, her major source of income. I had to cover her half of the rent this month, which was no easy feat, but that's what my emergency stash is for.

Because of that, shopping for this photoshoot was not an option. Sleek and trendy on a budget will need to be enough.

"I hope Elijah Hastings is there," Kyle says, and I try not to let it sting that he completely ignores my complaint.

Then again, I shouldn't be complaining about this opportunity to begin with. The money is amazing and definitely needed. But a shoot for the famous rock star's wife is also a literal dream come true. Unlike my new boyfriend, I'm more excited to meet said wife instead of her husband.

I read her book after it blew up on social media, and to put it lightly, I'm obsessed.

What I'm *not* obsessed about is doing the custom session with Theo freaking Lazaridis.

When I saw his name in Stormie's email, I called her right away in a fit of rage. She talked me off a ledge and rationalized what a big deal this would be for her and me both.

But it didn't explain why Pia Matthews chose him. Of all the viable—and delicious—possibilities, why did she have to pick the one guy I never want to see again? The woman has great taste, indicated by her choice in husband, but also, she puts hot as hell men on her covers.

Theo *is* hot as hell, unfortunately, but it's obvious she doesn't know what kind of person he is. His personality and dickish tendencies really ruin his appeal.

After Dakota interrupted us that night, she told me way more about their falling out, and she definitely saved me from a hellish nightmare. I would've slept with Theo, and if it would've ended half as badly as it did with him and her after they didn't even have sex, I'd be a basket case.

It's why I'm taking things slow with Kyle.

No need to jump in with both feet—and my lady bits—just yet. I need to see what he's really like first.

"I don't like all of his songs. Many of his newest are too sappy, but the guy rocks hard," Kyle continues as I finish packing my bag.

"Maybe don't tell him the first part of that opinion," I offer playfully. "But truthfully, I don't know if he's going to be there. Stormie just told me it's possible."

"That's enough for me. Besides, I want to see my woman in action." He tosses his phone onto the bed and pulls himself into a seated position, his sandy blond hair bouncing on top of his head, much like I remember Theo's hair doing in the soft evening breeze the night of our date almost two months ago.

It's the only similarity between the two men, and I welcome the difference. I'm still getting to know Kyle, but so far, he hasn't abandoned me in my time of need or texted other women in front of me.

So far, we're golden.

Plus, when he calls me his woman, it does send a thrill down my spine, and that counts for a lot.

"Come here." He walks his fingers down my forearm and grips my wrist. "Let's get silly before I hand you off to another dude for the afternoon."

I jerk out of his reach. "That's not what's happening. Theo doesn't have a chance," I assert.

"I didn't think he did." Kyle frowns. "I was just joking."

I squeeze my eyes closed as guilt floods my stomach. Why did I even say that? "You're right. I'm sorry. That was weird." I force a laugh, and it eases his frown into a suggestive grin.

"So... we can get frisky?" Kyle wiggles his eyebrows and tries to pull me on top of him. It's a move he's tried once before, and I thought I might even give in to the temptation—after all, I'm a woman with needs—but a nagging voice in the back of my head stopped me.

Just as it does now.

And it's a good thing it pesters me, because the door isn't locked, and Dakota barges in. That could've been awkward.

Kyle and I both jolt apart from the sudden intrusion as Dakota foregoes a greeting and jumps right into a question. "Hey, do you remember the lip gloss I stuck in your purse a few weeks ago?"

I pause in thought, recalling the one she texted me about the same day I met Theo—*curse him*. "Sure."

She scrunches her nose up in the same way she does when she

needs to say something difficult, like, "I forgot to take the trash out, and now the kitchen smells like onions," or "I got fired."

This time, it's, "I gave you some foundation when you ran out last week too, but I don't think you paid me back for either of those."

I chew on the inside of my cheek, acutely aware of Kyle's curious gaze bouncing between us, and the hair at the back of my neck stands. "Well," I start and swallow around the lump in my throat. "I did forget, and I'm sorry about that. But I thought since I paid all of this month's rent, that it wouldn't be an issue..."

She purses her lips, then almost immediately breaks into a smile. "You're totally right. I didn't think about it like that."

As quickly as she appeared, she spins on her bare heel and vanishes, leaving the door open behind her.

"Yikes," Kyle mutters and rubs his hands between his knees. "The balls on her, huh?"

Although I don't disagree with him, I bite my tongue and stick up for my long-time friend. "She's going through a rough patch, and we've all been there. It's understandable."

"You're far nicer than I am." He stands and glides his hands up my shoulders as he places a chaste kiss to my lips.

It barely reaches my toes.

"I'm going to hit the can and change my shirt before we head out." He gives me a squeeze, then disappears, and I'm left with a hollow ache in my chest.

There's no time to unpack that because Dakota reappears in my doorway. "Are you ready?" she asks, her smile more genuine and natural than before.

"*Blech.*" I huff and slump onto the edge of my bed, the cream bedspread light against my black, floor-length dress. "I should be so excited, but it's too hard to reach that level when I know I'm going to see Theo's stupid face today."

"His face *is* stupid. Do not let his charming grin fool you," she warns. "He's just the Devil in a Greek god's body."

And it is some *body*.

No matter how much I dislike him after learning how he treated my friend, it doesn't change the fact that I once desperately wanted to know what he would feel like on top of me.

"I mean... you do believe me about him, right? I know I haven't always been truthful in the past when it comes to guys, but I'm not lying about him." She peers down at me, her eyes twinkling with hope.

"Of course." I clutch my chest. "Theo is worm food, as far as I'm concerned."

"That's good to hear." She eases her hip against my rustic white desk along the opposite wall. "I know how easy it is to get wrapped up in him, but I don't want you to still be hung up on him."

"*Please*." I flick my wrist. "We had a drink one night several weeks ago. It didn't mean anything."

I swallow the lie, and it's as hard as keeping bile down after a spell of food poisoning.

But it has to be true. Theo isn't who I thought he was, and no matter how disappointed I was to learn this, I've moved on.

"Besides, I'm with Kyle now," I say.

"And he is so yummy."

I hum in agreement, although *yummy* isn't a word I've uttered myself to describe him. He's very handsome, nonetheless.

"How is it going with him? Have you two..." She lowers her voice and wiggles her eyebrows suggestively.

Sex. She's asking if we've had sex yet, and I have to let her down.

"No." I sigh as the sound of the sink being turned on filters through the wall. "I just don't want to rush into anything. The last time I did, I almost slept with the Devil."

"That's smart," she says, but it's not convincing. It's said in the same tone as the one I use when I'm trying to be optimistic about brussels sprouts—my least favorite food, but Dakota loves them.

Those, she devours, but juices are where she draws the line and are somehow worse to her. I'll never understand some things about my friend.

"Ready?" Kyle reenters the bedroom, a fresh red dress shirt clinging to his muscular biceps. It was definitely a good choice. He might've picked it to impress Elijah and the others at the photoshoot, but it's working on me too.

I hop up and grab my tote, purse, and phone, then give the crystals on my windowsill a once-over. They give the tiny room a little more flair. I'm not normally one to gravitate toward flash and sparkly things, but this room is far too dull. It desperately needs the crystals.

"Call me after, and let me know how it goes!" Dakota calls out right before we shut the door.

And suddenly, I'm off to see the evil wizard of broken hearts.

As it turns out, Elijah is not here, but Pia is. I got to fangirl over her latest book and how much I love the fake dating trope, and she told me more about her upcoming release too. It's the one we're shooting for.

It'll be the first book in a brand-new series—a marriage of convenience romance packed with angst and heat. In other words, my catnip.

When Stormie said they were almost set up and ready, I disappeared into the bathroom to freshen up my lipstick and fluff my hair. Half an hour on a subway does wonders to kill volume.

I don't get two steps out of the restroom before Theo corners me.

"Who's the boy toy?" He cocks a brow, and I know he's referring to Kyle.

Bracing myself, I peer up into his gorgeous face through my fake lashes. I reserve them for photoshoots, and Stormie insisted this was the perfect time to use them. "He's my boyfriend."

Something akin to doubt flickers across his tight grimace. "Bullshit. You brought him here to fuck with me, didn't you? Is he some kind of fake boyfriend like the one you obsessed over from Pia's book?"

My jaw comes unhinged. "Kyle is my *actual* boyfriend. We met at a wedding a few weeks ago. He asked me to stay for a drink once I was finished photographing the couple and their guests, and we —" I hold my hands up and raise my chin. "I don't have to explain myself to you."

His sinful lips settle into a shit-eating smirk, and it grates on my nerves. What the hell is he so smug about?

Rolling my eyes, I brush my shoulder against his and have every intention of marching past him, but he stops me with a low, grainy laugh.

"You brought him here so you could make sure to be on your best behavior," he says.

"What?" I snap, spinning around to face him again, and I applaud myself for being only momentarily distracted by how good he looks.

It's been several weeks since I last saw him, and I'd almost forgotten how sinfully sexy Theo is. How dark his eyes are below his thick, wild hair. How gravelly his voice is.

The top few buttons on his crisp white dress shirt are undone, and the shirt blossoms into a narrow V, which stops between his pecs. Velvety tan skin greets me each time Theo moves, and my mouth dries.

One look at him, and I'm weak in the knees.

But I refuse to be fooled by any of this.

It's in my best interest to remember that the man underneath is no picnic, nor is he worth my energy—or drool.

"You knew you wouldn't be able to keep your hands off me, so you brought the *boyfriend* in order to keep yourself honest." The jerk has the audacity to use air quotes around the word boyfriend.

"Ha! You are more full of it than Dakota said. She was being rather kind, but in truth, you are so damn arrogant," I say, my tone dripping with vengeance.

Something indiscernible blinks across his dusky eyes. If I had to guess, I'd say it's anger. Could it be because he knows I'm right? "There are two sides to every story, Raegan," he says, but it reaches my ears as more of a warning.

"Theo! Raegan!" Stormie's voice rings out through the studio.

With the help of her successful uncle, a commercial real estate mogul, my friend leased this place for her shoots. It's about the size of my own apartment but far more open, which is especially beneficial for our purposes. With several windows lining the walls, natural sunlight casts a glow over the room—another advantage.

The exposed brick wall offers a modern background, and a bed dressed in white sheets rests on one side, mocking me.

It watches me like the face in a painting as I move toward Stormie, my steps heavy with reluctance.

Is she going to make Theo and me take advantage of that bed?

If that's the case, bringing Kyle was a huge mistake. When he'd asked to tag along, I was hesitant. I didn't think it would be a good idea to invite my boyfriend to witness me posing scandalously with another guy for a steamy book cover, but Kyle insisted.

And I thought it was pretty adorable that he wanted to be supportive, even if he partly wanted to come in case Elijah would be here.

It's not so adorable now, as the prospect of literally crawling into bed with Theo looms over me.

The first thing Stormie asks him to do is stand behind me and wrap his arms around my waist.

"We'll take some shots here against the neutral backdrop, and then we'll move over to the bed. Does that sound good?" she asks over her shoulder for Pia's approval.

"That's perfect." She beams as she takes it all in. "I'd love to have some variety to choose from for the cover, plus teaser images." She turns to us. "Thanks again for agreeing to do this."

Theo and I each force smiles and grumble our polite responses.

We follow Stormie's lead, and I try to focus on Kyle over her shoulder, who nibbles on a cookie from the snack table my friend set up for us. Pia also brought champagne and a platter of meats and cheeses.

It all blurs, though, when Theo hugs me from behind, his strong arms holding me like he does this every day. It's easy to lose myself in them and the comforting warmth of his body.

His chest is harder than I remember from our first shoot.

When he rests his chin in my hair, I instinctively lean into the gesture.

My pulse quickens as the rate of Stormie's camera shutter increases.

Theo slides his hand up to tilt my chin toward his parted lips, and I willingly go where his touch leads.

"Amazing," Stormie gushes from behind the camera.

The background music playing from her Bluetooth speaker brings me back to reality, and I jerk out of Theo's hold.

"Sorry!" I blurt and shake my body loose from the evil tempter's spell.

"Are you okay?" Stormie steps forward. "You jumped like the time you got stung by a bee."

A nervous laugh escapes me as a sudden trickle of sweat skates down my back. Good thing I'm in a black dress that easily hides the evidence. A gross streak of sweat dampening my clothes would be embarrassing. "I'm fine. I just... felt a sneeze coming on. False alarm," I say, but my excuse is weak.

As I step back into position—into Theo's wickedly rugged arms—I hold my breath.

And the ass tsks before he whispers in my ear, his breath flitting across my flushed skin like a caress. "It's not too late to admit I was right. You still want me, don't you?"

I tighten my lips and force myself to find Kyle behind the camera and other equipment.

"Babe, you're doing something weird with your mouth." Stormie rises to her full height and checks the screen on her camera. "Are you comfortable? Is it your dress?"

She gestures toward the slim-fitting gown, the hem of which tickles the tops of my bare feet. To my delight, she told us we could leave the shoes behind since she'd only be shooting from the waist up.

I'm actually very comfortable in my attire. It's the sexy man's arms around me that's making my heart race.

And I hate it.

I hate him for doing this to me.

Is he purposely trying to mess with my head and make me look bad in front of Stormie—and Pia? It's possible I was too obvious with my admiration for her when we first arrived. Is this pig taking advantage and trying to humiliate me?

It looks that way. Why else would he insist I'm harboring some unrequited attraction to him?

Which I'm totally not.

Two can play this game.

"Actually, I could be *more* comfortable. In fact..." I spin in Theo's arms and hitch my leg to cling to the side of his waist that faces the camera. As if we've choreographed it, he catches me, sliding his hand up my exposed thigh, the slit in my dress perfect for this very moment.

"All right," Stormie cheers and almost drops her camera in an attempt to capture the spontaneous pose.

I thread my fingers through the thick hair at the nape of his neck and tug, parting my lips for the simultaneous purpose of giving Stormie a sexy shot—and toying right back with the annoying bastard.

"What the hell are you playing at?" he gruffly whispers against my mouth.

"Me? I'm not playing at anything," I answer sweetly. "I'm just doing my job. Try to keep up."

"You're in way over your head."

I arch my back, pressing my breasts into his chest and letting my loose hair flow behind me. "I'm just getting started," I whisper.

Theo chuckles darkly, the puffs of his amusement skating across my exposed throat. Heat involuntarily flares in my lower stomach as he drops his hands to grip my hips, his firm fingers mere millimeters above my ass.

I'm not wearing underwear underneath.

When I was getting ready, I didn't think twice about it. After all, it's not the first time I've gone commando in a fitted dress to avoid panty lines.

But I'm now thinking it was a terrible idea.

"You're not wearing anything under this, are you?" Theo deeply inhales, his lips brushing my jawline and sending a pulsating shiver down my spine. "That's pretty hot."

I grip his upper arm and maintain the pose, but it becomes increasingly difficult to remember there are people in this room.

I'm too aware of his blistering touch hovering over the exposed lower half of my body.

"If you would've returned my texts all those weeks ago, we could've been having so... much... fun," he punctuates each otherwise innocent word with sinister promises of what could've been.

"You lost the right to text me when you were an asshole to my friend," I snap, barely keeping my voice down.

He clucks his tongue as he takes an audible whiff of my hair like he's going to devour me by smell alone. "What did I say about two sides to the story?"

"I'd ask for your side, but it's likely riddled with lies. So why bother?"

He jerks me upright, spins me around, and yanks me flush against him like we were before, but we're much closer now. So close, I feel his heart throbbing against my back.

His touch is less tentative and warm than it was earlier. Rather, it's angry and possessive.

As he holds me, there's a hint of a plea beneath his grip. Am I imagining this?

"What? No comeback?" I goad, extremely pleased to be winning this little game he started.

He slides his hand up my side and pauses with his thumb on the outside of my breast.

A small, shocked gasp escapes me, and I clamp my mouth closed.

But it's too late.

It's out there, and my sole hope is that he's the only one who heard it.

Then again, of all the people in the room, he's the worst one to have heard it.

I feel his lips curl into a smile at my temple. As expected, he gloats. "I don't need a comeback. You're doing enough talking—and confessing—for the both of us."

"I've confessed nothing," I bite out.

"Admit you want me..."

I leap forward and shove him off me, breaking the spell once again. "Don't touch me," I warn.

"Umm..." Stormie's confused voice pulls me toward where she stands—and back to the room full of people, one of whom is my boyfriend.

"There," I blurt. "Don't touch me... there... on my side. I, um, nicked my side on the edge of my desk this morning, and it's still sore."

Theo covers his mouth with both hands, undoubtedly hiding a smirk the size of New York behind them, and it fuels my anger.

How dare he.

This is my job, and I'm damn good at it. But he's making me out to be a joke in front of my peers. All because I rejected him.

From what Dakota said, I figured his ego would've been so big and impenetrable that a few unanswered texts would've barely made a dent.

Guess the opposite is true. Theo's ego is fragile and riddled with holes of insecurities.

And he's taken his last shot.

Because if I have any plans of working with Pia or any of her friends in the future—and I'd really like to—I need to force a one-eighty on this session, stat.

Theo Lazaridis is going to regret messing with me.

"I promise that's the last interruption," I announce to Stormie, then smile at Pia, who nods sympathetically.

I fist Theo's shirt and pull him back toward me, but Stormie stops us. "I think we got all these shots. We can get a few individual ones here, then do a wardrobe change and move to the bed."

Firing him a final warning glare, I release his shirt and put much-needed distance between us.

I take shots on my own and use the time apart from the jerk to slow my racing heart. Once Stormie gives me a thumbs-up, signaling she's done with me for now, I excuse myself to change while Theo resumes my position for his turn.

I've seen enough of him today, so there's no need to stick around for more.

I know exactly what his pompous smolder looks like.

But before I storm off, he whips his shirt off while Stormie steps to the side, her camera covering her face as her finger works double time to snap several shots.

Theo leans on the wall, opening and closing a fist at his side and flexing his tricep. His brooding smolder deepens as he looks straight into the camera—and I keep my eyes trained on him.

His abs are cut from stone, hard and magnificent. A true work of art.

Stormie tells him to bite his lip, and my ovaries scream with delight.

Until his attention lands on me, exposing my obvious appreciation of his naked torso. I spin to escape this torture and race toward the bathroom, where I hope to compose myself in private, but I bump into Kyle.

"Didn't you hear me saying your name?" he asks, gripping my upper arm.

I blink, bringing him in and out of focus as my pulse spikes with hatred for the man I'm supposed to pretend to want. "Sorry. I was just... thinking about what to wear next."

"The red thing you tried on this morning is sexy as fuck. That's my pick."

"Maybe," I agree weakly, still dazed from the last few minutes.

"Here's a water." He produces an unopened bottle from his side and offers it to me.

As I accept, I run my gaze over him, searching for any indication of discomfort, but he seems at ease. Like he's at the Museum of Modern Art, one of his favorite places to visit in the city. Why does that piss me off? Is he not seeing what's happening?

Another man—a very *hot* man—is groping me, and my own boyfriend doesn't seem to give a shit. What the hell?

After I've swallowed a sip of water to wet my dry throat, I pry, "How are you? Doing okay with all this?"

"It's very new and different for me, but I think that's what is exciting. You're very talented." He beams. "I couldn't keep a straight face out there, if I were you. That's next level shit."

It's so kind of him to say these things, especially since I fear I'm butchering this photoshoot. But instead of thanking Kyle, I press, "So, you're... fine with everything?"

He shrugs and glances down at his phone. "You've got to be fucking kidding me. Jonah's taking his boring cousin Gerard to see the Mets in a couple weeks. The son of a bitch. I have to call him."

"Now?" I blink again, but this time, it's in disbelief.

Kyle doesn't answer me. Instead, he gives me his back, offering his full attention to his phone.

Which leaves me with so many questions, at the top being—did he mean what he said, or was he complimenting me while really thinking about the Mets game?

Replacing the cold Kyle left in his wake is a warmth I'd love to believe is only in my head.

Unfortunately, I'm not so lucky.

I refuse to turn around, my head and chest a storm of mixed emotions. "Don't start with me," I caution.

Theo's low voice flows over me in waves as he simply says, "I'm just here for a snack." He reaches his arm around me, gently grazing my hand to grab a couple of crackers and cheeses.

Exhaling, I squeeze my eyes closed and imagine I'm at the beach with my toes in the sand and a colorful cocktail in my hand. I've never been so angry that I needed to rely on my imagination to settle my nerves, but as it turns out, Theo has a knack for pushing me to the edge—and over it.

"Nice boyfriend of yours," he says evenly, but I'm not falling for it.

"We're really together, asshole."

"I believe you." There's zero indication in his tone that he believes Kyle is fake, but he's too casual. Something's up, and if I had to guess, he's still convinced I'm putting on a show like I'm a sad chick set on making Theo jealous.

I spin around to face him, and thankfully, he's fully dressed again. "What are you doing? What was that out there?"

"I'm just doing my job." He slips a cracker between his lips and onto his tongue, eating the innocent snack like he's in an erotic perfume commercial.

I don't even register the crunching sounds he makes as he chews. I'm transfixed on the way his tongue darts out again to swipe any remaining crumbs on his thin lips.

How can he make crackers so hot?

And why am I so turned on by him?

I've never wanted someone whose personality I hated, and

Theo is making me question my sanity. It must be that I'm just horny for anyone.

I haven't had sex in months, and maybe this whole afternoon is a sign that I need to do it with Kyle already. That, or I should really take a break from the sexy episodes of *Bridgerton*. Simon and Anthony are the stuff of filthy dreams, and they're messing with my hormones too much lately.

"What? Do I have something on my cheek?" Theo lifts his fingers to brush his face and smirks.

"Whatever you think you're accomplishing by being an ass—stop. Because it's not going to work." I grip my tote tightly until my knuckles turn white, then practically stomp off to the bathroom to change.

We succeed with the next part of the session, posing on the bed with as much intensity and heat as before, but I keep my breathing in check.

My mind on the prize.

And my heart still.

I try to, anyway.

Theo is relentless in his attempts to get a rise out of me, but now that I know his tricks, I'm better prepared to counter them.

Until Stormie asks us to look deep into each other's eyes. To portray longing and affection.

We do as she says, and I do my best to block out who he is. In fact, I pretend he's someone else entirely. It's only for a few seconds.

I can pretend for the sake of my job—and future.

Surprisingly, it's not so difficult. Because when I gaze into Theo's rich chocolate eyes, scattered black flecks swimming in their depths, I'm reminded of the guy I thought he was the night he kissed me.

His eyes had locked on to mine then too, captivating me in a realm of possibilities.

So thrilling.

The anticipation had rocked my core, and I would've given anything to find out where that kiss would lead us.

"Fantastic," Stormie compliments. "These are great, you guys!"

Theo licks his lips, and I eagerly follow the movement with my eyes, lost in the charade.

I angle my head to the side, casting my gaze over his sharp nose and strong cheeks. His citrusy cologne fills my nostrils, and the sensual smell teams up with my memories to further ease my defenses.

Dazed, I lean in until our foreheads touch, and Stormie calls out more and more encouragement, like she's cheering us on.

It drowns out the music and other voices in the room.

Goose bumps cover my arms as a current of electricity hums through my veins.

Everything goes dark as Theo's mouth covers mine... and I don't push him away.

Reason in the back of my mind screams at me, scolding my weak body for its betrayal as my lips effortlessly glide over his.

I savor his taste.

It's exactly as I remember—intense, heady, and explosive.

"We got it," I hear to our side, but it sounds far away. It could be meant for anyone else.

It could be coming from outside, for all I know.

I bring both hands up to Theo's neck and hold him there as I melt into our kiss, opening my mouth and drinking in his low groan, and my skin tingles from the heat of our connection.

"I said, we got it!" Stormie calls out, and I peel my mouth off my enemy's, snapping out of yet another trance this man put me in.

What is up with that?

He's just a person. He's not a god, or a vagina whisperer.

Have some self-control, Raegan!

But I didn't. I displayed a total lack of control and resolve by kissing him.

What did I just do?

FOUR

RAEGAN

THEO'S CHEEKS SPLIT INTO A SATISFIED GRIN. "IS THIS A GOOD time to say I told you so?"

I shove him off me and scoot to the edge of the bed, where I hop onto my feet and leap toward Stormie—to safety. "So, we're finished?" I ask, embarrassingly breathless.

She lifts her curious gaze from the camera screen, peeks over my shoulder, then back at me as she whispers, "You and Theo are finished with the shoot, but you and I are just getting started. What the hell just happened?"

I swipe my hair away from my clammy forehead, sweat pooling over my lower back and neck, which is likely obvious at this point in my satin floral top. "I thought it would be a good shot, that's all."

"I thought we hated Theo for what he did to Dakota, although I'm still shook by what she said." She chews on her bottom lip, her camera resting on her chest and separating us as chatter drifts over us from behind. "When I first met Theo, he was a sweetheart. And ridiculously hot, of course. Dakota was instantly hooked when we met him at the gym way back, and I couldn't blame her."

"Looks and first impressions are often deceiving."

Stormie returns her gaze to me, and I note a hint of doubt in her eyes. "I don't know. I guess you're right."

"What're you thinking?" I pry.

"I'm still surprised they went out to begin with. I mean, she flirted with him—we both did, and I'm not ashamed of it—but I thought that was it. I don't understand why she wouldn't tell me they went out."

"Maybe she didn't want you to feel weird since you work together," I rationalize. It would make sense.

She shrugs. "It's really great to work with Theo, and he's a popular choice. After Pia's cover releases with his face on it, he's going to be an even bigger deal."

"Okay," I draw out, still attempting to fill in the gaps she's leaving out and catch up on her trail of thinking.

"Is Dakota upset with me for working with Theo, or something? She's barely spoken to me in weeks, and she's been dodging all my invitations to hang out. I know she's mad at him, but this is strictly business for me."

"Me too," I insist, my cheeks still hot from the kiss.

My freaking lips tingle too. How long is that going to last?

"I'd take a stand against him, but..." She chews on her lip again, like she's afraid to tell me the truth. This whole conversation feels like it's difficult for her. "Can we really trust her judgment on this? This is the same girl who claimed one of her classmates in college only dated her to cheat off her during tests, but it turned out that's what she was doing to him. She also flirted heavily with the barista at our favorite coffee shop just for free lattes. She claimed he had a thing for her, but he had a boyfriend."

I stiffen.

"Dakota—God love her—hasn't always been totally honest with

us," she continues, "especially when it comes to shiny new guys. And Theo is *hella* shiny."

"We all did stupid things in college and made a ton of mistakes," I say. "But Dakota is our friend. She has nothing to gain from lying about Theo."

Stormie holds her hands up. "You're right. I'm just grasping at straws to make myself feel better for being a shitty friend, and doing so just makes me even shittier."

"You're not. Look, we live in New York. We literally can't afford to have extra rigid morals," I joke, but I'm also halfway serious. It's the reason I decided to be here today.

The rent isn't going to pay itself, unfortunately, and until Dakota finds a new job, I need to take any financial opportunity that comes my way.

"I just need to figure out a way to talk to her long enough to explain," Stormie says, but it sounds like it's more to herself than to me.

"That was amazing!" Pia cuts in and clings to my arm. "I cannot wait to see these images."

"We got a lot of good ones. Of course, this friend of mine makes it easy." Stormie nudges my shoulder with hers.

I'm about to return the compliment—she's the magician behind the camera, after all—but Kyle catches my eye. I immediately freeze with the hair standing up at the back of my neck.

He's distraught, with his shoulders slumped forward and a frown I could spot from space.

Shit.

"I'd love to take you all out to dinner tonight," Pia offers, her megawatt smile making my heart sink. "Are you free? Your boyfriend can join us too."

"That would be so great," I force out. It's hard to match her enthusiasm with the prospect of seeing more of Theo looming over us. "I'll ask Kyle."

"How about we pop this baby open already?" Theo appears

next to us, holding the bottle of champagne over his head like this is a New Year's Eve party.

If possible, Pia's grin grows wider, and Stormie shoots a questioning stare my way.

I need to find Kyle. I assume he wants to talk about what just happened, but I only get one step from the huddle when a pop echoes behind me, followed by cold liquid splashing across my neck and upper back.

I yelp and face the group again in time to catch Stormie's hands flying to her gaping mouth. Pia does the same, and Theo lunges forward, the bubbling champagne bottle still in his grasp.

Fizzy liquid spews from the top and over his hands, and my eye twitches.

Theo curses under his breath. "It was an accident. I'm—"

"You did it on purpose!" I screech and release a harsh exhale as champagne drips from the ends of my hair.

"I didn't," he argues. "It was an—"

"You aimed the bottle right at me—"

"—accident, I swear."

"—because you're an asshole."

"I'll get you some napkins," he offers, but I'm not buying this whole apologetic gimmick.

"Like those will help! I need a damn shower." I scoff as I scoop my hair over my shoulder and pull my sticky satin top away from my lower back. I was worried about the sweat earlier, but this is much worse. "My shirt is ruined. Satin and champagne don't mix very well."

"Neither do bitterness and delusion, but you make them both work," he shoots back. "You're fine. It's just a little champagne—not acid."

And my rage spikes.

I could strangle him.

"You're *so* clever, aren't you," I deadpan. "That flying cork you aimed right at my face could've blinded me, I hope you know."

"That's a stretch." He rolls his eyes.

While we were posing, and I thought he was trying to embarrass me, I didn't believe I could get any angrier.

I was very wrong.

This is the peak of my fury. I'd unleash it too, if Stormie and Pia didn't just rush back with napkins and a towel. I never even noticed them leave us.

"This is the only towel I could find, but it should help," Pia says, holding out a gray hand towel that's more like the size of a face cloth.

I thank her through gritted teeth and instantly regret how harsh I sound. It's not my intention. Then again, it was never my intention to let Theo get this far under my skin.

I squeeze the ends of my hair into the towel as Stormie dabs at my back with the napkins.

All this time, Kyle still hovers in the background with his attention glued to his phone, and it annoys the hell out of me that he's not trying to help.

Is it possible he's still outraged over the fucking Mets game?

If this wasn't my place of work, and I didn't have witnesses, I'd scream. Never in my life have I wanted to scream so badly, but there's a first for everything.

"Thank you," I say to Stormie and Pia, but this time, my words hold a gentler tone.

"We can do a raincheck on dinner if you want." Pia smiles sympathetically.

I shake my head and force a smile back. Even if Kyle is mad at me, or Theo will be attending this dinner, I can't pass on an opportunity to sit down with Pia and convince her I'm not a complete moron or rage monster.

It's my chance to show her I'm normal—fun, even.

"No. It's totally fine," I say. "I'll change my clothes, then order a drink I can't sip from my hair."

"We will definitely order drinks—strong ones." She giggles. "My husband will be meeting us too."

"Elijah Hastings?" Theo chimes in. If he were a dog, his ears would've perked straight up, and his tongue would be hanging out of the side of his mouth.

I'd say he's a fan of the rock star.

"I'm definitely game for dinner," Theo says, then quickly adds, "Not that I wasn't excited before knowing he'd be there. Besides, I never turn down a dinner with three gorgeous ladies. I'm just—"

"And my boyfriend," I interject with a scowl. "Kyle will also be there."

Theo flashes his own annoyed sneer my way and grinds out, "Yes. Of course. *Kyle*." He turns back to Pia and says, "I'm a huge Faint of Heart fan."

"He'll be happy to hear that, although I really don't encourage many compliments. His inflated ego can't take any more," she teases.

"Can I talk to you?" Kyle appears next to me and nods toward a more private corner.

I excuse myself from the group and follow him out of their earshot, interested to know why he didn't join us sooner.

Alone, he lets out a long exhale, or maybe it's simply long to me because the knot in my gut tells me I'm not going to like what he says next.

I can't make this about the champagne spill. It wouldn't be fair, not after I kissed another man.

"I know the last part must have been weird for you, and I wouldn't blame you for being upset," I say and hold my breath.

"Upset? That's putting it lightly." His laugh is humorless. "Is Theo an ex-boyfriend or something?"

"No," I assert. "We worked together a couple months ago, but that's it. He actually went out with Dakota before that, and he turned out to be a real piece of work. I don't even like him as a friend. He's truly terrible. A real blemish on humanity," I ramble.

"Seemed like you were more than just friends when you kissed him." His defeated gaze bores into mine, and guilt swells in the pit of my stomach.

"Kyle, this is... my job," I defend myself, but it's a weak and rather lame explanation. It's unconvincing to my own ears, but I continue nonetheless, desperately trying to make things right. "We're models for the cover of a romance book. Things get heated sometimes. It's common."

I'm not completely lying. Depending on what kind of story it is, the cover image could involve heavy petting and kissing. Some covers Stormie has shot are way steamier too, with a lot more skin.

But that's not what happened here, and Kyle and I both know it, unfortunately.

"You were fine in the beginning when we were all but kissing. Was it just the kiss that bothered you? If so, I—"

"I wasn't even paying attention in the beginning because my stupid cousin was being a selfish dick over the tickets."

I furrow my brow, and hurt replaces the previous guilt that gnawed at me. "So, all the nice things you said about my talent were, what? Lies?"

"Don't come at me about lies, Raegan," he says, condescension dripping from each syllable in my name. "You and Theo obviously have something going on, whether you want to admit it to me or not."

"We don't," I say, punctuating the T with added resentment for the implication.

"Is he the reason you won't sleep with me?"

I gape, unsure if my mouth is wider than my eyes bugging out of my head. "Is that what you're really pissed about? Sex?"

"The *lack of* sex."

"Unbelievable," I mutter under my breath and turn in place, jumbled thoughts racing through my mind.

"We're all packed up," Stormie interrupts from a few feet away.

Her expression scrunches into one of concern as she studies us. "Ready to head out?"

"Almost," I answer her. Before I turn, I catch a shadow behind my friend, but it quickly disappears. Roughly exhaling, I say to Kyle, "I don't think you should come to dinner."

He grimaces. "I wasn't going to. I'm so done."

I fold my arms over my chest and stare after him as he practically runs out of the studio like he can't get away from me fast enough.

How did one afternoon lead to such chaos?

"Is he meeting us at the restaurant?" Stormie asks with dubious optimism.

I close my eyes and shake my head. "I think we just broke up, not that we had much of a relationship to begin with."

"It was still new," she reasons.

"Apparently, not new enough. According to him, we should've been sleeping together already."

"Oh, babe." She closes the distance between us and hooks her arm through mine. "If he was pressuring you, then good riddance."

"That's the thing—I thought he was fine with taking things slow."

Kyle hadn't given me any pushback on my resolve to hold off on sex. Sure, he was disappointed, but it was in a playful way.

Or so I thought.

Did he really just believe the reason I haven't been sleeping with him is... Theo? That I've been using Kyle to fill the time or something?

At the end of the day, it doesn't even matter what Kyle was thinking. It's clear he was not the one for me, especially considering how easy it was for him to walk away.

I let out another rough, frustrated exhale. "I'm so gullible, aren't I?"

"Why do you say that?"

"Let's consider my track record this year." I tap my chin. "I was duped by Theo, and I believed the best in Kyle. Both turned out to be complete jerks."

"Those were just two, and they both fooled me too."

"What about Sloppy Sal, who drank so much on New Year's Eve that there was barely enough for the rest of us? To make that night even worse, he somehow convinced me to pay for bottle service at that high-end bar in Manhattan because he forgot his credit card, but he would *totally* pay me back. I'm still waiting. Anyone with half a brain would've immediately run the other way before charging a few hundred bucks they didn't have to their already pathetic account."

She winces. "I'll give you that one, but there's nothing wrong with *you*. You've just had some bad luck lately. It'll turn around, starting with dinner with an author you love and a rock star who's so incredibly yummy that I'm going to have a hard time focusing on the food tonight instead of him."

I inhale deeply and brush the hair out of my face. "You're right. Not even stupid Theo can ruin that for me. Although, he is partially responsible for breaking Kyle and me up, and he will pay for that."

"So, it wasn't just the sex thing, then?" She quirks a brow as she fishes a key out of the black leather belt bag slung across her chest.

"I'll tell you everything, but first, I need to get out of these clothes." I hoist my tote up from the floor and rush to the bathroom, ready to shed this champagne-soaked top.

I would've loved to wear this out. It matches my lipstick, which I notice from the mirror is smeared.

From the kiss.

Thanks to Theo's hypnotizing lips, my previously flawless makeup is ruined.

My heart thumps, the echoes of each beat loud in my head as I peel the sticky clothes off me and replace them with clean ones, then retrieve my cosmetics bag and touch up my lipstick, blush, and hair. After fussing with my clumped strands, I toss my hair into a low bun, my fingers still trembling with residual vexation over this evening.

But there's still time to turn it around. If I keep my focus on Pia, Elijah, and Stormie, I'll be fine. That's three people—more than enough to hold my attention. There's no need to even notice the fourth.

Unless he chokes on an appetizer. Could I get so lucky?

Happy with my fresh appearance, I exit the bathroom in the red jumpsuit Kyle said he liked, and I have to admit, it empowers me. Not because he liked it, or because it's dry. It simply feels good to be in it. The red pops against my fair skin, and the polyester material daringly clings to my natural curves.

While we turn out the lights, grab Stormie's things, and lock up, I fill her in on Kyle's ridiculous assumptions and accusations.

And the more I recount, the less upset I am over Kyle's rejection, and the more my temper boils to dangerous levels over Theo fucking Lazaridis.

FIVE

THEO

As I ride in an Uber for the short distance to the restaurant, soft taps of raindrops against the window blend with the ragged sounds of my labored breaths.

What the hell got into me this afternoon?

As soon as I laid eyes on Raegan—the effortless flow of her hair down her back, the gleam in her eye, the achingly sensual red tint of her bow-shaped lips—every pep talk I'd given myself before she showed up flew out the window. They were as useless to me as the three-pound dumbbells at the gym.

Instantly, I was filled with an irritating combination of lust, anger, and disappointment. I hate that lust was in the mix at all. I shouldn't want someone so narrow-minded, who insults my integrity and refuses her own feelings just because she blindly believes someone else's lies.

And I know Raegan harbors feelings for me, even if they are only physical. I can work with physical attraction, but she's being so damn stubborn in her misguided crusade to paint me as the bad guy.

Then there's the "boyfriend."

My vision fucking blurred when she told me she's seeing someone. The thought of him—or anyone else—touching her nearly punctured my spleen.

I lost my head and pushed her boundaries. Contrary to what she might think, I wasn't trying to embarrass or mess with her. I only wanted to test her. To prove I was right about her wanting me.

And right I was, even if she insists on digging her heels into the ground and denying it all.

If the way she so willingly—and eagerly—kissed me wasn't enough proof, there's the hushed conversation with her little boy toy too.

"Is he the reason you won't sleep with me?"

That's the only thing I heard while they talked, but it was enough to make me smirk.

Kyle isn't touching her, after all, and the confirmation made me deliriously happy, especially considering I might've had something to do with it.

I'm the first to arrive at the restaurant, sitting alone at a long table while I wait for the other five. I almost told the hostess there would only be four more joining me, purposely leaving Raegan's plus-one out, but I decided to be a good boy.

For now.

This war with Raegan is far from over, but I can play nice until the "boyfriend" disappears. Judging by the brief conversation I caught earlier, that might be sooner rather than later.

A server approaches the table and places both hands behind his back. "I'll give you a moment to peruse our wine menu."

"No need. Any kind of red wine will be perfect, please." I unbutton my suit jacket and open it in order to breathe more easily while I sit.

Before I left the studio, I'd changed back into my suit, the first thing I'd worn during our shoot—before she kissed me.

That kiss with Raegan was so fucking right.

I can't explain it. There's no logic or reason. I've just been drawn to her since the moment we met, and the last two months apart have done nothing to curb my need for her—and the need to battle her defenses until she dismantles them completely.

"Hey, Theo!" Pia chirps, and a guy dressed in all black is in tow.

Elijah Hastings.

His hands are on his wife's waist as he guides her to sit across from me, leaving the seats to my left open.

I stand and greet them both, offering my hand to Elijah, who gives it a quick shake. Niko is going to freak when I tell him I'm having dinner with one of our favorite musicians.

"Pia tells me the shoot went really well." Elijah beams over at her, and she blushes. "I wish I could've been there."

"You had to work. It's no big deal." She lovingly pats his hand on the table, then grips it, her petite fingers threading through his.

"What are you working on?" I venture, shifting forward in my seat as excitement rolls through me. It's a damn dream to be sitting here with him. As a once-in-a-lifetime opportunity, I'd kick myself if I didn't make the most of it, which involves prying into anything music-related going on in his life.

"The band and I are recording a new single. We've gone over it countless times, but something feels off." He winces.

"I still think Boone is to blame," Pia adds.

Elijah's mouth splits into a mischievous grin. "You blame him for everything, just like my sister."

"It's because of your sister that I do it."

"You should spend less time with her and more with me." He winks down at her.

The newlyweds are lost in their own bubble, much like Catherine and Todd were when they first got married. They're still deliriously—and sickeningly—in love, but having a kid redirected a lot of their affections, as she claims.

I've never been in any kind of love before, and I've never cared. I still don't. It's not what I'm looking for, and besides, I wouldn't have time for it. I'm too busy with modeling and building the podcast. Plus, my family obligations take up any free time.

A serious relationship isn't on the table for me, but having a supportive partner and a mutually encouraging relationship like Pia and Elijah seem to have don't sound unappealing. I could be on board with that.

Somewhere in the future, anyway.

Our server pops over to take their drink orders, and as soon as he disappears, Pia smiles crookedly at me. "I'm sorry, Theo. We've been droning on without you."

"No need to apologize. I have four siblings and very nosy parents. Our dinners often involve random conversations happening over each other, usually at an unnecessarily loud volume. I'm just happy to be in the presence of people who know what a normal decibel sounds like." I laugh, and they join me.

She pats Elijah's hand again but addresses me when she says, "For the record, their drummer, Boone, isn't all that bad, although he and I did not get off to a great start."

"Which he's still paying for, even if he doesn't always know it," Elijah adds, balling up his fist.

I'd love to hear more about that, but Stormie and Raegan show up before I get another word out.

I nearly swallow my fucking tongue.

Raegan's hair is no longer down. Instead, she's pulled it into a low bun at the base of her slender neck, soft wisps framing her heart-shaped face.

Her delicate curves are on display in the deep red jumpsuit she's changed into. It's much sexier than the black dress she wore at the photoshoot. Of course, she looks great in anything, but this... this is unfair.

She's messing with fire by wearing its color, which matches the stain on her lips. They're no longer swollen and smudged like they were after our kiss, as if she wiped it away.

But it happened.

No matter how much she might want to forget about it, we kissed, and it was better than any fantasy I've ever had.

"What did we miss?" Stormie attempts to sit at the end, but Raegan beats her to it, forcing her friend to sit next to me.

It's comical, really, how hard she tries to put distance between us, but her efforts are pointless. Raegan will be sitting next to me by the end of this dinner—that's a fact.

"We were just boring Theo with the band's stories," Pia answers, then gives introductions for Elijah and the women. After they exchange pleasantries, Pia glances over Raegan's shoulder and asks, "Is Kyle still coming?"

My head swivels in her direction, and I wait on the edge of my seat for her answer.

To my surprise, Raegan's gaze flickers to mine, although the malice in it is no surprise at all. "He's not going to make it tonight," she finally answers with a sigh.

"Next time," Pia offers, but Raegan simply shrugs, her expression now unreadable.

But I'm elated.

Their argument must've been a lot worse than I originally thought. Is he out of the equation altogether?

I plan on finding out, and soon.

When the server returns to our table, Elijah points around the group. "Should we order a bottle of champagne to celebrate your day?"

Stormie claps, but Raegan purses her lips. "None for me. I still have plenty of it in my hair from earlier."

"What kind of photoshoot was this?" Elijah teases.

"It was an accident," I clip for the third or fourth time tonight—

I'm losing count. I lean forward to get a better view of her, and her lips are still set into a firm line of aggravation.

She doesn't believe me.

Stormie holds her hands up like a referee might at a wrestling match. "Whether we order more champagne, wine, or hard liquor, we're definitely going to need something strong, or these two won't make it through dinner. Neither will we." She points to herself, Elijah, and Pia as she says the last part.

Elijah drops his voice for Pia's benefit, but he's loud enough for me to make out what he says. "I really wish I could've been there today. I missed out on all the fun."

Tsking, she elbows his side and picks up the menu in front of her.

After we place our order, Elijah turns to me. "So, four siblings, huh? Shit."

"You're Greek, right?" Pia asks. As I nod, she says, "You must have a ton of fun stories."

This makes me laugh, as a zillion memories instantly slam into me. My brother, sisters, and I practically grew up in our family's restaurant. The trouble we'd get into is what my mother claims prematurely turned her hair gray, but she often says she wouldn't have had it any other way.

She loved watching us play restaurant with plastic dishes and a fake cash register. She got a kick out of perching Niko onto the counter by the actual register, where he'd greet customers with a toothy grin and hand them their change.

Catherine would wear an apron three times her small size and take orders.

The restaurant bug stuck with them, but Angie, Kia, and I didn't find the same type of home there. Maybe because there's no more room for the three of us to make it our own. But each of us has found something else to fill our souls.

If only Dad would respect it.

"A lot of fun stories—yes," I tell her with a wistful smile. "My brother and I even have a podcast called *Growing Up Greek*, where we share those stories."

"Really?" Pia sits up straighter. "I'll definitely check it out, especially for book research."

"If you have any questions, I'm happy to help."

"That would be great. I probably have too many questions to help me flesh out the character. Google is great, but it can only take me so far." She giggles and sets her water aside to rest her hands on the table in front of her. "Do you speak Greek?"

"I don't." I give her a tight-lipped smile as disappointment floods my chest.

I shouldn't be surprised. It's a common question I've gotten all my life, so I should be used to it by now. But it doesn't change the fact that I wish I had a different answer.

Although I know a few words, the language as a whole is very difficult, and my accent is laughable. Trying to use what few phrases I'd once practiced on my dad proved to be futile. He didn't appreciate it as much as I thought he would, and he's the only reason I ever attempted to learn in the first place.

I thought it would strengthen our connection, given we don't share any of the same interests, but it turned out to be just another swing and a miss.

I could try to learn again for my own benefit in the case that I do visit Greece, which I'd like to someday, but learning to speak the language fluently would need to be a full-time job. As I've gotten older, it's become harder to dedicate the time and care it would require.

"What about the food? What're some common themes in the cuisine?" Pia continues, unfazed that I claim to be Greek but don't speak the language.

It's a relief, but it's also frustrating to feel like I need that factor to be validated in my ancestry. I think it would help bridge some of the gap between my father and me, and that's what really fucking stings.

Will that ever go away?

"Greeks love their extra virgin olive oil, oregano, and bread. With those three things, anything is possible." I chuckle.

Elijah lifts his glass. "I love it. Cheers to that!"

I clink my wineglass to his short one, which is filled with whiskey, no ice.

"And your favorite food?" This question comes from Stormie to my left.

"I'd have to say—"

"So, Elijah, Pia—you recently got married," Raegan cuts in. "The pictures online looked gorgeous."

We all stare at her, although my gaze lingers longer than the rest.

Raegan smiles. "Sorry. It's just the last time I had Greek food, I got extreme food poisoning, so I needed a subject change."

I nearly choke on the last drop of my wine. Is she referring to me as the Greek food in this scenario? That I'm the one who makes her sick to her stomach?

That's fucking rich.

"Plus, I'm a wedding photographer, so I'd love to hear all about your big day," Raegan adds.

Pia and Elijah make moony eyes at each other as she describes the wedding day using details of flowers and dresses I don't know the meaning of.

It wouldn't matter if I did, though, because irritation builds in my bloodstream, causing my pulse to spike and my dick to stir.

I'm still squirming halfway through the meal when Pia brings up the photoshoot again, filling Elijah in on the success of it.

"You two have such amazing chemistry," she says to Raegan and me. "When I saw Stormie's portfolio of your last session, I knew right away that I needed to book a custom shoot."

"It's true," Elijah confirms. "I was trying to enjoy the last day of our honeymoon in Paris, and all she could do was talk about her next cover."

Laughter buzzes from everyone at the table. Even Raegan smiles at that, but what does she think about Pia's compliment? She saw our connection from a few images long before she witnessed us in action for herself. My self-proclaimed archnemesis must have thoughts on that.

I have plenty of my own, including vengeful ways to get her back for the jab about Greek food—and to punish her for making my balls blue.

I seize the opportunity when Raegan excuses herself to go to the bathroom, her hips dancing to a beat of their own, ebbing and flowing like the wild waves of an ocean.

Silently, I rise from my seat, and my feet carry me in the same direction. I don't know what I'm going to say, but I just know I need to talk to her—alone.

Pacing outside the women's restroom, I jam both hands through my hair and sigh. This woman makes me crazy, and for reasons I can't explain, I crave more of it.

More of her.

I haven't been able to get her out of my head for two months, and I can't leave this restaurant without taking one last shot.

The door finally swings open, and I stop a few inches from her.

One hand flies to her chest, her fingers splayed over the V-neck of her jumpsuit. The ruffled straps are flirty and fun, but the deep neckline is sexy and inviting.

I want to touch her there. To slip my own fingers inside and find out for myself if she's wearing a bra. If her nipples are already hard, or if they'll harden under the heat of my touch.

What does she sound like when she's pleasured?

The need to find out consumes me—I'm like a fucking caveman.

"You scared the shit out of me," she hisses, and half her face disappears into the shadow of the empty hall. Thanks to the soft glow of the dim lighting above, I can still make out her adorable scowl.

She's not fooling anyone, though, least of all me. It's a cover to mask her true feelings for me.

"Don't tell me you're here to chastise me for cutting off the Theo show out there."

"Cute," I deadpan.

"You're the one who couldn't stop talking about yourself."

"Let's talk about you now. Why did your *boyfriend* not join us tonight?" I stuff a hand into my pocket, exuding casual indifference, but in reality, I'm cautious. What she says next might just crush me, although I have an inkling it'll do the exact opposite.

After all, I may or may not be the reason she never slept with the jackass, so what she says next might be the greatest compliment I've ever received.

"Stop saying it like that. Kyle was actually my boyfriend," she insists and crosses both arms over her chest, hiding my view of her cleavage.

"*Was*?" I cock a brow.

There it is. The truth I've been happily suspecting all night.

She clamps her mouth shut.

"Did your roommate talk shit about him too, so you ended it with him like you did me?"

"You and I were never together."

"We could've been." I tread toward her with care, stepping into the light as she backs out of it until she hits the wall. "Still could be, if you'd admit how attracted you are to me."

"*Please*." She scoffs. "I'm as attracted to you as I am to this wallpaper." She points a finger over my shoulder, and I take it in my hand, sliding my palm against hers as if I'm trying it on for size.

And look at that—it fits.

My hand covers hers as perfectly as a glove would, and the singe of her skin against mine sends a shot of adrenaline through my stomach.

"I don't believe you," I whisper.

"If I'm so attracted to you, why would I have gone out with

someone else? Kyle and I were *great* together, but thanks to you, he left me." She yanks her hand away, but she doesn't storm off. Instead, she pushes off the wall and shoves me backward. "It's because of your stupid stunt at the photoshoot that he left, and you're going to pay for that. I swear to God, you're going to fucking pay."

"I did you a favor. You should be thanking me." I stand my ground and press my chest against hers. With the help of her fuck-me heels, she reaches me in height, and it works out in my favor as the tips of her breasts brush against me.

I welcome the torture.

I run my teeth over my bottom lip and growl. "No man worth his balls sits idly by while another guy kisses his woman, and that's exactly what Kyle did. He didn't so much as flinch. No one is that cocky and secure not to even flinch."

I glimpse a flash of hurt cross her expression, starting in her eyes and ending with a frown on her lips.

She knows I'm right.

I cup the side of her face, and look at that—her cheek rests perfectly in my palm too. It's like our bodies were made for each other. "If you were mine, and I was the one watching you from the sidelines, I would've burned down the entire building had another man laid a finger on you," I whisper down to her.

"You're lying."

"You're right." I smirk, fire blazing in my veins as I say, "I'd never be on the sidelines. Not when it comes to you."

Her eyelids flutter closed, and her thick lashes fan evenly across the tops of her cheeks.

I rub the apple of one cheek, grazing the tips of those lashes with intrigue and fascination. Raegan is beyond gorgeous.

She's resilient and stubborn and loyal.

Although her loyalty to her friend is the reason she and I haven't been fucking each other's brains out all this time, I've come to respect such a trait in her. Even though she doesn't know the whole truth, she insists on being a good friend, instead of acting on what I know she desires. It's admirable, even if it comes at my expense.

A woman enters the dark hallway and breaks us out of our spell.

Raegan backs away to one side of the wall, while I take the opposite. Facing each other, we freeze on either side of the imaginary line drawn between us, down which the woman walks to reach the bathroom.

Once the door swings shut behind her, I meet Raegan's gaze, determined not to let the moment pass us by entirely. "Have you asked yourself why we have such good chemistry?"

"Because I'm a great actress?" she quips. "I hear people uncover all kinds of hidden talents in moments of great discomfort."

"Bullshit," I counter and step into the light again, closing some of the distance between us as I say, "It's real. We have something real here."

"You're delusional," she claims, but it's weak. Her voice is unsteady, and I detect a tremor in her bottom lip as I continue inching toward her.

Her walls crumble right before me.

I want her in my arms again.

Now.

"If you can look me in the eye and tell me you don't feel what I do, then I'll walk away. I'll never bother you again. In fact, I'll agree to never work together again." I stop just short of her, my chest and hands a breath away from hers.

She peeks into my eyes, her lips parted and begging to be kissed the way I know she likes—and she likes *my* kisses.

"Tell me," I press with an impatient edge cutting into my tone.

I can't help it.

Each second I spend with her, I grow crazier.

"I really wish I could," she breathes and drops her gaze to my mouth.

Fucking finally.

I cup both her cheeks in my large hands and zero in on her lips, but I don't land the kiss. The same woman who interrupted us before shoots out of the bathroom.

She might as well have struck a gong, the vibrations drifting over us as Raegan and I split apart once again.

"Not here." Raegan chews on the inside of her cheek, her eyes darting around us.

"My place after dinner," I say with finality.

It's decided. I will have her in my bed tonight. I can finally put an end to the ache in my gut. I can stop pining for her. I can quench this damning thirst that's been tormenting me for weeks.

We've been missing from our table for longer than it takes to piss, but I don't care. The curious stares we receive bounce right off my tense shoulders because in half an hour, I'm going to be leading Raegan into my bedroom.

Niko will be working late at the restaurant, so we'll have the place to ourselves.

But as soon as Raegan resumes her place at the opposite end of the table, thirty minutes suddenly feels like an eternity.

I dip my head and whisper to Stormie, "Do you mind if I sit next to Raegan? There's something I want to talk to her about."

She side-eyes her friend, as if to silently ask for permission, and I'm relieved when Raegan nods.

Stormie slides over, and I replace her in the seat, immediately slipping my hand under the white table linens and onto Raegan's thigh.

She stiffens at first, but as we resume our conversation, she relaxes.

"We were just discussing Elijah's tour dates this fall," Stormie says, catching us up on what we missed. "He'll be in town this October."

"You all should come," he says.

I ease my hand farther between Raegan's legs until my pinky reaches her sensitive heat, the material hot between her thighs.

As I tease her, she squeaks, "For sure."

I suppress a victorious grin and continue teasing and torturing her under the table while we wait for the bill. In the meantime, we chat about the pressure on Elijah to drop the new single before their tour starts in August.

At one point, I press my pinky more firmly into Raegan, imagining what kind of panties she's wearing underneath this sinful jumpsuit—if she's wearing any at all. She disguises a gasp with a cough, and this time, I can't hide my satisfied smile.

She has no idea how hard I'm going to make her gasp and moan and scream tonight.

SIX

RAEGAN

THEO IS TORTURING ME.

And I wish I didn't love it so much.

The angst. The anticipation. The promise.

It all lights a fire in my core and breathes life into my body.

I've never felt such a thrill from a touch under the dinner table.

I just need to figure out how to get to his place without Stormie asking questions. I can't tell her about the cardinal sin I'm planning to commit. I'm going to break the sister code all because I can no longer stand not knowing what it would be like to sleep with Theo Lazaridis.

If he fucks like he kisses, then I'm in deeper trouble with my soul than anything Dakota might do to me.

"I'll text you my address," he whispers in my ear as he stands, pulling his wandering hand from my thigh with him.

Outside, we stand in a line on the sidewalk with the rest of the group, flagging down cabs one at a time. I say my goodbyes and thank them for a wonderful evening, but I make sure to avoid Theo in order to uphold our pretense. Before I duck into the next available taxi, I promise to see Stormie tomorrow for our weekly coffee date.

I just hope I'll be able to look her in the eye and act normal.

In the silence of the car, I steal a glimpse of Theo through the window right as he lifts his head from his phone, the screen illuminating the glimmer in his eye.

And I receive his text.

I read it aloud to the driver, but instead of resting my back against the seat as I normally would, I remain on the edge, my heart racing.

My body hums.

My leg where Theo's hand gripped it is still warm and tingling.

A few minutes later, I pace in front of a closed gate, which leads to Theo's apartment building. Low lights shine from the front door, and a laundromat sits on the corner next to a small gardening store.

I bite my lip as a taxi rolls up to the curb, and a pang hits my chest.

What the hell am I doing?

This is crazy, right?

Theo steps out, his suit jacket unbuttoned and casual. The crisp white shirt is slightly wrinkled at the waist from where he'd been sitting next to me at the restaurant, and images of crumpling it into a pile on the floor flash through my head.

As he reaches me, I whisper, "This can't happen. It shouldn't, anyway."

A shiver vibrates down my back as the evening chill washes over me. I didn't think I'd need a jacket tonight. Then again, I didn't think we'd be going to dinner after the shoot, nor did I expect to be standing in front of this asshole's apartment.

I wasn't prepared for any of it.

A slow drizzle of rain dances along my flushed cheeks, and

lightning strikes in the distance between two tall buildings. It's a warning for a stronger storm on the horizon.

Dragging his teeth along his bottom lip, Theo shrugs his jacket off and slips it over my shoulders, then runs his hands down the sides of it. The tips of his thumbs brush the sides of my breasts, and my nipples harden.

That's all it takes.

Seemingly unfazed by the soft rain, he holds the lapels at my midsection together and peers down at me like he's in no hurry. "Is that what you came all the way over here to say?"

Another bolt of lightning flashes across the sky, and thicker rain drops fall more rapidly as if to say, "Your time is up. What's it going to be?"

"No," I whisper and crush my lips to his, abandoning all logic and resolve.

He tastes too freaking good.

A hint of red wine still lingers on his tongue, and I don't want to stop kissing him until I've lapped up every last drop.

But the rain urges us inside as it transforms from a light drizzle to a heavy shower.

Theo wraps his hand around mine and tugs me up the stairs and into the warmth of the plain lobby. I interlock our fingers as he leads the way up more stairs and into a dark apartment.

Inside, he presses me against the wall and grabs the backs of my knees like he's going to lift me up, but I stop him, jerking my mouth away from his.

"You better not drop me," I warn, my tone incredulous. I wouldn't put it past Theo to toss me on my ass and claim it was an accident, just like the champagne. "Are you sure you can keep me up while you—"

His grip on my legs is almost painful as he pushes me up, and instinctively, I wrap my legs around him. His hold is firm and secure, and it sends aching arousal through my heated core.

"As a matter of fact, yes. I could keep you up while I fucked you against the wall, but why do that when there's a perfectly comfortable mattress in my room?"

Still holding me, he whips us around, marches into a bedroom, and tosses me onto the bed with a bounce. I nearly swallow my tongue as he peels out of his drenched shirt and pants, remaining in nothing but his boxer briefs.

Streaks of raindrops glimmer in the moonlight filtering in from his naked window, and my lungs squeeze.

The outline of the bulge between his legs causes an eruption of heat in my lower stomach, need and impatience curling inside me.

I sit upright and reach behind me to work my jumpsuit's zipper free, then lift my hips to rid myself of the material.

All the while, our eyes remain locked on each other. Everything in the room stills except for us. We're alive and needy, with chests heaving and desire swirling around us.

He crawls onto the bed and over my bare body, resting his elbows on either side of my head and holding himself up. When I lift to smash my mouth to his, a sting reverberates from the side of my head. My hair is caught under the weight of his arms, trapping me.

"Ow." I wince. "You're pulling my hair. Move your arms, you damn brute."

He shifts to free me, but as I try to swipe my locks away, he beats me to it, wrapping my long strands in his tight fist and tugging. "How about this?"

"How about you just fuck me already?"

He growls against my jawline, then grinds his hard dick against me with angry rolls of his hips. "I'm going to fuck you until your smartass mouth is sealed shut. The only time you'll part those pretty lips is when you're taking my cock down your throat."

I hum my agreement and lick my lips, turned on by his filthy words. They're filled with lust and the special kind of desire that's rooted in hate. Guess he's not always a gentleman like I once wondered, much to my pleasurable delight.

"Let's do this," I breathe.

When he kisses me, I no longer taste the red wine from before. Instead, I'm greeted by hints of fresh rain and hunger.

This kiss turns clumsy and unyielding as his tongue clashes with mine.

He breaks our connection only to reach under his bed and reappear with a shoebox.

"Why do you keep your condoms under the bed in a shoebox?" I ask, rising onto my elbows.

"You remember how I told you I have a big, loud family? Well, they're also very nosy and like to snoop through my things under the pretense of cleaning my room."

"You should really—" I'm cut off by the sight of him bare.

Leaning his body to the side, he tugs his boxer briefs the rest of the way down, and there he lies in all his naked glory.

My God.

Once the condom is in place, he rolls on top of me again and smirks wickedly. "Now, what were you saying about fucking you?"

"Do it already," I command through heavy pants.

He slips his hips between my legs, hitches his knees to the backs of mine, and spreads us both wide until I'm completely at his mercy.

Lined up, he surges forward and plunges into me without abandon or care. In fact, it seems like a relief for him as his previously tight jaw loosens, and his resolve appears to snap.

His thrusts are manic, and I can't get enough. Theo turns my organs into a carnival ride, spinning and flipping, and I scream with pleasure, enjoying every dip and curve of the thrill.

My heels rise and fall against his ass as it contracts, rocking with each inch he buries inside me. The sensations he elicits from hitting just the right spots at such an angry, off-beat rhythm are erotic.

Feral.

Sexy.

When he brings me to the edge of ecstasy, he slows his pace, rolling his hips at an excruciatingly delicious angle—one that holds me hostage in purgatory.

I'm trapped between Heaven and Hell, where I can't afford to confuse these feelings for anything outside this bedroom, but I also can't bring myself to fully hate him.

My enemy.

The bane of my existence and *not* the object of any of my desires.

Yet, the latter isn't entirely true, no matter how badly I need it to be.

The back of my head hits the headboard, rattling the thoughts inside my mind like a cocktail shaker. "I... need to... come," I hiccup, clutching his shoulders with a grip so hard, my fingers ache.

"Not until I tell you to." A guttural sound rumbles out of him and sends vibrating waves of arousal throughout my body.

He's commanding.

As he pistons into me, our bodies easily slide up and down each other from sweat, and it turns me on.

I pant, and every burst of breath yearns to cry out his name.

I pull his head back by a tuft of his hair, then slap him. The strike sounds like the crack of lightning outside as the city drowns under the sky's wrath.

Theo blinks at me, momentarily slowing his hips, but his cock pulses and twitches inside me.

He liked it.

I blink back and bite my lip, surprised I did such a thing. I don't normally like any kind of slapping or spanking, but that felt good —*really* freaking good.

My heated cheeks split into a grin. "I've been wanting to do that all day."

"You're going to pay for that."

Theo pulls out, much to my disdain, but there's no time to

protest—or slap him again for leaving me on the edge of potentially the best orgasm I've ever experienced.

His nostrils flare as he reaches under my hips, flips me onto my stomach, and yanks my ass into the air until I'm steady on my hands and knees.

"What do you think about Greek food now? Addicted to it yet?"

I peek over my shoulder at him, and my words freeze in my mouth as I drink him in.

He watches me through a hooded gaze, his jaw clenched as tight as his abs, like he's trying to hold back.

"I need more convincing," I tell him and arch my back until my nipples brush against the soft sheets beneath me, my ass perched in the air.

I keep my head angled toward him, intrigued by the unholy darkness shadowing his expression as he chuckles under his breath. "You asked for it."

He drives into me from behind, and I cry out in pleasure, especially when he reaches around me to pinch my hard nipple.

A thrill zings through my body as the tension gathers in my lower stomach once again, and my arms wobble.

He makes it his mission to break this bed—that's what it feels like.

In fact, it's like he's trying to wreck me, and it's working.

I'm putty underneath him.

He spreads my ass cheeks as he thrusts into me at a hysterical pace, his hips slapping against my slick skin.

Another flash of lightning brightens the sky and this room at the exact moment my arms give out, and I collapse onto the bed, a blissful orgasm jolting my body into an explosion of ecstasy.

His balls tighten against my swollen, satiated heat, and he slams my hips against his as he shudders against me.

I squeeze every last drop of him dry, and even before I look back at him again, I know this was as good for him as it was for me.

Just what we both needed.

"You..." He inhales deeply. "You came before I told you to."

"I do... what I want," I manage, my cheek still buried into one of his pillows as his weight traps me down.

"Next time, you're going to wait for my command."

I snort. "There will not be a next time, Theo. This can't happen again."

He lifts his body from mine and turns me over. "Oh, this is definitely happening again."

"I'm serious. This was... it." I swallow, still trying to catch my breath, but it's difficult now that I can see him.

His hair sticks up in every direction, a rogue curl stuck to the sheen of sweat dotting his forehead. The dopey smile on his face is simultaneously lazy and smug, as are his devilish eyes.

He really is the Devil.

"You can't resist the dick you hate, baby." He winks, slides an arm under my back, and curls me into him.

"You're such a pompous ass."

"And your shrill voice is annoying."

I toss the covers aside, my legs already sore from the rough way he spread them open, but my body is heavily sated. It feels like I'm high on drugs. What did this asshole do to me?

Before my feet hit the floor, he grips my arm and pulls me back again, his touch hot and possessive. "So, want to fuck again?"

I quirk a brow over my shoulder. He didn't hear what I said about this being a one-time thing, and I can't blame him. I didn't sound very resolute. "You're hard again so quickly?"

"I'm not eighteen anymore, but I can sure as hell manage. Just put a pillowcase over your face and flash me those tits, and we'll be good to go." He smirks, and his grip on my arm tightens.

"Like I said, this can't happen again."

"Bullshit."

My attempt to wiggle my arm free proves to be futile, not that I really want to peel away from his sizzling touch.

And he knows it.

"Just remember how much you despise me," he rasps, inching forward until the tip of his nose invades the wisps of hair loose over my ear.

I do as he says and bring my distaste for him to the forefront of my mind, but instead of urging me to leave, as it should, it turns me on.

"I got champagne in your precious, silky hair," he continues, a low rumble reverberating in his chest as he whispers in my ear, his lips achingly close to my flushed skin. "Your boyfriend dumped you because of me."

I'm panting like I haven't had water in days.

Why is this working?

"Worst of all—and perhaps the most dangerous—you hate how much you love my hard cock inside you."

"God, I do hate you." I press against his chest until his back hits the mattress, and I throw my leg over his hip to straddle him.

Fisting one tender breast in each of his hands, he quips, "Right back at you, baby."

SEVEN

RAEGAN

I TAP MY FINGERS AGAINST THE SIDES OF MY LEGS, WAITING for Theo to let me in. I haven't seen him in a few days since I was visiting my mom on Long Island. We haven't spoken, either, other than the quick text I sent him to let him know I'm back in town, to which he replied asking me to come over.

He and I don't talk much beyond that, since our arrangement involves more sex than words.

In the last three weeks, we've been hate fucking in an attempt to beat both our personal records combined. It's more like we're trying to get each other out of our systems, but none of it has been enough. After each tryst, I tell him that was the last time, but I always come back for more like freaking clockwork.

And I haven't disclosed any of this to either of my best friends, one of whom would absolutely kill me in my sleep. I've felt so guilty over what Dakota would think that I haven't even mustered the courage to bring Stormie into the loop.

How could I face either of them, knowing how badly I've betrayed their trust?

Theo yanks me inside and traps me against the door, both of his impressive hands flying to the wall on either side of my head as he devours my mouth with urgency.

Kissing.

Tasting.

Fucking my mouth with his tongue.

And it's so sexy, my core automatically weeps with delight and desire.

Did he miss me that much? I was only gone for a few days.

He hoists me up and settles his hips between my legs, anchoring me to the wall with the weight of his powerful body.

My short, flowy skirt flies up to my waist, and his turgid length hidden beneath his jeans pushes against my panty-clad heat.

"You can't leave for so long again," he growls into my mouth.

"Are you going to punish me for it?" I prod.

"You have no idea," he answers, and the hint of warning underneath excites me.

He's likely going to tease me by twisting a hard nipple between his fingers or rolling his hips into me, taunting me with his long and thick cock until my mouth waters.

He's going to goad and torment me with his sculpted body and deliciously filthy words until I'm begging for him. It's a game Theo loves to play with me, and it's one I quickly lose at, waving my panties in the air in place of a white flag.

But he doesn't this time.

Instead of the intense foreplay I've come to expect, he aims right for the prize, shoving his hand between us and unzipping his pants. I claw at his shirt, my breath caught in my throat as all-consuming need darts through me, but he swats me away.

My feet flutter to the floor as he shimmies his pants the rest of the way down his thighs, bunched around his knees. I gawk as he sheaths himself, rolling a condom over his swollen tip until his veiny shaft is covered. Did he have that in his hand, ready to use the second I arrived?

I gasp when he reaches under my skirt and slides my panties to the side, exposing my wetness as he settles between my legs again.

He roughly jerks inside me, practically lifting me off the floor with a single, wolfish thrust. With the help of the sturdy wall and his even sturdier arms around my waist, I hitch my leg around his and hungrily meet his hips each time they surge forward.

But the give-and-take rhythm we establish doesn't last long.

He presses his body more firmly against mine, sliding me up and down his pulsing shaft, my back flush against the wall. He leaves zero room for me to move of my own accord, and I don't even care.

This feels too freaking good to fight him for control.

"Yes," I pant. "Right there. Right... there."

I feel him grin against my mouth, and if I could open my eyes, I'd bet it's a victorious one. But my eyes remain squeezed shut as I relish in the euphoria he elicits.

He fucks me at an angle that makes me forget my own name, and I'm mush.

Theo's dangerously close to tearing a hole in the wall, and I eat it up.

I bask in his passion.

There's something different about him today. He's more feral as he drills into me at a violent pace like... well, like he hates me, or this wall. If I had to guess, it's me.

That's been the case for weeks, no matter how many times we've torn each other's clothes off and ridden away into sexual oblivion.

But there's something different in the way he touches me today. Something like reverence and adulation underneath his dominating grip. It makes me feel surprisingly cherished, for lack of a better term. Not that he hasn't appreciated me and my body before, but this is on another, deeper level.

Theo slides his hand farther up the back of my leg until he claws a fistful of my ass cheek, and I scream his name for what may be the thousandth time since the first night we crossed the line of moral boundaries.

Once he shifts my leg higher, still holding me close, he bites my nipple over my shirt, then resumes pistoning into me.

My panties slide between his shaft and my throbbing clit, adding explosive friction to the mix, and I come—hard.

He follows suit, picking up my other leg and rubbing my body up and down the wall, my vibrating folds gliding along his length as I squeeze the last drop from him.

Panting, he cradles the side of my face in his palm, and I take deep breaths, my lungs shriveling and aching to keep up.

"What happened..." I clear my throat. "What happened to using the perfectly good mattress in your room?" I tease, recalling the first night we hooked up and how he carried me to his bed.

He rests his forehead against mine and releases a raspy chuckle. "I needed you too fucking badly, and the wall was much closer."

The confession follows me to the bathroom, the words dancing along the surface of my heart like they're begging to be let in.

He needed me—badly.

I gulp as a ball of emotions lodges in the pit of my stomach.

We don't have the kind of relationship that involves needing each other, which is much different than wanting to have sex. Than enjoying the sex and each other's guarded company.

But that's what we've been so far—guarded and reserved.

We've never left his freaking apartment together. In fact, we've rarely left his room.

Sex on the bed, in the shower, and against his dresser, sure, but we've never even been on a date. That's not the agreement we've made.

Why did my heart skip with glee at his words?

Why does the sound of a date with him sound so tempting?

I don't want to feel good about any of that, or about Theo in general. I can't.

I tiptoe back into his room, where he sits on the edge of the bed, his clothes back in place. The only things he's left bare are his feet. But I know he's hiding a long, lean torso underneath his plain black T-shirt. My fingerprints might even mar his tan skin right now from how hard I clung to him mere minutes ago.

I drink all of him in, taking my time to peruse every covered inch of him until my curious gaze lands on his tight expression. He stares at nothing in particular, and my chest squeezes.

What happened while I was away? What did I miss?

I shouldn't ask. No good can come of it, but I can't help myself. "Is everything... okay?"

His attention snaps in my direction like he forgot I was here. "Yeah" is all he offers.

And the mystery eats at me like a grizzly bear tearing into its dinner. "You can talk to me," I whisper and lean on the doorframe, deciding against joining him on the bed. We need at least *some* distance between us if he's going to close the emotional gap right now.

His low laugh lacks any humor, and I cringe as he tosses back, "Since when do you want to hear about my day?"

I hold my hands up and scurry across the room toward the door, calling over my shoulder, "Forget I asked. I don't even care. This can't happen again, anyway. We—"

"Seriously? You're saying that again?" he asks from behind me as he follows me into the living room.

I pass pictures on the end tables of his grandparents, plus ones of his siblings. I've never met any of them. He claims to live with his brother, but I've never run into him. Theo says it's because he works a lot, but maybe he doesn't want me to meet him.

It's highly probable that he carefully plans when to have me over to keep his brother from finding us together. Has Theo even told him about me?

It'd be for the best if he hasn't—I know this deep down—but there's a weird pang in my chest at the thought of him wanting to keep me separate from his real life.

How can I be upset about that, though? I'm doing the exact same thing.

"It can't happen again," I assert, whirling around to him. "What the hell are we even doing? We should've stopped sleeping together weeks ago. Actually, we never should've started in the first place."

"I disagree."

"What do you want from me, Theo? To have me as a booty call forever? You told me yourself that you don't want a real girlfriend, and that's fine. I accept it. But this thing between us has run its course. It's time we stop kidding ourselves and move on."

He roughly exhales, but it does nothing to relieve the pressure pushing his veins against his throat. "I admit—I didn't want a girlfriend. Last month, I prided myself on being single. I was happy focusing on other things. But ever since you stomped into my life with your stubborn... everything... I've realized I want more."

"More what?" I say, my lips trembling over the magnitude of what this could mean.

"More of *you*. I want you to be my real fucking girlfriend, Raegan."

"If that's really what you wanted, you would've introduced me to your brother by now—if he does in fact live here."

"Oh, he does." Theo widens his stance, firmly planting his feet on the rug in the middle of the room like he's settling in for a while, and I don't know whether it should scare me or not. "But I haven't allowed you two to meet for the same reason we always come here to fuck instead of going to your place."

I wince at the way he bites out the word *fuck*, but what did I expect? That's how it's been with us.

It doesn't sting any less, though, to hear it fall from his mouth so easily and curtly. This whole conversation shouldn't hurt as much as it does. I should run before it gets any more heated, but I can't move. My feet are frozen in place with relief.

Much to my surprise, I'm actually relieved to finally get all this out in the open.

He scoffs. "You can't tell your roommate about me because you still believe every shitty thing she's said about me."

I twist my lips as he shakes his head, and my stomach rolls. "You haven't given me a reason to think otherwise."

"Because you've never asked!" He throws up his palms into a prayerlike gesture. "If you want to know my side of the story, then just fucking ask me, baby."

"What happened with—" I purse my lips.

I can't finish my question. I can't ask for his side of the story because I'm too afraid of his answer. In truth, I'm afraid I'll believe him over one of my best and oldest friends.

And if that becomes the case, what would happen to Dakota and me?

I can't stand the thought of losing her, which would be a strong possibility if she finds out I've betrayed her. That I don't believe her, after all. How could she trust me after that?

"I should go," I whisper.

He marches over to the door, and right when I think he's going to throw it open and shove me through it, he spins to face me. "Before you do that, take a walk with me."

He doesn't leave any room for argument, and my curiosity is a force to be reckoned with. So, I follow on his heels, waiting out in the hall for him to lock his door. All the while, I try not to stare at the curve of his ass in his jeans.

I've seen him in sweats, slacks, and in nothing at all, but Theo in jeans that hug his backside is a rare, glorious sight.

The man himself is otherworldly, and I'm teetering on a dangerous emotional line by blindly following him.

Outside, we walk side by side, our hands barely grazing each other, but it doesn't feel like we're on an idle stroll. He walks with purpose, and I have to skip to keep up.

"Where are we going?" I finally ask him as we cross the street, and a small crowd of people surrounds us.

The noises of the city bring the street to life, but I might as well be in Alaska with nothing but icy winds and several feet of snow. Because not only does Theo not answer me, but he also throws me a cold stare over his shoulder.

Why does that hurt so much?

I shouldn't care that he's mad at me. In fact, I should've used our argument as an excuse to end things for good. I've been saying over and over that this can't happen again, but still, I find myself on his doorstep every time we're both free.

What is wrong with me?

When he finally stops, some of the tension has dissipated from his shoulders. As I reach him, I glimpse the name *Ethos Café* scrolled across the window, and he holds the door open for me. His grim, tight lips still make me want to crawl into a hole, but I follow his lead, nonetheless.

"Is this..." My voice trails off as a loud commotion greets us the second we step through the door to his family's Greek restaurant.

I assume it's his, anyway. For one, I've seen coasters at his apartment with the Ethos Café logo on them, and for two, why would he bring me to a different Greek restaurant?

More and more voices and chatter join the mix as we make our way to the back corner, opposite the wall with a giant mural covering it from floor to ceiling.

I freeze in place as I study it.

The green trees and brush covering the hillside are lush and vibrant. The church at the top with a clay tile roof is worn and dated, but it stands tall as a strong symbol.

The sun in the opposite corner shines bright light over it all, embracing it with each widespread beam.

It's breathtaking.

When I turn, Theo's hands are stuffed into his pockets. "I haven't told you what kind of person I am, but I'd like to show you."

Gone is the stony glare of anger he reserved just for me on the walk over. In its place is something that sets the butterflies in my stomach loose.

Vulnerability.

It's a big step bringing me here, and he seems hesitant and scared. Is he worried about my reaction? Does it mean that much to him?

Maybe he was telling the truth about wanting me to be his real girlfriend. Maybe he's been telling me the truth about himself this whole time.

My heart flips, joining the party in my stomach.

God... I'm in deep, *deep* trouble.

EIGHT

THEO

It's too late to turn back now.

Raegan's here—in the heart of my life—and I can't stop the chaos from descending.

The bubble we've carefully and rigidly constructed over the last few weeks is crashing, but hopefully, it won't be burning.

I just hope she realizes I'm laying it all out there by introducing her to my family, and I hope to God she doesn't squash me and what we have in the process.

And we sure as fuck have something amazing, whether or not she still has one foot out the door. After this, I'll at least know if we have a future or if this is the last afternoon we ever spend together.

"You didn't bring me here to have your father chastise me over my choice in jobs, did you?" Raegan's eyes widen, and although they hold a bit of amusement in them, I also detect a hint of hesitation.

"Why would I do that?"

She scans the restaurant as she slides her hands down the

outsides of her thighs. "You told me about your previous girlfriend. Introducing her to your father ended things between you."

Suddenly, it all clicks.

I step in front of her, shielding the rest of the dining room from her view. "That was different."

"How?"

"When my ex ended things, my feelings weren't strong enough to fight for her."

Placing my hand on the small of her back, I guide Raegan to my family's table. The surrounding ones are filled with patrons, as are most of the other tables. It's just after nine, and the end of the dinner rush is in sight. My family must be winding down in the back. It's the only explanation as to why my parents, brother, and big sister didn't race over to greet us the moment we stepped through the door.

"What would you like to drink?" I ask Raegan, switching on my server voice. I don't work here anymore, but as a teenager, I spent every summer, holiday break, and weekend helping out.

Things might have changed around here. My parents and Niko might've gotten a new register and updated the menu since then, but the restaurant-repreneur will forever live in my soul.

She asks for a soda, and I maneuver through the tables before slipping into the kitchen. Once the door swings closed behind me, the bouzouki playing through the speakers in the main dining room softens to a muffled tune.

"Niko, we need the fries before this order can go out. It looks to be the final one—*finally*," my father calls over the sizzle of a couple lonely steaks on the grill. Smoke rises as he scoops one up to flip it over. "Barry, don't just stand there. Take the trash out." He mumbles something in Greek as Niko carefully adds fries to two plates. Then our father slides both steaks onto them and hoists the two entrees onto the counter for Catherine to grab.

"Is this a bad time to put in a personal order?" I ask as my sister spins right into me and nearly drops the orders in her hands.

"Jesus, Theo," she hisses.

"Look who it is!" My father nods toward me, the sides of his face sweaty and his eyes red from the smoke.

Aside from the exhaustion marring his features, he seems happy to see me. I was afraid the opposite might be true because he's the reason I was in a sour mood earlier tonight. I came by yesterday to talk to Niko about a potential new producer, but our father halted the conversation with his own issues—issues he wanted to talk only with Niko about, effectively cutting me out.

I hate that it bothered me so much, but according to Niko, it was urgent restaurant business. Something about the price of lettuce and other produce increasing, and they needed to discuss this week's order from the food rep.

It made sense, and it's nothing new, to be honest. I'm just extra shifty lately with the uncertainty of Raegan looming over me.

But after tonight, I'll have the damn clarity I need.

"Did I hear Theo?" My mother rounds the corner, wiping her hands on a dish towel and wearing a large smile like she hasn't seen me in days.

In reality, I was here yesterday. And the day before that. And the day before that.

"Hi, Ma."

"*Γεια σου, χρυσέ μου.*" She kisses both my cheeks and pats my shoulders. "Want something to eat?"

"If it's not too much trouble."

"Never!" She rushes toward the cooler next to my father as he wipes his forehead on the corner of his shirt sleeve. My mom retrieves a silver pan and sets it on the counter as she calls out, "I made toutoumakia with chicken. I can heat this up for you, or we can throw something on the grill. What would you like?"

I scratch the back of my head, slow sweat from the heat back here accumulating above the neckline of my T-shirt.

What would Raegan want?

"We'll take some of the toutoumakia, please," I say. Raegan's here for the full experience, which she won't get unless she tries my mother's cooking.

"We?" This comes from Catherine, who returns to the kitchen in the *timeliest* of manners and quirks a brow.

The rest of the kitchen seems to freeze as Niko, Ma, and Dad stare at me.

"I brought... someone."

"A woman?" Niko asks.

The kitchen could be burning behind them, but they wouldn't care. They stare at me like I've grown two heads.

I shrug in an attempt to downplay the significance, but it's no use.

My mother tosses her hands into the air, then scurries around the counter, tugging at the string behind her back to loosen the apron around her waist.

Catherine leads the pack, shooting by me like the place is on fire, and the rest follow her.

To my joy and misfortune—a real mix of emotions—Raegan's still sitting where I left her. I'm glad she didn't run, like part of me nagged she might, but it also means we're about to get serious as hell.

Raegan's eyes widen as the small crowd descends upon her, and although I'm afraid of what outcome this will result in, I can't help but laugh.

"The honest-to-God Lazaridis experience," Niko muses, hanging back with me.

"Was this a horrible idea?" I ask.

"Nah." He clasps my shoulder and pauses. "Do I know her?"

"It's... Raegan Peters," I confess.

"The woman you care nothing about?"

I glare at him, and in my periphery, I notice our mom spitting on her.

"Oh, fuck," I mutter and rush to offer assistance.

"*Κούκλα*! You're gorgeous." Ma beams with a final spit.

"Let her breathe, okay?" I tell them as I reach Raegan's side and lean down.

"Did she just spit on me?" she whispers and smooths a hand over her hair. I assume she's searching for evidence of my mother's saliva.

Shit.

"Yes, and no. It's not actual spit—"

"It sort of is. It's so she doesn't give you the *Mati*, or evil eye, by complimenting you," Catherine cuts in. "I'm his oldest sister, Catherine."

I'm going to have to explain that more later so she doesn't think we're nuts, although we kind of are. I'd do it now, but my family has taken over.

I'm a mere fly on the wall.

"It's nice to meet you." Raegan offers her hand as she stands, but Catherine waves it away.

"Come here. I'm a hugger." My sister envelops her in her arms like she's known her for weeks.

And pain slices through my stomach.

They could've known Raegan for weeks. Had she not insisted on sex, mumbling vows to never let it happen again, then storming out of my apartment, we could've gotten the introductions over with ages ago.

But as I've said from the beginning, Raegan is stubborn as hell.

I just hope bombarding her and feeding her toutoumakia will finally break through her walls.

Okay, maybe this was *a terrible fucking idea...*

"Easy, easy," my father chimes in as he sits across from her. "We don't even know her name. What is your name?"

"Oh, it's Raegan." She smiles warmly at him.

He hums while my mom hurries back to the kitchen, muttering a list of foods she's going to bring out for us all.

I open my mouth to stop her from returning with a feast to feed a small army—I only planned on a small dinner—but Niko stops me. "Don't bother. You know there's no point in trying to stop her. She's a Greek mother, and food is the only way to anyone's heart, as far as she's concerned."

He's right.

My mother can't stand when we have guests and there's nothing on the table to eat or snack on. To her, friends and family gathered around an empty table is as bad as cursing in church.

"What is the Greek name for Raegan?" my father asks, but it sounds like the question is directed at himself.

Niko needs to check on the kitchen, and Catherine moves away to cash out customers at the register, leaving only the three of us—and Dad's bizarre question.

"I don't know. I've never thought about it." Raegan giggles and lowers herself onto the seat again.

"If you and Theo get married, you're going to need a Greek name."

And I feel the color drain from my face.

It's bad enough that Raegan doesn't trust me to even want to date me. I don't need to worsen matters by leaping to the topic of marriage.

"Dad, I think Barry and Niko need your help in the kitchen," I interrupt.

He waves me off. "They're fine."

"They're calling for you," I insist.

"I don't hear anything, but okay. If you say so." He shrugs and stands.

After he disappears, leaving me alone with Raegan, I occupy his seat and... hold my breath.

She tucks her dark hair behind her ears, the flush I put in her cheeks earlier long gone. "They're, um..."

"Yes?"

"They're very sweet." She eases into a smile that immediately reaches her eyes.

"Really?" I quirk a brow. "Even my spitting mother?"

This earns me a hearty laugh as she nods.

"Greeks spit to chase away bad luck. When they compliment someone, they fear jinxing them, basically. The spit wards off any evil curses. That's the gist." I wait expectantly.

"Makes total sense," she says with a smile and another nod. "What I find harder to believe is the fact that it doesn't seem like you bring many girls around here..."

Chuckling, I reach across the table and take her hand in mine. "Not usually, and of course, the one time I do, it's a woman who hates me."

She squeezes my hand back, and her light expression falters as she whispers, "I don't hate you."

"I'm hoping that's true—wait." My mind races back to what she said and catches on it like a fish on a hook. "Why do you find it hard to believe that I don't bring many dates here?"

"Here we go!" My mother sets a tray of various items onto the table next to ours, then proceeds to arrange it all in front of us.

Our drinks are followed by a basket of warm bread, a plate of sliced feta, and a bowl of traditional Greek salad—the works.

She turns to Raegan. "I can bring mozzarella sticks and loaded French fries too, if you'd like."

"This is more than enough. It all looks delicious, and I can't wait to try it," she responds. "Thank you."

Ma waves over the food. "Dig in. Dig in. *Καλή όρεξη*."

When we're alone again, Raegan asks me what that means, to which I respond, "It's like *bon appétit*."

"So, you do know some Greek."

"I know *some* French too, but I don't speak the language," I joke.

"Touché."

Niko returns, wiping his hand on the black apron around his waist before offering it to Raegan. "I didn't get a chance to introduce myself. I'm Niko."

"Of course." She slides her palm into his. "Theo's told me so much about you."

"I can't imagine there's much to say," he answers with a chuckle.

"The podcast, for one." She spreads her arms as she glances between us. "It's doing great, and it's hilarious."

"You've listened to it?" My eyebrows jump into my hairline.

This is news to me. Why wouldn't she tell me?

Then again, we don't really share these kinds of things. Not yet, anyway, but I would love to make open conversations a regular occurrence.

I want to know everything about her.

Raegan tilts her head and tosses me an odd look. "Why do you say it like it's so surprising? Even if I didn't know you, I would've listened to it after Elijah blasted it on his socials. I couldn't get away from it for weeks."

Niko laughs into his hand, and his eyes shine. He's proud of it, just as I am, especially since we've had thousands of new subscribers, thanks to Elijah's shoutout. Plus, hot new sponsors and producers are currently vying for a piece of *Growing Up Greek*.

I knew that photoshoot with Pia would change my life—I just didn't foresee the exact magnitude of that impact.

On top of the tremendous exposure for my business ventures, that day brought Raegan back to me too.

My family comes and goes as Raegan and I eat until our stomachs can't handle a single morsel more. Only one other table remains as I rise to my feet, my stomach stretching uncomfortably from the giant meal I inhaled.

But I was too engrossed in my conversation with Raegan to realize I'd eaten twice as much as normal.

That's the effect she has on me.

After we thank my family and wave goodnight, I fold Raegan's hand in mine and lead her outside.

But we don't get very far.

I stop her in an alley a couple blocks from the restaurant, desperate to spill the truth. After the giant meal we had, plus the excruciating suspense, it's no surprise I can no longer hold anything else inside. "Your friend faked her ankle injury," I blurt.

"What?" She slides her hand away from mine and wraps her arms around her midsection, her short skirt swaying to a stop as she freezes in front of me.

"Dakota—she wasn't actually hurt the night we went out, so no, I did not abandon her when she needed me." I rub my hands down my face as I reach into the recesses of my brain for the exact details.

After all, it happened months ago, long before Raegan and I started sleeping together. I may not remember what either of us was wearing or at what restaurant we ate, but the important details about this friend of hers are very clear. Those are what matter.

"She invited me over after dinner, but I didn't want to go. I didn't want to go out again at all. I made an excuse that Catherine needed my help with my niece, and that's the only thing I did wrong that night. Instead of lying to her about my sister, I should've been honest. I'm sorry for that."

"What should you have told her?"

"That I just wasn't into her. I didn't know exactly how to express it, but I didn't feel the fucking spark or whatever. Not like I did with—"

She furrows her brow.

"With you," I rasp.

Raegan squeezes her eyes closed and dips her head. Does she believe me?

"When I left Dakota that night, I put her in an Uber myself, and she was fine. She'd stumbled a bit when her heel got caught in a crack on the sidewalk, but that's it. She didn't mention a painful injury, and she didn't ask me to help her in any medical sense. I swear on my mother's pastitio—my favorite Greek food—that's what happened," I explain and crack a lopsided grin. "I'm not a monster, Raegan."

"It doesn't make any sense. Why would she lie to me about that? I mean, I helped take care of her the day after your date."

"I know she's your friend, so no offense, but I suspect she loves attention and will do anything to get it."

"What about all the girls you were texting while you two were out?"

"If I texted anyone that night, it was one—or all—of my sisters. You know I have three of them, and I have an aunt I'm also close to. Like I said inside, I'm not a serial dater, player, or whatever you want to call it."

She chews on her bottom lip, worrying it between her teeth in hesitation as people come and go along the sidewalk next to us. More people are out tonight to enjoy the summer night, especially since we've gotten relief from the humidity that plagued us this afternoon.

And I wish I was one of them.

I wish I was having fun. I did enjoy myself earlier while I had Raegan pinned to the wall, and even afterward while we talked and chatted with my family. Tonight was the first time since our very first date a few months ago that we had a real conversation.

I could actually see more nights like this in the future.

But judging from the disdain in her eyes, I fear this is the end of the line for us.

"You still think I'm a piece of shit," I say, speaking the words aloud for her in hopes she'll correct me.

But all she responds with is "I don't know what I think."

"It's been weeks, Raegan. You should know by now if you still hate the guy you're fucking." I swipe at the corners of my grim lips and brush past her, nausea rolling through my stomach.

Unease settles in my throat, rendering me speechless, not that there's anything left to say. I've put it all out there, and it's up to Raegan to do what she wants with it.

"Theo, wait!" she calls out after me and rushes to my side. "I just... I need to talk to Dakota, okay? We've been friends since I was eighteen. She was my roommate as a freshman in college, and I can't do this with you unless I come clean with her. You get that, right?"

I give her a tight-lipped smile, careful not to get my hopes up. Given how fucked up Dakota can make the most innocent things sound, there's no telling what she might say to convince Raegan I'm bad news. And she's believed her friend up until this point.

I'm not optimistic that'll change anytime soon.

Before I realize what I'm doing, my hand snakes up her arm to grip the back of her neck, and my mouth lands on hers.

My lips fuse to Raegan's as I kiss the hell out of her in the middle of the street, my body vibrating with the need to convince her we could be so damn good together.

I pull this woman into my arms, and she willingly tugs on me as if she doesn't want me to go. As if she doesn't want to *let* me go.

But she's right. No matter how much I despise our circumstances, she needs to clear this mess up with her friend, and I respect that.

It doesn't mean I can't send her off with a kiss she won't forget, though.

I just hope it's not the last one we'll share.

NINE

RAEGAN

Theo's face haunts me the entire way to my apartment.

The hurt and distress.

He truly cares about me, and I couldn't give him the benefit of the doubt all because I've used that energy on Dakota.

And there's a good chance she's lying.

After spending the evening with Theo and his wholesome family, it's too hard to believe he's the Devil my friend has spent the last few months cursing.

My pulse spikes as I attempt to unlock the door, but I drop my keys. With trembling hands, I scoop them up and try again, my heart hammering at an ungodly speed.

I finally throw the door open, but instead of marching into Dakota's bedroom, I freeze just outside the threshold.

Waltzing out of her room and tugging a shirt over his naked torso is...

"Kyle?" I blink once, twice, three times to make sure, but it's definitely him.

My ex-boyfriend.

"Oh... hey... Raegan." He grimaces as he fiddles with the hem of his shirt.

Dakota skips out from behind him, a purple robe tied loosely at her waist, and it's obvious she's naked underneath.

Are they together?

This can't be happening.

She smacks his ass and opens her mouth, but she quickly shuts it when her eyes land on me.

I'm still standing shocked in the doorway like I don't even live here.

"Hey, Raegan," she says evenly—*too* evenly.

Kyle, on the other hand, has the decency to look ashamed, crimson blotches coloring his handsome features the longer he stands here. "I thought you said she'd be gone for hours," he hisses.

But my friend simply casts her bored gaze onto her nails. "Oops."

"What the hell?" Kyle grumbles and shoves his hands through his hair.

Dakota finally lifts her gaze to meet mine. "I didn't think you'd be home from your mom's yet. If that's even truly where you went."

I glare at her, disbelief curling into a ball in the pit of my stomach. "You know that's where I went. I sent you a Snapchat from her front porch—with her in it."

"Just as well. I still figured you'd be out. You're late most nights." She draws out the S in the last word, holding the dreadful note with an accusatory tone.

Her eyes narrow too, and it's not a welcoming expression.

Is she mad at *me*?

"I'm going to go." Kyle points to where I stand frozen in the open doorway and starts to move toward me, but Dakota yanks him back and plants her mouth on his, adding a hum for... what effect, I can't be sure.

With both hands on her shoulders, Kyle nudges her back and

awkwardly pats her arms before he races in my direction. I jump out of the way at the last minute.

I'm not sure if he would've stopped or barreled right through me. Given his quick and jerky movements, I'd say the latter.

I slam the door shut behind him, leaving me alone with Dakota, plus the stink of betrayal. "Seriously—my ex?" I gape. "Have you always had feelings for him, or something?"

She scoffs, but it's weak and unlike her. This whole situation is unlike her, and I'm scared to admit I don't recognize this person.

There has to be an explanation, though. Right?

Dakota levels me with another menacing glare. "You didn't put out, so he crawled into the better bed—*my* bed."

"I take that to mean you don't have feelings for him," I state, although it sounds like more of a question. She doesn't deny it, or comment at all, and my hands twitch to shake her like a freaking pinata until she bursts.

I want some damn answers, no matter where they might lead.

"What the hell is the matter with you?" I snap. "Is this your way of getting back at me for working with Theo last month? Stormie and I both explained it was just business. Why didn't you just—"

"It's for fucking Theo behind my back for the last month," she snarls, and a mask of darkness covers her already glowering disposition.

"What? I'm not..." I swallow around the lump in my throat and wince. There's no sense in denying it. That's what I rushed home to confess, after all. She just beat me to it. "How did you know?"

"I saw his texts on your phone."

I lunge forward. "You went through my phone? That's so over the line, Dakota."

"Don't turn this around on me. You stabbed me in the back. So typical of you. Stormie too."

"What are you talking about?"

"You both think you're hot shit with all your success. It's like you think you're better than me, and you're fucking not. I got Kyle, didn't I? And I could've had Theo too."

I hold my hands up. "We do not think that at all. Where is this—"

"I know you two have coffee and dinner a zillion times a week without me. You've been cutting me out of your lives like I don't belong, or like I'm not worthy of being your friend anymore."

"We've invited you to join us!"

"Everything has come *so* easy to you and Stormie," she continues, blazing past my comeback like I didn't even give voice to it. "You have no idea what it's been like for me. I've had to work my ass off to survive in this fucking city, and it's still trying to knock me down. I lost my job, then had to take one at an even shittier gallery all because you nagged me over the stupid rent."

I shake my head. This is all so twisted that I can't even wrap my mind around it.

What she's saying is so not true.

I don't know whether to be outraged or to pity her. Maybe I'm feeling a little of both, but either way, the nausea settling in my stomach like bricks doesn't bode well.

"New York is hard, but that's no excuse to lie and cheat your way to the top."

She folds her arms over her chest. "I've only protected myself, seeing as how no one's going to do it for me."

My heart cracks as I slump against the door behind me. "What you've done is push away the people who love and trust you."

"You're the one I can't trust anymore."

I nod, and heavy tears sting the backs of my eyes. "Right back at you."

She rolls her eyes and tries to give me her back, but we're not finished here. In fact, we're far from done with this conversation.

I storm past her and stop in the doorway to her room, blocking her entry. "I actually came here tonight to come clean and apologize about Theo. I wanted to make things right with you and our friendship."

"Please! That's such bullshit!" She balls both fists at her sides, and rage lights her green eyes on fire. "You never cared about my feelings. You just wanted to make yourself feel better about sneaking around behind my back with him, but Theo should've never been yours."

"He was never yours, either. You were never together."

"Neither were you and Kyle. You didn't sleep together, so you shouldn't be mad that I did." She stands her ground, however misguided and fucked up I might think it is.

The truth is, she's right. I did want to feel better about my feelings for Theo. They're strong and very real, and my loyalty to Dakota has held me back. I wanted to clear the air so that I could be with him out in the open.

I'm tired of hiding.

But what she doesn't understand is that I truly wanted to earn back her trust. To rebuild our friendship. To work my way back into her good graces.

There's nothing left here to salvage, though. She's made sure of it.

We both messed up, but I never wanted to intentionally hurt her like she did me. I have felt guilty for weeks over acting on my attraction to Theo, but Dakota was petty by sleeping with Kyle. She did it to get revenge, and although I could forgive her in the future, I don't see myself forgetting about it. How could I? If this is the kind of *friend* she's going to be, then there's nothing left for us.

"I don't care about you and Kyle. If you want to fuck him, go ahead. In fact, if sex is all it is between you two, then you deserve each other."

"Like I need your permission." She clips, seemingly offended that I even offered somewhat of a blessing, although it was admittedly a double-edged sword.

I've had enough of this.

My heart is about to thunder right out of my chest, and if I don't stop this now, I'll really be in danger.

"I don't want to live together anymore," I say.

This shatters the salty exterior she's adopted since I arrived home—and it is *my* home. I don't want to live with someone I can't trust, and she's proved time and again that she can't be trusted.

No matter how painful it is to sever this bond between us, I know it needs to be done.

"I didn't even have to ask Dakota if she's been lying about Theo all along. It's obvious she has." I pace in front of a wide-eyed Stormie on the other side of the counter in her kitchen, on top of which both our coffees grow cold. "Can you believe her?"

It's the hundredth time I've asked her this since I showed up unannounced in the middle of the night, a bag of my pajamas and a few extra outfits slung over my shoulder. I'd barely finished asking her if I could stay here for a few days before she pulled me into a hug and said, "You can stay here for as long as you need."

After she pulled me inside and poured me a glass of our favorite wine, she asked whose ass she needed to kick. That's Stormie—her generous heart speaks before the loyal warrior in her.

As I filled her in on my secret bang-fests with Theo, she gasped and shook me like she might an uncooperative vending machine. She begged for all the details of how and when that had happened, and although I shared some delicious morsels with her, I left out the meat of it.

I was too upset over Dakota, so we spent most of the night hashing out those not-so-pleasant details.

"I hate to say it, but I'm not surprised." Stormie frowns. "I wish I was, but this is so typical of her."

Slouching onto a stool, I hang my head and rest it between my hands on the counter.

She's the one to pace now as she says, "I really thought she'd changed since college—I hoped she had, anyway. I mean, we graduated three years ago, but it seems she's more immature now than she was back then. Did she seriously have the audacity to say if she couldn't have Theo, you couldn't, either?" My one true friend walks backward toward the bag of sliced bread next to the toaster. "That's the kind of shit cartoon villains say."

"Right?" I slide forward until my forehead rests on the counter. My temples throb after a night of restless sleep, and my chest still aches from losing Dakota as a friend.

Because that's what's happened.

We yelled at each other while I packed a bag, after which I warned her to be gone before I return from Stormie's at the end of the week. She didn't have a leg to stand on during that argument since the lease to our apartment is in my name, something I hadn't been thrilled about at first but that had turned out to be a good thing.

It's yet another blemish on our relationship. She'd given me a sad tale of her tarnished credit and convinced me it would be in my best interest to leave her name off the lease.

Looking back, I'm sure she simply didn't want to be liable—it would be on brand for her, in light of recent events.

Toast pops out of the toaster, and as she grabs it, Stormie asks over her shoulder, "Why didn't she tell me from the beginning that she went out with Theo? I was there when they met. She could've told me."

"She said you acted like he was too good to be with her, so she couldn't trust you." I twist my lips as I repeat the words Dakota spoke to me last night.

"She's playing it fast and loose with the idea. Does she even know what trust means?"

I shake my head in answer to her question, although it is rhetorical, and I accept the plate she sets in front of me.

"I'll be honest—I haven't trusted her in some time. I just didn't want to be a bad friend, but I never should've doubted my gut. It doesn't lie."

"And I shouldn't have kept making excuses for her. See?" I drop the torn piece of toast back onto my plate and stare at her. "I told you I'm so freaking gullible."

"Babe, this is not a *you* problem, okay? She was your roommate all those years ago, and she became a friend when you needed each other the most. The first year of college is hard for most people. It was easy and necessary for all three of us to lean on each other through that transition." She takes a large bite of her toast with a loud crunch like she's angry at it, then shakes the bangs out of her eyes. They've grown so much they can hardly be considered bangs, though. I teased her last week that she needs a haircut—or Bobby pins—if she hopes to be able to see through her lens.

We had a good laugh, and thinking back on times with her, I realize I've done something right with Stormie. She's always made me feel safe and comfortable.

She accepts me as I am.

I did as much for Dakota, but as it turns out, I'm not really sure who she is. She's only shown me bits and pieces of herself, most of which have been lies. During our confrontation last night, I didn't even recognize her at all.

She was a completely different person.

"It's not our fault we were both duped by her wide-eyed innocence. I totally believed her sob story of growing up in a small town and dreaming of building a kickass life in New York City. And it was probably true, but she went about it horribly wrong and burned so many bridges in the process," Stormie continues around the last bite of her small breakfast, tiny crumbs floating across the cream-colored counter.

"I really wish it wouldn't have come to this." I push my own plate away, the nauseas knots in my stomach holding my appetite hostage.

Stormie reaches for my hand and squeezes. "Me too."

I smile and thank her for being here for me—she always is.

But the one thing she can't do for me is what a hot shower can. I need a second one to wash the stink of last night off me, so I take my mug of coffee and slip off the stool.

I drag myself through the motions of a shower, letting the lavender body wash in Stormie's bathroom soothe my erratic nerves. It all works to calm me down too, until my mind wanders to Theo.

I left him high and dry last night.

I've kept my distance from him since we met in order to avoid establishing anything akin to an emotional connection.

Seeing him with his family last night, though, was a different story. He let me into his real life outside the walls of his apartment, and I joyfully drank it all in like I do this coffee as I stare at myself in the mirror.

The truth is, I can see a future with Theo—one where we're both happy. One where we're both in love, even.

The thought of it is terrifying, to say the least, especially since I've only experienced true love through a lens at the weddings I shoot. I've never been in love myself, not even the dopey, reckless kind that most teenagers fall into. Sure, I had a major crush on the boy next door once upon a time, but he liked my friend Brandi. Nothing ever came of us, or any other crush I might've had back then.

I've never felt the spark Theo mentioned last night until he came into my life, and I immediately tried to snuff it out once I discovered his history with Dakota.

Everything's different now.

Can I love someone I've tried so hard to hate?

The ache in my stomach only grows throughout the day as I edit photos for my latest dreamy couple. The way the groom holds his bride on the most romantic day of their lives is breathtaking. It was easy to capture beautiful shots of them because all they had to do was stare at each other, and their love was obvious and pure.

Whether they were standing far apart or close together, it was so easy to do my job.

By the time the sun sets, the ache from this morning has traveled to my chest and squeezes my heart. I've just grabbed two wineglasses and the remainder of the wine from last night when Stormie bounces onto the couch. "So, what are you going to do about Theo?" she asks.

"I don't know..." I sink onto the loveseat, one foot underneath my ass as I sip from my glass. "But I need to do something."

Theo and I have the chance to start over—to start fresh—and I want to do that with him. I want to do this for real without any reservations or walls keeping us from experiencing the true extent of our connection.

Simply telling him I want to date him feels too meager and insignificant. I need something more.

Stormie does a mini cheer from her spot, then swipes the other glass from the coffee table, a mischievous gleam in her eye as she says, "I have a few thoughts."

TEN

THEO

"Did you see what she was wearing last Sunday?" Thea Dimitra gapes as I unintentionally sneak up on them. I'm not trying to hide my presence, but they're deeply engrossed into whatever scandal befell the two women's social circle last weekend. "It was church, and she skipped inside wearing a tiny skirt like she was ten years younger and parading into a club."

My mother shakes her head as she lifts a cup of coffee to her lips.

"Who are you two gossiping about?" I tsk, and my aunt rises to her feet to kiss each of my cheeks.

"Don't pay us two petty ladies any attention, Theo." My aunt laughs.

"Is Niko around?" I scan the restaurant but come up empty.

"I thought he was home." My mom furrows her brow. "He's not here."

Right then, Niko strolls in, his strides easy and comfortable. It's much different than his long, purposeful steps.

He's been unusually cheerful this week, and I thought it was because our podcast has grown exponentially. We're going to actually make good money from it this year, which has been the goal from day one.

Even without the financial rewards, it's been a fun project for us to work on together. He and I don't share the same love affair with the restaurant, and the podcast has been a welcomed joint activity.

But what is he really up to?

I can't help but think there's more to his newfound joy, and my skepticism over such happiness has nothing do to with my bitterness toward Raegan.

She hasn't called since she left here earlier in the week. Not a word since she told me she was going to straighten things out with her roommate.

I've gotten countless questions from my family about Raegan and when she's coming back. When I'm going to ask her to marry me. What dessert she likes.

They're mostly questions my mother bombards me with, but I get a lot of heat from the rest of the Lazaridis clan too. Angie and Kia still complain that they weren't here to meet her.

I haven't had the heart to tell any of them that they may never see her again, unless she stops by the restaurant for a gyro.

And if I get beaten out by a few strips of lamb, I'm going to fucking scream—albeit the urge to scream is already strong enough. I put it all out there, and she still rejected me.

At least, I think she did. She hasn't explicitly said as much. The last thing she said is that she needed to talk to Dakota, but her silence is speaking volumes.

Maybe I need to accept that she still bought whatever bullshit her roommate spewed and that anything we had—or could've had—is out of the question.

I knew not to get my hopes up, but I did.

Fucking pathetic.

"Where have you been?" my mother asks Niko.

He glances around and shrugs. "I went for a walk. Why? Do you need me to do anything?"

"You said you were going home to work on the podcast with Theo, but Theo is here." She points to me standing next to Niko like he can't see me.

"We can work on it later." He wraps his arm around my neck and puts me in a chokehold. I'm so stunned that I don't move to free myself.

The last time he did this to me was after we saw the first *Spider-Man* all those years ago. We convinced ourselves we could be superheroes; we just needed the practice, and who better to practice on than each other?

"Aren't we a little too old for this?" I say, my voice strained. "*You're* definitely too old for this," I goad.

"Such a jokester." Niko lets up and ruffles my hair.

What the hell has gotten into him?

"Are you talking about the podcast?" My father joins us, a glass of water in his hand and an apron tied in place over a plain white T-shirt—his usual getup.

I bite down a snarky response. He's probably only asking in order to berate us and uses a simple question as a disguise, but I refuse to take the bait.

It's never simple with him, unless he's referring to the décor in his house. According to Dad, any flair would be a waste of money, just as our podcast is a waste of time.

Even though our recent influx of downloads and new subscribers is insane, he wasn't too impressed when we gave him an update last week. He hadn't asked for one, but I felt like I needed to tell him in hopes of a pat on the back, at the very least.

I was very naïve—yet again. All I got in response was a grunt and an order to finish eating my lunch.

Thankfully, Niko jumps in. "Yes. We're shopping around for a producer, who will help us take *Growing Up Greek* to the next level."

My dad grunts, much like he did last week, then takes a sip of water, and I brace myself for the ridicule.

But it doesn't come.

Instead, he shrugs, and I might even detect a smile on his face. "I liked the last episode. It made me laugh."

"What?" I blink.

I didn't know he ever listened to it. As often as we have to explain it to him, I figured he didn't even know the name of the podcast.

I'm also surprised he knew where to find it. After all, his favorite show is from the eighties, and he watches said show on a thick TV that looks to be from the same decade.

He's not tech savvy, so I suspect Kia had something to do with this.

"I have an idea for you to use." He waves for us all to sit at the table my aunt Dimitra and Ma just vacated. "We went to Moretti's a couple of weeks ago after your mother insisted we needed to try something new. Like Italian food is new—*pfft*."

Niko shifts next to me, angling his body toward us as he rests his back against the wall.

"Anyway, your mom, Niko here, Kia, and I went to Moretti's, and of course, the chicken was overdone. The breadsticks weren't even warm, and the plates themselves looked like they'd seen better days. The only pleasant thing there was the waitress. She was cute and very funny. It's hard to find polite young people these days."

I chuckle as Niko shifts again.

Why is he so squirmy?

"Dad, you never like eating at other restaurants," I say. "You spend the entire time either complaining about the overdone, dry chicken, pointing out how much better Ethos does everything, or talking about ways you could incorporate new things around here."

"Exactly. It's funny." He bursts into laughter, and it finally makes sense.

This is the idea he wants us to use, and it's pretty good. I'm surprised we haven't used it before. Then again, our father rarely ever tries new restaurants. I've been out to eat with him only a handful of times myself in my twenty-eight years of existence.

I make a note of it in my phone as Niko mumbles something about getting a soda. My father follows after him into the kitchen in search of a snack, and when Niko returns, he's light and upbeat again.

"Let's talk." I nod toward the front door and lead him outside for privacy. The thick humidity hugs my face, and immediately, I cringe. Summer in New York City is great, but these hot July afternoons can be especially brutal.

"What's up, little bro?"

I clear my throat and ask, "What's up with you? You're practically dancing in there. Has the bouzouki music finally driven you insane?"

"No. I'm acting totally normal." He displays his hands out like he's waiting for me to give him something.

And I do. I give him a doubtful glare. Does he really think I'm buying this? We've lived together since I was born. We may not share the same room anymore, and he might spend ninety-nine percent of his time at the restaurant, but we still live in the same apartment.

I know my brother better than anyone.

"You met someone," I venture a guess.

After all, I was in this position myself a few weeks ago. I went so far as to sing to the bouzouki music, and I didn't even know the Greek words. I just made up my own and didn't give a shit if my dad gave me the side-eye, because I was so deliriously happy that Raegan and I finally slept together, not that I could tell them that.

"You did. You met someone," I repeat, and my cheeks split into a smug grin.

"Keep your fucking voice down," he hisses, checking our surroundings. Then he grabs me by the shirt and pulls me around the side toward the dry cleaners next door.

"Who is she?" I press. This is the best news I've heard all week —all year, even.

He buries his face in his hands, muffling his voice when he says, "She's the waitress from Moretti's."

My jaw drops. "You're kidding."

"I'm not. I wish I was because Skylar is thirteen years younger than me, and she's not *a nice Greek girl*. Not one bit." Niko hangs his head. "Don't tell Dad. He'd flip."

"Come on." I rattle his shoulders until he meets my gaze again. "You heard him. He thought she was cute and polite."

"He thought she was good at her job. He would not be happy to hear I'm secretly seeing her."

My brother is obviously having a crisis of faith—the religion being our father's dreams and principles—but I can't help the laughter bubbling out of me.

It's too funny.

Perfect, parent-pleasing Niko has fallen from his pedestal. With a woman so much younger than him, no less.

It's fucking hilarious.

"This isn't funny," he warns. "He's going to kill me."

This only makes me laugh harder, but this time, it's more out of pity for the both of us.

"Look at us. Two Lazaridis brothers hopelessly in love with women we shouldn't want."

"Whoa. I don't love Skylar. I just met her."

"But you're already afraid of Dad, so you know it could be serious. You *could* love her."

"Shut up." He shoves me backward, and I can tell I'm two words away from another chokehold.

"Romance is an adorable look on you," I tease, but in truth, it's nice to see him happy over a woman. He dates a lot less than I do.

In fact, the last girlfriend I remember him introducing us to was probably Denise from six years ago. Dad threw a fit over what he referred to as Niko's fling and told him to get serious about finding a wife. Apparently, Denise was not the kind of woman he had in mind for Niko.

Two weeks later, he broke up with Denise, and he hasn't dated since.

And the thought gives me pause.

"Wait." It all comes crashing down on me at once. "Is Dad why you broke up with Denise and haven't dated anyone else since you turned thirty? You're *that* afraid of him?" I place both hands on my hips and stare at my big, strong brother in disbelief.

He spins in a circle, tilting his head back like he hasn't gotten enough sun, but we've been standing out here long enough for sweat to pool at my back at an embarrassing level.

"Am I right?" I urge, abandoning my previous notions of patience and space with him.

Normally, I'd let this go. I'd give him room to come to me if he so chose, without pushing him, but we're past all that. This is too huge, and if Niko can't talk to me—his own brother—I fear he's going to explode. He can't keep his shit bottled up forever.

"I'm not afraid of him," he says on an exhale. "He respects me, and I want to hold onto that. It's why I don't fight him on things I want to do differently with the restaurant. He refuses to fully give me the reins, and I let him do his thing because I don't want to disappoint him. You of all people can understand that."

"Sure, except all I do is disappoint him, and I'm still alive, aren't I?"

Niko rolls his eyes.

"Seriously, though." I clap my hand around his shoulder. "You can't live to appease him. He's going to find something wrong with our choices no matter what. Just last week, he got onto Kia about wanting to start a travel blog and all the trips she wants to go on next year. He told her it was a waste of money and that she needed a real job. He said that to our youngest sister." I emphasize the last two words with extra force, hoping he understands the magnitude of it.

Our father has never been so callous with any of our sisters, least of all the baby of the family.

"As long as you're happy and healthy, Dad will be fine," I say, reminding Niko of our mother's words. "He's always proud of you, no matter what. Me too, even if it's not always obvious—and it's usually not."

Niko chuckles, and although it's still a nervous sound, there's some relief in it too. I'm getting through to him.

"Love can't be stopped," I continue. "It catches us by surprise. We can let it pass us by, or we can fight for it, no matter what anyone else has to say."

"And what about you?"

This question doesn't come from him. The familiar voice behind it sounds from our side, and I'm afraid to turn in that direction.

Amusement flashes across Niko's expression as he tells me, "I need to get back to work. Thanks for the chat, little bro."

I grumble an incoherent response as blood rushes to my ears. In truth, it feels good to help my big brother. So often, he's the one helping me. After all, he has nearly ten years on me and a lot more experiences from which to draw wisdom.

"So?" Raegan starts. "Which is it for you—are you going to let it pass you by, or will you fight for it?"

As I fully turn toward her, the softness in her eyes deepens. Her face is free of makeup, and her hair is pulled high on her head. She's breathtaking.

Absolutely, completely, painfully breathtaking.

The sight of her momentarily distracts me from her question.

"It depends. Is there something still here for me to fight for?" I ask, pulling her into the hot seat.

And my chest swells when she nods. "I'm sorry for the way I've treated you. I've been so harsh and totally out of line."

My lips sink into a tight line, unsure where this is leading, but it's off to a good start, right?

A couple enters the restaurant, pulling my attention toward the windows. Somewhere during my conversation with Niko, we drifted back toward the front of Ethos Café, and through the cursive letters of the name on the glass window, I see several eyes on us, peeking and prodding.

My nosy family.

It's not just my mother, Catherine, Dad, and Niko, either. I don't know when they arrived, but Kia and Angie are there too, fighting my father for a peek.

I step to the side and open my arm to lead Raegan away from their view, which is when I realize she's holding an envelope. What's in there?

Once we stop, she swipes a loose wisp of hair from her mouth and licks her lips. "Dakota moved out."

I stiffen. "Bullshit."

"She did. I asked her to leave." She gulps and fidgets with the envelope between her fingers. "As it turns out, she's not the great friend I thought she was."

I squeeze the back of my neck and frown. "Look, I never meant to be a wedge between you two. I didn't want to end your friendship, and I hate the thought of being some kind of... homewrecker."

Her laugh is soft, and it washes over me with warmth.

At this point, I'm boiling underneath the sun's hot rays and her presence.

"It's not your fault," she reassures me. "She has some doubts and insecurities to work through."

"And you?"

"I..." She takes a deep breath and laughs again through the exhale. "I have more crystals to grow because she broke them all—her parting gift before she left."

"Ouch."

I've never seen these crystals she grows, but she has talked about them before, one of the very few things she's offered me when we've hooked up in the past.

But fuck, it kills me not to know more about them—and her.

What's even crazier is that I meant what I said to Niko. Even though I only know bits and pieces about this woman, I'm falling for her.

She stands up for herself and the people she believes in, although they might not always return the sentiment.

Raegan's ambitious and hard-working. She's clever and talented, and she's sexy as hell.

The need to wrap my arms around her is fucking gutting me.

"There are tons of cool things about crystals." She bites her lip and leaves an air of intrigue between us. "They require such simple ingredients to grow, most of which are already in your kitchen, and they grow in wild shapes, depending on what method is used. But no matter what, they sparkle and shine. It's pretty magical."

Nodding, I step closer to her, and not because I'm trying to make room for a big group of pedestrians racing toward us on the sidewalk. It's because I like where she's going with this crystal overview, and I hate to keep the distance between us.

"In any case, they can take weeks and weeks to grow. It's a slow process, but... the end product is so worth it." She flashes her bright eyes up at me, soft lashes fanning around them with total freedom from any mascara or fake products.

Is she talking about us and the slow, excruciating process of reaching this moment?

I hope to God she is. Otherwise, she's just pouring salt in my wound.

But she seems to be in good spirits. There's a carefree energy emanating from her that I don't normally have the pleasure of experiencing. She's normally too busy casting glares and disdain my way, but I like this change, to say the least. And it's infectious. It eases the tension in my shoulders from days of uncertainty and misery.

"I have something for you." She slides a glossy photo from the envelope, presents it toward me, and smiles. "It's us."

In the image, I'm holding her in my arms. My thumb and finger cradle her chin, angling her face toward mine, and she gazes longingly at me.

It's one of the pictures from the shoot for Pia, but it's not just that. A turquoise title pops over Pia's name.

"Is this her cover?" I ask, taking the photo in my hands. There's a signature at the top, and upon closer inspection, it's Pia's.

"It is," she whispers.

With the black attire Raegan and I wear, the bright color of the text is the perfect contrast. But what stands out is the way Raegan and I are looking at each other.

There's wonder and true affection.

The chemistry is not the kind that can be faked.

"I want you to have it," she says.

I shake my head and place the photo back into her hand. "This is yours. It's your favorite author."

"Oh. I should've clarified—I got my own. This one's for you." She giggles, and I laugh too. Of course she wouldn't sacrifice such a memento just for me, and I don't even blame her. "I wanted to come here today to tell you how I feel. To tell you how sorry I am for what I've put you through. But nothing I thought to say seemed to be enough. Instead, I..." She licks her lips and continues, "I wanted to *show* you how I feel about you. I think the photo says it all, don't you agree?"

"I do," I rasp as I finally scoop her into my arms and hoist her up until her feet kick the air behind her. "Raegan Peters, I'm falling for your stubborn ass," I mumble into her hair. Then I settle her back onto the sidewalk but don't pull away.

Not without a kiss.

Sparks fly when my mouth lands on hers, and I welcome the fire this kiss ignites. I'm fucking consumed by it.

It should probably embarrass me to kiss her this way out in the open, but it's hard to care.

What does make my cheeks heat, though, is the obnoxious applause sounding from somewhere behind us. We both turn, and my family stands outside the restaurant a few yards away, smiling and hugging each other like they did the summer of 2004, when Greece won the Euro Championship.

I groan. "They are unbelievable."

"They're the best, you mean." Raegan tucks herself into my side and clings to me.

"My spitting mother and all?" I peer down at her, eyebrow cocked.

"She's my favorite, actually."

"Don't let my sisters hear you."

"I still need to meet the rest of your sisters," she says, and there's a genuine desire in her tone and expression to do just that.

And she's in luck—well, I'm also in luck, but for different reasons.

"I hope you're ready for this." I squeeze her as we walk toward the boisterous bunch. "My aunt and all my sisters are here today, so you get an extended version of the last dinner."

"Perfect." Raegan stops us and cups my rugged jawline in her delicate palm. "I'm ready for anything and everything with you because I'm falling for you too, Theo. I tried to fight it, but as it turns out, you're stubborn too. Because you just couldn't stop until you wormed your way into my heart."

"Part of my charm, isn't it?" I tease, but her words affect me.

A special kind of warmth settles over me, and it's not from the sun.

"It is," she says seriously.

Emotion balls in my throat as I plant another kiss on her lips, momentarily disappointed that I won't get her alone for a while.

But there's plenty of time for it. There's no clock or deadline between us. For the first time since we met, I don't feel like the other shoe is going to drop. Sure, it might seem too good to be true, but that's the beauty of it.

Of us.

Since my family disappeared back inside, and we don't have many witnesses, I swat Raegan's ass and pull her into my side again. "It's weird when you're nice to me, but I think I could get used to it."

"I wouldn't get too comfortable. I still think you're pompous and arrogant. I mean, you are way too good-looking, and you know it. It's obvious from that one cover photo alone, and that's the real issue here," she ribs me, and I fucking love it.

"Your ass is going to get smacked again if you keep this up."

She hums like she just tasted something phenomenal. "I'll keep it up, then."

I groan.

This woman is going to be the death of me—and what a damn perfect way to go.

The End

ABOUT THE AUTHOR

Georgia Coffman is an author of steamy contemporary romances and romantic comedies. She has a Master's in Professional Writing and loves the TV show Friends, as well as shopping. She and her husband enjoy working out and playing with their two dogs.

View more from Georgia Coffman:
www.georgiacoffman.com

BETTER LUCK NEXT TIME

BRIT BENSON

ABOUT THE BOOK

The enemy of my enemy is... my boyfriend, apparently

Vale Banks is my nemesis.

I want to win the Randolph Marshall Fellowship, but so does he.

We've been competing for it all semester, and I refuse to lose to some arrogant, irritating, playboy hockey player.

But when I catch my boyfriend of thirteen months cheating, Vale offers to help me out. Get even with my ex by pretending to date Vale.

You see, Vale isn't only *my* nemesis, but my ex's as well.

Vale and Jaxon both play for the Butler Ice Dawgs, and Vale wants my ex-boyfriend's team captain title.

The plan should be simple.

Fake date Vale and make Jaxon jealous enough that his performance on the ice tanks.

I get even, and Vale gets the coveted captain's C.

You know what's not simple?
My feelings.

With each passing day of this charade,
The lines between fake and real start to blur,
And I start to wonder if this plan was a good idea.

But just like they say,
The enemy of my enemy is...
Well,
my boyfriend, apparently.

ONE

I FLICK MY EYES TO THE CLOCK AT THE FRONT OF THE LECTURE hall.

The *tick tick tick* of the second hand drowns out the sound of my biochem TA. He's going over the questions missed on the latest exam, which ones were thrown out and which ones were kept. Reminding us about office hours. Encouraging us to download the free study materials from the website.

Blah blah blah.

None of this applies to me. I know it doesn't. The questions most people missed? I could answer those with my eyes closed and one hand tied behind my back. The free study materials? I downloaded all of those and put them in color-coded binders the moment the syllabus hit my inbox at the beginning of the semester. And as far as office hours go, the only time I want to step back into that dank old building is to accept the Randolph Marshall Fellowship.

I place my hand on my knee to stop its bouncing, then check the clock again.

Three minutes.

The longest three minutes of my life.

The honor of attending the Randolph Marshall summer undergraduate research program at the Chicago Children's Hospital has been my goal since I was a freshman. My biochemistry professor awards the fellowship to one student from his class every year. Just one.

Tick tick tick.

Two minutes.

It takes all of my strength not to groan and dart out of here now. I packed up my stuff fifteen minutes ago. If I have to listen to my TA answer another question about number five on the exam, I will explode.

One minute.

I take my bag off the floor and set it on my lap, then turn my knees toward the aisle. I sit on the end for just this purpose. Then, against my better judgment, I let my eyes wander across the lecture hall until they meet a waiting pair of familiar blue ones.

He raises a dark brow, and I scowl on impulse, then look away.

He's such a dick.

Thirty seconds.

Twenty-nine, twenty-eight, twenty-seven...

"Have a great weekend," the TA calls. "And don't forget to—

I'm on my feet the moment the clock strikes, sprinting up the aisle to the doors that lead into the hallway where the grades are posted. Would it make more sense for our professor to just post grades online instead of tacking them up on this ancient bulletin board after every test and quiz? Yes, of course, it would. But he calls himself "old school." Says this way of doing things "encourages healthy competition."

I think he's full of crap.

I wouldn't be surprised if he's sitting in some office watching the security footage like he's President Snow and we're some sort of academic hunger games. I send a glower to the camera in the corner as I hustle into the fray.

There's already a crowd around the bulletin board, which is a downfall of sitting in the front row, and I see a mop of black hair looming above everyone else, standing at the front.

Damn him and his long legs.

"Sorry. Excuse me. Sorry," I say, as I push through bodies, ignoring the collective groans and complaints my classmates are making about their exam scores. I don't care if they all got Cs and Ds. I only care what my grade is.

The moment I'm in front of the board, my eyes seek out my student number. It's always 32nd from the top in the first column. When I find it, I dart my eyes to the score and smile when I find a 97.34. That's good. That's really good. But before I can celebrate, I have to find...

"97.81," a deep, annoying voice says from above me just as I find his student number.

"No," I whisper, and he laughs. "No way."

"Yep. You lost this one, Ten."

I whip around and tilt my head back so I can look into his stupid, stupid face. He's smirking that stupid smirk with his stupid full lips, and I want to kick him in his stupid massive shins.

"I had a head cold last week," I say, and he rolls his eyes.

"Sure."

He turns toward the exit, so I speed walk to follow.

"I did. If it weren't for the sinus pressure, I'd have wiped the floor with you two exams in a row."

He turns his head and glances down at me.

"I beat you fair and square. Just accept it."

His statement is so arrogant, and when he drags his eyes away from me so he can send a flirty wink to some random girl wearing a Butler Ice Dawgs shirt, I contemplate sticking my foot out to trip him.

"Don't do it, Ten. My reflexes are better than yours, too."

My attention flies from his feet to his face and I huff when I see his mocking smile.

"You didn't beat me," I say, "you just—"

"Beat you. I know you hate it, I can see the steam rolling out of your tiny ears, but I still beat you."

"You didn't."

"I did. The numbers don't lie."

I growl. Damn it, he's right. This is exactly why we asked the TA not to round our scores. The decimals matter, and the numbers don't lie. I take a deep breath, and his smile grows.

"It won't happen again."

"We'll see," he taunts, grinning down at me like some sort of gorgeous evil circus clown.

I open my mouth to tell him as much, but his eyes move to something behind me and his smile morphs into a scowl. I whip my head around to see why he's looking murderous and find my boyfriend walking toward us. I turn back around and hit him with a glare.

"Don't be a prick, Vale."

"Maybe don't *date* pricks, Piper."

We meet Jaxon at the end of the sidewalk. This is where Vale and I usually part ways with one last barb or scathing glance, but this time he stops walking at the same time I do, and I roll my eyes.

Great. Here we go again.

Jaxon wraps his arm around my shoulders and pulls me to his side as he and Vale stare at each other. I swear, they're both trying their damndest to be the tallest and if it wasn't the millionth time I've seen it, I'd find it funny.

"Kane," Vale greets, folding his arms across his chest.

"Banks." Jaxon nods and pulls me tighter into his side, then smiles broadly. "You were looking a little slow on the ice this morning, Vale. You feelin' okay?"

Vale's own lips turn up into a lopsided smirk, then he tilts his head to the side slightly.

"Did I look slow? I guess you'd know better than I would since you're usually behind me." Vale looks down at me and grins. "Better vantage point, right, Ten?"

I narrow my eyes at him as Jaxon's fingers tighten on my shoulder.

"It's probably best if you show up early for the pregame skate tomorrow, Banks. Wouldn't want Coach to think you're slacking."

I watch Vale's face to see if Jaxon's thinly-veiled threat hit home, but he's the picture of unbothered. He's all lazy smile and laughing eyes. As captain of the Butler U Ice Dawgs, Jaxon spends a lot of time with Coach Brower, and since he's got a year of seniority on Vale, his word carries weight. I hate it when Jaxon throws his influence around, to be honest, but it doesn't seem like Vale cares at all.

"Of course, Captain," Vale says cheerily, then slides his eyes to me. "You gonna come cheer *me* on tomorrow night?"

I can actually feel Jaxon's body vibrating with anger. Vale did that on purpose—say *me* instead of *the team*—and I narrow my eyes at him. These childish games he likes to play are unamusing and annoying.

"I have to study," I say flatly.

He pokes out his lower lip in a pretend pout then starts to walk backwards, away from us.

"Probably for the best considering your last exam grade, Ten. Better luck next time."

He winks at me, and I have to swallow back a scream. Then he turns on his heel and saunters away. He's not made it eight yards before the girl in the Ice Dawgs shirt from earlier plasters herself to his side, and I can't help but scoff.

"He's such a slut," I grumble.

Jaxon grabs my hand and tugs me hard in the opposite direction. My shoulder and wrist hurt from the force of it, I can tell from the way he's speed-walking that Vale got under his skin. Vale *always* gets under Jaxon's skin.

"He wants my C," Jaxon snaps, and I shake my head.

"He doesn't. He's just an asshole."

"He wants my C, Piper." Jaxon snatches his hand out of mine and walks faster, so I have to practically jog to keep up. "You don't see him at practice. You never come to games. He wants my fucking C."

"So, what, then?" I say, my breathing labored from the fast pace. "So let him want it. He won't get it. You've got seniority. You've played for the Dawgs for four years. You've been captain for two. And anyway, you're going free agent after graduation, so what Vale Banks wants or doesn't want shouldn't matter."

Jaxon grunts but says nothing.

I've said all of this to him a hundred times since Vale transferred last year. It started out just some weird rookie hazing thing. As captain and an upperclassman, Jaxon liked to give Vale a hard time. But when Vale started to dominate on the ice, Jaxon's irritation grew. He couldn't stand being shown up by a sophomore. Then, when Jaxon learned that Vale and I have a lot of the same classes since we're both biology majors, he was livid. Irritation turned to hatred, and now they can't stand each other.

And me?

Well, I'd dislike Vale in solidarity with Jaxon just because I'm a good girlfriend, but since Vale's also an annoying, arrogant jerk who wants my fellowship and uses me to piss Jaxon off, I dislike him even more.

"You know I hate when he calls you that," Jaxon says finally, and my shoulders fall.

"You know that's *why* he does it, right?" Jaxon gives me an irritated side-eye and I huff. "I didn't know! Jesus, Jaxon, I was a sophomore, and it was a generic t-shirt, and you and I weren't even officially dating yet. There's no way I could have known it was his number."

Jaxon stops walking and sighs before grabbing my shoulder and pulling me in for a hug, the gentle touch a direct contrast to the rough way he was tugging me around moments earlier.

"I know," he says into my hair. "I'm sorry. It's not your fault. It just bugs me knowing he'll be here with you next year."

I pull away with a laugh, then swat Jaxon in the side.

"Yeah, we'll be here on campus while you're out playing in the pros and being swarmed by puck bunnies on the regular." I shake my head and start walking again. "Seems like your worries are minuscule compared to mine."

"C'mon, Pipes," Jaxon says with a sly grin. "You know the only puck bunny I want is you." Jaxon grabs my waist and pulls me against his body, kissing my lips before burying his face in my shoulder. "How about I come up and show you just how much."

I sink into him, closing my eyes and letting myself get a little lost in the feel of his lips on my neck.

"I have to study," I say finally, shoving him away with a giggle. "After the game tomorrow," I tell him. "After the win."

He groans.

"You never come out after the games anymore. All you do is study this year."

My smile turns into a frown, my shoulders slumping. He keeps bringing this up, and it makes me feel like a bad girlfriend. But it's just for this semester. It will be different after I win that fellowship.

"You know how important this is to me," I say, guilt lacing my words. "I don't mean to neglect our relationship, but I'm doing the best I can. I need the Randolph Marshall Fellowship. Attending that summer research program would be a dream come true. Please, please don't be mad."

Jaxon sighs and tilts his head to the sky.

"I know, Pipes. You want the fellowship and the only way to get it is to study 24/7."

I nod. "It's not forever, okay?"

"Yeah."

He sounds annoyed, like he's sick of having this same conversation. But what else can I do? I *am* trying, but studying *has* to come first right now.

"I'll text you after the game," Jaxon says, and I force a smile.

"I'll watch it on television. You'll run MSU right out of town."

His smile is fake, but his eye roll is real. "Later, Pipes."

"I love you," I yell at his retreating back, but he's already putting his earbuds in, so I turn and drag my feet into my dorm.

TWO

The Ice Dawgs won against MSU by one.

That's not why I'm hauling my ass across campus tonight, though. A win is great. I'm thrilled for the team. They deserve the raging house party they're probably throwing right now—more power to them—but I'm worried about Jaxon. He made only one of his six shots tonight, and the one he made was assisted by Vale. And to make matters worse, Vale scored the winning goal.

I know Jaxon's pissed.

I could tell he was upset when I spoke to him after the game. He told me not to worry about it, that he'd be fine, but I can't stomach the thought of him brooding in that house while everyone else parties. He thinks because he's captain, he has to be there, and he'll torture himself in the name of leadership. We've been dating for a little over a year, so I know how he gets, and it's something I need to be better at handling since he'll be in the pros next year.

Poor Jaxon. He just needs to feel supported and loved right now.

The closer I get to Jaxon's house, the louder the music gets. There are people dancing on the front lawn, couples making out on the porch, and a beer pong game going on in the driveway in the beam of someone's truck headlights.

"Hey Piper," one of the guys greets me as I step onto the porch. "We won!"

"Congrats," I grin. He's so drunk. "Have you seen Jaxon?"

"Kanerrrr," he slurs. "Last I saw the captain was on the couch."

"Thank you."

I walk through the front door, say hello to a few more of the guys, and push my way into the living room. My eyes scan the couch, but instead of finding Jaxon, they land on Vale. I can't stop the way my upper lip curls into a sneer.

He has some girl sitting on his lap, running her fingers through his shaggy brown hair while he chats it up with some of the younger guys. My attention is only on him for a matter of seconds before he turns his on me. The moment he sees me, his eyes flare wide, and he moves quickly to shift the girl off his lap.

I raise a brow and watch, amused, as he stands, says something to the guys, then makes a beeline for me.

"Piper," he says. "What are you doin' here?"

I cock my head to the side and put my hand on my hip.

"I came to see Jaxon, obviously."

"Hm." He takes a sip of whatever is in his red plastic cup, eyes never leaving mine. "You watch the game?"

I nod. "You played well, if that's what you want me to say."

He smirks and shrugs. "Just another day on the ice."

I roll my eyes and move to step around him, but he sidesteps so he's still in front of me. I huff and tilt my head up so I can direct my irritation at his face.

"Where ya goin'?" he asks, and I narrow my eyes.

"To Jaxon's room." I try to step around him again, but he moves his body in front of mine once more. "Vale, what the hell are you doing?"

He purses his lips and bounces his eyes between mine.

"What if you come have a drink with me?"

My jaw drops with a laugh, and I'm about to tell him to get lost when I realize he actually looks concerned. The way his brows are furrowed. The way he won't let me pass him...

My heart starts to race, and I dart my eyes over Vale's shoulder to the staircase that leads to the second-floor bedrooms. There are people lining the stairs and the hallway. There's a bathroom up there that gets a lot of traffic during these parties. I squint, staring harder as if I can see past the crowd and into Jaxon's bedroom.

When I look back at Vale, his eyes are pleading. He shakes his head once, and I clench my hands into fists.

"Who are you trying to protect?"

"Only you," he says, all but confirming my fears.

This time, when I push past him, he doesn't try to stop me.

I don't run. I don't shove people out of the way. I don't speak. I take measured, calm steps up the stairs, and when I reach the top, I keep my eyes on the door at the end of the hall. It's closed, but that's not uncommon. His door is always closed, especially when there are parties here. I came to a lot of them last year—that's actually how Jaxon and I met—and everyone knows to stay out of the room at the end of the hall.

I walk past the line of people waiting for the bathroom, and step up to Jaxon's bedroom door. I put my hand on the cold metal knob, then stare at the white fake wood while chewing on my lip. I don't know for sure what's going on inside this room. He could be sleeping. He could be studying. He could be playing video games.

This could be nothing.

But I know it's not.

I could turn around and go home, and no one would be the wiser. Only Vale and I would know I was here tonight. No one else has paid much attention to me except the drunk guy on the porch. I could turn around and go home and nothing would change. For a minute, the thought is almost tempting. But could I really pretend?

No. I couldn't.

I straighten my spine, take a deep breath, and turn the knob.

Locked.

I huff. On impulse, I reach up and knock. When no one answers, my nerves start to ease. Maybe he really is sleeping. Or playing video games with his headphones on. Maybe Jaxon is actually downstairs at the party, and Vale just sent me up here to fuck with me. I knock again while reaching for my phone with the intention of calling him, but my movements freeze when Jaxon's voice sounds from behind the door.

"Occupied!" he yells, followed by laughter.

Female laughter.

Surprisingly, after the shock, my first emotion isn't hurt or sorrow. My first emotion is rage. Without thinking too deeply, I turn and walk back to the bathroom line, stepping in front of a random girl with long red hair.

"Hey," I say, and she looks up at me with glossy eyes and a smile.

"Hi!" she says cheerily.

"Um, weird question, but do you have a bobby pin?"

"Oh..." she reaches up to her hair and pats around for a second. "I don't. Sorry. But hold on." She pulls her phone out and starts typing on it. "I think my girlfriend might... Yep! She's on the way."

"Thank you." There is literally no one kinder or more helpful than a drunk girl you meet in the bathroom line. It's the epitome of sisterhood. "I'm Piper, by the way."

The girl looks back at me with a smile.

"I'm Zoey." She scans my hair, her smile turning curious. "What do you need a bobby pin for? Your hair looks great."

"Oh, thank you." I laugh awkwardly and wave my hand toward the bedroom door down the hall. "I need it to pop the lock on my boyfriend's door so I can catch him cheating on me."

Her eyes widen and her jaw drops.

"Really?"

"Yeah, it's one of those button-type locks. You know, you just gotta shove the bobby pin in the hole and..."

I act like I'm jiggling an invisible bobby pin, my hand shaking slightly with the adrenaline, and she nods. She looks back over my shoulder at the door just as a girl with dark hair bounces up next to us and brandishes a handful of bobby pins.

"Voila," the girl sings, then gives me a wink. "You the damsel in hair distress?"

"More like *dating* distress," Zoey chimes in, snatching a bobby pin out of her friend's hand and pressing it into mine. "Piper, this is my girlfriend Giana. Giana, this is my new friend Piper. She's about to break into that bedroom and catch her asshole boyfriend cheating."

"What?" Giana gasps, and her expression mimics the one Zoey made moments before.

I lift my shoulder in a half-hearted shrug, trying and probably failing to hide my sky-high nerves and plummeting emotional state.

"Thanks for aiding and abetting," I say shakily, forcing a laugh, but Giana doesn't join in.

"Girl, are you okay, though?" she asks with genuine concern. "You need backup? After you bust his ass, you want to come with us to go get pizza?"

"Thank you," I say honestly, then close my eyes and take a few breaths. "I'll let you know."

"You can do this," Zoey says, patting my shoulder. "You deserve better than him, anyway."

"That's right. You're way too good for his busted ass. Pop that lock, catch him with his ass out, and then kick him to the curb," Giana adds, patting me on the other shoulder.

I open my eyes and meet theirs.

"I am too good for him," I say, and they nod. "I deserve better than this."

"You do, girl. You do," Giana says, and then they start talking, off and on, taking turns giving me advice and encouragement.

"Don't let him sweet talk you."

"That's right. Don't let him try to make it seem like your fault, either."

"Because it's not."

"It's definitely not."

"And don't let him try to blame it on the girl he's with, either."

"Right! He is in control of what he does with his dick."

"You just march in there, tell him to fuck himself because he's done fucking you, and then march back out like the bad bitch you are."

"Yeah," I say. "I am a bad bitch. I deserve better than this bullshit."

See? Literally no one kinder or more helpful than drunk girls in the bathroom line.

"Okay," I breathe out. "Here I go."

I turn toward Jaxon's bedroom and start to walk. I hear Giana and Zoey behind me whispering *you got this* and *show him you know your worth*, and I let myself focus on their words as I take the bobby pin and bend it so it's straight, then stick one end into the door knob. It takes all of three seconds for the lock to pop, but I wait for a few more before opening the door.

I look back over my shoulder at Giana and Zoey.

You got this, they mouth while flashing me thumbs up. Giana mimes throwing a punch. I furrow my brow and nod, then turn back to the door. I put my hand on the knob, take one last breath, then open the door.

It takes a second for my vision to adjust to the dark, the only light coming from the glow of the computer in the corner playing what I immediately recognize as Jaxon's sex playlist. I feel my eyes start to well with tears. It's a bunch of 90's R&B that I will now never be able to listen to again. That might actually piss me off more than the fact that he's currently butt-naked pounding into some girl while she's face down, ass up, fake moaning into *my* silk pillowcase.

Did he really just ruin 90's R&B for me?

Jaxon doesn't notice me right away, so I take that opportunity to step into the room and turn on the light.

"What the fuck!" he shouts as the girl shrieks.

My boyfriend whips angry eyes at the door without taking his hands off the girl's ass or halting his thrusts, but when he sees it's me, his anger disappears, his movements stop, and his face goes pale. His mouth gapes open, then shut, then open again. The girl turns her head toward me and gasps, then scrambles away from Jaxon to try and hide herself. I catch the exact moment his unprotected, hard dick slides out of her, and I want to vomit.

"Piper," Jaxon finally says. "Piper, it's not what it looks like."

I laugh angrily, dragging my eyes off his dick to look at the girl.

"Hi. I'm Piper," I say, my voice light despite the hot tears streaming down my face. "Was my boyfriend just fucking you doggy style?" The girl blinks at me but doesn't answer, so I look back at Jaxon. "Because that is certainly what it looks like to me."

"Piper. I'm sorry." He jumps up, one hand cupped over his still hard fucking dick and looks around the room for his pants. "I'm sorry. She came on to me and—"

"Are you fucking joking?" the girl shouts, and I shake my head. Like I'm going to believe a damn word he says.

"Piper, fuck, baby, I'm sorry. You know I love you. You're my future. You're my everything."

I take my trembling hands and wipe away some of my tears, watching as he tries to talk his way out of this mess while naked and trying to put on clothing. Everything about this hurts.

"Fuck off, Jaxon," I force out.

"No, Piper, baby. No. Wait—"

I don't listen. I turn and run out. Sobbing, I make eye contact with Giana and Zoey. I shake my head no and hope they understand before darting down the stairs. When I reach the bottom and am just a few strides from the front door, a big body steps in my path and I run right into his chest.

"Piper," Vale says, pulling me in for a hug.

I relax into it, just for a moment, then I pull back and smack right across the face.

I don't even fully understand why I do it—excess adrenaline or misplaced outrage, perhaps. But even though I don't fully understand, Vale seems to. His head shoots to the side, his handsome face scrunched up from the sting of my palm, and then he turns back to meet my eyes and nods. Just once. As if we're in agreement over something, only I don't know what.

I open my mouth to ask him just how long Jaxon's been sleeping around when I hear my name called.

Vale and I both turn to look at the stairs and find Jaxon staring at us. He's shirtless and his jeans aren't even done up, but he still has the audacity to look angry with me. Like *I'm* the one doing something wrong.

"Who do you hate more," I ask Vale. "Him or me?"

"Him."

I turn back and look into his eyes. "Kiss me."

He hesitates for just a moment, just enough for a single shaky inhale and exhale before his big hands cradle my face and he brings his mouth down to mine.

THREE

The softness of his lips surprises me, the way they tentatively caress and glide over mine.

The kiss coupled with the way his thumbs gently massage my jaw sends goosebumps down my arms, and I want to explore it more, but Jaxon's loud voice brings me back to reality, and Vale and I break apart.

"What the fuck are you doing?" Jaxon shouts, glaring daggers at Vale.

I turn and plant my body between them.

"Don't look at him," I say to Jaxon. "Look at me. I'm the girl you've been playing for god knows how long."

I shove at Jaxon's chest, and he reluctantly drags his angry eyes to mine. I fist my hands at my side and stare him down.

"How dare you make a fool out of me," I seethe. "Thirteen months. Thirteen fucking months. All those empty promises, all our plans. You just stomped all over them for a post-game fuck."

"Pipes, you don't understand. It was a mistake. Please. I'm so fucking sorry."

"I don't want to hear any more of your lies."

I shake my head and take a step back, bumping into Vale's chest. When his hand lifts and rests gently on my waist, I don't remove it. Instead, I rejoice in the way Jaxon's face turns murderous, and his anger briefly extinguishes my hurt.

"I deserve better than someone who will tell me he loves me one day, then screws another woman the next."

And without a condom, I want to say. He didn't even have the decency to wrap it up.

"Piper, I—"

"Stay the fuck away from me. We're done," I say calmly, then I turn around and walk out.

"Ten, hold up," Vale shouts as I rush out of the lecture hall.

I glance over my shoulder, but I don't stop walking. He catches up to me in seconds anyway. Those damn long legs.

"What do you want, Vale?" I ask, exasperated. "I'm stressed, I haven't slept, and I have only fifteen minutes to make it across campus. I don't have time for you to gloat about your grade on the pop quiz. I was in the room when the TA congratulated you for having the highest score. You don't have to rub it in."

Our TA doesn't usually do that, but Vale's grade was drastically higher than everyone's, so obviously the universe wanted to rub salt in my wounds. Joy.

"I mean, the fact that I beat you twice in a row is pretty great," he says, and I roll my eyes. "But that's not what I want."

I don't ask him to elaborate. Instead, I walk faster and try to ignore him, but he keeps up with me as if we're out for a leisurely stroll.

"What's your appointment for?" he asks, and I side-eye him.

I consider telling him to fuck off, but my defenses are depleted, and I don't have to energy to spar. Besides, what's the point of protecting Jaxon? He lost my loyalty when he disrespected me. So, I tell Vale the truth.

"I have to make sure my cheating, skeezy boyfriend didn't give me any STIs since he was apparently barebacking his way through campus."

I found out this weekend from numerous DMs on social media that Jaxon's whoring ways were actually pretty well-known amongst the team. A number of the guys sent me messages to apologize for not telling me. They were afraid of the repercussions of pissing off the captain or some bullshit. I told them all the same thing—thanks for fucking nothing. He really did make me look like a fool.

Then, the thought hits me and I stop in my tracks, whirling on Vale.

"I see you multiple times a week, Vale. I know we don't get along, but you hate Jaxon. Why the hell wouldn't you tell me he was cheating on me?"

He winces but has the decency to still meet my eyes.

"Would you have believed me?" he asks, and I scowl.

"No," I say honestly, "but you still should have told me."

I turn and start walking again, and he follows.

"I did try to hint at it though," he says, and I scoff. "I did, Piper. Think about it. How many times did I tell you he was an asshole? That you shouldn't trust him and that he wasn't as great as you thought he was."

My steps falter and my brow furrows as I run back through my memories. Vale's right. He's said all of those things. He's even gone as far as flat-out suggesting that I shouldn't believe I was the only girl Jaxon was seeing.

I blew him off every single time.

I hate that he's right.

"Fine," I snap. "You made your point. Literally, everyone knew except me, and I was the idiot who refused to see the signs. You can go."

"I can't, actually," Vale says, and I groan, tilting my head to the sky. "What did you get on the pop quiz?"

I whip my head toward him and hit him with a glare, my jaw so tight it feels like it could shatter. I expect to see him gloating, smirking that damn arrogant smirk, and mocking me with those stupid blue eyes, but he's not. His face is contemplative, and his attention is fixed on the sidewalk in front of us.

I study him for a moment, trying to suss out the game he's playing, and just as I open my mouth to beat it out of him, he sticks his hand out in front of me and stops my walking.

"Glass," he says, then grabs my arm and maneuvers me so I'm walking around what appears to be a shattered bottle on the sidewalk.

"Oh," I say softly. "Um, thanks."

He nods, then releases his grip on my arm and shoves his hands in his pockets.

"So, the pop quiz?" he says, and I groan again.

"Vale, haven't I been through enough? You beat me. Congrats. Don't rub it in."

"No, that's not what I'm doing," he says, glancing down at me and then back to the sidewalk. "You've never let me beat you twice in a row, and I have a feeling your grade on this pop quiz was shit. I saw you come into class. You looked like the walking dead."

I growl at him, and he throws his hands up.

"I'm just saying, you weren't yourself, and I think we both know this bullshit with Jaxon is to blame."

I sigh. He's not wrong. He's dead on, actually.

I spent all weekend oscillating between sadness and rage. I scoured my text threads with Jaxon, his socials, everything looking for some sign that I missed. And to my dismay, I found so, so many. I pride myself on being observant. On being able to read between the lines. I thought I was a good judge of character, but hindsight really is 20/20. How had I been so careless with Jaxon? And for over a year, too. I lost my virginity to him. I thought I was going to marry him.

The joke was on me the entire time.

"I got a C," I confess. I wait for Vale to gloat, but instead, he pivots the topic.

"Jaxon's been shit at practice. He's moody and sloppy. He's an absolute mess."

I jerk my head back.

"So what? Don't tell me you're here to argue his side. Get me to take him back in the name of the team?"

Vale barks out a laugh and shakes his head.

"Absolutely the opposite, actually."

We turn off the main path that will take us to the student health center and stop walking just before the staircase leading inside. I turn to face him and raise my eyebrows.

"Well?"

"I think we should fake date."

My jaw drops and I can't stop the laughter that bubbles out of me. Maybe it's fueled by the lack of sleep and the empty well of emotional fortitude, but I can't stop laughing. I laugh for so long that I have to clutch my side and wipe tears from my eyes. When I finally catch my breath and look at Vale, the annoyed way he's frowning at me just starts me laughing again.

"Are you going to be done soon?" he asks with an unamused sigh.

I nod and wipe more tears off my cheeks.

"Yes, okay," I squeak out. "I'm done, I think. It's just...you want to *what*?"

He rolls his eyes. "You heard me right the first time."

"Did I?" My voice is high-pitched and breathy from trying to hold back more laughter and Vale just blinks at me, face full of irritation. "We can't date. We'd kill each other. And anyway, I'm never dating another hockey player. I'm done with all of you."

"*Fake* date," he corrects. "It would just be for show. Just to piss off Jaxon. To get him back for being a sleazy prick."

Any lingering laughter disappears, and I tilt my head to the side, assessing him.

"Is this because you want to be captain?" I ask, and he shrugs.

My first instinct, ingrained from a year of steadfast loyalty to Jaxon, is to tell Vale hell no. But then I think of Jaxon's face at the party on Saturday. How his anger at seeing me with Vale made my heart feel a little less broken, a little less humiliated. Would fake dating Vale be the mature adult way to get over a breakup? Of course not.

But could it be worth it?

The alarm on my phone chimes before I can answer him, reminding me of my student health appointment.

"Shit," I say, checking the time. "I have to go."

"Think about it, okay?" Vale says, and instead of going with my impulses, I nod slowly then turn and head into the health center without giving Vale another glance.

My appointment at student health is a weird blur. I have to fill out a questionnaire where I check "one" next to a question that asks the number of sexual partners I've had (in a year? A month? My lifetime? Doesn't matter. The answer is the same). Then I write "My boyfriend was a cheating whore" in the section that asks if I have any more pertinent information to share.

The doctor comes in and thankfully is a woman. She's very matter-of-fact, which I appreciate, and the whole ordeal—speculums, swabs, everything—is over in about thirty minutes.

"We'll have results for you in a few days," the doctor says, and then I'm sent on my merry way.

On the walk back to my dorm, I'm scrolling through my social media when I get a message request notification. I should ignore it since I've been getting tons of DMs about Jaxon and his indiscretions, but I'm a glutton for punishment, so I open it anyway.

It's a message from Zoey, the girl with the bobby pins from Saturday.

Hey Piper. Me and Giana wanted to check in and make sure you're okay and not thinking about getting back with your douchey ex.

I grin immediately as I respond.

Hanging in there. Definitely NOT getting back with him.

GOOD! Meet at Maria's Pizza in thirty?

I consider the invite. I need to eat, and in the last year, I've sort of lost any casual friends I had when I started dating Jaxon. Yes, I was *that* girl. The girl who dedicated all her free time to her boyfriend and neglected everyone else. My life was studying and Jaxon. Jaxon and studying. I didn't think I needed or wanted anything else.

Ugh. Hate that for me now.

See you in thirty, I type out before I can overthink it.

I file all thoughts of Jaxon, my pending test results, the Randolph Marshal Fellowship, and Vale away for later, and change my direction, heading straight for Main Street instead of my dorm. Vale said I look like the walking dead, and he's not wrong, but something tells me Zoey and Giana won't care. I need pizza and girlfriends, stat.

FOUR

"IN A RELATIONSHIP!!!" I SHRIEK INTO THE DARKNESS, dropping my phone right onto my face.

I shoot upright, swing my legs over the side of the bed, and snatch my phone back up. My hands are shaking as I scroll through the profile that was sent to me.

Ashlyn Little, the girl Jaxon was banging from behind at the party on Saturday, has changed her social media profile to say *in a relationship* and then put heart emojis around Jaxon's hockey number. There are no pictures of him on her feed, but there's a selfie in his bathroom and a picture of the tree out his bedroom window.

I unblock Jaxon's profile and inspect it, but I find nothing.

Not a single mention of this girl. No relationship status. No pictures. No comments. His feed is still full of me, in fact, but I don't trust any of it. He's proved to be an expert at sneaking around, and her profile tells me everything I need to know.

It hasn't even been a week.

What a slap in the damn face.

The fact that I'm crying makes this even worse. I don't want to hurt over him. He's a waste of tears. I don't want to care, but I do. I care that he lied. I care that I fell for it. I care that my heart aches more often than it doesn't right now.

I jump back to Ashlyn's profile. She's pretty. Tall and blonde with big boobs. She's basically everything I'm not. I usually don't play the comparison game, but right now, I can't help it. How am I supposed to feel when the guy I thought I would marry cheated on me with someone my polar opposite?

I hate him, and I latch onto that feeling.

Heartbreak sucks. Anger is better. I don't want to waste any more time crying, but I don't want to just get over it, either.

I want to get even.

How do you get back at someone who humiliated you and broke your heart? You date his nemesis, obviously. I can look past the fact that Vale is also *my* nemesis.

I close out of the social media app and pull up my contacts. I still have Vale's number saved from that first party—the one where I met Jaxon. Technically, I met Vale first, and I never questioned why I didn't just delete his number. I'm glad now that I didn't. I hit call and wait.

"Ten," he answers, his voice rough from sleep. "What time is it?"

I pull my phone back and look at the time.

"It's three am," I tell him, and he groans.

"What do you want?"

"If you're going to be my fake boyfriend, you'll have to work on how you talk to me," I say flatly, and he goes quiet. I don't even hear him breathing. I pull the phone back and check to make sure I didn't lose him, but it's still connected. "Vale. You there?"

"You wanna do it?" he finally says, and my lips twitch up at the disbelief I hear in his voice.

"Yep."

"Why?"

I sigh.

"Someone sent me Ashlyn Little's social media profile. She's got Jaxon's hockey number in her bio with a bunch of stupid hearts." I flop back on my pillow and close my eyes. "I want to ruin him."

He chuckles, and I ignore the way goosebumps prickle my arms at the sound.

"Then let's ruin him."

The enemy of my enemy is my...*boyfriend*, apparently.

"QUIT FIDGETING."

"I can't help it," I snap. "I'm nervous."

"Why? It's just us."

"I'm a terrible actress, Vale. I'm a logical, analytical mind. I'm not creative, and I'm a terrible liar." I rake my hands down my face and groan. "How the hell am I supposed to convince people I like you?"

Vale scoffs. "It's not like it's going to be easy for me, either. I mean, you're not exactly my type."

My jaw drops and I scowl at him. "And I suppose your type is, what, blonde hair and big boobs and Ashlyn Little?"

"Nah, Ten," he says with a shrug and a raised brow, "but my type does typically include someone who actually likes me."

"Oh." I wipe the sneer off my face and nod. "Yep. I'm not your type."

Vale rolls his eyes and taps the paper in front of him.

"Focus, please. No wonder you can barely keep up with me in class." I growl and hurl a couch pillow at his head, but he bats it away effortlessly. "As I was saying. If we can do this for a month, it will get us to the playoffs. Jaxon will self-destruct and I'll be made captain leading into the most important string of games."

"Okay but what if he self-destructs so badly that he is a hindrance to the team?" I ask, and Vale waves me off.

"I can easily take over as right wing, and we can move Gavin Barker to center. He's actually really fucking good, but he's a sophomore and Jaxon purposely makes sure he doesn't get the ice time."

"Really?"

I'm shocked. I've heard Jaxon complain about Gavin Barker numerous times. I thought it was because he was a slacker.

"Yeah, really. See, I'm a better right wing than Jaxon, but until this year, I was also the best center we had. Enter Gavin Barker. Kid is good, and Jaxon knows that if given the chance, Gavin Barker could fuck things up for him."

"Wow. I had no idea." I drop my head back on the couch cushion. "God, I was such an idiot."

"You weren't," Vale says. "Jaxon was just a really good liar."

I turn my head to face him. "You weren't fooled."

"He didn't *try* to fool me," he says with a shrug. "He's got Coach and half the team snowed, too. It's not just you."

I sigh. Everything about this sucks.

"Okay," I say finally. "One month. I'll go to the home games—"

"And the after parties," he cuts in, scribbling something else on the paper, and I shake my head.

"No way, Vale. I can't take that much time away from studying."

"It won't be believable if we don't rub it in at the parties." Then he goes for the kill. "And anyway, that's when Jaxon always fucked around."

Ouch.

"Fine," I grit out through clenched teeth.

"And I'll swing by your dorm and walk you to and from class."

"Fine," I repeat, then groan. "Do I have to hold your hand?"

"If you want it to look real, yeah."

Ugh.

"Alright, stand up. Let's get to the important stuff."

He jumps to his feet and looks at me expectantly. I study him with narrowed, suspicious eyes.

"I thought your list *was* the important stuff."

"Don't be dense, Ten. You want this to be convincing?"

"Yeah," I say, making my irritation noticeable in both tone and body language. He ignores it and plows forward.

"You want to, and I quote, *ruin him*, yeah?"

"Yes, Vale, that is what I said. That is what I want."

"Okay, then. Swallow back your attitude." He claps his hands and rubs them together. "Stand up, come here, and let's make out."

I start laughing, but when he doesn't join in, my laughter dies, and my eyes go wide.

"Absolutely not."

"You kissed me Saturday," he says pointedly. "Pretty sure you didn't hate it."

I scoff. "Um, I totally did."

"Okay, fine," he says, bending back down and scribbling something on his paper. "Hand-holding is fine. Kissing is not. We'll just have to work on your facial expressions. No one is going to believe this is real if you keep looking at me like you want me dead."

I roll my eyes, but I don't argue. I don't want him *dead*. I just want him gone. Alive and well, but messing with someone else's fellowship. Not mine.

"Last thing," he says, head bowed over the paper, before brandishing his hand dramatically and presenting the list to me. "No falling in love."

I snort. "Easiest part of the whole thing."

He nods, his lip curled up in disgust as he drags his eyes over my body, and I huff, throwing another pillow at him. He bats it away without flinching, and I scowl. Hot, smart, and impeccable reflexes. He's so annoying.

"Okay," he says quickly, "get out of my house. I have to study for the next quiz so I can kick your ass." I swallow back a growl and stand, giving him a forced sweet smile. He tilts his head to the side, studies me, then sighs like I'm the annoying one. "Nope. Still terrible. Go practice in the mirror. See you tomorrow."

THERE'S A KNOCK ON MY DORM DOOR THE NEXT MORNING.

When I open it, I'm momentarily confused to see Vale before I remember he's here to walk me to class. I fling the door wide and let him in, then go back to packing my bag. I watch him as he surveys my room, glancing at the photos and notes I have tacked to my bulletin board, then picking up a small elephant figurine I have sitting on my desk.

"Quit touching things," I grumble, and I hear him laugh under his breath. I sling my bag over my shoulder. "Let's go."

He follows me into the hallway and then down the stairs, but before we push through the doors to step outside, he puts his arm in front of me. I glance at him questioningly and he extends his hand with a fake-charming smile. I roll my eyes and slap my hand in his.

"Your hands are sweaty," he says, and I throw my shoulder into him.

"Are not," I snap. "At least mine aren't all callusy."

"It's from handling my stick," he says suggestively, sending me a wink. "Thought you'd be used to that, having dated a hockey player and all." I glare at him, but he ignores me. "Ready for the quiz?"

"More than ready," I say, and he nods.

"Me, too. Probably going to get the highest grade in the class again."

"Shut up, Vale."

He grins, but he's quiet the rest of the walk to the lecture hall. I get lost in my thoughts. Imagining what it will be like when Jaxon learns of my new relationship. Will he be angry? Jealous? Will he even care?

Before I realize it, we're in the lecture hall and Vale is trailing me to my seat in the front row.

"You're not sitting next to me," I say to him, and he raises an eyebrow. That eyebrow says enough. How's it going to look if we don't sit next to each other in class? *Ugh.* I throw my bag into the seat immediately beside me. "Fine, but the bag stays between us. I don't want you copying my answers."

Like usual, we spend the first fifteen minutes of class taking the quiz electronically, then the rest of the class is spent on lecture. Unlike exams, quizzes are graded and posted immediately, and I'm on the edge of my seat waiting for the class to be dismissed so I can check the board.

The second the class is over, I'm on my feet, shoving past Vale, and speed walking out of the lecture hall. I'm in front of the board long enough to check both my student number and his before Vale lumbers up next to me, and I whirl on him.

"Ah ha!" I shout, poking him in his smug, rock-solid chest. "98.72." I watch as his eyes scan the board and stop on his number, then I answer for him. "98.1." I spin away from him and throw my hands in the air, then point at him mockingly. "Suck it, Banks. Suck. It."

"No one likes a cocky winner, Ten," he says flatly, and my smile grows.

I open my mouth to say something smart-assy, but my words die on my tongue when my eyes catch on a familiar face through the glass doors leading to the quad.

Jaxon.

My heart falls to my feet and shatters.

He's got Ashlyn Little pressed against the stair railing leading into the lecture hall and they're laughing about something. Her hands are fisted in his shirt, his lips are inches from hers. I feel a single tear slide down my face, then my line of sight is blocked by a broad chest.

I look up into Vale's concerned face.

"He did this on purpose," Vale says. "He's literally never been outside this building after class. He's doing this to get to you. Do *not* let him win."

The last sentence is what does it. It feeds right into my competitive nature. I can't let him win. I nod curtly, and Vale's smile turns wicked.

"Time to win an Oscar, Ten."

He grabs my hand and pulls me closer, then uses his thumbs to wipe the tears off my face. He places his finger under my chin, then tilts my head up so I'm looking right into his ice-blue eyes. His eyes and smile turn softer, and he caresses my jaw lightly with his thumb.

"Ready?"

"Ready," I rasp, trying to keep my heart from pounding out of my chest. Am I ready? To face Jaxon and Ashlyn? To act like my heart isn't broken, and I haven't been humiliated?

Damn it, I sure hope so.

Vale takes my bag out of my hand and slings it over his shoulder, then pulls me into his side and drapes his arm around me, so I slide mine around his waist. He gives me one last encouraging smile, then we walk out the doors and head straight for the stairs.

Ashlyn sees me first, and her face goes pale. I keep mine blank. Jaxon turns my way with a smug smile, basically confirming that this was a setup to try and hurt me, but the smile disappears when he sees who I'm wrapped around. His eyes bounce between me and Vale, and then he sneers.

"Oh," I say, feigning surprise, "I didn't see you guys out here."

I tilt my face up to Vale and try to focus on him. My hands are shaking, so I tighten my grip on his side. I hold his gaze and he gives me a small, encouraging smile. I nod, then force a laugh. It comes out shaky and nervous, but I plow forward, and I make a show of wincing before looking back at Jaxon and Ashlyn.

"Have a great, um, date, I guess," I say with a shrug. I make sure to address them both. I want them both to see just how unbothered I am.

Not heartbroken.

Not humiliated.

Not affected by either of them at all.

"Later Kane," Vale taunts, then I let him steer me away from my ex and one of the many girls he cheated on me with.

"You okay?" Vale bends down and whispers into my hair, then runs his hand up and down my arm. "You're shaking."

"Yeah," I croak out, though I don't feel it. I focus on the feel of Vale's hand on my bicep, rubbing gently, and his warm breath tickling my scalp. "You think I was convincing?"

He chuckles. "Very. He went from white to red to green. Gnarly."

I peek over my shoulder and see Jaxon still watching us, face murderous, so I sink further into Vale's side and slide my hand into the back pocket of his jeans. His chest vibrates with a laugh, and the grin that takes over my face erases the hurt I felt moments earlier.

Did it suck seeing Jaxon with Ashlyn? Yes.

But did it feel good using Vale to make him jealous? Definitely.

It felt *really* good, actually.

But which part felt good, exactly? Jaxon's irritation, or Vale's... well...everything.

Vale tightens his arm around me as we walk and I push the question out of my head. It doesn't matter *why* it feels good, I lie to myself, just that it does. If my breakup with Jaxon is a competition, I'm finally pulling ahead thanks to having Vale as my teammate.

And I refuse to fall back again.

FIVE

I DO A SPIN IN FRONT OF THE FULL-LENGTH MIRROR ON THE back of my closet door, making sure to check out my butt in these jeans.

It looks good. All of me looks good, honestly, which is necessary if I'm going to make it through this game tonight.

This will be the first BU hockey game I've ever attended not as Jaxon Kane's girlfriend. I let my eyes drop to the number on my BU Ice Dawgs shirt.

10. Vale's hockey number.

I haven't worn this shirt in over a year. I'm surprised I still had it considering how much Jaxon used to hate it. The night Jaxon and I met, I was wearing this shirt.

Vale had approached me first. He said it was fate that I showed up to a party after his first home game at BU wearing his number, and we swapped phones to enter our contacts. I remember feeling giddy that an attractive hockey player was flirting with me. I remember developing a pretty big crush almost immediately. But then he left to use the bathroom and never returned.

Then Jaxon appeared.

And then he kept appearing.

Outside my classes. In the dining hall. In my DMs on social media. When he asked me out on a date, I said yes, even though a part of me was still holding out hope that Vale would call or text or DM.

He didn't.

I didn't hear from him again until he showed up in one of my classes a few weeks later. But by then, I'd already fallen for Jaxon.

I frown at myself in the mirror. What a stupid, stupid girl.

I part my hair down the middle and plait it into two French braids. Then I put a blue BU stocking cap on my head and snap a picture of myself, making sure to get the number 10 in the photo. Before I can overthink it, I upload the photo to my social media with the caption "Go Dawgs" and tag Vale.

Take that, Jaxon Kane.

Then, I head to the ice rink.

The game is a good one, and not in small part because Jaxon is playing exactly as Vale predicted. I felt bad at first, but then I recognized Ashlyn Little wearing a shirt with Jaxon's number and holding a bedazzled cardboard sign with GO KANER printed on it in glitter paint and all my sympathy flew out the window. Ashlyn is surrounded by a bunch of other girls, and it takes every ounce of strength I have not to stick my tongue out at them. I should have asked Giana and Zoey to come with me. Next time, I will. I need backup.

When the game ends, we've won by three and Vale scored three goals. Jaxon scored none. I practically skip to the hall outside the locker room, giddy with evil glee at his dismal performance. I'm nearly cackling to myself, but then I hear a familiar voice and skid to a halt.

Ashlyn Little's voice.

So, apparently she's in the hallway waiting for Jaxon. Perfect. Great. Awesome. Love this. I don't know why I'm surprised. Her social media bio did say *in a relationship*. Why wouldn't she be in the partner and family hallway? I hate it.

I lean on the all just outside the hallway and listen. It's not just Ashlyn, but all of her friends, which is annoying. I cross my arms over my chest and huff, leaning back on the cinderblock wall. Surprisingly, I don't feel jealous or hurt. Just annoyed. Then, I hear their conversation switch to other, more interesting topics. Me.

I can't believe she's here...

Thinks she's going to get him back...

Trying to make him jealous...

Doesn't she know he's been sleeping with you for months?...

Never loved her...

Now I feel annoyed and challenged. Why the hell is she threatened by me? I haven't even attempted to talk to Jaxon, but if she wants to make this into some stupid, petty competition, fine. I don't lose.

With my teeth clenched so hard they might break, I take out my phone and shoot Vale a text.

Feel like winning an Oscar? I say, and his chat bubble appears instantly.

Give me thirty seconds, he replies, so I shove my phone back in my pocket and round the corner into the hallway just in time to see Vale stride through the double doors.

His charming smile is already in place and his gaze eats me up in a way that almost makes me forget about the tittering off to my right. I roll my eyes and flick them toward Ashlyn, and his attention follows. Quickly, he glances back at me, winks, then walks faster until he's dropping his giant hockey bag onto the floor and lifting me by the waist. I throw my arms around his neck and wrap my legs around him on instinct.

When his blue eyes meet mine, there's a question in them. He doesn't say anything, but I know what he's asking, and I nod.

His lips are on mine immediately, and I open my mouth for him, allowing his tongue to slide over mine. I feel the kiss in a way

I've never felt any other kiss. All the way to my toes. With just a few glides of his tongue over mine, my core starts to throb, and my heart threatens to beat out of my chest. This man can *kiss*.

A small moan leaves me, and Vale tightens his grip on my body, pulling me closer. I put my fingers in his hair, still wet from his post-game shower, and move to deepen the kiss, but then he pulls away.

"Hey babe," he says with a grin. "I missed you."

I don't miss how he's a little breathless. Good. So am I. His lips twitch in amusement at my dazed expression, which snaps me right out of it, and I remember we're supposed to be putting on a show. I glance over Vale's shoulder just as Jaxon pushes his way out of the locker room doors. Our eyes catch and hold, and when he takes a step in our direction, I tear my eyes off him and smile sweetly at Vale.

"I missed you too, babe. Let's get out of here."

Vale presses one last kiss to my lips, then sets me back on my feet and we leave the hallway without giving Jaxon or Ashlyn another glance. And the Oscar goes to...

Me, damn it. Take that, Jaxon Kane.

Vale drives me back to my dorm in silence. It was an unspoken agreement to skip the after party, and I don't know why he's not talking, but I know why I'm not talking, and that's because I feel weird as hell. I cannot stop replaying that kiss. My nipples are still hard, and it's been ten minutes. I can't like kissing Vale Banks.

I *hate* Vale Banks.

He's...Vale. He's annoying and arrogant and irritating, and he wants my fellowship. Not to mention *this isn't real*. Italicized and bolded and double underlined, even.

Fake. A *performance*.

But...damn. He sure can act. Is there anything he's not good at? The question makes me shiver, and I have to squeeze my thighs together.

I've even gone as far as trying to recall bedroom romps with

Jaxon just to push Vale out of *that* part of my head, but not even my most explicit moments with my ex made me feel this way. And it was just a kiss. It lasted thirty seconds, tops. But I really, *really* liked it.

When he pulls up outside of my dorm, I have every intention of saying goodnight and climbing out. I have every intention of holing up in my dorm for the rest of the weekend to study and not talking to Vale again until class on Tuesday.

These are the things I *intend* to do, but I don't do any of them.

Instead, the moment our eyes connect, we pounce. He and I collide with equal force, lips and hands and tongues and teeth. I want to climb over the center console and straddle him right here while he's parked at the curb, but when I try, I bang my knee and grunt out an *ouch*. He laughs into my mouth, so I jab him in the stomach, making him grunt a similar *ouch*.

"Come up," I whisper against his mouth.

"You sure?" he whispers back, eyes boring into mine, searching. I don't look away, I don't blink. I nod.

"God, yes."

We stop kissing long enough for him to pull into an actual parking spot, then we both hustle into my dorm building and up the stairs to my room. We don't speak. The only sounds are our feet on the linoleum and our labored breathing, but the moment we're in the comfort of my dorm room, all restraint snaps.

His mouth and hands are everywhere—on my lips and neck and breasts and ass—but when I try to take off my shirt, he stops me.

"You don't want to get naked with me?" I ask, incredulous, and he smirks.

"Oh, I want to get naked," he says, stripping off his shirt. "But I want you *half* naked."

I raise an eyebrow, and he undoes the button on my jeans. I let him pull my jeans down over my ass and I step out of them, so I'm standing in front of him in just my panties and my hockey shirt.

When it dawns on me what he's doing, I roll my eyes, but I don't fight my grin.

"I want to fuck you while you're wearing my number, Ten," he says bluntly, and his low voice makes my nipples peak in my bra.

He pushes his own pants and underwear down his slender hips and massive thighs until they're pooling at his feet, then closes the distance between us. He searches my eyes and places his hands on my waist. I feel his fingers flex into the soft skin there.

"You okay with that?" he growls, and instead of answering, I grab his neck and pull him down to me.

Mouths fused, I walk him backward to my bed, then push him onto it.

I grab a condom out of my bedside table drawer and toss it on his chest, then I slip my fingers into the band of my panties and shimmy out of them. When I stand back up, I gape at the sight of Vale stretched out on my bed, hard cock displayed impressively against a sculpted abdomen. I don't breathe as I take him in. His big muscular thighs and thick defined biceps could be chiseled from marble. When he takes his cock in his hand and strokes once, I almost swallow my tongue.

"C'mon, Ten," he croons with a smirk. "Don't be shy, now."

I send him a glare, then reach up the back of my shirt and unhook my bra. Swiftly and with some careful, practiced maneuvering, I pull my bra out of my sleeve and drop it to the floor. Vale's eyebrows raise into his hairline.

"What kind of magician parlor trick was that?"

I bark laugh and strut toward him, climbing on the bed.

"You want the shirt on, fine," I say as he places both hands on my waist and helps me straddle his thighs. "But I don't want to have to wear a bra."

I take one of his hands and slide it under my shirt, shivering when his callused fingers flick over my hard nipple.

"No complaints here," he growls, moving his free hand to my other breast and squeezing. I drop my head back and whimper. I'm sure my arousal is dripping onto him. I never realized I could be this attracted to him, but I don't question it. I let myself feel it, revel in it.

I want him, I admit it, and I want him now.

He snags the condom from the bed beside him, and I watch in fascination as he slides it down his thick shaft. I haven't used condoms in a long time—I only bought the box I have out of spite after my breakup. Which reminds me—

"Dick head didn't give me anything," I say quickly, almost as an afterthought. I've never been in a position where I needed to share my medical history with a partner before, and I scowl. Fucking Jaxon and his whoring ways. "The tests were all negative."

Vale grabs my bare ass, then lifts me to my knees and guides me over him.

"Okay," he clips, then growls, "but no more talk of him. You're fucking me, now. Only me. Got it?"

I nod once. "Got it."

He swipes the head of his dick through me, pressing it hard on my clit once before moving it back to my entrance and slowly pulling me down around him.

"Fuck," he groans, eyes stuck on where we're connected. I nod in agreement.

"Fuck," I gasp, then I swivel my hips. "Vale, this is...this is..."

"I know," he says.

I'm so *full*, so tight. It's heaven.

Vale drags his hands up and down my body, then grips my hips hard and thrusts up into me once. I cry out at the pleasure and prop my hands on his hard chest.

"Go ahead and move on me, Ten," he says, lacing his hands behind his head and watching me with interest. "Show me what you can do."

Normally, I'd tell him to fuck off for trying to tell me what to do, acting like I'm some sort of trick pony for his entertainment, but something about the way he's looking at me...

I don't want to fight him right now. I want to fuck him.

So, I move on him. I swivel my hips in circles before rocking back, grinding down on his pelvis. When I start to speed up, he hisses, then moves his hands back to my hips.

"Fuck, Piper," he groans out, squeezing my hips and then moving to grip my breasts. "Fuck, baby, look at you."

I hum then flash him a smirk before changing tactics, bouncing instead of thrusting, and the guttural moan that escapes him almost has me coming on the spot.

"Good God," he gasps, and I speed up, squeezing around him, making it a game.

I want him to come undone. He said he wants to see what I can do. I can make him lose it.

"Feels so good," I whisper, making my voice breathy. I drag one hand up my body, then pinch my nipple through my shirt. "Oh, Vale, yes."

I close my eyes and tilt my head back as I ride him, giving my best performance, but before I can do anything else, I'm quickly flipped around and hit the bed with a bounce. I yelp as my head hits the pillow, and when I open my eyes, Vale's sporting a wicked grin.

"You think I don't know what you're up to?" he says, kissing me once before thrusting slowly. "You think I don't know when you're faking it? No more Oscars, Ten. Tonight, I want you real."

I scoff and open my mouth to argue, but he angles his body to hit a new spot inside me and I groan instead. He takes my legs and hooks them around one side of his body, so I'm lying on my back with my hips twisted toward the wall. The new depth is enough to make me cross-eyed.

"Grab onto those sheets, baby," he growls, then starts to speed up. "I'm done letting you drive."

SIX

VALE AND I DON'T SPEAK ON THE WALK TO CLASS TUESDAY.

Saturday night was the best sex of my entire life. Not that I'm super experienced, but I'm also not a prude. I'd been sort of adventurous with Jaxon. But Vale...

I didn't know a tongue could do those things.

A shiver skates down my spine just thinking about it.

We fell asleep almost immediately, and then I woke up Sunday to an empty bed. It's been radio silence since.

I'm not dumb. I know that the hockey team has open ice time on Sunday, and logically, I know that's where Vale went. It's also not uncommon for us to only see each other on Tuesdays and Thursdays for lectures. We don't hang out during the week. He doesn't owe me anything.

It's not like we're dating for real.

Tonight, I want you real...

I shake my head to clear it of Vale's deep voice. The sexy things he said.

No more Oscars.

But that was just for the night. We're back to acting. To faking it. I know this, but damn if it still doesn't sting a little. I'm just weeks off a massive heartbreak and now I'm nursing yet another rejection.

You're fucking me now. Only me.

My heart speeds up, and I shake my head again. Ugh, stupid girl. Stop fantasizing about hockey players. They're trouble. Haven't I learned my lesson?

I'm so angry at myself that when Vale shows up to walk me to class, I greet him with a scowl and take his hand reluctantly. We don't talk the whole walk to class, and when we get to the lecture hall, he trails me to my seat, and I plop my bag between us just like I've been doing.

"Ready?" he asks, and I shrug, refusing to even glance at him.

"I'm always ready," I say, which is actually a lie.

I had one hell of a time trying to study for this damn quiz. I spent all Saturday night with Vale in my bed, then all Sunday & Monday worrying what the hell I did to make yet another guy think I was so easy to discard. Is something wrong with me? I know it wasn't the sex. That was phenomenal. So I guess the problem lies with my personality or something.

Dumb. I'm a bad bitch, just like Zoey and Giana said. Stupid Vale. Stupid hockey players. I should date an accountant.

Vale finishes the quiz four minutes before I do. That's what I stress about for the whole class. Then I sprint to the board in the hallway and hold my breath until...

"Damn it," I spit. "Damn it!"

"Better luck next t—" Vale starts to taunt, but I whirl on him and cut him off.

"This is your fault," I growl. "This was your plan!"

His mouth drops with a laugh. "Are you kidding me right now?"

"No. You distracted me. You messed with my head so that you would...so you could..."

"What? Beat you by point three percentage points?" He steps

toward me. "You think I'm fake dating you so I could score better on the quiz?"

"Shut up," I whisper, looking around frantically to see if anyone heard him. I grab his hand and pull him down the hall and into an empty classroom. "What the hell, Vale? You want everyone to know our business? You want it to get back to Jaxon that this isn't real?"

He shakes his head slowly, eyes eating me up and nostrils flaring.

"You think it's not real, Piper?" He steps up to me and I step back, bumping into a desk. "Were the three times I made you come not real? Hm? What about those little whimpers? Those aren't real, too?" He takes my hand and presses it to his chest. Under my palm, I feel his heart racing. When he speaks again, his voice is a whisper. "That feel fake to you, Ten?"

"Shut up, Vale," I say again, but this time my voice is a breathy, needy whisper. Instead of pushing him away like I should, I dig my fingers into his shirt and pull him closer. "It's not real. It's all fake. It's just for sh—"

He kisses me, hard and deep, and I kiss him back, opening for him immediately. He lifts me onto the desk, and I wrap my legs around him as he presses his hard cock against my core. Even through my jeans, I can feel his heat.

"Does this feel fake?" he growls into my mouth, and I shake my head no as I grip him over his jeans. "Jesus, I could fuck you right here on this desk."

"Okay," I say, pulling him closer, but he takes a step back.

I watch as he drags his eyes off of me and pushes a hand through his hair.

"You make me fucking crazy," he groans, and all I can do is nod. "We have away games this weekend, but there will be a party when we get back in town on Saturday."

"You want to go and make Jaxon jealous," I say with a raised eyebrow, ignoring the way my heart stings. *Not real. Not real. Not real.*

He chuckles and shakes his head.

"Hell no. I want you to come to my house. My roommates will all be at the damn party, so we'll have the place to ourselves."

I try to fight my grin, but I fail.

"What about studying for the exam on Tuesday?" I ask with a cock of my head. "I'm sure our course grades are neck and neck. This could be the deciding factor for the fellowship."

He shrugs. "We can study together after we fuck."

I roll my eyes, then stand from the desk and walk toward the door.

"I'll think about it," I tell him, but I've already made up my mind.

"PIPES, WAIT UP!"

Ugh. Instead of looking behind me, I walk faster.

"Damn it, Piper," Jaxon yells, and I hear his feet pounding on the pavement behind me. It takes him mere seconds to catch up to me.

"What do you want, Jaxon?" I ask, making sure he can hear my disgust. "I'm busy."

"What the hell are you doing with Banks, Piper?" he spits out, and I roll my eyes.

"Dating. Having fun."

He grabs my arm hard and makes me stop walking.

"You can't trust him."

I rip my arm out of his grip and scowl at him. "That's ironic, coming from you," I spit out.

His face changes to sorrow, the picture of regret, and my stomach flips just a little before I stomp it back into submission. Not falling for this asshole's lies anymore.

"I'm sorry I hurt you, Piper. I made a huge mistake. I know that."

"Yeah, you did."

"I gave into peer pressure," he starts, and my brows lift in disbelief. "It's the culture of the team—everyone does it."

"Everyone cheats on their girlfriends of thirteen months after making them believe they wanted to marry them?" I say sarcastically, not believing a damn word coming out of his mouth, but he nods.

"Vale's the same way, Piper. You think he's not screwing around? It's like an unspoken rule. It's expected of us, and you have to know that Vale is only using you to get to me."

God, he's such a jerk. How did I not see it in the year we dated? I roll my eyes and click my tongue.

"So?"

He blinks at me. "So? SO? You don't care if he's just trying to fuck with me?"

I shrug and check my nails.

"Don't care who he's fucking *with* as long as I'm the one *getting* fucked *by him*."

"Jesus Christ, Piper." The fake concern in his voice is gone. Now it's just ire. "And what if I told you he's also trying to keep you from getting the highest grade in biochem?"

My head jerks back involuntarily and my eyes whip to his. He looks pleased—too pleased for this to be a lie. He'd only look that happy if he thinks he's won something.

"You're a liar," I say through my teeth, and he shakes his head.

"He wants that fellowship. He's trying to do everything he can you keep you from winning."

I shake my head, but he continues.

"Why do you think he helped you catch me with Ashlyn? He thought the breakup would derail you, but when it didn't, he had to adjust and get closer to you."

"You're so full of shit, Jaxon." I turn to leave, but he says one last thing that stops me.

"So how have your grades been, then?"

I let the question settle, but I don't answer. Without turning back to him, I start walking and I don't stop until I'm in the comfort of my dorm.

Jaxon is wrong.

None of what he said lines up. First, it's not like Vale invited me to the party the night I caught Jaxon cheating. And second, my first grade after the breakup was bad on its own. It didn't need interference from Vale.

But maybe it wasn't bad enough?

No. *No.* Shut up, Piper. This is ridiculous. Absolutely ridiculous.

But...

I think about Saturday night and my grade today. *We can study together after we fuck*, he said.

No.

Jaxon is an idiot, and I would be an even bigger idiot if I believed anything he said.

FRIDAY NIGHT I WATCH THE AWAY GAME ON THE TELEVISION.

We win, and Vale plays great, but it's Jaxon's performance that has me bouncing on my dorm bed.

He was benched.

Jaxon was benched, and the exact line swap Vale predicted took place. Vale was moved to right wing and that sophomore Gavin Barker was moved to center. It went down beautifully, and even though I feel a little bad, I feel a lot more vindicated.

I send Vale a text with a little celebratory firework emoji. I start to type something like "can't wait to see you tomorrow," but then I erase it.

Not yet. We're not there *yet*.

As much as I want to deny it, I think I've gone and caught real feelings, like an idiot. But even more, I think Vale might have done the same. Maybe.

God, I hope so.

But I'm still hearing Jaxon's voice in my head. *Culture of the team*, etc. I shouldn't let the dick get to me, but I spent thirteen months conditioned to believe what he said. Old habits are hard to break.

After the game, I drop my phone on my bed and grab my bathroom caddy. I walk to the dorm bathrooms and take a long, hot shower. I condition my hair twice, then use my blow-dryer on cool to get rid of most of the dampness. It's late, but I still want to get some studying in.

I wasn't kidding when I said the exam on Tuesday could be the deciding factor in the fellowship. I've been keeping rough track of Vale's grades based on the quiz and test scores. We really are neck and neck. I have to do well on this exam. I might actually have feelings for Vale, but my future depends on getting the Randolph Marshall Fellowship, and my future trumps my feelings.

I settle onto my desk and start going over my notes when my phone pings.

Then it pings again. And again. I turn and look at where it lies on my bed and another chorus of notification pings sounds from it. First, I'm excited that it might be texts from Vale, but then I'm filled with dread.

I pick up the phone and find a string of texts from an unknown number. When I open the text thread, my stomach falls to my feet and my heart breaks.

I'm assaulted with pictures of Vale with some girl all over him. She's sitting on his lap and they're making out on a couch I've never seen before. They're surrounded by some of the hockey guys, but I don't recognize anyone or anything else.

This must be from the post-game party tonight.

I know that for away games sometimes some of the guys will find local parties and sneak out after curfew. Jaxon used to do it all the time. Still does, apparently. And apparently, so does Vale.

The same feeling I felt when I found Jaxon cheating on me with Ashlyn blankets me, heavy and thick and suffocating. I hate it. I hate it so much. I hate it even more when I start crying. I feel used and humiliated.

Who is this? I text the unknown number.

No response.

Where is this from? When?

Chat bubbles pop up and I hold my breath until the text comes through.

Tonight in Ohio after the win.

I read the sentence over and over, the words blurring with my tears.

Did Jaxon put you up to this?

Why are you lying?

Who is this?

I send the texts one after another and then hold my breath as the chat bubbles appear once more.

If you don't believe me, text him.

I swallow hard. *Text him.* Meaning Vale. I know they mean Vale. My hands are shaking when I close out of the text thread with the unknown number and pull up Vale's. I contemplate what to say, but then I decide to just be blunt.

Are you making out with some girl on a couch? Are we done?

The response is almost immediate.

We had fun. Thanks for your help.

Gutted. That's how I feel. Gutted. I press call on his contact, but it's denied immediately and followed up with a text.

Don't make this harder on yourself, Ten.

I gasp and stare at the text.

Jaxon was benched tonight. I guess this is what Vale wanted. I wouldn't be surprised if I see him sporting the captain's C on his jersey next. Mission accomplished. Oscar acquired. *Thanks for your help*, he says. What a damn douche.

I stare at the text for three whole minutes before I finally close out of it and block Vale's number. Then I block the unknown number and Jaxon's number.

These hockey fucks can find some other girl's heart to stomp all over. I'm done.

I STAY THE REST OF THE WEEKEND AT ZOEY AND GIANA'S apartment.

I was climbing the walls in my dorm, especially after a video started circulating on social media of a fight on the ice between Vale and Jaxon at the Saturday game. It was brutal. The video shows the two in a heated back and forth, but you can't hear what they're saying. Jaxon gets in Vale's face first, but Vale throws the first punch.

I watched it twice before I had to log out of all of my accounts and bail.

The fight has been nagging at me, though. Something doesn't add up. Vale's not the type to get into fights on the ice. Jaxon does all the time, but it's rare for Vale.

Is Vale mad that Jaxon sent me those pictures?

But if so, why would Vale text me what he did? Unless it wasn't Vale...

I bark out a laugh.

Like it's some sort of conspiracy theory. This is my junior year of college, not some Liam Neeson film. Vale wasn't kidnapped, and his phone wasn't hacked.

It's much more likely, unfortunately, that I got played. *Again.*

But still... That fight? I don't understand where it fits in this confusing ass jigsaw puzzle that is my love life. That's what nags at me constantly until I get back to my dorm Sunday night and find a note taped to my door.

Lecture Hall. Monday. 10 am. Please.
-Vale

I stare at the note with a furrowed brow, trying like hell to ignore the way my heart speeds up with excitement. I know even before I finish reading the note that I'll meet him, but the *please* is what erases my dread. The *please* is what tells me that I might like what he has to say.

There's just been something about Vale, something different yet consistent, that makes me want to trust him. Even when I loathed him, I still trusted him. I still considered him a good guy, albeit annoyingly arrogant. None of that has changed.

What has changed, though, is the way my heart kicks up when I think of him. The way I get shivers when I picture his ice-blue eyes and gentle, calloused hands. The way I miss him when he drops me off at my door, and the way I long to see him every minute until our next lecture.

I sigh. I've gone and caught stupid feelings for him. I admit it. And that's ultimately why I unblock Vale's number and send a single text.

10 am.

He sends me back a heart, but nothing else, and then I turn my phone off and go to sleep.

SEVEN

My chest aches when I see him leaning against the cement railing outside our lecture hall Monday morning.

His head is bowed, and the concern on his face makes me want to hug him. His lip is split and his cheek is sporting an angry bruise, and I just want to kiss it away and soothe him even though it was my heart that was broken on Friday night.

"Hey," I say softly, and his eyes shoot to me.

"It's not true," he blurts, and I nod.

He hasn't even explained, but I believe him already. I believed it even before I left my dorm this morning, but he still plows forward.

"Those pictures were from last year. The guys went to a party Friday night, but I didn't. I stayed at the hotel and slept. I did not make out with anyone Friday night. I haven't been making out with anyone—haven't even been *touching* anyone—except you. I swear."

God, the way those words lift days' worth of bricks off my body. I want to rush him and hug him and kiss him, but I still need to know one thing.

"The texts? That wasn't you?"

He shakes his head adamantly.

"I was asleep, and Jaxon had the guy I was rooming with take my phone. I didn't even know anything had happened until Jaxon started talking shit at the game on Saturday. Trying to throw me off, you know? Get his spot back. And then everything came out. Jaxon promised the guy playing time if he stole my phone."

My jaw drops.

"Oh my god," I breathe out. "I can't believe he'd go to those lengths to hurt me."

Vale closes the distance between us and pulls me in his arms.

"I think it was more an attempt to win you back and fuck me over," he says into my hair. "But it backfired. He lost Captain and has been benched for the next five games."

I jerk back. "What? You told coach?"

"I didn't have to. We got into a huge fucking fight, and everything came to light after."

I study Vale's face, grazing my fingertips over the bruise on his cheek, then his swollen split lip. He definitely looks like he got into a doozie of a fight. Vale brings his hand to my face and smooths his thumb over my lower lip.

"You should see the other guy," he says with a grin, and I roll my eyes.

"You think you can still kiss like this?" I whisper, and the humor in Vale's blue eyes is replaced with heat.

"Only one way to find out," he says and brings his lips to mine.

I moan into his mouth. This kiss is everything I've been needing, craving, since seeing those photos on Friday. The reassurance I feel in every swipe of his tongue, every nip of his teeth, fills me with so much warmth that I could ignite. I'm seconds away from climbing his big body like a ladder when I'm shoved violently to the ground.

My head hits something solid and I land on my hip so hard that my teeth rattle and pain ricochets through my body. Tears flood my eyes as something warm hits my neck. My whole body throbs and I'm dizzy.

"Oh my god," someone says, and I blink up into the eyes of a stranger.

I open my mouth to answer, but the scene behind him steals all my attention. Vale and Jaxon are locked in some sort of bear hug, grunting and shouting. I don't understand. When did Jaxon get here?

"What...what is...?"

I bring my hand to the back of my head and gasp when I feel something warm and sticky. I bring my hand to my face, confused and woozy at the sight of blood.

"Oh shit," the stranger says. "Hold on, I'm going to get help."

I nod slowly at the person speaking, then look beyond them at Vale and Jaxon. They're a moving blur. One of them shoves the other off and Jaxon's fist flies at Vale's face.

"No!" I shout, my head pounding, and Vale whips his eyes to me just as Jaxon lands a jab to his jaw.

He turns his attention back to Jaxon and throws a punch to his stomach, and I try to push myself to standing, but my hip aches and my head spins.

"Stop it," I yell, the pressure in my head unbearable.

I groan and close my eyes, gently letting my body rest back on the stone railing. I can hear a crowd gathering. Lots of mumbling and shrieking, but I can seem to open my eyes.

Jaxon yells something that sounds like *stay away from my fucking girlfriend*, while Vale shouts back something like *keep your fucking hands off her*. Then callused fingers are gently tipping my chin up and I open my eyes to find Vale's blue ones assessing me. I feel his gentle hands on my head and I let my eyes flutter back shut.

"Where's it hurt, Ten?"

Before I can answer, Vale is jerked backward by Jaxon, then turns and shoves Jaxon to the ground.

"What the fuck is wrong with you, asshole?" Vale yells. "You fucking hurt her. Stop acting like a goddamn idiot. She's fucking bleeding. She needs help."

Vale's voice is full of fury. It might be shaking with it, but sounds start to fade in and out, mixing with the throbbing in my head. Someone says something about a concussion. I hear someone mention the emergency room. I just want to take a nap.

"I need you to keep your eyes open for me, okay, Ten?"

I nod my head. Or, at least, I try to, but when Vale's fingers brush my cheek, I realize I can't see him anymore. I can barely feel him. I imagine tightening my grip on him.

"It's okay," I hear him say.

"I'm scared," I whisper, and I feel his lips on my cheek. Something wet. He sniffles.

"You'll be okay, Ten, I swear it. I swear it."

And then everything goes black.

I WAKE UP TO THE SOUND OF A STEADY, RHYTHMIC BEEPING.

When I open my eyes, all I can see is a blurry white ceiling. All I can feel is an itch somewhere on the back of my head. I raise my arm to scratch it, but it's heavy and awkward. I glance at my hand to see an IV and finger monitor. I stare at it, giving my fingers a little wiggle before turning my attention to my other hand.

It doesn't have an IV on it, so I lift it to scratch the spot on my head that's driving me crazy only to find gauze. Some sort of gauze wrap. I explore my head with my free hand. There is gauze everywhere. And...

Shit, something hurts.

I glance around the room—a hospital room, it looks like—and then my eyes land on a blurry figure in a chair. I blink twice, squint and let my eyes adjust, and the figure becomes clearer.

"Vale?"

My voice is a raspy, whispered croak, but he still shoots up from his chair.

"Piper," he gasps out, launching out of the chair and coming to my bedside. "How do you feel? Do you hurt? Do I need to call a nurse?"

His hands hover over me, arms and legs and face, but he never touches me, and I feel lost. As his eyes bounce between mine, I notice deep purple circles under them. The whites of his eyes are bloodshot, and I worry for him until I recognize the bruised cheek and the split lip.

The fight.

Jaxon and Vale.

"What happened?" I ask, and his face falls.

"You were shoved and smacked your head on the pillar outside of the lecture hall."

I bring my hand back to the gauze and it finally dawns on me. Fear rackets in my chest, the beeping speeds up, and Vale takes my hand in his.

"You're okay," he says soothingly, rubbing his thumb over the back of my hand. "You have a concussion and a gnarly contusion, but you're okay now. You'll be okay."

"What day is it?" I ask, and his smile falls.

"Tuesday. You've been out for a bit."

"The exam," I shout, but when I move to shoot upright, my head throbs and I fall back down on my pillow. I clamp my eyes shut and speak through the pain. "Did I miss the exam?"

"I talked to our TA," Vale says. "You're excused from the exam, considering everything. You don't even have to take it. Your grade is fine without it."

I imagine myself shaking my head, but in reality, the movement is barely a flinch.

"I can't. Our grades are too close. I need to...."

Ouch, this hurts. I close my eyes and bring my free hand to my forehead. I feel like I might pass out.

"Your grade is the highest in the class," Vale says. "You don't need to take the exam. You'll still get the fellowship."

I open my eyes and focus on Vale's smirking face.

"But not if you score higher," I say, and his grin grows, "then I won't have the highest grade in the class. What? Why are you smiling?"

"Well," he says slowly, "I'm not taking the exam either."

I furrow my brow.

"Why?"

He shrugs. "My grade is good. I don't need to take it."

I stare at him, studying the smirk on his lips and the playfulness in his eyes. I'm still foggy and confused, so I feel like there is a joke I'm missing.

"But what about the fellowship?" I ask finally. "This is your opportunity to nudge ahead of me and win the fellowship."

Vale chuckles and shakes his head slowly.

"I don't care about the fellowship, Ten," he says with a grin. "I never did."

My jaw drops. "What? But...but all semester... We've been neck and neck this whole time. You were always taunting me about it. What do you mean you never wanted it?"

For the first time since meeting him a year ago, Vale actually looks sheepish. His smile turns softer, and I swear I see a blush color his cheeks.

"I just liked riling you up," he confesses. "You wouldn't give me the time of day unless it had to do with the competition for the fellowship. Pain in the ass, too, because I've literally never studied that much in my life."

"You... you..." I swallow and blink a few times before trying again. "You did all of that just to...tease me?"

Vale rolls his eyes. "To interact with you. To talk to you. To have your attention on me for a few minutes. And, yeah, to tease you, I guess. But only because I fucking love your reactions."

I bounce my eyes between his, letting all of this information settle into my dully-throbbing head. Vale doesn't care about the fellowship. He never did. And he's been here with me since Monday...

Sleeping in that chair in the hospital.

Talking to my TA for me.

Watching over me.

"Vale Banks, are you saying you have a crush on me?" I say, mouth stretched into a shocked smile.

"Guess so, yeah."

"Since when?"

"Since that first party," he confesses. "I told you, Ten. You were wearing my number. It was fate. You were there for me all along."

I think back to that night over a year ago. Vale and I exchanged phone numbers. I liked him. A lot. But then...

"I chose the wrong hockey player," I whisper, and he smiles.

"Yeah, you did." Vale takes my hand and presses a kiss to my knuckles. "But I'm pretty sure you're going to have better luck this time."

EIGHT

Vale

"Good game, Cap."

I shout the words to Gavin through the locker room, and his grin is bigger than I've ever seen it. Kid was shocked when we voted to give him the C after Jaxon was kicked off the team. First, because he thought I wanted it, so when I suggested him for captain, he was floored. Second, because he's a sophomore, which makes him the youngest team captain in Ice Dawgs history. But seriously, there is no one better suited to lead this team.

I've only got a year left before I go free agent. Gavin's got two more, plus our team is a young one. Gavin can grow with them.

I know what you're thinking. *But Banks, wasn't your whole plan to fake date Piper supposed to get you the captain's C?*

To that, I say *nah.*

I didn't want the C. I just wanted Ten.

I saw an opportunity and I jumped on it. I'm resourceful like that. Same reason I pretended to want the fellowship. I might know way more about biochemistry than I ever thought I would, but it was worth it.

I got my Oscar trophy in the form of a tiny, sassy brunette who likes to bust my balls and then kiss them better. She's intelligent and brave, and absolutely gorgeous.

And now she's mine, which is exactly how it was always supposed to be.

Fuck, I love her.

My smile is dopey as I sling my bag over my shoulder and head out of the locker room. When I push through the double doors, Piper is waiting for me in the hallway, and she's wearing my favorite shirt. I drop my bag, pick her up, and kiss her breathless.

"Good game," she pants against my lips with a smile. "You're such a show-off."

I smirk and kiss her again.

"Gotta remind you that you picked the right hockey player," I joke. "Wouldn't want you trying to trade me out."

She laughs then wiggles free and grabs my hand after I pick my bag back up.

"I think I'm pretty happy with my selection," she says, winking, as she tugs me out of the hallway. "For now."

I huff out a laugh and move to smack her ass, but she darts out of my way so fast that all I do is graze my fingertips against her jeans and woosh the air.

"Ah ah, Banksy," Piper teases, skipping quickly down the hallway. "A missed shot. Better luck next time."

Then she turns and runs, and because I'm not one to back down from a challenge, I drop my hockey bag and sprint after her.

Next time is now.

And this time, it's real.

The End

ABOUT THE AUTHOR

Don't want to wait to read more by Brit Benson?
You can find her books and all pertinent information at the links below.

Instagram @britbensonwritesbooks
TikTok @britbensonauthor
BookBub www.bookbub.com/authors/brit-benson
Facebook www.facebook.com/britbensonbooks/
Website https://authorbritbenson.com/

NOT SO NEIGHBORLY

ELYSE KELLY

Editing: Kat Pagan, Lunar Rose Editing Services

ABOUT THE BOOK

It all started with a flooded condo...
Now, I'm stuck temporarily living in Satan's lair.

Oh, I mean rooming with my neighbor, Jack Stalling—the man I can't stand who hates me right back. He thinks because he's a billionaire and eight years older that he's got life all figured out and I'm just a wealthy princess who knows nothing.

Yet somehow, between his condescending attitude and constantly telling me what to do, I've noticed there's more to the gorgeous devil than I thought. Especially when he gazes at me, thinking I don't notice. And if the way he held me close when I accidentally fell asleep in his arms is any indication, then maybe he doesn't hate me as much as I thought he did.

Either way, whatever is happening between us is definitely not so neighborly.

Perhaps I should stick around a little longer and see where it goes...

ONE

Cassi

THE CORNERS OF MY MOUTH TIP UP AS I LOOK DOWN AT SIR Wigglesworth III. The cute little cockapoo sits at my feet, wagging his tail against the marble floor of the lobby in my condo building. He's been my baby for two years, and I completely adore him.

Who wouldn't?

Wiggles is sweet and smart. And when it comes to snuggling on the couch, he's an expert. "You look so handsome in your new collar, Sir." I swear he understands my compliment, tilting his head to the side and making his floppy ears shift with the movement.

I bought the collar this morning—an impulse buy that I couldn't resist when I was picking up a bag of his high-quality dog food. *Only the best for my little man.* It has a big navy-blue bow with small rhinestones lining the edges.

The elevator in front of us opens, and Sir Wigglesworth follows me inside. He knows the routine since we usually go on walks at the same time every day. His new collar was a big hit at the dog park today, getting lots of praise from the other dog moms.

I press the button for my floor, and my eyes shift to the lobby just as my neighbor hurries toward me, his powerful steps made with purpose. I frown and mash the *door close* button, hoping to avoid riding in the small metal box with a man I can't stand.

But luck isn't on my side.

He reaches the elevator before the doors close, shoving his arm into the narrow space and causing them to open for him. He slips inside with a smirk on his face. "You'll have to be faster than that to keep me out, cupcake."

A scowl scrunches my face. *He's such an ass.*

Jack Stalling got under my skin the first time we met. The day I moved in last year, he brought his nosy ass over to my condo to introduce himself. I don't know why, because I've never seen him talk to anyone else here. And it wouldn't have been so bad if he wasn't in such a hurry to patronize me while asking about my age and whether or not I could handle living in *such a big condo all by myself*. Apparently, being younger than Jack makes me incapable of independence and basic survival skills.

If that wasn't bad enough, he also expressed concerns about Sir Wigglesworth being *yappy*. According to him, dogs were hard to control, and he didn't pay an astronomical housing fee to be living next to a barking menace. The insult to my baby was the final straw, and I haven't been able to stand him ever since.

"You could have just taken the next elevator, you know," I grumble, folding my arms across my chest.

"I've had a long day at work, Princess, and I'm ready to get home. But I'm sure you wouldn't know anything about that."

If my eyes roll back any farther, I'd see my brain. "This again? Don't you ever get tired of giving me a hard time?"

"Just stating the truth." He shrugs, the corner of his mouth quirking up in a half grin.

I grind my teeth together while my nails dig crescent moons into my palms. It's always bothered him that my parents bought my condo for me. I'm not sure why, since it's none of his damn business, but he seems to think I'm a spoiled princess because of it. As if I demanded they do this for me and it wasn't their choice.

Like I said, he's *patronizing*. And I want to smack him in the face just to shut him up. "You know, my parents wanted to make sure I'm taken care of, and last I checked, that's not a crime." I give him my most sickeningly sweet smile. "So, don't be jealous because yours didn't do the same for you."

"I think we both know that my parents could have easily purchased my condo. *I* didn't want them to. Because it's important to me to earn my own money. Not be given everything in life like a pampered pet." He glances at Wiggles, then snickers.

My lips pinch together as I take a deep breath. "Having a real job doesn't make you better than me."

"A *real* job, huh?" He chuckles. "Maybe you should consider getting one of those. You could learn what it's like to work for a living instead of taking handouts from Mommy and Daddy."

This man has a way of talking to me with a teasing lilt to his voice that grates my nerves every time. *So damn arrogant.*

I sniff and turn my head away from him, but I can't resist responding. "I know what it's like to work hard, Jack. I work with several charitable organizations."

"Well, that's something, I guess."

Why does this guy's dismissal bother me so much? I hate that he has the ability to get under my skin so easily.

Sir Wigglesworth moves from one side of the elevator to the other, drawing Jack's attention. He looks at my pup and curls his lip in disdain. "That collar is a bit much, don't you think? He looks ridiculous."

I glare at Jack. "He *likes* it."

"How can you tell? He's a dog. He can't exactly tell you how he feels."

Annoyed by his words, I step closer to the panel of buttons and jab at the one for our floor over and over, hoping to speed up the damn elevator somehow. *Why does it have to move so slowly?* This is an exclusive, luxurious building with multi-million dollar residences. You'd think we'd be able to get to our floor faster.

Jack laughs at me. "You know that isn't gonna help, right?"

I do know that, but I won't admit it to him. Instead, I angle my body away from him and stare at the doors, willing them to open soon.

Jack

I force myself not to notice her breasts as she crosses her arms over her chest, pushing the delectable mounds together. The girl is already showing plenty of cleavage in her V-neck top, and how she's standing right now only calls more attention to it. Her skinny jeans hug her curvy ass in a way that should be illegal, and I swallow hard as an unwelcomed wave of desire courses through me. This woman drives me insane, but I can't deny she's beautiful to look at. Not that I'd ever admit it to her.

Gazing down at the cockapoo at her feet, I shake my head. I've never understood people who dress up their dogs like humans. The huge bedazzled bow on his collar *is* over-the-top but saying something was clearly a mistake. If looks could kill, the death glare Cassi threw my way when I criticized her canine's fashion sense would have struck me down on the spot.

Finally, the fucking elevator reaches our floor, and she rushes forward like the damn thing is on fire. She can't wait to get away from me, and the feeling is mutual. Too bad we're heading in the same direction, though. We both have corner condos, with our front doors facing each other.

I easily keep pace with her hurried steps, even though she's practically running down the hall. I'm 6'2, and my legs are much longer than hers, but it's amusing to see the irritation on her face.

When we reach our homes, I waste no time opening my door

and stepping inside while Cassi digs in her purse for her key. I've just closed my door when I hear what sounds like a scream of frustration come from her place.

I'm immediately exasperated by her lack of respect. This is a condo building, not a fucking barn. Which means we should be thinking of the people around us. People like me, who like things quiet.

But doubt starts to creep in, and I second-guess myself. What if that wasn't a frustrated scream? What if something's wrong and she's hurt? My mind conjures up the image of her walking in on a thief or someone else inside her home with ill intent. I'd never forgive myself if I didn't investigate and something happened to her.

My exhale is loud as I walk out of my condo. Seeing her door has been left partially ajar, I don't hesitate to push it open and step inside.

Cassi stands just beyond the entrance. Observing that she's okay, I'm ready to lay into her about disturbing neighbors who are tired and want to rest. And also about how reckless it is to leave her door open, giving any stranger the ability to walk inside and hurt her. But my words die on my lips as my gaze shifts to the living room. Now, I see what she was yelling about, and I honestly can't blame her. I'd have done the same thing.

The floor is covered with pools of water. It looks like a pipe has burst, and the results are disastrous. I'm speechless as I take it all in. The rug under the couch is soaked, and the dog's bed is the same. I can see water dripping from the ceiling, some of it right over the TV, which is no doubt ruined now.

Cassi scoops Sir Wigglesworth off the floor, clutching him to her chest as she turns to see me standing behind her. Her shocked expression crumbles, and she bursts into tears.

TWO

Jack

I'm surveying the damage, trying to avoid the distraught look on Cassi's face that causes my chest to tighten. "What the fuck happened in here?"

She's wiping the tears from her cheeks, yet they keep coming. I don't know what to do in this situation. I should probably comfort her, but I doubt she'd accept it coming from me; she can't stand me. So, I shove my hands into my pockets while she tries to get her emotions under control.

I don't like this innate desire I have to soothe her or fix her problems, especially when it's not an entirely platonic feeling, no matter how much I try lying to myself.

"I thought you went to college," she snaps. "What the hell do you think happened in here?"

Her bitter words make me wish I'd stayed at home, but I'm here now. And I know she's projecting her anger on me simply because I'm available and standing in front of her. But her attitude reminds me that she drives me crazy on any given day. Cassi is the embodiment of a privileged person with no real responsibilities. Maybe it's not her fault since she was raised to be this way, after all. But I can't help feeling jaded about it. I grew up in the same situation, with a wealthy family that could provide me with anything I wanted. The difference is that I'm out here proving I'm more than just a pretty boy billionaire.

"Yes, Cassi, it's obvious what happened here. My question is why did it happen?"

"*Why*?" she repeats as if it's the stupidest thing she's ever heard. "It doesn't take a physicist from NASA to see that a freaking pipe broke." She throws her hands in the air before resting her fists on her hips. "I can't *believe* this is happening."

She turns away, hiding her face as she lets out a choked sob. For a moment, I consider reaching out to place a hand on her shoulder, but I restrain myself.

I feel bad for her; that's all. I'd feel bad for anyone in this situation. Doesn't stop me from being a jerk, though. "You should probably call maintenance to take care of this before more damage is done." I'm unable to keep the condescension out of my voice, and I know it drives her crazy. But I can't help it. She's just standing here while water continues to leak from the ceiling and flood the place. What is she waiting on?

"I know what to do," she bites back. "I'm a little stunned and need a minute to get my bearings."

She pulls out her cell phone, still holding on to her dog, as she finds the number for maintenance. I huff and shake my head. I guess this is the thanks I get for coming to check on her. Knowing that this is in no way my problem, I leave her to it and go back to my place, making sure to close her door securely behind me. If she won't think of her safety, at least I will.

Making a conscious effort to finally relax after an exhausting day, I strip out of my suit, put on some gym shorts, and kick back on the couch with a new crime book I've been reading. An hour passes, and I don't hear any more commotion coming from across the hall. I deem that a good thing, assuming Cassi has everything under control now.

I grab my keys and leave the condo, only to pause in the hallway when I notice Cassi's door has been left open once again. Does she *want* someone to come waltzing in and rob her?

I swear, if she were mine, I'd spank her ass for this.

She's careless but acts like *I'm* the jerk for pointing it out. She should move back in with her parents if she can't remember basic things like personal safety.

As I extend my arm to close her door, her heated tone snags my attention. I should mind my own business, but I can't seem to make my feet move away from this spot. In fact, they take me a step closer, as if they have a mind of their own.

"I can't believe all the problems I've had since moving in here," Cassi exclaims. "This is absurd! It's been one headache after another from day one, and I need to know what you're gonna do to help me."

There's a mumbled response from a masculine voice that I can't make out, but her discontented sigh comes through loud and clear.

"All the issues with my condo *must* be fixed. It's completely unacceptable for things to continue this way. If my home can't be made suitable, then you owe me another one."

I assume the person she's talking to is from engineering, not maintenance. This skyscraper is one of the tallest residential buildings in the world, drawing in celebrities and ultra-wealthy individuals. Yet, because of its magnificent height, there have been construction issues from the beginning, most notably electric and plumbing problems. They've had to call in world-class engineers and architects more than once over the years to address these ongoing concerns. But it still remains one of the most sought-after, luxurious, expensive, and exclusive addresses in existence.

Cassi proceeds to give the guy the riot act, and I'm surprised that she's being so forceful. We bicker a lot, though I've heard almost nothing but snarky comments from her. She's never had this kind of fiery passion when she talks to me.

Who'd have thought it would be so fucking sexy?

I shake my head. What the hell am I thinking? Sure, she's attractive, but that doesn't mean I want her. There are plenty of stunning women in the city besides this one. *This one* I can't stand, and I'm pretty sure she hates me. I might get amusement out of riling her up, but I refuse to think of her as *sexy*.

Annoyed with myself, I turn away, preparing to leave unnoticed to get some dinner. But then, I stop in my tracks when I hear Cassi's next words.

"What do you mean you have no place for me to go? There has to be somewhere in this building for me. I *can't* go to a hotel. I-I... I just can't."

Her panic at the mention of hotels has me once again stepping closer to her door before I even realize I'm doing it.

Why the fuck am I so drawn to her? And why is she freaked out about hotels?

I push her door open wider and peek inside, my eyebrows shooting up when I see it's not one of the design engineers she's speaking with; it's the building executive. Her condo is a mirror image of mine, with an open concept. The two are standing in the gourmet kitchen, one of the few places where the water didn't reach. It's finally stopped leaking from the ceiling, and I notice a sump pump on the hardwood floor, sucking up the liquid.

The man has his back to me, but Cassi sees me. Surprise flickers across her face as she wonders what the hell I'm doing here, but she waves me inside anyway. The building executive shoots us a questioning look while his gaze darts back and forth between me and Cassi. I'm sure he's drawing some wildly incorrect conclusions, watching me make a beeline for her—because I apparently can't help myself—but he doesn't say anything.

Landing his focus back on Cassi, he starts, "Look, I know this is an inconvenience..." He pauses when Cassi stares at him with a mix of fire and fear in her eyes. "But there are no condos available for you to move in to while repairs are made. This is a highly coveted place to live. There's been a wait list for months and months."

Cassi's shoulders slump, and her pretty face distorts into the most defeated look I've ever seen.

"Like I said before," the man continues, "the only option is for you to go to a hotel, which we are more than happy to pay for."

My eyes are on Cassi, and the trepidation in hers is unmistakable when he mentions a hotel. There's a story there, and I *have* to know it, despite how I feel about this woman.

"I-I-I just can't," she stutters. "I won't go to a hotel."

The angst and hopelessness that hangs over her like a storm cloud are both strange and pitiful to see. It makes me realize how vivacious Cassi usually is in contrast to this moment. It's somewhat gut-wrenching to watch whatever is happening in her head affect her like this and I can't fucking stand it. Between this and her tears, I wonder if I'm having a mild heart attack with the periodic chest pains I've been experiencing since I got home from work. This girl is going to be the fucking death of me, but I can't let her go to a hotel. Something inside me tells me that it's wrong and I refuse to stand by while she's in distress. Why? I don't know because I owe her fucking nothing. But the clenching in my lower stomach is telling me I have to do this.

"You can stay with me." The words leave my mouth before I can think this cockamamie idea through, and my heart rate speeds up. It goes directly against my better judgment, and the way Cassi looks at me with wide-eyed astonishment indicates that she didn't expect this offer any more than I did. But I've already put the suggestion out there, and I'm an honorable man, so I won't take it back.

I'm frozen in place while I wait for her to respond, wondering what the hell I just got myself into.

THREE

Cassi

I THINK MY BRAIN JUST SHUT DOWN.

Why on Earth would Jack ever offer to let me stay with him? We have a mutual dislike of each other, and I would never have expected this in a million years.

I blink rapidly as if that'll restart my internal hard drive. "I don't think that's a good idea."

He rears back at my response and I bite the inside of my lip. The problem with Jack is that he has no idea how to relax and unwind. He lives for work, which makes him uber-uptight all the time. Frankly, he's a giant pain in the ass. But, despite that, I *am* grateful for his offer.

I know I'm being silly and immature. Staying in a hotel is a perfectly reasonable solution and it's listed in the occupancy agreement I signed for my condo when we purchased it. But I just *can't*. I wring my hands as I remember the past, knowing I should be over it by now. I'm an adult, damn it, and I need to let it go. But apparently, childhood trauma is the kind of irrational thing that lingers, no matter how much we wish it didn't.

I dealt with years and years of being left alone to fend for myself in cold, unwelcoming hotels when I was growing up. I remember it happening when I was as young as seven years old. Every time we would travel as a family for vacation or business trips—which was at least a monthly occurrence—I was left on my own in an unfamiliar space with unfamiliar things. My father was off working, even when we were supposed to be on vacation, while my mother went to spas and salons and fancy meals with friends. Places where a child would cramp her style and be deemed not suitable to attend.

So, the thought of being forced to stay in one more hotel room makes my chest tighten with anxiety. The apprehension of feeling lonely, and sad, and abandoned floods my mind until I'm almost breathless. I wouldn't have many of my personal belongings with me or the familiar comfort of my home.

It would be a nightmare. One I don't want to relive ever again.

A male voice cuts through my panicked thoughts. "I don't get it," Jack says, and I sense from his patronizing tone that his next words are going to make me angry. "You're being stupid about this."

What in the actual fuck?

My emotions instantly shift from dread to fury. "Well, when you put it like that, I don't see why women aren't beating down your door to get to you. Especially when you're so understanding." I raise an eyebrow as the intensity of my stare burns a hole into his face, or at least I wish it would.

"I'm just trying to help you out, and it's not like I'm known for doing good deeds. So you should probably take me up on it and not say *no*. Besides, where else are you gonna go?"

I look at Jack, hating that he has a point. *Is* this the better option? His agitated expression says he's not excited by the idea of me sharing his space, even though it was his suggestion and it would obviously be temporary. I can't pretend that I'm thrilled by it either. But I would be close to my home, with my own things right across the hall. And that fact calms my nerves. I also know that all the residences here have similar layouts, so Jack's place likely wouldn't feel foreign like a hotel. Still...

I run through my other options in my head. The first one is the hotel and no matter what, that isn't going to work for me. My second option is crashing with one of my friends, but I'm reluctant to do that. I love them and enjoy spending time with them, but all of my friends are partiers. *Serious* partiers. We may be in our mid-to-late twenties, but they still live wild lives, and I've started to outgrow that, despite what Jack thinks and says.

Finally, I consider staying with my parents. They still live in the house I grew up in outside the city, which gives the idea a certain appeal. That house was the only home I knew for a long time. But I've been on my own now for two years and staying there would feel like taking a step backward, even if I was only there for a few weeks. And I'd have to deal with my parents' constant arguing and bickering. I swear the longer they're married, the less they like each other. They're worse than me and Jack.

The alternatives seem exhausting and unviable.

I meet Jack's eyes and nod. "While I do have other options..." He fish-hooks his left brow. "Staying with you would be very helpful. Thank you for the offer."

Damn, that tasted like a mouthful of vinegar.

This might be the first time I've said something pleasant to him since he pissed me off when we met. But I suppose he's more than earned it by giving me a place to stay. Jack's tense shoulders drop a fraction, and a look of relief flashes on his face for just a second. His expression is curious to me, but he neutralizes it so quickly that I think I might have imagined it.

The building executive gazes back and forth between the two of us for a moment, his eyes narrowed. "So, are you two..."

His hint is heavy, and Jack and I talk over each other as I respond. "Oh, no. Not at all."

And Jack blurts out, "Not happening, man."

An awkward silence settles over the room, and I shift my weight from one foot to the other. The man continues to appraise Jack and me as if he's trying to figure out a jigsaw puzzle.

Wanting to get us back on track, I shift the conversation. "So, the repairs? How long will they take?"

He shrugs, which doesn't instill much confidence. "Can't say for sure until we get the maintenance team up here. Couple of weeks, maybe. It depends on how much damage was done to the flooring before we got the water shut off. And, of course, I'll have to consult with an engineer about the pipe problem. If it's more extensive than I think, it could be a while. But I'll have more information in the morning."

I pinch the bridge of my nose and exhale through my mouth. I know it's not his fault this building has architectural problems, but I can't help being upset. This is the first home that's all *mine*, and I hate that I've had so many issues here. I hate that I'll be staying with Jack even more.

I turn to face him. "I'm gonna pack an overnight bag. Tomorrow, I'll come back for the rest of my things."

"Take your time and come across the hall when you're ready." For once, his tone sounds kind and I wasn't expecting that.

I watch the two men walk out before exhaling loudly, feeling like I've been holding my breath for the last half hour. This is surreal. When I woke up this morning, I would never have imagined my day would end like this. And tonight, I'll be sleeping in Jack Stalling's home.

Shaking off the weirdness of my new reality, I head up the stairs to my bedroom. Sir Wigglesworth is lying on his posh, four-poster pet bed—a mini replica of my own—and I cross the room to him and smile.

"You won't believe where we're going tonight, boy." I scratch behind his ears while I relay the plans to him.

I grab a leather weekender bag out of my closet and rummage

through my drawers for clothes. I decide I might as well change into something more comfortable before I go so that I have to pack less. Pulling out some loungewear, I sense a strange combination of nervousness and excitement wash over me.

What is there to be excited about?

I recall Jack's piercing blue eyes and the way that his T-shirt stretched over his broad, muscular pecks when he appeared in my kitchen. I've rarely seen him without a suit on, since I usually catch glimpses of him on his way to or from work. Casual clothing looks good on him and shows off his fabulously sculpted body.

"Stop it, Cassi," I say out loud.

I will *not* think about him like that. Who cares if the guy is drop-dead gorgeous? He's a jerk, and every time I interact with him, I'm left feeling flustered and frustrated, and not in a good way. Firmly reminding myself that he's the enemy and not a friend, I finish packing my bag and scoop Sir Wigglesworth off the floor.

Let's get this shitshow over with.

FOUR

Jack

I PACE THE FLOOR IN MY CONDO, SECOND-GUESSING MY decision to provide Cassi with a place to stay. I don't know what the fuck I was thinking. The woman gets on my nerves enough as it is. I don't need her here.

Did I do it because I'm attracted to her?

That must be it, but if so, that's a dumb-as-fuck reason. She's gorgeous, but I don't have time in my life to chase after some spoiled little rich girl. My job comes first. I'm the VP of Finance for Bennett Enterprises and my focus needs to be on the global market, not the sexy curves of my female neighbor.

Why wouldn't she just stay in a hotel? Her reaction to that idea was peculiar at best, yet I can't stop wondering what it was about. I'll have to find the right time to bring it up again and get an answer out of her, just to make sure there isn't some skeleton in her closet that I should know about.

Now that I think about it, I can't understand why she'd agree to stay with me instead of calling her parents. Wouldn't that be the best solution? Although, I never see her parents come around or hear her talk about them much. Not that I'm with her enough to know for sure who she talks about. But we live so close to one another that even with my busy work schedule, I would surely see her mom and dad if they came by with any frequency whatsoever.

I've always been so focused on how much she annoys me that I never thought about how strange that is. She's a fairly young woman, who's living in a big city alone, and her parents never come to see her. Don't they want to make sure she's okay? If I had a daughter as beautiful as Cassi, I'd be worried fucking sick about her being unprotected in these streets. I wouldn't let her out of my sight for more than five seconds.

I stop pacing and groan while brushing my hair back off my forehead. Why can't I stop thinking of her as beautiful?

Looks aren't everything, so get your shit together, Jack.

Cassi will be here any minute and my gaze darts around my home, wondering what she'll think of it. It's definitely got a more masculine vibe than her place, with heavy, leather furniture and natural-colored walls. The dark curtains are pulled shut over the windows, blocking out sunlight during the day and the artificial glare of the city lights once the sun goes down.

Normally, I wouldn't give a damn if someone likes my place or not. I love it, it's perfect for my needs, and I worked hard to afford it without getting help from my parents. So, why do I feel the compulsion to straighten up the place, even though it doesn't really need it?

Do I want to impress Cassi?

These conflicting emotions are driving me fucking crazy. I can't think of a time I've wanted to impress anyone. I've always had the attitude that people will either like me or they won't. In fact, I usually consider it to be a red flag when a woman is too interested in material things from me. Coming from money will do that to a man.

But Cassi is a different story. She comes from wealth herself, so I'm not sure why I care what she thinks.

Heading down the hall where the bedrooms are, I enter the larger of the two guestrooms, which is the one right next to the master suite. The room is fully furnished with white oak furniture and a king-sized bed. My housekeeper comes once a week and keeps the linens fresh, even though I rarely have overnight guests. The white comforter is smooth and the pillows on the bed match the navy curtains and the rug.

It's modern, but still looks like a comfortable place to stay. Moving to the bed, I reach over and fluff the pillows. I've done two of them before I stop myself, taking a step back as I shake my head.

"What the hell am I doing?" I ask out loud. This is getting ridiculous. I've already gone out of my way enough for this girl.

Get your head out of your ass.

I drag my hand down my face, as if I can wipe away my thoughts. I need to shelve these out-of-place emotions and act normal. I release a sigh when I hear a knock at the door, knowing it must be her.

I leave the bedroom, heading back through the living room to the entrance of my condo. Cassi is standing there, and I find myself staring at her like an idiot. She's changed her clothes, making herself more comfortable and somehow even sexier.

Don't get me wrong, she's always beautiful, with not a hair out of place and impeccable makeup. Regularly wearing designer clothing and the latest fashion trends. A flawless princess.

But, right now, she looks completely different. Her golden hair is pulled up in a messy bun at the top of her head with a wispy tendril hanging down to frame her angelic face. Her black yoga pants mold to her sensuous hips and thick thighs, and the slouchy off-the-shoulder sweatshirt she's wearing displays her smooth, pale skin, which also shows me she's not wearing a bra.

Fuck, what's this girl doing to me?

Desire surges inside me and my dick hardens as my gaze settles on her face. For the first time, I can see a hint of freckles on her cheeks and nose peeking through her foundation and notice the cherry color of her full, plump lips. This dressed-down version of her somehow makes Cassi even more appealing. Then, a sudden realization slams into me: this is the most stunning woman I have ever seen.

And I hate it.

Cassi

A long moment of awkward silence stretches out as I stand in the hallway between my condo and Jack's. He's gawking at me, but I can't tell what he's thinking. *Is he judging me for the way I'm dressed?* I don't usually leave my home looking so casual, but I figured it made sense to do it now if I'm going to be staying with Jack for a couple of weeks.

Maybe he doesn't like how I look. Is that why he's not saying anything?

That thought has me feeling self-conscious, which makes no sense, because I don't care what this man thinks of me. Deciding to steel my emotions, I lock down my expression so he won't know that he's getting to me right now.

"Well, are you going to let me in or are we gonna eyeball each other all evening?" I ask with a hand on my hip.

Jack clears his throat and straightens his posture, like he's coming out of a temporary fog. When he moves back to let me inside, I step over the threshold and place Sir Wigglesworth down on the floor while I look around.

His home is like I imagined, in regard to the layout, but it's decorated completely different from what I thought it would be. It's a total bachelor pad, without a hint of femininity. Again, that's not a surprise, but it's not my personal taste. The urge to comment on his lack of style is on the tip of my tongue, but I hold myself back. I don't want to offend the man who offered to let me stay with him while my place is being fixed. I need to play nice.

"This is lovely, Jack."

Sir Wigglesworth wanders over to a leather club chair, sniffing around and becoming comfortable with his surroundings. I would never tell Jack this, but I'm dying to warm the place up a bit. It feels cold and impersonal as it is now. And dark. He needs color in here... and light.

Jack is such a workaholic, so I'm sure it doesn't make much difference to him that his space isn't a warm and welcoming environment because he isn't here much. Maybe if it were more inviting and soothing, he'd relax a little. I glance at him, wondering if I'm right or if it's impossible for him to take the stick out of his ass.

"Thanks," he replies to my compliment. "Let me take your bag."

I hand it over and drop Sir Wigglesworth's travel dog bed in the corner. Jack jerks his head in the direction of a hallway that I know from my own layout leads to the bedrooms.

"Come on, I'll show you your room."

I follow him, silently noting that the walls are mostly empty. Hasn't he ever heard of décor? Art or pictures of loved ones would really add a lot to this place.

He leads me past a door and opens the second one. I walk inside, looking around. This room is nice and impeccably clean.

"I like the navy color," I exclaim, looking at the curtains and pillows. There's still no décor or knickknacks in here, but it'll be comfortable enough for the duration of my stay.

"The bathroom is through that door over there." He gestures with a hand before shoving both into his front pockets.

"And your room?" I'm not sure why I even ask that. I know it's right beside mine, but I guess I just want him to confirm it.

"I'm right next door."

A thick silence settles in the air, and I can't stop my traitorous mind from conjuring up the idea of something happening between us in the night. He's going to be so close, probably sleeping in just a pair of pajama pants. I bet he looks amazing without a shirt on...

I shouldn't be thinking like that. He's hot, but that doesn't mean I want to sneak into his room in the middle of the night, no matter how tempting my imagination makes it seem.

Jack glances at the bed, and I wonder if he's thinking the same thing I am. I suppress a shudder at that possibility while questioning if the temperature just Cassi in this room because it's suddenly a lot hotter.

"Are you hungry?" His inquiry is abrupt while he steps toward the door as if he can't wait to get out of here.

My shoulders sag with relief and I smile at the mention of food. "Yeah, I'm actually starving." I was supposed to go to dinner with some friends tonight, but the disaster at my condo made me cancel my plans.

Jack leaves the room without another word, so I follow him to the kitchen.

"I can order something. Or..." He opens the freezer and I see trays of frozen food neatly stacked inside. "I have some prepared meals that my chef made for me. I just have to pop them in the oven and heat them up."

"Dinner in thirty minutes?"

Jack smirks. "Give or take."

"Then let's do that, please." I internally jolt when I perch myself onto one of the metal barstools lined up along the kitchen island. I'm not sure why I expected it to be comfortable, but at least it's functional.

Jack lists a few meal options and I select a penne pasta with grilled chicken and pesto. A pleasant beep sounds in the room, then he places two small aluminum trays into the oven and sets the timer. Afterwards, I sense he's avoiding eye contact with me while he stiffly moves about the kitchen. I get the distinct impression he wishes I wasn't here, but he's being polite and won't say that to my face.

What if this whole thing was a mistake? Regardless if it's temporary, I can't stay here if I'm uncomfortable and walking on eggshells. I refuse to spend the next few weeks living with strained silence and constant awkwardness. Maybe if we address the elephant in the room, we can move past it.

Closing my eyes, I fill my lungs with air before slowly releasing my breath and folding my hands on top of the kitchen island. "Listen, I know you don't like me, and the feeling is mutual." Jack turns his full attention to me, his eyes narrowing as I speak. "But *you're* the one who offered for me to come here and acted like it was my only suitable choice." I hold his gaze, daring him to contradict me, but he doesn't. "And now that I'm here, it's like you've changed your mind."

He rushes to reply. "I didn't."

"I think we can make this bearable for however long it's going to be, but it'll take some work on *both* our parts. I promise, Jack, I'm not as bad as you think." I offer him a small, yet sincere smile as a gesture of peace.

He stares at me for a moment, and I start to squirm under his scrutiny. "And I'm not as bad as *you* think." That remains to be seen, but I'm going to stay positive.

"Great! So, why don't we call a truce, then? Let's be on our best behavior. Deal?" I hold out my hand, hoping he won't leave me hanging. Thankfully, he doesn't. Gripping my palm with his, he shakes it, shooting a warm, pleasant tingle up my arm. My eyes widen as if I've been shocked by a surge of static electricity.

"Deal," he agrees and abruptly drops my hand. I tell myself I'm not disappointed by the brevity of our contact.

"Now, can we *please* stop making this so damn weird?" I chuckle with nervousness.

The corner of his mouth twitches, and for a second, I think he might smile. "What's that supposed to mean?"

"It means we should have a civilized conversation for once. I'm already out of sorts being away from my own home, even if we are just across the hall. And I don't want to think about the complete mess my condo is in right now or how long it'll take for all the repairs. I'm stressed and I'm emotionally exhausted."

Genuine sympathy softens his face. "And what kind of civilized conversation do you have in mind?"

That question stumps me. I don't know enough about Jack to have a clue where we could find common ground, and my shoulders slump with defeat. "I didn't have a particular conversation in mind. I can't even think straight right now. I'm just... tired."

I glance up from my fidgeting hands to see concern etched on his face as he watches me. *That can't be right, can it?* Jack doesn't care about me or my hard day. And this is confirmed when after a few seconds, all traces of emotion are wiped away as if they were never there at all.

"Alright, well... dinner will be ready in a few minutes." He grabs two glasses from a cabinet. "How about some wine?"

My head drops back and I lift my face to the ceiling. "God, yes! That sounds perfect."

Jack produces a bottle of white and deftly opens it. Our fingers brush when he hands over my glass, but I pretend not to notice. "You need to relax, Cassi." For once, that bossy tone of his doesn't bother me so much. "Head into the living room to enjoy your wine, and I'll let you know when the food is ready."

I give him a grateful smile, mouthing the words *thank you* to him as I slide off the hard, metal stool. Sipping the dry white wine, I sink down onto the oversized couch, noting that it's cushy even if it's not as attractive as something I'd select. I slip off my shoes and tuck my feet under me, snuggling into the corner with a throw pillow. I glance into the kitchen and observe Jack getting a couple of plates for our meal.

I'm a little upset he didn't attempt to initiate any conversation with me. It would be nice if he'd try to get to know me for once, instead of using surface-level observations and assumptions to criticize me. Maybe if he actually talked to me, things could be different between us.

Perhaps, for now, I should be thankful we're not bickering. I'd rather sit in this living room alone and drink my wine than trade snarky comments with my hot, grumpy neighbor, especially after the evening I've had.

FIVE

Jack

HER PLUMP LIPS WRAP AROUND HER FORK AS SHE TAKES A BITE of her pasta. "Mmm, this is delicious."

We're sitting at my dining table, sharing our first meal together and a million thoughts are running through my head, none of which are neighborly. My eyes keep lifting from my plate to her face, so I stab my food to redirect my focus. I'm trying to get a lock on my dirty thoughts by reminding myself that Cassi may have a pretty face, but that's all there is to her. There's nothing deeper there that will make me care about her. We eat in silence and I wonder if we're ever going to shake this horrible awkward tension that hovers around us.

I feel a nudge against my ankle and glance down to see Sir Wigglesworth at my feet. He looks at me with his head tilted to the side and his little tail thumping against the floor. He's been trying to get my attention all evening, but I've denied him.

"He wants to play with you." My gaze cuts to Cassi and I see a small frown on her face.

"Are you... jealous?" I smirk.

I've always pretended not to like the little guy—mostly because I know it pisses her off—but I love dogs. The only reason I don't have one is because I'm not home enough to take proper care of it.

"No," she snaps, confirming she *is* jealous of the dog wanting to spend time with me. I'm amused and her reaction makes me want to win the pup over even more. But I'll wait until after dinner.

Cassi's glass is only half full, so I get up to grab the wine for her refill. While I'm up, I also grab the salt and pepper from the kitchen to place in front of her just in case she wants some.

"Thanks, Jack." Her tone is sincere and we finally manage a little small talk as we continue eating. It's stilted, as if we're strangers, and doesn't get personal. But we discuss *the usual,* such as the weather and current books we're reading.

Our conversation is polite but undeniably strained.

When we're both finished, I stand to collect our dirty dishes, shaking my head when she starts to help.

"I got this. I'm just going to put the plates in the dishwasher."

It's proper etiquette to take care of my guest, but I'm surprised at how much I like taking care of her. It comes naturally. Maybe it's because I saw her cry earlier, and I'm trying to make up for the helplessness I felt in that moment.

Yeah, that makes sense.

I'm cleaning up the kitchen when I sense her presence behind me. I pivot around in time to see her tip her wine glass up to the ceiling as she drinks the last few dregs. My gaze latches on to her throat as she swallows, and a deep longing squeezes my chest.

Oblivious to my gawking, she carefully hands me the empty stemware. "If you don't mind, I think I'm gonna lie down. I'm wiped out."

"Sure. I'll carry your bag to your room for you."

She smiles, but I ignore the way my heart skips a beat. "I can handle it. Thanks, Jack."

She pads down the hall with an easy cadence before a soft click is heard from the closing of her door. That's when I rub at my eyes and release a long breath, as a buzz of energy courses through me. My body feels like a live wire, and it's disconcerting, particularly because I know where it stems from. If I can't get over this attraction, I won't be able to relax and unwind in my own home. Not while Cassi is here.

I just *had* to be a knight in fucking shining armor...

Going to bed myself, I try not to think about the woman in the next room. But it's not easy. My mind won't turn off. So, after an hour of kicking at the sheets and rearranging my pillow for the eighth time, I toss back the covers in search of a drink. Maybe a Scotch will help me drift off.

It's dark in the hallway, and I'm not paying much attention to my surroundings when I collide with something warm and soft. So fucking soft. A startled, feminine yelp pierces my ears and I automatically reach out, grabbing a stumbling Cassi by her upper arms. My vision adjusts to the darkness, and I note her pink satin pajama set. The skimpy camisole and shorts leave so much delicate skin exposed that I suck in a sharp breath at the sight of it. This brings the scent of warm vanilla to my nose, and my eyes close while I inhale her fragrance.

The urge to tug her closer is overwhelming, so I drop my hands and take a step back. Words escape me as I stand here, my mind struggling to process so many conflicting thoughts. The reason for leaving my room has disappeared and my head is a jumbled mess as my cock grows as hard as steel. My hands itch to touch her again, and my mouth waters, wanting a taste of her plump lips.

I'm thankful for the cloak of darkness when my body tenses while her gaze drifts down my bare torso. I hold back a groan of frustration as her eyes meet mine, and she bites her bottom lip.

"Uh... were you heading to the kitchen too?" She sounds almost hopeful, but I must be mistaken.

"No," I rush to say, scrambling for an excuse not to join her. "I forgot something in my room. I'll just see you in the morning." I don't know why my tone comes across as angry, but I hope she doesn't think it's directed at her.

I'm backing away as I speak, and she watches me with obvious confusion on her face. I wait until she turns to head for the stairs before I retrace my steps to my bedroom.

I can't ignore my aching cock and decide I have to do something about it now. As soon as I'm behind closed doors, I push down my pajama pants and boxers. Stumbling to my bed, I lie across it on my back and grip my rigid shaft in my tight fist. With my eyes squeezed shut, I drop my head onto the mattress and think about Cassi and her sinful body. Her smooth skin and silky hair. The warm smiles she gave me this evening. Every dip and sway of her voluptuous curves.

It all flashes through my mind like a pornographic slideshow as I stroke myself harder and faster. Precum is dribbling from the tip of my cock and provides me with enough lube to keep going. My brain shifts from real memories to illicit fantasies and I picture her here, in my bed, while I slowly strip her of her clothing, kissing every inch of flesh as it becomes exposed. I want her to scream and writhe beneath me.

My hand moves faster, and I grind my teeth as I bite back a groan threatening to escape. I don't know how long she'll be downstairs, but the last thing I want is for her to return to her room and hear me fucking my hand while calling out her name.

However, my imagination is still running wild, and I envision her coming through my door with a hungry look in her beautiful hazel eyes. She seductively saunters toward me, offering to take over while eyeing my dick like it's the most delicious thing she's ever seen. Her soft hand glides over my hard cock as she strokes me, over and over, faster and faster, until she gets to her knees and takes me into her hot little mouth.

She swirls her tongue expertly around my tip, until the head of my cock hits the back of her throat and she gags. The image of her mouth stretched wide around my dick as her eyes water while she eagerly sucks my throbbing cock is enough to send me over the edge, my muscles flexing while I shudder through my orgasm. My release spurts onto my stomach until my lower abs are covered with cum. Fuck, I needed that and it felt good, but I know being inside Cassi's sweet pussy would feel so much better.

I just hope this short burst of pleasure is enough to take the edge off my desperate need for her, at least for a little while.

SIX

Cassi

A MELODIC BEEPING COMING FROM MY PHONE WAKES ME from my peaceful sleep. As my brain comes online, part of me thinks the events from last night must've been a bad dream, but when I glance around at the room I'm sleeping in, I know that's not the case. After the drama of yesterday's flooding disaster and having to temporarily move in with Jack, I need something to take my mind off everything. So, the reminder text from my friend, Allie, about our hot yoga class couldn't have come at a more perfect time. I rush out of bed and dress in some fitted, but stretchy and comfortable workout clothes, ready to leave my stresses behind me, even if briefly.

I take Sir Wigglesworth outside to potty and set him up with a food bowl in the corner of the living room, before scrounging around in the kitchen. My friends and I are going to grab lunch later, but I'll need a light breakfast to hold me over until then. Doing hot yoga without anything in my stomach is a good way to get nauseous, so I decide to eat some yogurt and an apple.

Turning, I jump back with a yelp when I see Jack standing in the doorway of the kitchen, staring at me. I place a hand over my racing heart. "Holy shit! I didn't realize you were home. I figured you'd gone to work already."

I tell myself not to pay attention to how sexy he looks in his suit. I've seen him wear one every day, so why am I suddenly struck by the thought that he looks gorgeous?

"I didn't sleep well. Decided to go into the office a little late." I raise a single eyebrow at him without saying a word, but he seems to read my mind because he shrugs. "There's a first time for everything," he adds.

He takes a step into the room and I swear his eyes sweep over me in a heated gaze. There's a rush of awareness that skitters across my skin, settling at my core and causing goose bumps.

Wait. No, that's crazy.

I have to be imagining this because he'd never look at me that way.

There's a scurrying of puppy paws against the hardwood floor coming from the living room. Then I see an overly excited Sir Wigglesworth bound into the kitchen, his little tail waving wildly while I stare with wide eyes as he pounces on Jack.

He *never* does stuff like this. I made sure he was trained not to jump on people. I'm shocked and a little embarrassed that he's pawing Jack's expensive suit, but my neighbor takes it in stride, bending down to pet the dog as if it's no big deal. I just stand there, watching, not sure what to make of it. Sir Wigglesworth has a big puppy grin on his face as Jack runs a hand over the dog's head, like he's completely smitten with him.

What alternate universe is this?

Still petting my pup, Jack glances up at me. "So, where are you off to with barely any clothes on?"

I look down at the black yoga pants and yellow fitted tank. A laugh escapes me as my eyes dart over to meet Jack's. Surely, this man isn't trying to tell me what to wear?

"I'm dressed appropriately for class. You act like I'm half-naked or something."

"You *are* half-naked or something."

I roll my eyes. "Thanks, Grandpa. I'll keep that in mind. If you must know, I'm going to a hot yoga class and then my friends are taking me out for lunch. Apparently, they want to tell me about some guy they think I'll hit it off with. But why do you care where I'm going or what I'm wearing?"

"What guy?" he asks, ignoring my questions. If I didn't know better, I'd say he seems almost jealous.

But why would he be?

"I don't know," I answer honestly, taking a bite from my apple. I chew quickly and swallow. "That's why I'm going. So that I can find out. Again, why do you care at all?"

"I *don't* care," he scoffs. "I just think you should cover up. That's all."

He turns away from me, getting a cup of coffee. I consider his words, my brows scrunched up while I eat my apple. "I don't get you," I finally say.

"Whatever," he replies, his posture dismissive. "There's nothing to get. I really don't care what you wear."

What is wrong with this man?

"What a jerk," I mutter under my breath.

Jack sets down his coffee and stares at me. "What was that?"

I toss my apple core in the trash and stand in front of him. "You know what, Jack? As I said last night, it was *your* idea for me to move in here."

"What's your point?" There's that damn patronizing tone again that sparks anger inside me every time.

"My point is that you need to pull your head out of your ass." The last word comes out forcefully, and his eyebrows pop up as he straightens his back.

"Pardon?" He takes a step toward me.

"You heard me," I snap.

He holds up a hand in an unmistakable *stop* gesture. "Look, Cassi—"

I press on, talking over him. "I'm thankful that you're letting me stay here. Really, I am. But I also don't want to be treated like a child or made to feel like a burden. I've already been displaced from my home, and this isn't exactly the ideal situation for me either."

Jack takes a deep breath, stretching his neck to the left and the right, as if he's trying to loosen up some of the building tension. His jaw is tight, and he won't meet my eyes. I'm not sure if he's going to respond at all, but after a long pause, he does. "You're right. I'm sorry." He mumbles the words like they're painful to get out, and I have to fight back a smile.

"What was that?" I ask.

"Don't push it, smartass."

I decide to take the win and let the subject drop. Huffing, I grab my gym bag off the counter and start toward the door. "I guess I'll see you later, then."

"Yeah, you will. Be careful out there."

"I'm always careful." Heading out the door, I feel a pang of sadness when I pass by my own condo on the way to the elevator.

Instead of dwelling on what's happening inside my place, I think about the interaction I just had with Jack. If this is how things are going to be for the next few weeks, I'm not sure how we're going to make it.

It's not just that I'm living with a jerk. He also happens to be the hottest jerk I've ever seen in an expensive suit.

I STAY OUT OF THE CONDO FOR MOST OF THE DAY AS IT SEEMS easier to avoid the place for now. When I get back, I know Jack is probably home because I always see him coming into the building around the same time. So, I'm not surprised to walk in the condo and find him in the kitchen.

The lack of a shirt is unexpected though. *Very* unexpected.

I caught a faint glimpse of his bare, sculpted chest last night, but it was so dark in the hallway. Here, the bright lights are shining down, highlighting his chiseled form and naturally tanned skin stretched over hard muscle that my fingers itch to trace. His jeans sit low on his hips, showing off the V-shaped indents on each side.

I'm standing just inside the entryway as I stare at him with my mouth open.

At first, he's busy preparing dinner, but he must feel my gaze on him because he looks over and notices me ogling him. "You know, you're going to catch flies in your mouth if you don't close it."

Embarrassed and annoyed, I glare at him before setting my things down on a side table. Then I walk toward the kitchen without dignifying his words with a response.

"Where have you been?" he asks, his attention on opening another bottle of white wine.

"Out." My reply is terse, but I don't care.

"Do you always have such a snarky attitude?"

"Do you always have to act like you're my dad?" I ask, folding my arms across my chest.

Jack pins me with an unamused stare. "Maybe if you didn't act like a child, I wouldn't treat you like one."

Asshole.

He turns his back to me as he checks whatever food is on the stovetop and misses the scowl I shoot at him. Why does he think he can always boss me around? Didn't we just talk about that this morning? He clearly can't help himself.

Then again, I have to admit that he's definitely one hot-ass *daddy*.

"What the fuck?" I mutter, my shockingly sexual thought making me more annoyed with him.

Jack turns around, leaning his ass against the counter. He

crosses his arms over his chest, causing the muscles of his pecks to bulge. "Watch your mouth," he says in a low voice.

I try to hold on to my anger—I really do—but I can't help being distracted by Jack's hot body. I hate that it makes me feel weak, but I can't remember ever having such an intense desire for a man before. The worst part is that I'm terrible at keeping my thoughts and emotions from showing on my face. Jack definitely knows that I'm attracted to him, if his present smirk is anything to go by.

Great. Now I'm flustered.

Feeling the need to preserve my pride, I open my mouth to tell him off, but Jack spins back around to the stove before I can get a word out. He stirs something in a pan. I can't see it from here, but it smells fantastic. He pulls it off the heat and looks over his shoulder at me. "Did you eat while you were *out*?"

"Yes, but it's been a while." Since lunch, actually.

"Sit down. I'll fix you a plate."

"Oh no, that's okay," I shake my head, worried that if we spend more time together, we'll just fight. "I'll grab something quick and head to my room."

"Quit being stubborn and just sit down," he says, placing a glass of wine on the kitchen island in front of me.

I hesitate. "Do you *always* get your way?"

He flashes me a mischievous smile. "Yes."

Oh my god. Is this some kind of hate flirting? Is that what we're doing right now? Though, an even more pressing question would be: *why can't I stop myself?*

My stomach rumbles, so I give up fighting him and plant my ass on one of the uncomfortable stools at the counter. If given the chance, these ungodly things would be the first things I replace. I notice it's awfully quiet here, and I glance toward the dog bed in the living room to find it empty.

"Where's Sir Wigglesworth?" I ask as Jack scoops some kind of noodles onto two plates.

"Asleep on my bed." He doesn't offer any further explanation, and I don't know what to think. I thought he couldn't stand my dog.

Jack comes around the island to place a plate of what looks like seafood alfredo in front of me. I expect him to sit and eat, but he stays standing beside my stool. He's way too close, and not only can I feel the heat radiating from his sexy body, I can also smell his spicy cologne.

What's happening to me? I'm supposed to hate him because he's always a jerk to me. Why am I feeling so attracted to him right now? Just because he has a nice body?

That doesn't change his personality.

Maybe it's low blood sugar affecting my brain. I take a bite of the pasta, and it's fantastic. I can't hold back the moan while my eyes drift closed. When I open them, Jack is staring at me with his fork paused midair.

"What's wrong?" I ask, grabbing a napkin and quickly wiping my face, just in case I have food there or something like that.

Jack gulps. "Nothing. Nothing is wrong."

I watch him curiously as he shifts his weight back and forth, but he resumes eating. I do the same, but I could swear that I'm picking up on even more heat emanating from his body.

As soon as we're done, I stand. "I'll clean up this time."

I expect him to decline my offer like he did yesterday, but he just nods and turns away. I watch his muscular back as he retreats toward the bedrooms without saying anything. I don't know what to make of his odd behavior. I could have sworn that we were flirting just a few minutes ago. Now it seems like he's eager to get away from me.

What the hell?

"Is everything okay?" I call out as I gather up our plates.

"Yep," he says over his shoulder. "Everything is fine. I'm just tired." But right before he rounds the corner, out of sight, I see him reach down and adjust his dick.

Huh. *Well, that's interesting.*

SEVEN

Jack

I've been staring at my computer screen for the past twenty minutes, unmoving. I can't concentrate on my work. All my fucking brain can think about is the sexy-as-sin girl living in my condo, who is apparently much smarter than I ever gave her credit for.

Why is that so damn annoying?

Yesterday, I overheard her talking on the phone with a friend, giving the woman shockingly insightful financial advice. So many people who grew up with money don't know a fucking thing about how to properly manage it. I thought Cassi was one of those people, but I guess I was wrong.

She's also in the process of planning a charity gala with one of her friends, but from what I can see, Cassi is the one doing all the work. If someone had told me that before she moved in, I would have assumed she'd complain and whine about having to step up, but it turns out I would have been wrong about that too. Cassi has kept her head down and focused on preparing for the event.

And for some reason, I don't like it. I urged her to confront her so-called friend about pulling her weight with the planning. Yet Cassi surprised me once again when she agreed that she would be confronting the woman, but *after* the gala. She wanted her friend to meet her obligations first. It turns out the friend is a spiteful brat who would probably bail if Cassi pushed her to do more. And Cassi needs her at the gala for appearances.

Yep, she's definitely smarter than I thought. She doesn't just put thought into the execution of her plans; she also has the necessary social skills that allow her to understand how to work with difficult people.

The fact there's obviously more to her than money and a pretty face is troubling me.

A knock on my office door shakes me from my thoughts, and I call out for my assistant to come in. I try to refocus my attention on my computer screen as Ella walks inside.

"I have those documents you wanted for the Goldstein file," she says, crossing to my desk and placing the papers on the corner. "And I scheduled a meeting with Chase for tomorrow morning."

I nod without looking away from my computer, where I'm checking my email. "Thanks, Ella." I know she's still standing in front of me, even though I'm not focused on her. "Was there something else you needed?"

"Actually, yes, there is." Her voice drips with sarcasm. "It turns out I'm pregnant with Taylor's baby. And I embezzled $500,000 to support myself while I decide what to do. Oh, and I'm too ashamed to come to work here anymore. So, you're on your own, pal. Good luck with that."

"Okay, sounds good," I murmur. Then, some of what she said seeps in, and I look at her. "I'm sorry... what?"

Ella puts her hands on her hips and tilts her head to the side. "What has gotten into you lately? You've been walking around in a fog for two weeks now. Are you on drugs?"

"What?"

"It's drugs, isn't it?" she continues, narrowing her eyes at me. "Spill it, or I'm calling your father."

My eyebrows wrinkle as I stare at her. "Why the fuck would you do that?"

"I don't know," she replies, waving a hand dismissively. "You're just being weird."

"Sure, but calling my father is a bit extreme, don't you think? Considering I haven't spoken to him in almost two years. Might be better to ask your boyfriend first. I mean, Taylor is my best friend..."

Ella looks thoughtful for a moment before shaking her head. "Nah. I prefer to keep my future husband separate from my work one."

That makes me grin. "Probably a good idea. So... maybe consult with Chase, then?"

"I guess that's fair," Ella agrees. "As CEO and your boss, he *would* be the best one to approach."

I roll my eyes. "Chase is Taylor's cousin, you know. There's still a familial connection."

"If you don't want me to call Chase right now, then quit being weird."

There's been a playful vibe to this conversation so far, but I can see that there's real concern in Ella's eyes. It's not surprising. She's like a sister to me.

"Seriously, Jack. I'm not leaving until you tell me what the hell is going on."

I groan. Her eyebrows are raised, and her lips pinch together in stubborn determination. She's not going to let this go.

Exasperated, I exhale a huff of air and throw my hands up. "Fine. But the least you can do is get me a donut while I bitch and moan about a fucking woman, like some teenage idiot who doesn't know what to do with a pussy."

Ella's smile is triumphant. "Maybe the donut should be for me while I listen to you bitch and moan."

"Fine. We both get a donut," I agree, not willing to compromise on this.

"Fine," she mimics me. "I'll be back."

"Fine. I'll be right here." I can't resist riling her up a bit.

"Fine," she says through gritted teeth. "You can wait for me."

"Fine. I—"

"Oh my God," she cuts me off as she spins toward the door. "Shut up. I'm getting donuts, and I'll be right back. Just keep sitting there, staring into space, and wait for me."

It only takes five minutes for Ella to return with two fresh raspberry-filled donuts and two cups of hot coffee. She settles into the chair in front of my desk, making herself comfortable as I spend the next twenty minutes telling her all about Cassi and our current living situation. By the time I finish, Ella is bent over at the waist, laughing at me with tears in her eyes.

I glare at her. "What is so fucking funny?"

"Please tell me I get an invitation to the wedding," she says, wiping at her face.

Her words fill me with bewilderment. "Are you insane? Did you hear anything I just said?"

"Oh, I heard you. And I stand by my statement." She can't seem to rein in her giggles.

"You know what? I—"

Before I can finish my sentence, the door swings open and Taylor walks in with a smile on his face that gets brighter at the sight of Ella.

"I heard laughter from the hallway," he says, coming to the side of her chair and placing a hand on her shoulder. "What's going on in here? You trying to steal my girl?" His words are lighthearted. He knows things aren't like that between me and Ella.

"No, but apparently she's crazy and talking out her ass. I may need to reconsider her employment."

"Hey!" she cries out, putting a hand on her chest. "Don't be mad at me because I'm right."

"You're right about what?" Taylor asks.

I interrupt before she can answer. "Nothing. She's right about nothing. Now, why don't you two get out of here? I have work to do."

"Sure, if you can stop thinking about your new *roommate* for five minutes," Ella says with a teasing grin before making kissy faces.

Taylor's eyes widen. "New roommate? What new roommate?"

Ella is clearly shocked as she looks back and forth between me and Taylor. "You didn't tell him?"

"Tell me what?" Taylor asks, irritated. He's always hated feeling left out of the loop.

"There's nothing to tell," I mumble.

Ella laughs again. "Oh, this is too good."

"*What's* too good?" Taylor presses, agitated. "Somebody tell me what the hell is going on."

"Nothing," I say, but Ella speaks at the same time.

"Jack has a girlfriend," she announces.

I sneer at her. "I don't have a fucking girlfriend." Looking at Taylor, I gesture to Ella. "Can you get your woman out of here? This is one of those times I wish my assistant wasn't dating my best friend, and I could fire her ass."

Ella stands with a grin. "You'd never fire me. You need me too much."

"We'll see about that," I mutter.

Taylor's eyes light up, and he grins. "Wait a minute... Are we talking about the hot neighbor you're always staring at?" Ella smacks his arm and gives him a dirty look. "Babe, I'm talking about Jack," he quickly clarifies. "That's gross. Ew. Yuck." *Okay, that's a little much, man.* "I don't think she's hot. Jack does."

"No, I don't." Even as I say the words, I picture her in those tight fucking yoga pants.

"Yeah, right." Taylor joins Ella in laughing at me now. "Anyone with a brain and partial eyesight can see that you're into her. But you fight it like a dumbass. I don't understand why. It sounds like you've got a perfect opportunity to make a move, if you ask me."

"I didn't ask you." I sigh, running a hand through my hair. "She needed help. I gave it to her. I'm not hitting on her."

"So, you'll finally admit that you're into her?" Ella pushes, smiling like she knows some big secret.

"No. Now, get the hell out of my office."

"I'd think about it if I were you," Ella says, still not leaving. "Someone else could come along and steal her away. You'll miss your chance if you're not careful."

"I'm not going to miss anything because I'm not interested." I don't want to think about why my stomach is suddenly twisted into a knot.

Taylor chimes in with a smirk on his face. "Keep telling yourself that, man." These two are driving me fucking crazy.

"Come on," Ella says, taking Taylor's hand. "Let's leave him alone with his feelings. It's been a big day for him."

"I will fire you, woman," I growl.

"Don't worry, baby," Taylor tells her. "You don't need to work."

I'm officially at the end of my patience. "Out," I demand, pointing toward the door.

They're still laughing at me as they finally go. I shake my head and force myself to focus on my damn job. I don't need this shit from either one of them. I don't want Cassi. Yes, she's hot, but that doesn't mean anything. I'm just doing her a favor until her place is ready, being a good neighbor.

In fact, I'm not even going to look at her gorgeous body from now on. I'll ignore it until she's gone. I should only have to tolerate her presence for a little longer, and she'll be back across the hall where she belongs. Her and her cute fucking dog too.

EIGHT

Cassi

I HAVE TO ADMIT THAT JACK HAS GOOD TASTE IN SELECTING comfortable furniture. This condo might be a total bachelor pad, but the couch is cushy. That's why I'm spending my evening curled up with Sir Wigglesworth, trying to find a movie to watch on Netflix. I've finally decided on one, but before I can start it, Jack walks into the room in nothing but a pair of low-slung sweatpants.

"Don't you own *any* t-shirts?" I ask, exasperated.

"It's my house." He shrugs. "I want to be comfortable. You don't have to look if you don't want to."

"And how would you feel if *I* walked around shirtless?" My mouth snaps shut as soon as I say those words. My cheeks heat as a broad grin spreads across Jack's face.

"As a matter of fact, I think I'd like that very much. Feel free to start now."

"Shut up," I mutter, unable to meet his eyes.

"How about I make us some snacks?"

I appreciate his suggestion and change of subject. Then, I realize what he said. "Wait... you're joining me?" I ask.

"Is that okay? I can go back to my room if you'd prefer."

"No, of course, you can stay." I bring my hand to my lower belly, hoping to ease the sudden fluttering. "Like you said, this is your home. You can do whatever you like. Or I can go to my room if you want."

"How about we both stay and just watch a damn movie. We've gotta stop being so fucking weird."

I laugh awkwardly. "Why *is* it so weird?"

"I think we both know the answer to that," Jack mutters, his voice so low that I'm sure I wasn't supposed to hear it.

"What did you say?"

"Nothing. I'll be right back."

Sir Wigglesworth nuzzles against my hand as I pet his little puppy head. He's keeping me occupied while I wait for Jack, who returns a few minutes later with a smorgasbord of treats. I watch as he covers the coffee table with every snack I can think of. Cookies, popcorn, chips, and soda. It's a ton of junk food that I know he doesn't eat.

"Holy fuck," I exclaim. "Where did all this come from?"

Jack laughs as he takes a seat on the couch beside me. He's close but not touching me, since the dog is between us. "I have a secret stash."

"Obviously. I can't believe you've been holding out on me. Why didn't you say anything?"

He opens a can of Coke and takes a long sip before answering. "Honestly, I forgot it even existed. I rarely allow myself to indulge like this, so I mainly keep it on hand for guests."

"But... you never have people over."

He arches a single eyebrow. "How would you know?"

I fiddle with the corner of the blanket draped over the back of the couch. "I never see anyone else coming or going. It's just you going to work or the gym and coming home again."

"Are you stalking me?" He sounds amused, but I immediately shake my head no.

"Don't be ridiculous. I just notice things occasionally." I reach for the popcorn to give myself something to do. Jack lets the subject drop and I start the movie, hoping things will feel less strange if we focus on the screen and not each other.

Jack

The movie we watch is actually quite funny. I suppose I shouldn't continue to be surprised by Cassi, but her above-average taste in films is yet another unexpected element of her personality. I relax on the couch, as the two of us snack on junk food and laugh at the screen.

I forget myself as I focus on the TV. Before I know what's happening, the two of us inch closer and closer until our arms are pressed together. My confused gaze travels down the couch, and I realize the dog has moved to the loveseat.

Little traitor. I was counting on him being a buffer between us.

I think about scooting away from Cassi, but when I glance at her face and see that she's completely focused on the movie, I stay put. Not because I'm enjoying the warmth of her body seeping into mine or the scent of her heavenly perfume. I just don't want to stir things up between us again.

But staying put might have been a mistake, because the next thing I know, I'm waking up. We fell asleep watching the movie together, and now I'm spooning Cassi, my chest pressed to her back and her ass nestled against my rock-hard cock.

I peek open my eyes and catch the TV's logo displayed on the screen. The movie is long over, so it must be sometime in the middle of the night. My arm is wrapped tight around her middle, and I'm considering how I'm going to slip out from behind Cassi without disturbing her when I feel her body shift. Her breathing adjusts, and I know she's not sleeping anymore. But she's facing away from me, so she must not realize that I'm awake too. Then her ass moves against me, and she freezes.

Shit.

This is awkward. I hold perfectly still, willing my cock to go down. But then... Cassi continues to rub her lush little ass against my hard dick. Electricity zips through my veins, and I stifle a groan, not wanting her to know that I'm awake or worse, embarrass her. When she moans her pleasure, it's all I can do not to reach around and slide my hand into her panties to play with her sweet pussy until I make her come.

Fucking hell.

When she pulls away from me a moment later, I'm disappointed, but I miraculously pretend to still be asleep, closing my eyes as she stands from the couch. The air shifts when she turns to face me, then her smooth fingertips gently trace the curve of my cheek. I don't know what to think as my heart races, but I don't dare move, wanting to experience her touch for as long as she lets me.

Then, Cassi pulls the blanket from the back of the sofa and covers me with it. I listen to her footsteps as she walks away, waiting until I hear her bedroom door close with a snick before I sit up and bring a hand to my face, wondering what she was thinking while she caressed my skin.

After a couple of minutes, I finally peel myself from the couch and turn off the TV. As I head to my room, the only thing on my mind is trying to forget what just happened and sleeping in my warm bed. However, all that goes out the fucking window when I pass Cassi's door, and a familiar buzzing has me halting in my steps.

What is that?

I listen closely, certain I've heard this sound or something similar before. Like the information is lingering in the back of my mind, and I'm on the cusp of identifying this mystery noise. And once Cassi moans, it all clicks into place.

Holy fuck, she's masturbating.

Of course, it's a vibrator. The picture that flashes in my mind makes my dick throb, and I have to force myself not to bust down her fucking door like a caveman and offer to do it for her.

I'm about to pry myself away from this spot when she cries out, louder this time. I can't resist staying to listen, not when the throaty sounds she makes are so erotic and sensual. I need to commit them to memory and keep them forever. I damn near press my ear against the door as I listen to her pant and whimper. She must be close, and a strange excitement builds inside me, almost as strong as the desire and lust pulsing through every inch of my body.

I'm barely resisting the urge to stroke my aching cock when she finally comes, louder than I think she intended or even realizes. My pulse is pounding in my ears as I hold back my own orgasm threatening to release, but there's no mistaking the word that's called out from her mouth.

Cassi shocks the shit out of me when she comes hard with *my* name on her tongue.

NINE

Cassi

A month later, and it's taking much longer to fix the issues with my condo than anticipated. I'm annoyed by the whole process, mostly because my parents paid a lot for me to live in this exclusive building, and it feels like it's been money wasted.

On the other hand, things aren't so bad living with Jack, not like they were in the beginning. We've settled into a routine, and I find myself being home most nights by the time Jack gets off work. I'm not sure if that's just a coincidence or something I'm doing on a subconscious level. But either way, I've started to enjoy our evenings together, even if I'll never admit that out loud.

We have dinner, usually at the condo, but we've gone out a few times too. There are plenty of places to eat near here, and we've ventured to a couple of them. Jack has started to be much more at ease around me, and it's nice to see the tension leave his body when he walks in the door and gives me a smile. I wish he'd be like that more often because he truly is one of the most gorgeous men I've ever met.

There have even been moments between us that feel almost intimate. I could have sworn several times that he was going to kiss me, but right as I got closer, he'd find an excuse to pull away and put distance between us. It's happened three times over the last two weeks and it's annoying as hell.

Like the time he was comforting me—which I did not expect—while I was reading this gut-wrenching book that tore my heart out and had me crying on the couch like a baby. I wasn't prepared for one of the characters to die and I completely lost it. So, Jack slid down onto the sofa behind me and held me gently, wiping away my tears. And when I looked up at him with watery eyes, he held my gaze for the longest time, like he could read my soul. I just knew that was going to be the moment he kissed me. But he handed he handed me a fresh tissue, excused himself, and brought me a glass of water instead. *Annoying*.

When I moved in, I thought I hated this guy. But now, I realize that I hated how he acted, which most of the time was like a crabby-ass jerk. Although, I'm sure I wasn't the nicest to him either. Since getting to know him better, I see he's not who I thought he was, and that I don't hate him so much after all. But the question is how does he feel about me?

The midafternoon sun heats up the kitchen while I gather the ingredients for a turkey sandwich. Multiple voices are blabbing through the speaker of my cell phone sitting next to me on the counter top.

"Is the asshole there?" Michelle cuts in, and I roll my eyes at the nickname my friends have given Jack.

He's really not an asshole. He's just annoyed by people who think they're entitled to things they aren't. "No, he's still at work."

"Well, forget about him," Heather says. "We should be talking about which guy we're setting you up with anyway."

I groan. "I don't know, guys. The last few blind dates you sent me on were disasters." I shudder, recalling the guy who criticized my clothes, then had the nerve to say my small talk was *unoriginal and boring*. That I should be trying to *wow* him and not ask the same tired questions that everyone always asks on a date. I couldn't get out of there fast enough.

Sierra sounds way too excited for me to like what she's about to say. "This one won't be. Not this time," she assures me. "I have the perfect guy for you. I just know it. And the best part is that he's nothing like your douchebag of an ex."

I snort. "Well, it's hard to beat a narcissist who puts you down and somehow makes you feel like it's all your fault."

"What?" Jack's voice cuts through the air from behind me. I whirl around, dropping the butter knife coated with mayonnaise onto the floor. "Who are you talking about?"

"Don't worry about it." I bend to pick up the knife. "He's long gone and moved on to someone prettier, skinnier, and richer."

Jack grinds his teeth together, looking more pissed than I've ever seen him. I don't understand it and I'm not sure what I've done to upset him.

"Forget about that dick bag, Cassi," Sierra encourages through the speakerphone. "We have a great guy for you anyway."

"The best," Michelle adds. "If you play your cards right, you'll be out of Jack's hair and spending all of your time with a new man soon enough."

"Whatever," Jack mumbles under his breath before storming out of the kitchen. I stand there, frozen for a moment, watching him go.

What the hell was that about?

TEN

Jack

SWEAT TRICKLES DOWN MY TEMPLE, AND I SWIPE IT AWAY with the back of my hand. My workout playlist is blaring in my ears, drowning out the sound of the weights smashing together as I use a machine targeting my triceps.

I like this gym. It's right down the street from my condo building, and they have an impressive array of equipment that keeps me in shape. I come here most days after work, focusing on my body and clearing my mind. It's also private, so I don't have to worry about people knowing who I am or how much money I have. I get to be just like everyone else, and that brings me great peace.

But today is different. I can't get my mind off what I heard in the kitchen yesterday. Cassi's friends are setting her up on a date, and I hate it. It's like there's an angry beast trying to claw his way through my fucking chest at the thought of a man putting his hands on her. I know it's jealousy, but that's fucking stupid.

Cassi isn't mine.

She's also not the vapid party girl I thought she was. Her friends might be, but not her. She's different and I was wrong.

Fuck, that tastes bitter.

Still, I'm not sure what I want to do about it. Am I really thinking about a relationship with her? Dating her? Asking her out? Am I ready to change how I live my life to make room for a woman I still don't know that well?

My thoughts are a jumbled mess as I work through my weights routine, frustration driving me to push myself harder until I'm completely exhausted. Hitting the shower, I try to force my mind to focus on something else, anything else. It's doing me no good to run the same scenarios over and over again without a solution. I'm merely driving myself crazy.

When I get back to my condo, my efforts to stop obsessing over Cassi fly out the window the moment I see her. She always dresses nicely, but tonight is different. She's gone all out, with her blonde hair styled in big, soft curls and her makeup heavier than usual. She pulls off the natural look just fine, but her smokey eye shadow highlights her cerulean-blue eyes. And those kissable lips painted candy-apple red are making my dick strain against my zipper.

Prying my gaze away from her face, I can't stop it from trailing down her body. Her pink dress clings to her generous tits and flows like water to her midthigh. Those long, shapely legs are on full display, toned and accentuated by the sexy stilettos on her feet, bringing her whole look together.

Fuck, she's gorgeous, and I don't like it one bit. She looks *too* good, and I have a sinking feeling in the pit of my stomach about what's coming next.

I cut the distance between us until I'm close enough to smell her perfume. That fucking heavenly vanilla perfume. "Where are you going?"

She doesn't look up while she checks the contents of her purse. *Is she searching for a condom in there?* There's that flare of jealousy again. *Motherfucker.*

"My friends finally convinced me to go out with the guy they were talking about yesterday." She still doesn't glance my way. She's too busy checking her reflection in the mirror by the door, making sure she looks good for another man.

My fists clench at my sides. "You're going to dinner?" I'm not sure why I'm asking. I don't want to know what she and her date have planned.

"Yeah, he's taking me to a French restaurant. Petit Chou." I'm very familiar with it. It's a four-star restaurant with a wait list. Obviously, her friends didn't set her up with a nobody, so at least there's that.

I'm struggling to keep the discontentment off my face when I hear knocking at the front door. I'm closer—and honestly I want to see who this motherfucker is—so I offer to greet her *guest*. The tall man in a black suit looks familiar to me, but I can't quite place him. I'm staring, trying to remember how I know the guy, when his gaze shifts over my shoulder, and I know Cassi has joined me at the door.

"Hi, you must be Peter," she addresses him with her angelic voice. "Come on in."

Reluctantly, I take a step back to allow him inside, even as my instincts scream at me not to let this guy anywhere near her. And then, his name clicks in my memory, and I'm reminded of who he is.

This asshat used to work at my company last year, and he was bad fucking news. A womanizer with a god complex. I was thrilled when he quit Bennett Enterprises, especially after he cheated on his girlfriend, who works in our marketing department.

Fuck no. Cassi cannot go out with this jerk.

ELEVEN

Cassi

"I NEED TO TALK TO YOU IN PRIVATE FOR A MINUTE." JACK'S request catches me off guard because he knows I'm about to go out on a date.

"Can't it wait until later?"

He's already shaking his head as he approaches me. Taking me by the elbow, he starts to lead me into his office. But I dig my heels in, smiling back at Peter and trying to act like this is perfectly normal. "I'm sorry. Just have a seat and I'll be right back."

Peter winks at me and nods. "Take your time. We have a few minutes before our reservation."

We walk down the hall and Jack shuts the door before he releases me. I cross my arms over my chest and glare at him. "What the hell is going on?"

He paces in front of his glass and black metal desk. "You can't go out with that guy."

I scoff. *He can't be serious.* "That's not up to you, Jack. And why do you care, anyway?"

He ignores my question. "That douche used to work for me. Well... worked at Bennett Enterprises. And I'm telling you he's not a good guy."

"Are you... *jealous*?" That's the only explanation I can come up with. But that makes no sense. I've been living here for *weeks*, and Jack hasn't made a single move.

He stops pacing and looks at me. "No, don't be crazy."

"So, I'm not good enough for you?"

His face goes red and he starts to step toward me, but thinks better of it. "Of course, you are. But you're too good for that idiot out there who doesn't deserve you."

"So, like I said, you're jealous." My eyes narrow as I barely contain my anger.

The tone and volume of his voice significantly lowers. "And like I said, no, I'm not." He's too defensive to be believed, yet he hasn't and won't do anything about it. And I don't understand why. I thought we were at least friendly now, but I guess not.

"Oh my God, you are so jealous, Jack." I rub my temples, feeling completely overwhelmed. "This is so fucking ridiculous. *You* don't want me, but you don't want anyone *else* to have me either."

"Don't be stupid," he snaps, and I'm not sure if he's angry with me or himself, but I'm sick of his shit. "I'm just trying to protect you from making a big mistake."

"Since when? When have I needed your protection?" I pause for him to answer but he just stares at me. *That's what I thought.* "You've been a pain in my ass since the day I moved into this building. And, yeah, we might have come to a tentative truce when I moved in here—Lord only knows why you agreed to that because I sure don't, and I don't think you do either—but don't act like you give a damn about me. You don't." Pain radiates through my hands as my freshly polished nails dig into my palms.

"Would you stop acting like a fucking brat and just listen. This guy isn't right for you, Cassi."

Not only is he jealous, but now he insults me. I shake my head at his audacity. "You know what, Jack? This living situation isn't going to work out. I don't know what I was thinking in the first place."

"What are you talking about?" His face crumples with confusion, but it's all very clear.

"I don't know when they'll have my place ready for me, but I can't stay here. I'll leave first thing in the morning." I pivot for the door.

"Cassi, wait—" He reaches for me, but I step out of his grasp.

"But for *now*..." I glare at him and he holds my stare. "I'm going on my date. Good night, Jack."

He looks completely taken aback by my words, but he doesn't continue to argue. In fact, he just stands there as I turn on my stilettos and rip open the door, walking out of the office and away from him. It shouldn't feel like my heart's been rolled in shattered glass, all because he let me go so easily. But it does.

"Come on, Peter," I command, my tone more aggressive than I intend.

"Uh... everything okay?" he questions, rising from the couch to meet me.

"Yep. And I'm suddenly starving. So, let's get outta here."

He doesn't question me further, which is a relief. Jack wouldn't let me off the hook like that.

Nope. Stop thinking about him.

But that's easier said than done. Peter is quite handsome, with a dimpled chin and deep-brown eyes. He's charming with a great smile, and he gives me his full attention as we sit at the restaurant, casually chatting about easy topics and current events. It's typical first-date small talk, but I try to enjoy myself anyway.

If only I could get Jack's hurtful words out of my mind.

Peter deserves to have the same courtesy he's given to me, but I'm struggling to reciprocate. On paper, he's a great catch, attractive, and successful. But I can't help wondering about what Jack said. Is he just being a controlling and jealous asshole, or does he have a reason for disliking Peter so much?

When I agreed to this date, I considered sleeping with him, thinking it might help me get over my ex. *And* get over this... whatever it is I'm feeling for Jack.

Isn't that what they say? The best way to get over a man is to get under a new one?

But I just can't. Everything about this man says he *should* be the right guy for me. Yet, by the time dessert comes, I know I'm not into Peter enough to sleep with him. Although, I can tell that he feels differently. Or maybe he doesn't feel a spark either, but he doesn't care. I know a lot of men will have sex with an attractive woman whether they feel something for her or not. And I'm not judging anybody—male or female—for that. It's just not what I'm looking for right now.

I muster through the end of the date, allowing him to get closer than I'd prefer, when he places a hand on the small of my back and leads me to the car as we leave. But as he turns to me with a hopeful expression, I know what's coming next.

"So... you've got an interesting living situation. You wanna come back to my place?"

Wow, presumptuous.

I offer him a weak smile. "I don't think so. Can you just take me home, please?"

He rears back in shock, and I can tell by the disappointment in his eyes he's not used to being turned down. But still, he doesn't argue. There's tension in the car on the way back, and I nervously bite my thumbnail while I stare at the city lights out the window. When he parks the car, Peter turns to face me before I can open my door.

"You know, Sierra was right. You *are* quite stunning. I had a great time tonight, Cassi." He tucks a loose curl behind my ear.

My heart beats faster as the intensity of his gaze heats up. He leans in close, and I know he's about to kiss me. This is a pivotal moment for me, my last opportunity to give this guy a real chance or shut him down and close the door. I don't have much time to decide. But as he inches closer to me, there's only one person I'm thinking about and it's not Peter.

I just can't do it. My stomach doesn't fill with butterflies the way it does when I'm around Jack. That tingling awareness that rushes over my skin with every casual touch he gives me. I don't feel anything when Peter's fingertips graze my cheek, and that's not good.

No matter how frustrating Jack is, I've grown attached to the jackass, and even just kissing Peter will feel wrong, all wrong. Like I'm using him, and I don't want to do that. So, I grip the handle and open the door, causing the overhead light to turn on. Peter flinches from the sudden brightness, giving me enough time to turn away.

"Good night, Peter. Thank you for a lovely evening." I step out of the car, closing the door behind me. I was going for polite but firm, and I hope he's not insulted by my rejection. But as I lean down to wave through the window, he pulls away, letting me know he's probably cursing my name at this very moment. Even if that's the case, I don't feel bad about my choice. I know it was the right thing to do.

I sigh as I walk inside, stretching my neck and preparing for the onslaught of emotions I put aside during dinner to come flooding back as soon as I get to Jack's condo. The whole date was a bad idea and I shouldn't have gone. Deep down, I knew I was starting to feel something for Jack, but I didn't want to admit it if he didn't feel anything for me. But now I'm all twisted up in knots, and I can't pretend these feelings don't exist anymore, even if I'm pretty sure they're one-sided.

As I enter the quiet condo, I don't know if I want to find him awake or not. Would we argue again? Would he apologize?

Slipping off my heels, I tiptoe down the hallway and see that his door is ajar. My curiosity gets the best of me and I peek into his room, where I find him passed out on his bed. I stand in the doorway for a couple of minutes, wrestling with the longing deep inside my chest.

I meant what I said earlier tonight. This isn't working. Jack treats me like a child half the time, patronizing me in a way that I can't stand. As annoying as that is, it's the other side of him that's driving me away. Because I like that part of him, the man who can be kind and thoughtful. I'm falling for him, but I know he doesn't feel the same.

As big, fat tears well in my eyes—my decision made—I creep the few feet back down the hall to my room. My *temporary* room. As much as I don't want to, I'm going to call my parents in the morning and ask if I can stay with them.

I hate this, but it's better this way.

TWELVE

Jack

I TRY TO LET CASSI GO. I REALLY DO.

She said she wanted to go on her date *and* move out. And who the fuck am I to stop her?

But I can't do it. I'm too damn weak. So, I follow her to the restaurant where that arrogant prick is taking her. I've been here enough times that they know me, and I manage to get a table without a reservation. It's my luck that I'm seated in a dark corner, allowing me to go unnoticed by Cassi but still able to watch her.

I can't hear what's being said from here, but Peter lavishes her with attention, his eyes riveted to her face. She has no idea that Mr. Charming is probably already thinking about how he's going to fuck her, then cheat on her as soon as he gets an opportunity. Or maybe *she's* going to be his sidepiece.

Either way, it pisses me the fuck off.

He doesn't deserve the smiles she throws his way or to hear her soft laughter. The date looks like it's going well, which makes my mood plummet further, if that's even possible. I shouldn't have come here, but I can't make myself leave.

I pick at my dinner, my appetite nonexistent. Cassi doesn't seem to have that problem, and I find myself wishing that I'd brought her here first, sharing the food with her that she appears to like so much.

Shit.

There's no denying it to myself anymore. I've caught feelings for my little neighbor. I'm not sure when I let that happen, but the desire I have for her is strong, and it's not just physical. Fucking her would be amazing, but I want more than that.

However, it's too late because I fucked it up.

The couple leaves the restaurant, and I narrow my eyes at the sight of his hand on her lower back. They look way too cozy, and I'm sure this guy is wasting no time getting Cassi into his bed.

To hell with this.

If she's going home with her date, I'm heading back to my own place to get drunk and forget all about this fuckery. I may have feelings now, but I'll be damned if I'm going to keep them. Some Scotch should wash it all away, at least for tonight.

And after that, I'll go back to being the asshole I'm known for. I'm good at that. Really good at that.

My fucking alarm goes off at the crack of dawn, and my head pounds with a hangover. Groaning, I roll out of bed and stumble toward the kitchen, in search of a bottle of aspirin and some water. As I pass Cassi's room, I'm surprised to hear her voice. Apparently, she's so eager to get away from me that she left Peter's bed bright and early just to get the hell out of here.

Her voice gets louder as I approach the kitchen. "Thanks, Mom." She must be on the phone. "I'll pack up my stuff and be home in about an hour."

I stomp down the hallway, getting my aspirin before returning to my room. It's the weekend, so I don't need to go into the office, but I can't stand the idea of being here when she leaves. I throw on some sweats and shove my earbuds in, heading for the gym.

Cassi is still in her bedroom when I slip out the front door. Telling myself that it's a good thing she's going, and better for both of us, doesn't help the anger coursing through me. Maybe working it off on the punching bag or the weights will do me some good.

My intentions were solid, but the moment I walk into the place that usually brings me peace, I spot Cassi's date from last night. I've never seen Peter here before, but it's a popular gym, so that doesn't mean anything.

What bothers me is watching him hit on someone else. There's a petite brunette in a sports bra with an obviously enhanced rack working with some light weights by the mirrors. And Peter is drooling all over her, clearly showing off and getting way too handsy, if you ask me. I immediately see red and storm over to him, consequences be fucking damned.

"What the fuck are you doing?" I snap, getting up in his face. The woman he was flirting with shuffles backward to avoid me, which is smart, even if she doesn't know it. She should steer clear of this asshole.

"Woah, what's your problem, man?" Peter asks, clearly shocked to see me.

"My problem is that you spent the night with my gir—roommate. And now I find you here trying to get into someone else's panties. Not even twenty-four hours later."

"What?" the brunette shrieks. "You're not single?"

"I didn't spend the night with her," Peter claims. "We went on a date, but she couldn't handle me."

I jerk him closer and pin him with my stare. My tone is low and deadly. "You wanna try that shit again? How about this time, you tell me the fucking truth before I smash your face in?"

His eyes widen; he knows I'm serious. "Fine, alright. I couldn't close the deal. Fuck, let me go." I set him down, but give him a look that demands he continue to explain. "Honestly, I got the feeling there was something or *someone* else on her mind. Like she couldn't wait for the date to be over and to get back home. So I dropped her off and I left, man. That's it."

"If you're fucking lying to me..."

"I come off like a punk in this scenario. Why would I lie?" The little fucker has a good point. But that means...

I feel like I've been slapped. She didn't sleep with him? Something inside me shifts at that spectacular news. My anger dissolves. Resistance fades. I have to get home.

Without sparing Peter another word, I leave the gym, scrambling to return to the condo. Cassi said she'd be at her parents' house within an hour. What if I already missed her?

I rush the few blocks from the gym to my place, hauling ass as quick as I can. Hurrying down the hallway to my front door, I reach for the knob just as it opens, and I'm flooded with relief. I didn't miss her.

But before I can say a word, she walks out, pulling a large suitcase behind her, with Sir Wigglesworth nestled protectively in her other arm. When she sees me, she frowns and I can read the heartbreak all over her beautiful face.

"I'm leaving. I'll send for the rest of my things later."

The fuck you are.

"You're not going anywhere, Cassi." I grab the handle of the suitcase and wrap a palm around her wrist. Before she can even think to resist me, I tug her back inside and shut the door. The wheels of her luggage screech on the marble tiles of the entryway when I set it aside, before I carefully extricate Wigs—as I've started calling my little buddy these last several weeks—and place him on the floor.

"What do you think—"

I cut her off by crashing my mouth to hers. Her body is flush against mine, all soft curves and warmth. She melts into me for a moment, gripping on to my biceps for support. Heat licks down my spine, and I run my tongue along the seam of her lips, hoping she'll part them for me.

Instead, she stiffens, as if she's come to her senses. Her hands shift to my chest, and she pushes me away. I've barely registered the movement when she brings her arm up and slaps me across the face. My breath leaves me in a rush as my head whips to the side.

"What the fuck are you doing, Jack?" she demands with fire in her eyes.

"You didn't go home with him last night." I smile but she steps away, out of reach.

"That is none of your business. I said I'm leaving and you're not gonna stop me." She sniffs, lifting her chin in the air, and attempts to take a step around me. But I move to block her path.

"No."

"Move, Jack."

"No, don't go. Please." I want to touch her so badly, but I know I need to wait.

She stares at me with hurt in her eyes. "Why should I stay?"

"Because I want you here. I want you to be with me."

Her eyes narrow as she studies me like I'm a puzzle she's trying to solve. "You *want* me to be with you? In what way?"

Isn't it obvious?

I reach out and take her hand. This time, she doesn't pull away, but I can see the distrust in her eyes. "I care about you, Cassi. I want you to be mine."

She shakes her head as conflicting thoughts compete in her brain. "But... I don't understand. You've always treated me like shit. Talking down to me and judging me. How can you possibly say that you want to be with me?"

"I know I've been an asshole. I just... I made assumptions when we met. I thought things about you that aren't true, and certainly weren't fair. I was wrong. And I don't deserve you."

If this woman wants me to beg, I'll fucking do it.

"What assumptions?"

I swallow hard. I want to lie. I don't want to tell her the truth because it'll upset her, and she just might walk out that door. But I know that I have to be honest because I care about her too much.

A nervous chuckle escapes me, followed by a loud exhale. "I thought you were a spoiled little rich girl. A princess who's mommy and daddy bought her a grown-up house to play in. I thought you'd been coddled your whole life and didn't know anything about the real world or life or how to earn something for yourself." My chin drops to my chest in shame.

I'm such a fucking dick.

Now, she does pull her hand away from mine. "That's not fair, Jack. You never once bothered to get to know me." Her voice quivers with distress and I hate myself for being the cause of it. "You didn't even try. It's not my fault that my parents are wealthy. So are yours, for that matter. So why take out your personal problems on me?"

"I know. You're right." I step closer to her as desperation overwhelms me when she glances toward the door. "I was so fucking wrong, Cassi. I see that now. Please, forgive me. Just one more chance." I'm not a man who begs. I come from a billion-dollar family and I can literally have whatever I want. I've never had to plead for something in my life, but I'm doing it now for Cassi. She's the only woman I want. I know I've fucked up, but I need her. And I don't need anything.

The corners of her mouth tip up ever so slightly, and the tension in the center of my chest slowly begins to loosen. "If I give you another chance, what will you do with it?"

Hope sparks to life inside me, and I feel like the Grinch whose heart grew three sizes. Invading her personal space, I take her hand in mine, getting as close to her as I can. She tilts her head back, looking up at me through her eyelashes. I cup her cheek, running the pad of my thumb over her soft skin. Her lips slightly part, and this time, I lower my head slowly, giving her a chance to deny me.

She doesn't.

She opens for me, allowing me to lick my way inside her mouth. I devour her, holding her against my chest. Her hands go to the back of my neck, pulling me close as our tongues collide.

I lift her into my arms, wrapping her legs around me and taking us down the hallway to my bedroom, never breaking the kiss. We tumble onto my bed, pawing at each other's clothes in a frenzy of movement. I whip her dress over her head, revealing a garnet-red lingerie set that shows her hard nipples through the thin lace. My shirt is off next, and she runs her fingertips along my muscular chest, tracing the ridges between my abs.

Her touch leaves a trail of fire, and my cock is pulsing with the need to be buried deep inside her wet pussy. I release the front clasp of her bra, freeing her full tits and eagerly capturing one of the rosy tips in my mouth with a groan. Cassi holds on to the back of my head, and I wrap my arms around her waist, pressing her soft, supple flesh farther into my mouth.

Her curvaceous body is perfection, and the whimpers of pleasure she makes drive me fucking insane. When I bring my mouth back to hers, she shocks me by nipping at my bottom lip. Hard. The unexpected sting of pain makes my cock ache, and I only want her more now.

I sit up, pulling her over to straddle my lap. I still have my basketball shorts on since I never did get my workout in, but I can feel the heat of her pussy as she settles over my cock. She rocks against me with a moan, and electricity sparks through my body.

"Jack." Her voice is an impatient plea. "I need you."

"I know you do, baby. You've been thinking about me at night, haven't you? When you use that little vibrator of yours?"

She stills and stares at me with wide eyes. "How did you know?"

I smirk. "I've heard it."

She looks away as her cheeks turn crimson. That intrigues me. I don't want her to ever feel embarrassed about giving herself pleasure, doing whatever she needs to make herself feel good. If anything, I want to watch and participate.

"Where is it?" I ask, my hands on her ass as I rock her cunt against me again.

"W-what?" she questions, her eyes hazy. I love that she's so turned on that she can't follow the conversation. She wants this just as much as I do, and I circle my thumb over her panties, across her pulsing clit. She lets out another moan.

"Your vibrator, baby. Did you pack it to take to your parents' house or is it in your room?"

She licks her lips, trying to focus. "It's still... in the nightstand."

"Stay here," I set her onto the mattress as I slide off the bed and hurry to her room. Locating the vibrator—a little pink thing—I rush back to Cassi, where I find she's taken off her lingerie. She's naked, and I pause for a moment, gazing at her beautiful, voluptuous curves.

This girl is thick as fuck and I love every inch of her body. So fucking soft and feminine, with those huge, bouncy tits, hourglass hips, rounded belly, and thighs so juicy I want to be buried between them for days.

She's a goddess, and I will worship her every day for as long as she lets me.

When she spreads her legs—knees bent, feet planted on the mattress—her pretty pussy is already glistening for me. Smirking, I crawl onto the bed, lifting her vibrator into her line of sight.

"I want to watch you use it," I exclaim, and she bites her lip nervously.

"I don't know... I've never..."

"Never let a man watch you make yourself come? Then, let me be the first."

I hold it out for her, and she hesitantly takes it. Leaning back on the pile of pillows, I watch her turn it on to her favorite setting. The buzzing sound is exactly what I heard that first night when she called out my name in her room. And a few other nights since then, if I'm honest. She brings the rounded tip of the fake cock to her pussy, gliding the thick head between her wet lips. Her cunt is dripping onto my sheets, and she uses her arousal to lube up her toy. She coats the shaft of it, whimpering each time the vibration hits her clit. Then, her mouth drops open as she pushes the vibrator inside her drenched cunt with a moan. She fucks herself with it while her free hand goes to her breast, kneading it and tweaking her nipple.

This is the most erotic thing I've seen in my life.

I lose my shorts and boxers, freeing my throbbing cock as I watch Cassi pleasure herself. Her eyes are closed, and she's thrown her head back on the pillow. A pretty flush covers her cheeks and neck, spreading all the way down to her chest, where I watch her delicate fingers pinch and play with her hardened bud. She's pumping the vibrator in and out, rough and fast, so I match her pace as I stroke my cock.

Fuck, it feels amazing, but I know I can't wait much longer to be inside her. I need this woman like I need air to breathe. And I can't stop until I have her.

She pulls the vibrator out and moves it to her clit. Her body spasms, and the loudest moan yet fills my bedroom.

God, she's gorgeous when she comes.

Diving in, I lift her legs onto my shoulders and move closer. Cassi's eyes fly open and she starts to slide the vibrator away as I line my mouth up with her entrance, but I shake my head. "Keep it against your clit, baby. I want to taste you when you come hard." She nods and does what I ask. "Good girl, Cassi. Good girl."

I suck and nibble on her swollen lips as her taste explodes across my tongue. *So fucking delicious.* Her heels dig into my back and I know she's close, especially with a toy to help. I slip two fingers inside her, curling them against her G-spot while I feast on her pussy and wait for my sweet reward. A few more seconds, and she moans again, deep and throaty, while she writhes against the bed, clawing at the sheets and filling my mouth with her sweet honey.

I could drink her down every day for the rest of my life.

When she's had a few moments to catch her breath, I toss the vibrator aside and tap her thigh. "Turn over, baby. Ass in the air for me." She's still breathless as she looks at me wide-eyed. "I promise I'll be gentle next time, but I'm about to fuck this pussy up. I need it, and so do you. Now, on your knees, face down on the bed for me."

Her cheeks flame red, but a small grin breaks out across her lips before she gives me her hand to help her sit upright. My dick is dripping precum onto the bed, dying to get inside her. I stroke my thick length a few times while she gets into position, and knowing she's been primed, I don't wait before I slam my fat cock deep inside her.

"Fuck!" I groan at the same time she screams my name and grabs handfuls of the sheets. I hold still while her whole body trembles beneath me. "Tell me you want me to fuck you, Cassi."

"Plea—" she pants, struggling to speak. "Please fuck me, Jack. I... we need this."

"Fuck, you're perfect." I grip her full hips and begin slamming my cock into her gushing pussy. It feels like fucking heaven and I can't stop. I won't stop until I fill her full of my cum and maybe even my baby.

Fuck!

Tears leak from her eyes as she moans and whimpers in bliss while I fuck the hell out of her. She's gorgeous like this, taking all this dick so pretty for me. I lean forward, thrusting hard inside her while massaging her tits and teasing her nipples. My hand slides down to her clit, and I feel it pulse between my fingers.

Whispering in her ear, I ask, "You ready to come on my dick, baby? Let me come deep in that pussy?"

"Y-y-yes... yes, Jack."

I see her vibrator is within reach, so I grab it and hand it to her.

"You know where to put that, don't you?" A blissed-out smile spreads across her face as she moves the neon-pink toy down to her swollen nub.

I grasp firmly onto her hips, which are made perfectly for my large hands, and begin fucking my girl like my life depends on it. My head drops back with a loud groan as the familiar tingle builds at the base of my spine. Cassi screams my name, and her cunt spasms around my cock as her next orgasm takes over her. It's just what I need to send me over the edge too, so I pick up my pace, and after a few more thrusts, I come hard, deep inside her.

I'm moving slower but still flexing my hips as I slide my cock lazily in and out, her pussy milking every drop of my cum. *Damn, she was made for me. I'm sure of it.* I ease out of her heavenly body and she slides forward, lying down, motionless on the bed. I collapse next to her and tug her over me so I can finally hold her.

Mine.

Cassi quivers, and I turn my head to press a kiss to her temple. "You okay?"

Her laugh is faint, but happy. "Better than okay."

This was amazing. Everything I needed and didn't know I wanted. More than I could have even imagined, and I roll to my side, gathering Cassi in my arms with a grateful sigh. I know I don't deserve her after the way I've treated her, but as she snuggles into my embrace, I'm silently thankful that I have a second chance with her. I swear I won't let her go. She belongs with me now, and I'll never be that fucking stupid again.

EPILOGUE

Cassi

1 Year Later

Jack offers his fork to me, sharing a bite of his breakfast. "Try this. You'll like it."

I open my mouth, allowing him to feed me a sample of the strawberry and cream-stuffed crepe. I hold his gaze as I close my lips around the utensil. The sweetness of the mascarpone and mild zing of the berries explode on my tongue, and my lashes close with a moan.

Lust flares in Jack's eyes. "There's my favorite sound in the world. Although, I prefer to hear it when I can get my cock inside you."

My cheeks warm as I swallow the mouthful of food. I glance around the restaurant where we're eating brunch. It's far from private, but at least no one is close enough to overhear.

"I admit I like making that sound." I give him a wicked smile.

"Especially when you're the one eating."

Jack groans. "I love it when you talk like that. You've become such a dirty little girl."

I know we're both thinking about last night. We've been together for a year now, but our sex life is just as wild as ever. If anything, it gets better each time.

My thighs squeeze, and Jack grins like the cat that ate the canary. He knows the effect he has on me and it must be obvious what we're talking about to anyone who looks our way.

That thought is confirmed a moment later when we're joined by Taylor and Ella. I was introduced to Jack's best friend a week after we started officially dating, followed by meeting Taylor's girlfriend, who happens to be Jack's assistant. Ella and I instantly hit it off, and now I consider her a close friend.

"What are you two talking about?" Taylor asks as he pulls out the chair beside Jack and takes a seat. "Because it certainly looks like we're interrupting something."

"Nothing," I say quickly, but Jack just chuckles and shrugs.

"Aren't you guys adorable?" Ella praises, sitting beside me. I lean over and give her a one-armed hug.

Jack sips his espresso. "Of course, we are."

"I can hardly believe that you tried to say you weren't interested in her," Ella comments nonchalantly as she scans her menu.

"It was pathetic, really," Taylor teases.

I look at Jack, confused. "What are they talking about?"

Ella beats him to a response. "Oh, he didn't tell you about his extreme state of denial?"

Jack groans and shoots her a warning look. "Stop giving me a hard time, woman." Reaching across the table, he takes my hand to address me directly. "I... might've told these guys that I didn't have feelings for you."

"Before we were together, though. Right?" I enjoy the panic in his eyes when he thinks he's about to be in trouble.

"Absolutely. Ella thought I liked you, and Taylor said you were hot."

Taylor's mouth drops open, then he glares at Jack. "I said that *you* thought she was hot." He kicks Jack under the table. "Are you denying it?"

I arch an eyebrow. "Yeah, are you?"

Jack's eyes dart between the three of us. "I thought this was a double date, not an opportunity for you assholes to gang up on me."

I give him a mock warning look. "So, I'm an asshole, am I?"

"No, baby. Them, not you."

I laugh, squeezing his hand. "Don't worry, Jack. You're not in trouble."

He gazes at me with sincerity. "You know I had feelings for you then," Jack says, looking relieved. "Ella helped to open my eyes to them. I just wasn't ready to act on those feelings."

"But now, here we are, together."

Jack's stare is intense, and I feel like we're the only two people in the room. Affection swells inside me, and I know that things have worked out just the way they were meant to.

Then, Ella's voice breaks our intimate moment. "I'll be looking for my raise on Monday."

We all laugh and get back to eating our brunch. I know that Jack would have come around eventually on his own, but I'm glad Ella helped nudge him in the right direction.

We recently decided that I'd sell my condo. I've been practically living with Jack since day one anyway. The place is less of a bachelor pad these days with my things in there as well, and Sir Wigglesworth is constantly spoiled rotten by the man who always claimed not to like my dog.

Jack slides his hand up my thigh underneath the table and gives it a squeeze. "It's always been you, Cassi."

I smile at him adoringly. "There's no getting rid of me now."

"Good. I wouldn't want it any other way."

ABOUT THE AUTHOR

Hi, I'm Elyse Kelly!
I'm just a true southern girl, reading and writing books, asking you to love me! My books are extra steamy, contemporary romances, all with HEAs and no cliffhangers! They're short, smutty, and tastefully trashy.

If you love over-protective, sexy, alpha book boyfriends who make you swoon and reach for your favorite... *bookmark*, then you've come to the right place.

When I'm not writing books or doing bookish things, I'm probably listening to music, designing smutty stickers, adding to my spectacular band t-shirt collection, or learning how to do something new like arm-knitting because I'm neurodivergent AF!
And yes, I really do know how to knit with my arms.

Learn more at:
https://elysekellybooks.com/